The MEDDLERS

Also by Claire Rayner

MADDIE
CLINICAL JUDGEMENTS
A STARCH OF APRONS
A TIME TO HEAL

CLAIRE RAYNER

The MEDDLERS

MICHAEL JOSEPH
LONDON

MICHAEL JOSEPH LTD

Published by the Penguin Group
27 Wrights Lane, London W8 5TZ, England
Viking Penguin Inc., 40 West 23rd Street, New York, New York 10010, USA
Penguin Books Australia Ltd, Ringwood, Victoria, Australia
Penguin Books Canada Ltd, 2801 John Street, Markham, Ontario, Canada L3R 1B4
Penguin Books (NZ) Ltd, 182-190 Wairau Road, Auckland 10, New Zealand

Penguin Books Ltd, Registered Offices: Harmondsworth, Middlesex, England

First published in 1970
Reissued by Michael Joseph Ltd in 1991

Printed and bound in Great Britain by
Butler & Tanner, Frome, Somerset

A CIP catalogue record for this book is available from the British Library

ISBN 0 7181 3401 X

For Dizzy
for all the obvious reasons

prologue

The fat orderly on the third floor of the Maternity Unit was worried. It showed in the way she moved aimlessly from single room to three-bedded room, from corridor to Sister's office, with a damp gray rag wadded in one pudgy hand, a bottle of all-purpose cleaner in the other. It showed in the way she washed the staff coffee cups after the mid-morning break, drying each one for a full minute as she stared blankly out the window at the bulk of the Physical Medicine Building across the courtyard.

Not that anyone would really have noticed much difference in her. No one ever did notice her, unless they wanted her for something, and even then they would simply call irritably, "Where's the orderly? The fat one?" because hardly anyone bothered to remember her name. She was so blank an individual, so ordinary, that she seemed to melt into the background even when being directly spoken to. She was as much a part of Maternity as the green gloss paint on the corridor walls, the piles of gowns and sheets in the linen cupboard and the heavy swinging doors that led to the labor room. Not even Sister Field, who was rather hot on human relations and concerned herself a great deal with the quality of communication between staff and patients, could see the fat orderly as a person. With so negative a personality, how could anyone see her as a person?

And yet she was worried. This was a rare experience for her, because she was not an individual who took herself at all seriously, in many ways sharing the general view of her own nonentity. Other people had personal problems with their husbands or their children or their boy friends or the people they worked with, but not Edna. She had her job and her room in the Maids' Home, and her weekly magazines full of love stories—in all of which she believed implicitly—and her television serials equally full of real people, and that was enough for her. To grapple with a moral dilemma, as she was now doing, was a very new and bothering experience.

Not that she knew she was grappling with a moral dilemma. All she knew was that something wasn't right about the patient in room eleven. It wasn't so much that she had no outside visitors like the other patients; lots of unmarried mothers were delivered in the Unit, and Edna accepted unquestioningly the loneliness that surrounded them. It wasn't just that she was in a single room when she was making perfectly normal progress, and such rooms were usually kept for mothers with infections or special complications, or doctors' wives. These facts merely added to the oddness of the situation.

The really odd thing was the number of important hospital people who were around. When she had gone into strong labor the day before, you'd have thought it was the Queen or Elizabeth Taylor or someone like that, the way they had come rushing. The doctor who worked over in the converted Isolation Unit near the back gates of the hospital, he'd come together with six—six!—people who seemed to be his assistants. And Miss Guttner herself had come to do the delivery, and Edna knew after eleven years of working in Maternity that she only came after the midwives and the registrars and everyone else had tried to manage and couldn't. And this girl had had a perfectly ordinary labor, something else

Edna knew from her eleven years of being part of the Unit's furniture.

And there had been the Hospital Secretary, and Matron, and no less than three of the specialists—the one from the Children's Unit, and the one from the Endocrinology Unit, and Sir Peter Apthorp, the Chief of Staff.

And after the baby was born, and they'd said it was a boy, seven pounds eleven, full term, no problems, perfect Agpar score (Edna didn't know what exactly an Agpar score was, only that a perfect one meant the baby was fine), look what they'd done. They hadn't put him in the nursery like the other babies. They hadn't given him to his mother, not once. Edna knew that because Sister Field had walked out of the labor room the minute he'd been delivered, holding him wrapped up in a bloodstained green towel. Edna had been standing just outside the door when that happened, cleaning the wheels of the spare anesthetic trolley, and had seen through the door to the mother on the table, and her face had been all flat and blotchy because she was under anesthetic—Dr. Palmer was just turning off the machine—so she couldn't have seen her baby. Yet they had taken him right away, out of the Unit altogether.

And so many people were still buzzing around today, sitting crushed in Sister's office and drinking all that coffee, and talking and talking and talking. It was funny about the way they talked. She knew they talked English—she could tell that—but what they said couldn't be understood, not the way you understood the way the nurses talked, and the mothers. They were a dirty lot, the mothers. Some of the things they said really upset Edna sometimes. People who had just had the glorious experience of childbirth, who had had love affairs and weddings first the way people ought to, they shouldn't talk dirty like the mothers did. But at least you could understand them, not like those people in Sister's office.

But even though she couldn't really understand them properly, she picked up some things from what they said as she poured out their coffee and carried plates of biscuits from one to the other. Computers, for example. What had computers got to do with a baby with a perfect Agpar score and a mother like the one in room eleven?

And, drying the last coffee cup, Edna thought about the mother again, because she was the one that really bothered her most.

A pretty girl, with black hair and blue eyes with long black curly eyelashes—"Blue eyes put in with a smutty finger"—like the girl in the story about the governess who got mixed up with a gang of kidnapers. But not like her otherwise. The governess had feelings and felt them all the time. But this new mother who ought to be having feelings a lot, she just sat in bed reading, and when Edna had said to her this morning while she was dusting her locker, "How's your little baby? What are you calling him?" she had just looked at her blankly over her book and had shrugged her shoulders and said nothing.

And she wasn't feeding, that was another thing. Every mother in the Unit had to feed her baby, even if she was going to have it adopted. It was a rule, and in eleven years the only time it had been broken was for mothers from the TB Unit, and there had only been two of them. This bothered Edna a lot. That poor baby! Where was he, and what were they doing about feeding him? It was all wrong! And if Edna knew it, wasn't Edna the person to do something about it?

When she went off duty at seven, she had solved her dilemma. She had a problem, and people who had problems wrote to magazines for help—that was what they were for. She would write to Margaret English, the one who gave her Warm Wise Advice to the whole family. She'd tell her. She'd know what to do.

"What do you think of this one?" Brenda said and pushed the three sheets of scrawled paper across the desk to Mrs. Barber. "I've read it twice, and I don't know. I thought at first it was just another nut gone overboard on the September serial—she goes on about babies being kidnaped and mothers being hypnotized, and that's a straight lift from Part Three. But I don't know. There're some things she says . . . Agpar scores, I mean. What the hell is that? There was nothing about that in the serial."

"We ran a piece on it a couple of years ago," Mrs. Barber said. "Something to do with examining babies at birth." She read swiftly and then read the letter again. And shook her head. She had been one of the six letter answerers who added up to the mythical Margaret English for five years—longer than any of the others—and she had an enviable nose for a crank. If anyone could spot a phony or a weird one it was Mrs. Barber.

"I'm not sure," she said. "She certainly believes it—I mean, that a baby's been kidnaped and the rest of it—but she seems to think the whole hospital staff are in on the plot. That's really off. But she seems to belong to the place. Lives there. I don't know. We could follow it up, I suppose—if there is something in it—we don't want another Nottingham."

Brenda grimaced. Indeed they didn't. It would be a long time before they would forget the man who had written saying he'd kill his wife, and they had written back soothingly, and then he had.

She took the letter back and read it again and then sighed. "I suppose we should. Police? Or what?"

Mrs. Barber shook her head. "Keep it in the family. Ring the Dr. Hunter page. They've got that chap—what's his name?—Dennis, David Dennis. He's a good researcher, always going round the hospitals, and he'll find out what's going on there. If it does turn out she's a nut case—well, we'll know what to do about it. But get Dennis to find out what he can, just in case."

So Brenda rang the Dr. Hunter page and spoke to David Dennis. And when he heard that the hospital in question was the Sillick Memorial, and that the letter had mentioned Dr. George Briant, he rang Mike on the *Echo* because Mike had said something at the last meeting of the Chapel about him. That he was a geneticist onto something that might be worth following up—if it ever came off. Mike might be interested.

Mike was.

1

Even before he was fully awake he felt the oppression of unpleasant memory, the threat of worse to come, although he couldn't remember exactly what it was that he remembered. And then he turned over and saw the empty crumpled pillow beside him, and it hit him in a great wave. Last night. He'd upset her thoroughly, and obviously she was still sulking, because she would never have got up before him otherwise.

She was going to use the sainted patience ploy, the one he found most difficult to handle. He would have much preferred the hysterical crying, the accusations of lack of love for her to that. But he'd had that last night—or rather, in the small hours of the morning. And now she was going to pile it on thick and heavy.

And with a short night's sleep behind him and a miserable hour ahead of him before he could get away to the hospital, the day would be spoiled before it started. He almost groaned as he got out of bed.

As he came out of the lavatory, Ian slammed the bathroom door behind him and went past in a wave of Old Spice.

"Morning, Prof!" he said with a loud cheerfulness. "Late this morning, aren't you?" And not waiting for an answer, he went into his room, moving jauntily.

So they'd been talking about it already. Ian knew perfectly well that his father loathed being called Prof, disliked intensely the way the boy went between the bathroom and his room with his towel flung over his shoulder so that he could flaunt his nakedness. That he had done both this morning made it perfectly clear that he knew George had upset her again.

As he shaved, he tried to organize his thinking. Apologize and promise her that he'd make it up somehow—take her out to dinner? But that wouldn't do. With the amount of work that was to be dealt with during the coming months his chances of getting away from the hospital much before eight or nine any evening were very slight. It would only mean he might let her down again, and that would be asking for it. Try again to get her to understand the implications of what he was doing, the possibility of a Nobel, and all that could mean? But she hadn't the patience for that. If he hadn't managed to convince her during the past eighteen years, he was unlikely to succeed this morning.

She was fully dressed, even wearing shoes rather than slippers. Her red hair was carefully arranged and her face made up, and she was grilling sausages and frying potatoes. Oh, God, he thought as he closed the kitchen door behind him. It's worse than I thought.

"You look nice," he said carefully.

"Do I, George? I'm glad." And she gave him a bleak little smile and put a plate of hot rolls on the table. "I hope these are all right. They were left over from last night."

"Oh, God, I'm sorry, Marjorie! All I can say is I'm sorry. I know you think I did it deliberately, but I assure you I did not. The project just—"

"Matters more than anything else. I know. I should be used to it by now. I'm sorry I'm not, and I know I'm at fault. How many sausages can you eat? Four?"

"You are not at fault. You have every right to be angry. I let you down in front of your friends, and I'm sorry. Please don't punish me any more!" And he tried to keep the impatience out of his voice.

"Punish you?" she raised one eyebrow at him as she put a plate of food at his place at the table. "How am I punishing you? If I were sending you off without a decent breakfast you could say that, but as it is . . ."

And I only get this sort of breakfast when you're angry, he thought. "Which I can't eat while you're still upset."

"Oh, I'm over it now. I can't deny that last night I was . . . very hurt. I know you don't much like them, that I should have asked a couple of the hospital people as well as people who share my interests—"

"Marjorie, please, will you accept what I tell you? It wouldn't have mattered *who* was here last night—and I don't dislike them in the least. They're very interesting. It's just that I got so involved with what was going on that I completely forgot! If I hadn't been so snowed under I'd have phoned myself, and you could have reminded me. And you could have told the girl on switchboard to remind me—she'd have given me the message, I assure you."

"And let *her* know that you cared so little for me that you had to be reminded? Oh, no, George. Bad enough the entire drama group will be gossiping this morning; I don't want all *your* people laughing at me too."

"No one will be laughing at you!" He began to eat his breakfast, not enjoying it in the least. But then, she knew he wouldn't. It was all part of his punishment, to give him food he liked when it couldn't be appreciated. "Surely people have better things to do than make a great song and dance about missing a dinner party."

"I am not making a great song and dance about it," she said in a softly dangerous voice and, with a hint of ostentation in her movements, stirred a saccharin tablet into a cup of black coffee.

"You ought to eat a proper breakfast." He responded obediently to the black coffee. Why did every bloody argument have to follow such a pattern? Didn't she realize that he saw through every trick she used? "And I didn't mean to imply *you* were making a song and dance. Only that intelligent people can surely accept that a man who has a job like mine can accidentally forget that his wife is giving a dinner party without immediately assuming his lapse is due to lack of concern for her."

"Oh, I know my friends aren't on a high intellectual plane like yours! They're only interested in theater, and music, and art, and things like that! A very dingy lot compared with the great minds you spend your time with." Her voice rose shrilly.

"Oh, for Christ's sake! Do we have to go through all that again?" He dropped his knife and fork with a clatter and leaned back in his chair. "I'm sorry, I'm sorry, I'm sorry! What more can I do than apologize? I do not despise your interests. I do care about you. I did not intend to embarrass you deliberately, and I will do all I can to ensure it doesn't happen again! What more do you want?"

"To be important to you." Now she was using her pathetic pleading little voice, the one that still could affect him even though he knew she was performing, using all the tricks she used to keep her place as the most important member of her bloody drama group. Yet, obvious a performance though it was, behind it lay a real anguish and he knew it, and knew he couldn't help it.

"You are important to me," he said helplessly. "Last night, I thought you could have told from last night—"

"You use sex the way I use makeup," she said with a sudden abandonment of her act. "To cover up the blemishes. Don't you think I can see through that? Making love and loving aren't the same thing."

"They are for me."

"No, they aren't. The only thing you love is the workings of your own mind. I'm here to be made love to when you need to, or when you think I need to, just to cover up. Like makeup. Oh, what's the use?"

She stood up and began to clear dishes from the table. "I take second place to your work, and I'll have to settle for that, I suppose."

"Why does this present project matter so much more?"

"More? More than what?"

"More than it's ever mattered before. I've been in research of one kind or another all our married life. Haven't I? Yet now you mind more. The time it takes, the inevitable abstraction I show when I'm involved with something big . . ."

For the first time she was really listening, not going through the motions of an argument. He felt suddenly a brief return of the closeness they had used to enjoy when the children were small and she still felt important to them and minded less his involvement with his work. He put out his hand toward her.

She looked at it and then shrugged and turned away, and the brief light that had illuminated him spluttered and died.

"It's always mattered. You just never noticed, that's all. I ought to be used to it, but I'm not. That's all there is to it."

"No—" and then the door swung open, and Ian came in, ostentatiously noisy, making sure his father knew that he, Ian, was aware there was an argument going on.

"Will I do, Rusty, my own?"

She turned and looked at him, and her face lit up joyously, and George looked at Ian and tried to keep his own face expressionless.

"You look splendid!" she cried. "If they don't cast you, it'll be because they're blind as well as stupid. I *know* you'll get it, darling. It's meant! Just you remember that, and you'll get it. Can't you see it? Ian Briant, up in lights!"

And then they were both looking at George, and he stretched his neck in his collar, tortoiselike, and said, a little gruffly, "Where are you going?"

"I'm auditioning for a new show." Ian's voice was slightly defiant, and he dropped his head and with a careful casualness flicked away some nonexistent dust from his high-buttoned silver jacket.

George looked with distaste at the rest of his outfit—at the indecently tight green trousers, the silver-shot green scarf in the neck of the jacket, and the way the boy's flaming red hair curled against it.

"I see. And these—garments—are the sort to impress?"

Ian laughed loudly. "What would be more impressive would be nothing at all, since they're casting another protest show. Most of the cast'll be starkers for the second half." He slid his eyes at his mother, and then said a little maliciously, "How much will you object if I *am* cast?"

"As long as I don't have to see it, not in the least," George said dryly. "But if a willingness to display nakedness is an essential part of the . . . job"—he couldn't help letting some of his scorn show —"it was hardly worth spending money on such clothes, was it?"

"Oh, don't worry about that!" Marjorie said, and her voice was high and brittle. "We couldn't have afforded to buy them anyway. They're borrowed from the costume store. My drama group people may be rather dim, but they're generous. But take care of them, darling. I hate to think what we'd do if they had to be replaced. Scrag end of mutton for weeks." She kissed Ian warmly. "You'll get the job, darling—I'm sure you will. But I wish you'd have some breakfast before you go."

"No, thanks, dolly-chops," Ian said and rumpled her hair. "But pop a poulet in the pot for me, and I'll be back for lunch. And keep your chin up. I'll be here by one, I promise." And he raised his own chin at George and went out, slamming the door behind him.

There was silence for a moment after the front door too slammed, and then George said carefully, "I would prefer you not to discuss our disagreements with the children. You know that."

"I didn't discuss. I simply mentioned it. Anyway, I don't see why I shouldn't talk to my own son if I choose. I have to talk to someone. And *we're* very close." And she placed the emphasis delicately but unmistakably.

But this was no time to complicate things by being sidetracked by Ian. George looked swiftly at his wristwatch as she turned away, and then leaned back in his chair.

"Marjorie, you were about to tell me why this project annoys you more than any other project ever has. I'd like to know."

I've got to know, he thought. The adoption shouldn't affect her, they shouldn't take her into account, but Kegan thinks they might want her token agreement, so I've got to handle this right. Oh,

God, why did I have to forget her wretched dinner party last night of all times?

"I told you. It doesn't."

"But I suspect it does. And that makes me rather unhappy."

"Why?" She shot a sharp look at him. "Maybe I should be asking what's so extra important about it to you."

How can a woman who is so intelligent be so often stupid? George thought suddenly. Or is it intelligence? Is there such a thing as intuition? I've never believed it, but sometimes she makes such leaps of comprehension . . .

He pulled his mind back. "You know why. Because it will be my definitive work. Because if I find the answers I'm seeking, it should be worth—oh, an inestimable amount. Its application could—I think I can say it might revolutionize life by the end of this century. You know that."

"And it might get you your Nobel, you'll take your place in scientific history alongside the Curies and Rutherford and the rest of them. I've heard all that before! But is that all?"

"It's a pretty big all."

"It's a pretty big might. When I used to get all excited about the projects you got involved with years ago, you used to slap me down with that. Told me I was jumping to conclusions and weaving fantasies and all the rest of it. And now you're doing it. Now I wonder why?"

She seemed to have completely forgotten her anger over the dinner party, which was one comfort. But she was being a little too shrewd for real comfort. If he didn't get this across to her properly and she chose to be obstructive she could make so many complications that the very project could be damaged. He spoke particularly carefully.

"This time I'm onto a . . . a big thing. I've been working towards it from the start. I can see that now, even though I had no idea at the beginning where it might all lead me. This one is—it involves so many factors, you see."

He stopped, a little helplessly. "I hardly know where to begin. I've told you something of the plan—"

"As much as you thought I could cope with. Not a lot."

"It was nothing to do with whether you could cope or not. It was just that I dislike going off half-cocked, talking too much about a project before I can see where it's leading."

"Yet now, all of a sudden, you want to know why I think it's so important. That's what you mean when you say it annoys me, isn't it? You think the things that are important to you annoy me the way the things that matter to me annoy *you*. You're—what's the word?—extrapolating. That's it. You're extrapolating from your own feelings to mine. If I needed any proof that I bore you, that you don't care about me—"

"No!" He almost shouted it. "That isn't just, and you bloody well know it! I just want to know if your anger is because of the way the project has absorbed me lately, or if it's simply the ill-mannered forgetfulness I showed last night—which I don't deny, and for which I again apologize."

"Wasn't it enough? And I've accepted your apology. I've had to."

"Not completely. And it isn't only last night I'm talking about. You've been edgy for months."

"Have I? I hadn't noticed particularly. Of course, I've been worried about Ian, and the way you and he—"

"Please, not that. Not now."

"—and I've not been well. Or hadn't you noticed?"

"Of course I have! And it's worried me. But I suspected you were—well, feeling the way you did because of the way I've been wrapped up in work, rather than because of any change in your condition."

She produced a smile of pure triumph. "I knew you hadn't noticed. How all occasions do inform against you, George! Sir Peter says he wants to do another pyelogram soon. He's been talking again about the possibility of dialysis."

"What?" George stared at her. "But I saw him only yesterday! He said nothing to me!"

She smiled sweetly. "I told him not to. Insisted that he respect my confidence as a patient. He knows how busy you are, of course, and quite understood."

"Marjorie! Why do you do this to me? You say I shut you out of my work, but you shut me out . . . If you're ill again, I've got to know!"

"Oh, it's not as bad as that," she said, clearly enjoying herself. "Not really. You know what an old woman Apthorp can be. Forget it. There's nothing really new. I've got a bit puffed up again, had a few headaches. Nothing very much. And I suppose you could be right."

"How do you mean?"

She sat down opposite him and propped her chin on her hands and gave him the look of limpid honesty at which she was particularly gifted.

"I have been—well, a little more resentful of this project than any others. Two years now, isn't it? And you've retreated further and further into it, and I've been jealous. I can't deny it."

She's done it again. She's made me angry with her anger, and then turned it around so that I'm eaten up with guilt because she's been ill and I haven't noticed, and now she's taking the blame on herself and making me feel worse than ever. Oh, God, how convoluted can a woman's mind be?

George stared at her and suddenly ached to get away, to take his coat and his briefcase and get into the car and escape to the haven of the Unit and work and the baby and . . . which brought him back to the reason for his starting to probe her feelings about the project. Complication on complication, Pelion on Ossa!

And then he said it aloud: "Pelion on Ossa."

"What?"

"I should join your drama group. I'm thinking in quotations."

"Why Pelion on Ossa? What's piling on what?"

I'll have to plunge now, he thought. I'll have to, and risk it.

"Complications. I'm going to need your help with the project."

She stared at him, her mouth slightly open so that her rather small even teeth gleamed in the thin October sunshine that was now filling the kitchen. "My help?" she said slowly. "*Mine?*"

"Yes. Well, perhaps cooperation would be a better word."

She closed her eyes for a moment, and when she opened them he was puzzled by the blankness in them.

"Oh. For one mad moment I thought—well, never mind. What

sort of cooperation? Do you want to move into the hospital altogether, and get me to put up with losing the little of your company I do get? Or are you going to start getting even less money than you do now, and want me to take a cut in the housekeeping? Which is it?"

"It's just a matter of giving your token consent to something that—"

The telephone buzzed sharply, and he turned his head quickly. "What's the time? Nine? Who the hell can . . . the infant . . ." And he moved rapidly toward the door, anxiety welling up in him.

When he came back his face was grim, and she looked at him with surprise. "What's happened? Is there something wrong?"

"It's a bloody nuisance! Are the papers here?"

"Ian took the *Echo*. There's just the *Times*. Why?"

"It's in the *Echo*. Nowhere else apparently. They've found out about the baby."

"Is that bad? You'll be publishing anyway, won't you?"

"But not yet. Oh, God, this is a nuisance. Kegan says they're driving him mad already and he wants me there right away to talk to some bloody newspaper people. And I won't. But I'll have to go."

He looked at her appealingly. "Marjorie, I've got to talk to you about this business, but I can't do it now. Not properly. Please. Am I forgiven for last night?"

Her eyes filled with tears suddenly and she nodded.

"Thank you. I really am sorry, you know. And this other thing—look, what are you doing today?"

"I promised to help make costumes for the next production. Why?"

"Somehow, I'll have to get away in time. I'll have to. We'll go out for dinner."

"I can't do that. Ian's got some friends tonight. I promised I'd cook for them."

"Oh." The chill that had gone for these brief seconds settled again. "Yes. Of course. Then it'll have to wait, I suppose. But it's important, Marjorie. Try not to brood about last night, so that you're angry again by the time I can talk to you."

"I'm not that petty," she said and turned away from him. "I should have known it was only because of something to do with work that you were so anxious to be with me. I'll never learn, will I? Oh, go, will you? I'll be here when you get back, the way I always am, and I'll *cooperate* with whatever it is that's so important to you. I suppose it's something to be grateful for that I can do anything useful for you, so stop worrying. It might interfere with your work if you worry, and that would never do."

Which leaves us just where we started, he thought drearily as he turned and went. If Kegan had waited another few minutes I could have got it settled. Now I'll have to start all over again.

And as he climbed into the car and started the chilled engine, he had to make a very strong effort indeed to close the door on the compartment of his mind where Marjorie belonged and open wide the door to careful logical thinking about the project and this newest complication.

But before he could banish the memory of the expression on Marjorie's face as she stood in the thinly sunlit kitchen, one thought slid through to settle painfully into his consciousness. I wish I could love her as little as I like her.

2

"And suppose I refuse?" Briant said. "What then? They'll give up and leave us to get on with some work, I imagine. So I refuse. End of problem."

"Not quite," Kegan said. "In fact, far from it." He was trying to keep his voice as dry as Briant's, to be as coldly objective, but it was difficult. Remarkable how emotionally involved one became with a situation like this — on the one hand wanting to keep the hospital's backwater unrippled, on the other finding the stir and the fuss and the questioning exciting, even rather agreeably so.

He walked over to the window and looked out at the courtyard below, busy with ambulances and patients clutching appointment cards as they peered hesitatingly at signs pointing the way to Casualty and X-ray and Outpatients, with the birdlike figures of caped nurses changing shifts, and the white coats of housemen hustling importantly from ward block to ward block.

Behind him, Briant sat calmly, legs outstretched, his hands thrust into the pockets of his near-white coat, his eyes fixed on the toes of his highly polished shoes as he rocked his crossed ankles in a slow rhythm.

Matron, sitting tidily in the chair on the far side of him, allowed herself a barely audible sigh of impatience and looked pointedly at her watch, and Briant slid his eyes sideways at her and smiled slightly, raising his eyebrows at Kegan's back view. Matron preferred not to accept his invitation to join in a professional contemptuousness of a fusspot hospital secretary and looked blankly back.

"Look here, Dr. Briant," Kegan said, "there are—what?—fifty, sixty people down there? And I can promise you that more than one of them has no right to be there. Newspaper people—they don't take no for an answer, you know. If they don't get cooperation from us, they'll do without it. And God knows what sort of a mishmash they'll make of it. I can assure you, from some very solid experience, it's asking for trouble to be obstructive."

"Who's being obstructive? If anyone is, they are. Obstructing me in the course of my work. Obstructing you and everyone else in the place, come to that. You're behaving as though they have a right to come nosing where they aren't wanted."

Kegan came back to his desk and sat down again, looking across at Briant with an attempt to appear as calmly reasonable as he did. But he felt irritation rising in him. Bloody man! Bloody arrogant dried-up man. Really, doctors were, by and large, a hateful species.

"I am not sure they haven't," he said carefully. "News is news, and newspaper people would argue that they have every right to report it. The point is, they'll report it one way or the other. I am simply trying to suggest that we do our best to ensure they report it accurately. If we—you—cooperate, then they'll be satisfied and, as you say, leave you to get on with your work. I can assure you, I hold no brief for these wretched people, but as I said, I have had some experience—"

"Yes, I know." Briant for the first time allowed some of his own irritation to show. "When James Torquay died here, and everyone carried on as though he were God incarnate instead of the superannuated useless politician he was. I've heard you on the subject before."

"It wasn't easy," Kegan said, nettled. "We were besieged here for weeks, and life was very complicated for everyone. I don't want it to happen again."

"Nor I, Dr. Briant," Matron said unexpectedly. "I really don't think we could cope with another such situation. And this would be worse. Already, Sister Field is almost at her wits' end. The Maternity phone never stops. Reporters have been ringing there since eight this morning. And three times since breakfast she found unauthorized people prowling around—one of them in the labor room, no less! I must say I agree with Mr. Kegan—"

"I'd like to know how the hell they got onto it," Briant said with a sudden cold fury. "I've been working on this project for two years—two full years with God knows how many people involved. And not a hint got out, not one damned hint. Yet the minute we have to use a hospital ward, newspapers start buzzing. I would have thought you could control your staff's tongues rather more efficiently, Matron."

"My staff have nothing whatsoever to do with this, Dr. Briant!" Matron stood up, thrusting her head forward so that the starched bows under her chin disappeared into folds of flesh. "For one thing, not one of my nurses knew anything about the project; you've kept them almost completely in the dark! Of course, there may well have been conjecture when so many people invaded Maternity when the infant was delivered, but that was something *you* permitted."

"I understand from the *Echo* man that it was your paper in *Nature* that put him onto the track," Kegan said maliciously. "He's a specialist journalist, you know—B. Sc. and all that. He seems to have a considerable amount of information about what your work implies."

"That paper was merely a preliminary one and was published months ago!" Briant snapped. "And no journalist, B.Sc. or not, could have picked up anything from it. This is an internal leak, and that's all about it. So whoever is responsible for the leak can clean up the mess it's made. I'm damned if I will. I've wasted quite enough time this morning already. *You* deal with it, Kegan. Or you, Matron. I told you, I refuse." And he stood up and stretched his neck with his characteristic tortoiselike movement and turned toward the door.

"There is another point, Dr. Briant," Kegan said hastily, regretting the self-indulgence that had allowed him the dig at Briant. "Money."

"What about money?" Briant stood still, his hand on the doorknob.

"You'll need a considerable sum yet to complete this project. Your application for a further grant from our endowment funds comes to committee next month, as you know, and as I told you when you first mooted it, the chances are—well, chancy." He looked at Briant under his lashes and, pleased with the expression on the other man's face, went on smoothly. "I'll do my best of course, as I promised—canvassing a few people—but if the hospital's in an unnecessary turmoil over this, it won't be easy."

"That's blackmail," Briant said after a moment. "Is that what you're trying to do? Blackmail me?" He let go of the doorknob and thrust his hands back into his pockets. "Christ, isn't it bad enough that I have to scrape for every bloody penny to do a piece of vital research, without being forced to turn my project into a circus for a lot of gawping idiots who won't have the least comprehension of what I'm trying to do? Have I got to jump through hoops, ride bareback in spangles, before I'm allowed to do my job?"

With Briant really showing some emotion at last, Kegan felt much better, much more in control. "Not at all, Dr. Briant," he said kindly. "Not at all. I'm just pointing out cold facts. And as for the gawping idiots—haven't you thought how useful a little judicious publicity could be? Get public sympathy and you'll be in a much stronger position altogether—outside the hospital more than in. Even if the committee agree to a grant, it can't be more than a couple of thousand—not enough to keep you going for a few months. But with public interest high, you can go to the big foundations in a far from cap-in-hand way. And they've got hundreds of thousands in their gift, remember."

There was a silence in the big carpeted room with its heavy polished desk and tasteful reproductions of Van Gogh on its lemon-colored walls, as Matron, still looking slightly ruffled, and Kegan, a ludicrously hopeful expression on his face, stared at Briant's bent head as he stood rocking gently on his heels.

"That is an aspect that had not occurred to me," Briant said, and the angry color that had blotched his narrow cheeks receded. "You may well indeed be right. And of course there are the individual philanthropists. There are a number of men only too anxious to buy themselves a knighthood who might be most attracted to a project that catches the public sympathy."

He produced one of his rare smiles and came back to his chair. "I am a practical man, Kegan. A scientist. When you produce an argument that makes practical sense, then of course I'm prepared to listen. Had you said this first, instead of producing emotional gush about the hospital's welfare, we could have saved a good deal of time. So, what precisely do you want to do? I'll cooperate as far as I can, on the understanding of course that I remain in control—full control—of anything to do with my project. I want no pompous official tours of my unit, you understand? And there will be no access to either the infant or the mother. That must be quite clear at the outset."

"Of course," Kegan said and reached for the intercom on his desk. "Matron, do sit down and be comfortable. I'll send for some coffee and we can plan this. Miss Bassett, coffee for three, if you please." He snapped off the machine and settled back in his chair as Matron with a soft rustle of starch rearranged herself in hers.

"I suggest an immediate preliminary press release. I'll write it if you wish, Dr. Briant, and you can vet it. Then a press conference. In the board room. You can appoint one of your own people to act as press liaison officer after that, or I'll lay on someone for the job. That's up to you."

Briant frowned sharply. "You expect more press interest even after the conference? If so, what's the point of having the conference at all? If we're still to be bombarded by these people—"

"There may be some follow-up interest, that's all," Kegan said soothingly. "But it shouldn't last more than a week or so. The press conference will satisfy the newspaper people to start with, but there are the weekly and monthly magazines, foreign press agencies, television people, and so on. We need a plan for them. As I said, I've had some experience. Ah, coffee. Thank you, Miss Bassett. Now, Dr. Briant, suppose we plan the conference for—say tomorrow at ten? That will satisfy the evening papers. Otherwise they'll go on nagging today."

Briant nodded, resigned. "Ten o'clock. I must be away by eleven at the latest, though. We do the daily rundown tests then, and I must be there. There are one or two feeding problems with the infant, and I can't delegate until they're ironed out."

"By all means," Kegan said. "Ten it is. Now I can at least get the pressure off a little. Excuse me."

He clicked the intercom again and said, "Miss Bassett, all calls regarding the Briant project are to be switched to me from here on in. Tell switchboard, will you? And we'd better clear all Maternity calls through here as well. I'll get Matron to handle them"—he looked up at her, and she nodded—"and tell all press callers that a press conference will be held here in the board room at ten A.M. tomorrow."

It had been raining heavily since dawn, water sluicing the gutters of the courtyard, creating rainbows of the patches of oil on the tarmac of the consultants' car park. The people filling the board room steamed gently as they sat huddled together on the rows of chairs arranged neatly in front of the big desk. Sitting in a heavily carved chair to the right of it, George Briant took a sardonic pleasure in the manifest discomfort of the men and women in front of him who moved uneasily in their damp coats and tried to find dry patches on their laps on which to rest their notebooks.

Serve them right, he thought vindictively and then, irritated at his own childishness, turned his head to look at the other people arranged alongside him, the desk's shining expanse of polished wood reflecting their faces as twisted white blobs.

Immediately beside him Kegan was fussing with sheets of paper, arranging and rearranging them into neat aligned squares. He had taken a lot of trouble with his appearance this morning, Briant noticed, his heavy gray hair carefully slicked across his head, his knitted red tie carefully arranged against the collar of his pink shirt. Vain idiot, Briant thought, suddenly conscious of the obvious age of his own gray suit and the shabbiness of his faded blue shirt.

It never failed to anger him—the clearly apparent greater affluence of hospital administrators as compared to his own lack of money. He knew beyond any shadow of doubt that his own contribution to the hospital was worth infinitely more than that of a hundred Kegans. He genuinely had little concern with making money for its own sake, but he could not fail to be infected by Marjorie's martyred attitude to their shortage of cash, and he resented being reminded of it by Kegan's sleekness.

But this was no time to be thinking about Marjorie again and her nagging about their poverty; the morning would be complicated enough, God knew, without allowing Marjorie to invade his mind. So he looked at Matron, tight-faced and armored in starch, at Miss Guttner sitting lumpishly beyond her, her glasses shining blankly as they picked up the overhead light that filled the room with a necessary illumination against the heaviness of the sky pressing grayly against the windows. Dismal woman, Briant thought and dismissed her too from his mind, turning his head again to look at the people in front of him.

Considering the amount of pressure they had been exerting, there should, Briant felt, be a different atmosphere about them. They should seem eager, anxiously expectant, but they merely sat waiting, apparently more concerned with their private conversations than with the people they had come to hear. Even Michael Bridges, the *Echo* man (Kegan had leaned over to Briant and pointed him out as soon as he came in), sat sprawled in seeming boredom in his chair at the end of the front row.

I'll have to watch him, Briant thought. He had made a point of reading some of his articles last night, and the man knew what he was writing about. He spoke Briant's own language.

And suddenly Briant felt better. These people were professionals, like himself. They had a job to do and did it well. Briant might despise the job, despise the way they presented facts to the gawping idiot public, but he could recognize ability when he saw it. And these people had it; their very casualness, their absence of wide-eyed eagerness showed that.

Beside him, Kegan moved, stood up and coughed self-importantly. "I think we can commence, ladies and gentlemen," he said. He coughed again and spoke a little more loudly. "Your time is as precious as ours. And Dr. Briant"—he bowed slightly in Briant's general direction—"must leave at eleven sharp. Now . . ." He took a deep breath, coughed yet again, and picked up one of the sheets of paper before him.

"Dr. Briant wishes me to make clear at the outset that he is not entirely happy that this matter should have become a subject of public discussion. He would point out that scientific projects need a great deal of time to come to fruition, and premature publication of, er, data can damage progress. What appear to be facts at an early stage may well be disproved before the work is completed. However, since some information about his project seems to have leaked out, Dr. Briant has kindly consented to give some of his valuable time to an explanation of the work he is doing."

Kegan looked up from the paper he had been reading and looked a little hopefully at the faces in front of him. "It would be . . . well, interesting to know just how you came to hear about the infant's birth, and why you felt this birth was . . . well, interesting. We, er, we're naturally concerned to know whether there are, er, people working here who have a direct contact with the newspaper that first reported the child's birth and linked it with Dr. Briant's work."

He was looking directly at Bridges, but Bridges looked imperturbably back, and after a few moments of heavy silence Kegan coughed and returned to the paper in his hand.

"Dr. Briant proposes to read a short account of his project to you and will then be available for questioning. In order to cooperate with you fully, we have prepared copies of his statement and some brief notes about Dr. Briant himself, which we trust will be of assistance to you."

Again he looked up from the paper and smiled conciliatingly at his audience. "To be quite honest, ladies and gentlemen, we hope that by offering you all the assistance we can that you will respond by being sympathetic to our, er, request for—shall we say, unsensational coverage? As I said, premature, er, excitement about new scientific facts can damage progress."

Again they sat and looked silently back at him, and again he coughed and turned his head and said a little gruffly, "Dr. George Briant," and sat down.

Briant put his hand in his inside jacket pocket and pulled out the folded sheet of paper that carried his statement, and, a little startled at the sudden wave of apprehension that swept over him, he stood up.

Immediately, the cameramen who had been standing at the sides of the rows of chairs moved, and the flash of lights and the clicks of their equipment bewildered him slightly. He stood blinking against the effect of the lights on his eyes and felt the apprehension disappear under a new wave of feeling—anger. They had made him both look and feel foolish, and that was infuriating.

But he was glad of it. He knew that he always operated at full efficiency when driven by anger; from now on, he was suddenly sure, he was in control of this bloody conference. "This is my statement," he said dryly and bent his head to read.

"As a biologist, my main interest has for some years been human genetics, the study of the way in which various characteristics are passed from parent to offspring. Much investigation has been made by myself and others into the patterns of physical inheritance: body build, eye and hair color, and so on. We know a good deal now about the way in which the genes act."

He looked up and stared at his audience with the slightly accusing look he used for classes of students. "I had better recapitulate for you. Human body cells contain chromosomes, forty-six in each cell. And each chromosome carries some fifty thousand genes, which are the structures that carry inheritance information from parent to offspring. I trust that is quite clear?" Without waiting for a response, he returned to the paper in his hand.

"The research results of the people who defined the structure of DNA—deoxyribonucleic acid—and others working in related fields suggested to me that it might be possible to identify specific genetic details in a newly fertilized human egg cell, since DNA is the substance of which genes are made. Since there are some fifty thousand genes in each chromosome, you can imagine the difficulty inherent in recognizing differences in such microscopic structures. I cannot possibly explain to a lay audience the techniques I used to study these genes—although I can tell you they involved the use of a type of radio microscope, and considerable extremely complex computer work—the programming alone involved almost a year's work. Anyway, in the course of these preliminary studies I succeeded in identifying certain exceedingly small but specific bodies in genes. Those of you who have read my papers in *Nature* may know that these are now known as Briant Bodies, and fall into four distinct groups, which I have labeled Alpha, Beta, Gamma and Delta. Briant Bodies Alpha and Beta carry physical characteristics including hair, skin and eye color, and body build. Briant Bodies Gamma and Delta—the most interesting in my estimation—carry certain personality traits, including intelligence, aggression, equanimity and emotional stress tolerance.

"In other words, it became technically possible for me, some three years ago, to make certain accurate predictions about a human individual by studying the structure of a newly fertilized female reproductive cell, in conjunction with detailed investigation of the adults who produced the ovum and the spermatozoon that fertilized it."

"Dr. Briant?"

Briant looked up, frowning at the interruption. Michael Bridges was still sprawled in his chair, but his face was alert. "Could you clarify that point, please?" he said. "You are saying that if it were possible to remove a fertilized egg cell from a woman after she had conceived, you could examine it and say what the resulting child would be like?"

"Precisely."

"But what's the point of that?" The man sitting next to Bridges leaned forward. "I mean, if you remove the cells, then they can't develop into a baby, can they? You've done an abortion."

"If you can contain your impatience," Briant said dryly, "these points will be explained. You will have ample time for questions when I have completed the reading of this statement."

He returned to his paper. "We also now have a technique that makes it possible to control the production of female ova—egg cells. If we give a woman controlled quantities of a substance called human gonadotrophin, we can make her produce ova to order, as it were. Researchers working with this substance set about trying to remove a fertilized ovum from a woman during the few days that elapse between actual conception and the implantation of the cell into the uterus—where it must be to develop into an infant—and then replacing it. They succeeded, thus making it possible for me to make predictions which could afterwards be verified.

"Now, as a biologist, I have long been somewhat suspicious of the assumptions about human behavior and motivation made by psychologists and sociologists. These, er, workers"—his voice took on a faint sneer as he said the word—"these workers suggest that most human behavior is learned, that we are controlled in our actions not by our inheritance but by what happens to us after birth. They feel nurture is of infinitely greater importance than nature. As I say, I doubt these assumptions, and some interesting studies have confirmed my doubts. For example, babies born carrying a particular extra chromosome are mongols, individuals with well-recognized facial characteristics, lowered intelligence, and an affectionate disposition. Also, it has been noted that men who carry another extra chromosome—in this case a Y chromosome, which is the one that determines maleness—are unusually tall and display aggressive antisocial behavior. In other words, these men are born criminals.

"This knowledge has been of great use. Some researchers working on the removal and examination of fertilized cells have been able to reject those which were clearly mongoloid, only replacing those known to be able to produce normal infants.

"With all this background work on which to draw, I decided two years ago to mount an experimental project which would define the difference between nature and nurture. I would select potential parents and investigate their genetic structure in detail, and then arrange for a conception to take place. I would then investigate the cell structure of this conception, predict the individual, and implant the fertilized cell into the uterus to develop to a full-term infant.

"Thereafter, the child would be reared in a carefully controlled environment, constantly observed and monitored. When he reached maturity, we would be in a position to know precisely which of his behavioral patterns he had inherited and which he had learned.

"The practical uses of such an investigation would be considerable, I thought. For example, if aggressiveness can be undoubtedly shown to be an inherited trait rather than a learned response—as it is in those men with the extra male chromosome—we would be in a position to reject all conceptions which would produce an excessively aggressive individual. We could eventually remove from human life all the characteristics which make for human distress—criminality, war-making, and the like."

He looked up and let his eyes move across the rows of faces before him. The blankness had gone from them, he noticed with satisfaction. They were sitting and staring at him in complete absorption. Aware of the complete control he had over them, and enjoying it, he went on with more deliberation.

"I selected potential parents from university students. Much genetic data was collected from some two thousand young men and women, and using the computer services of two cooperating universities, I eventually selected six potential mothers. I will not now detail the reasons for failure with the first three women—we lost some seven selected conceptions—but go straight to the one with whom we succeeded.

"She is a young woman of considerable intelligence and physical health—a splendid specimen of humanity. She cooperated fully in the project in a most commendable spirit of scientific interest. After several months of trials with human gonadotrophin and conceptions which were made in vitro—the mother of course never met the donor of the sperm which fertilized her ovum—a conception was selected and detailed predictions made—"

"Dr. Briant, would you permit another interruption?" Michael Bridges' voice cut across. "It would help if you would define the term 'in vitro,' I think."

"What? Oh." Briant allowed himself a small sigh of irritation. "Very well. Recent work, notably in Cambridge as well as in the United States, has demonstrated the feasibility of exposing a female ovum to spermatozoa outside the human body—in which such exposure normally takes place—in a special medium. Fertilization can then take place and the first cell divisions can occur. Thereafter, the zygote—the name given to the resultant collection of cells—can be implanted in the uterus. This process is called inovulation, and can be likened to artificial insemination, in that the egg cell is deliberately removed from the woman's body, and reinserted after fertilization. Does that answer your needs?"

"In other words, a test-tube baby?"

"In your words, perhaps. Not a term I would use myself, since I do not find it particularly felicitous. If you cannot use the terms I have offered you, the choice of another is up to you. May I now proceed? Thank you.

"Very well. After a series of trials, a conception made in vitro was selected, predictions were made about it, and it was implanted in the uterus of our volunteer mother. We could have used a different host mother—using ova from one woman, and allowing another to act as the incubator for the conception—but we preferred to use the donor of the egg cell as the incubator, mainly to avoid any risk of rejection. We thought it possible that we might get an auto-immune reaction otherwise—similar to that which occurs when a patient rejects a heart or kidney transplant. So, the selected conception was implanted, and the pregnancy went to full term. The infant, which was incidentally precisely what we predicted he would be in physical makeup, sex, coloring, and so on, was born here seven days ago. It is this fact that . . . leaked—and causes your presence here today.

"From now on, the infant will be reared as I explained, and not for at least twenty years will we be able to report in much detail on the results of our investigations, although preliminary papers will be published in the professional press from time to time. I must here point out to you that any attempts on the part of people outside the project to have any contact with the child will be vigorously rejected. Such contact may seriously invalidate an experiment into which a great deal of work and effort has already been put. I trust you will therefore treat this matter with . . . responsibility."

He sat down and, thrusting his hands into his trouser pockets, stared coolly at the audience which sat in complete silence before him.

But then a wave of movement rustled across them, and several people jumped up waving notebooks.

It was a woman who got the first question in, her voice rising shrilly above the others.

"Dr. Briant! Are we to understand you have made a test-tube baby? That you are going to bring him up in a . . . in a *laboratory?* A human baby is a *guinea* pig?"

The horror in her voice was almost ludicrous, and Briant raised his eyebrows slightly. "As I have said, 'test-tube baby' is not a term I would ever use. What I have described to you is a controlled conception. As for rearing the child in a laboratory, the unit prepared for him is not equipped with bunsen burners and retorts and animal cages. He will have every comfort and care, I assure you—probably in excess of that provided for any human infant ever."

"But what about his parents? Where do they come into it? Have they agreed to let their baby be treated in this fashion? What sort of parents can they be, to give up their baby like this?"

Only a momentary tightening of the jaw showed Briant's irritation. Emotional idiot! he thought, but tried not to let his contempt show in his voice.

"You appear to have misunderstood what I have told you. The father is known only to myself and the computer, and none of the young men who cooperated in giving us specimens of their sperm knew for what purpose it was given. The child's natural father has no idea that he is a father." He smiled thinly. "Not, perhaps, an unusual experience for virile young men."

"But the *mother*!" The woman reporter almost wailed the words. "She knows she has a baby—is she giving him up just like that? Doesn't she *care*?"

"I told you she entered into the project in a spirit of most admirable scientific curiosity. I must point out that she was selected with considerable care. She is not a woman with an interest in maternity. She at no time had an emotional link with the father of the infant—she never met him, as I must again repeat—or an emotional involvement with the pregnancy. She saw her role as purely an incubatory one, and will now return to her own work as a biologist—although not of course on this project—having made her most valuable contribution to my work. She will no doubt maintain her interest in the progress of the project, but not in the child in any possessive sense. She's too intelligent for that." And this time he let the contempt enter his voice.

"What's intelligence got to do with it?" This came from a man standing behind the shrill woman. "What about good old-fashioned mother love? Don't tell me intelligent women don't love their children! My wife's got a degree in mathematics, but she loves her kids!"

"No doubt. But mother love is a compound of involvement with the father and care of the infant. We know of course that this mother has the normal strong biological drive to care for her offspring, and if she did handle him would no doubt develop an emotional involvement. But, as a scientist, she was and is prepared to tolerate this drive while it lasts without satisfying it. We have done our best to protect her; we ensured she would not see the baby at birth, removing him from the Maternity Unit as soon as he was delivered. It is already apparent to us that she has no emotional link with the child; she is indeed now only anxious to return to her own work, which she will do in about ten days' time."

"Hence the kidnaping story," Bridges said, and Briant looked at him sharply.

"What was that?"

"We . . . heard that the child had been kidnaped with the full collusion of the hospital staff," Bridges said blandly.

"Who told you that?" Briant snapped.

"Ah, I'm sorry, Dr. Briant. Must protect my sources, you know."

Another journalist cut in then. "Dr. Briant, this mother never saw the father either?"

"I keep saying that!"

"Christ! A virgin birth, no less!"

"Hardly," Briant said sharply. "And may I suggest that this is precisely the kind of overheated sensational attitude I would most strongly deplore. This woman may be technically a virgin in that she has never experienced intercourse, either with the father of this infant or anyone else. It was necessary to the experiment that we select a sexually mature but inexperienced woman. Previous intercourse may have in some way altered her—set up antibodies of an unknown kind. We do not yet know whether this can happen, but we could not risk invalidating the experiment by using a sexually experienced woman. Also, if a woman at twenty-six is still a virgin it suggests she is not an overemotional type. That is, she would be in part protected by her own nature from the complications of emotional involvement."

"But the knowledge derived from psychological studies into the human personality suggests that sexually frigid women are just as liable to emotional involvement as anyone else," Bridges cut in. "Maybe she's the chilly type you describe because of psychological problems. Couldn't that damage your baby?"

"I have little faith in the unsubstantiated assertions of psychologists," Briant said dryly. "I can assure you this woman is what she appears—an intelligent scientist untrammeled by the usual preoccupations of women."

"You sound like a misogynist, Dr. Briant!" Bridges said. "That isn't really relevant, I suppose, though it would be interesting to know whether you inherited the trait." He looked at Briant a little wickedly and rode smoothly over his attempts to retort. "But to return to the baby. His mother may, as you suggest, have no need to love him. But hasn't he a need to be loved by *her*? Might I remind you of the work of Dr. Bowlby, who pointed out the effects of mother deprivation on children? Of course, he is perhaps more a sociologist and psychologist than a biologist, but still . . ."

Anger was getting close to being out of control, Briant suddenly realized, and he made a conscious effort to push it down.

"I am fully aware of the infant's need for a permanent mother figure, and this has been taken into account. The child is receiving his direct physical care from a carefully selected woman who will be his nurse-cum-mother for the next few years. And you may like to know that we have not neglected the infant's *biological* need to suckle. This woman, although not recently delivered, once bore a child, and so we have been able, by the use of selected hormone therapy, to establish lactation again."

"A wet nurse! Back to the Middle Ages!"

Briant ignored that and looked instead at a man waving his notebook eagerly from the back row.

"What about the legality of this, Dr. Briant?" he called. "Can you rear this child this way? Whatever the mother's feelings, she's got rights, hasn't she?"

"Of course she has. And she has assigned them to me. In other words, I will in due course adopt the child. As his legal guardian, I am then legally able to decide his care."

"But it's so *cruel*!" the shrill woman cried. "There'll be an outcry, bring up a human baby as though he were some sort of experimental animal! The authorities surely can't allow it!"

"Cruel?" Briant stared at her as though she were demented. "Madam, I do not intend to beat, starve or in any way maltreat this child. He will have every possible care, has an inheritance that ensures perfect physical health, high intelligence, an even disposition, and an inquiring mind. I can assure you that any busybody would be hard put to it to prove maltreatment! If you are so concerned with the kindly nurture of infants, I suggest you turn your journalistic—*conscience*—to those children begotten by inadequate stupid parents being reared in appalling conditions in slums all over the country. A newspaper campaign to prevent breeding by some of the substandard individuals with whom society is saddled would be much more to the point than vapid maunderings about the welfare of a child who has been endowed with an almost perfect inheritance, and is being given the best possible care!"

He suddenly became aware of Kegan beside him, sharply tugging at the edge of his jacket, and turned to stare at him, blotches of anger flaming in his cheeks.

"Ladies and gentlemen," Kegan said loudly, "I am sure you will understand Dr. Briant's . . . distress at the imputation of cruelty.

I must give you my personal assurances that this infant is receiving perfect care. The unit in which he will live is within the hospital grounds, and was most carefully prepared and equipped. As well as by Dr. Briant, he is supervised by our Dr. Saxby, a most eminent pediatrician—child-care specialist. We have assigned considerable staff to cooperate in his care—dietitians, physiotherapists, all sorts. You really need not fear that Dr. Briant will be anything other than an excellent father to this child. After all, he is a father himself! He has a daughter of sixteen, a son of seventeen, both charming and most happy young people! It is natural that any suggestion of lack of . . . of affection for this child should so upset a man who is of the highest integrity—"

"Thank you, Mr. Kegan," Briant said sharply. It was infuriating to have let anger steal his tongue as it had. He had been pushed into this bloody situation by the need to attract public sympathy, and yet had been stupid enough to let the manifest idiocy of his questioners drive him to make a most unsympathetic exhibition of himself. And it didn't help to have that idiot Kegan see what he had done and try to extricate him.

Remember what you're here for, he told himself and turned back to his audience.

"I must indeed apologize for my . . . irritation," he said and produced his most disarming smile. "My feelings were hurt. Will you forgive me, madam?" And he looked directly at the woman who had been the origin of his biting anger and smiled again. She reddened and bobbed her head and sat down a little awkwardly.

Bridges' voice came clearly again. "Dr. Briant, *why* are you doing this work?"

"I thought I'd explained that!"

"Oh, yes, you explained about what you want to find out. All very interesting. And that it may have practical applications. But *why?* Do you want to make it possible to rear a race of supermen? Bit . . . well, Hitlerish, isn't it?"

Careful. Careful, Briant thought, and he paused a moment before speaking.

"I can assure you that I have no political motives whatsoever. Politics bore me, frankly. But I am a biologist, a scientist. And that means I'm a realist. We surely have all faced the fact that the world is in real danger of overpopulation?" He looked around at the rest of the journalists. "That the time must inevitably come when we will have to control the right to reproduce? How it will be done is outside my brief at the moment. I . . . well, I want to find a way to ensure that we have a method that will help us produce only the best and happiest of individuals, so that when the time comes for control to be applied, it can be done gainfully. How much better it will be to say to people, 'We can ensure that the children you have will be the best possible children, the ones with the best inheritance, the ones who will make the world a really good place to live in instead of the misery it so often is.' "

I've got them! he thought with sudden joyousness. I've got them.

"You can't really want the handicapped, the mentally dull, the physically frail to reproduce themselves ad infinitum? In the early days of man's evolution natural forces ensured that these individuals were weeded out of the human race and could not reproduce, but science has altered all that, made it possible to rear such frail specimens. Survival of the fittest was a superb natural mechanism which we damaged. Now, as a scientist, I am trying to repair that damage. Isn't that a laudable aim?"

"Oh, undoubtedly," Bridges murmured, and he was clearly heard, for Briant's oration seemed to have completely flattened the other listeners. "Although I can't help wondering whether you may be creating a tool which could be dangerously used. Do you never fear the possible misapplication of your work?"

"A scientist cannot be swayed by such fears and still remain true to science." Briant paused, seeking the words which would explain what he meant without antagonizing this man. He was no longer aware of the other people present, only of the lanky figure in the front row.

"Take Rutherford. Had he worried about the possibility of atomic warfare when he was attempting to split the atom, he would never have gone on; and we would have lost the many benefits nuclear physics has given us, such as freely available power and treatment of disease. No, Mr. Bridges. In the search for knowledge what matters is the truth that is knowledge. How it is used becomes the responsibility of others, not the searchers. And anyway, my search for knowledge about human behavior—surely it can't be dangerous? To help people to be better people, happier people, how can that be dangerous?"

There was a short silence, and then from the back of the room a very young man stood up.

"Now you know how to select these perfect babies, Dr. Briant, will the treatment be available on the National Health Service?"

And suddenly the room shook with laughter. The prosaic simplicity of the question seemed to release and dissipate their suppressed anxiety and resentment, and the young man went scarlet with shame. But Briant was grateful to him.

"A most reasonable question!" he said loudly above the noise. "Most reasonable." The laughter subsided. "It will be some time before the results of the experiment can be applied; not until the child reaches maturity can we evaluate our findings. And as for the National Health Service, well, it isn't financing my work now! I have to seek such support from charity. And unless more charity comes my way, the whole project may founder."

Leave it at that, leave it at that, he thought. Don't shout too hard for money, but leave it at that. It's enough.

The shrill woman stood up again. "Dr. Briant! Can you tell us what the baby's name is?"

For one brief moment Briant was nonplused. He had frankly given no thought whatsoever to the child's name; he had not yet thought of him as an identity anyway. Perhaps that was why. But to say as much to this sentimental woman's-magazine lady would be asking for trouble, undoing all the efforts he had made to assure them all of his true warm humanity—emotional lot! And it would be a picture of his true warm humanity that would bring the money in for the project. He had then one of his occasional flashes of utter brilliance. "Why," he said, smiling kindly at her, "George Briant, of course. He is, after all, to be as a son to me."

3

He left them just before eleven, well satisfied with his morning's work. He'd made mistakes, but he had salvaged them. They had seemed quite satisfied with his answers to their further questions, piddling little questions about the baby's weight and hair and eye color, about the progress of the birth. He'd handed those to Miss Guttner, as the obstetrician involved, and she had confused them considerably with talk about the obstetric details, which pleased Briant a good deal. While she was ponderously explaining what an LOA presentation was, they couldn't probe at him.

He had deeply resented the questions about himself as a personality, but had accepted Kegan's whispered warning about antagonizing them again, and had submitted with the best grace he could muster. Yes, he was medically qualified, as well as being a biologist. Yes, he was a professor—an associate, not the holder of a chair, and did teach, but preferred to be referred to as Dr. Briant rather than Professor. No, his son was not at present intending to follow his father into a scientific career, although his daughter was (and these questions he found particularly intrusive, but then thoughts of Ian and his activities always were an intrusion anyway). And no, he could not discuss the question of his wife's involvement with the infant at this stage. She was of course interested in his progress, but as he had already told them, a mother substitute had been appointed to give the child his direct physical care.

He frowned sharply as he thought again about those particular questions. He had still not been able to talk to Majorie about the adoption. When he had reached home the previous evening, she had gone to bed. "Feeling ill, poor darling," Ian had told him with a hint of malice underlying his display of concern. "She cooked dinner for us—she always keeps her promises, doesn't she, no matter how she's feeling?—but now she's bushed."

And George had found her apparently asleep, and had slept uneasily himself, impatient to get the whole matter properly thrashed out, hoping to discuss it in the morning. But she had woken with one of her banging headaches, so that was that.

Perhaps tonight I'll get a chance, he thought now, with a lift of optimism. With a successful press conference behind him, he felt a new confidence in his ability to handle Marjorie, even though she was clearly well launched into one of her periods of being thoroughly tiresome. That she was being merely tiresome was undoubted. He had talked to Apthorp about her the previous afternoon, and it was clear she had exaggerated his anxiety about her health. There had been no new developments at all.

Yes, he'd deal with Majorie tonight, and he'd get her to agree to make her token agreement to the adoption. But he was glad he'd been able to fend off too many probing journalistic questions about her; he didn't want them publishing any comments about her at this stage, that was sure. Such premature publicity could make her positively obstructive instead of merely difficult.

Indeed, he told himself as he walked briskly across the courtyard toward the covered way that led past Pathology and Pharmacy to the rear of the hospital and his own unit, it was not quite as bad as it might have been, taking it all around. And now at least he'd be left in peace to get on with some real work.

The thought of work brought its familiar comfort, and as he pushed open the door of his unit he switched his mind tidily from the press conference to the tests waiting to be done. He had an enjoyable job of work waiting for him, and asked for no more than that. And he had six people to work with who wouldn't waste time on stupid questions about the baby's emotional welfare, who saw as clearly as he did the greater fascination in the sheaves of data they had already collected on the child since his birth.

At seven days, we may be able to get some sense out of the graph on the effects of vacuum decompression during the pregnancy, he told himself happily and walked into his crowded office with a spring in his step.

Isobel moved softly as she carried the pile of fresh disposable diapers to the cupboard. He was a good baby, didn't startle and wake at the least noise, like some did, but there was a pleasure in being gentle and slow about things. And the least I can do is make sure he has some peace and quiet while he can, poor little scrap, she thought.

She stacked the diapers neatly on the top shelf, checked the gowns and vests, and then closed the cupboard and turned to look approvingly around the room. All tidy and comfortable, though she would have preferred to see a little color about the place. All that buff paint—it was so unbabylike; a nursery should have some pink and blue and lemon in it, like sugared almonds. But when she had asked if they couldn't warm the place up a bit with some pretty colors, Dr. Briant had said sharply that they had to avoid confusing their color appreciation tests later, and she'd have all the color she wanted then.

She moved over to the cot and looked down at the baby. He really is a dear little thing, she thought, rubbing a little at her right breast. It was sore. She had told Dr. Saxby, and he'd said he'd mention it to Dr. Briant; it could be she was having a bit too high a dose of the red capsules. She certainly had a lot of milk. She thought herself it was because he was such a hungry baby—suckled so vigorously she felt sometimes as though he was pulling out her middle. Not that she had said that to Dr. Saxby. They had warned her at the start there would be complicated things going on, and not to try to understand them, that her job was looking after the baby. So, obediently she kept her own counsel. She wasn't going to risk annoying them as she had about the color of the paint.

The baby moved his head, and she winced slightly as she looked at him. Those things strapped to his poor little scalp—they must hurt him, no matter what they said. But he didn't wake, even though he was lying right on two of them, so maybe they were right. Electrodes, that's what they were; she had seen them used on the baby in the next cot to Jenny in the hospital, just a few days before she had died.

Strange how she could think about Jenny now without feeling so sick. For a long time after she had died, she hadn't been able to think about her at all, it had been so awful, but now she could. And in this last week, ever since she had started the job properly, it had got even easier. The baby had helped a lot.

She sat down in the chair at the head of the cot and very carefully slid her forefinger into the baby's hand. His grasp tightened around it automatically, and she found herself smiling. Dear little thing he was, just like Jenny had been at his age.

She felt a sudden stab of guilt, comparing him with Jenny. No matter what they had said to her at the hospital, it had been her fault she had died. She should have known she was ill, got a doctor to see her earlier, not waited until the bronchitis had turned to pneumonia, so that none of their injections and treatment had been any good. But she had been so ashamed. They had advised her to have the baby adopted, told her she'd not be able to earn a living for them both, but she'd been willful and gone her own way.

And when Jenny had got ill, she had been willful again, told herself she could manage to get her better without having the doctor to see her. And she knew now the reason she hadn't wanted the doctor, knew it was because she was afraid they'd take Jenny away from her because she wasn't fit to look after her. So it was her fault Jenny had died. She would carry the knowledge of that all her life.

Yet who'd have thought I'd be given another chance like this?

she thought. When she had decided to go after a job with children, the best she had hoped for was a mother's-help place; she wasn't trained as a nanny or anything like that. Yet she'd walked right into this marvelous chance, with no mother who would get jealous of her with the baby, only this bunch of doctors to deal with. It was like having a baby of her own again. It really went to show that God was good; when you'd paid for the things you did and you were really sorry, He gave you something good to make it up to you. And He knew she'd paid sorely for having Jenny, paid in her own shame at being caught by a married man at her age, paid in being the cause of her death.

The baby moved again, opened his eyes, and puckered his face as he pulled his hands up toward his mouth; and Isobel smiled again as he mouthed at his fingers. He really was a baby and a half, this one! He'd taken a full seven ounces at ten, and in just ten minutes on each breast too. Even Miss Hervey had remarked on it when she did the test weigh; seven days old, and taking so much already. And now he was curling his mouth and going for his fingers as though he could start all over again, not two hours later! Really, a baby and a half.

Her nipples tingled a little as she looked at him. She oughtn't to want him to wake properly, but she did. And she couldn't ring for them unless he was really awake. They'd told her, on no account was he to be allowed to cry for a feed, but that at the same time he wasn't to be put to the breast unless he really wanted to. She'd soon develop a judgment about it, they'd said, and she was beginning to.

He moved again, and gladly she leaned over and pressed the bell on the wall beside the cot and got up to get the breast tray. By the time Dr. Briant and Miss Hervey came in she was ready.

"He's hungry, sir, I think," she said as Dr. Briant walked over to the crib. "Though he took a lot at the ten o'clock feed."

"Splendid!" Dr. Briant said. "Splendid! Look, Barbara. Really a most well-defined rooting reflex, isn't it?" He touched the baby's cheek with his forefinger, and Isobel could see even from her chair between the cameras that the baby's lip curled at once toward it.

"I've rerun the film twice," Miss Hervey said. "It's a little early to be sure, but there certainly seems to be a pattern to it. The time lag in the nocturnal response is quite marked—averages point nine plus of a second greater. Most interesting. And it seems undoubtedly to be more rapid when he's put to the breast. You'll see when we see today's film run that this response won't have been nearly as rapid as the one he'll show when Miss Quinn takes him."

"Which suggests a considerable ability to modify a reflex with learned behavior," Dr. Briant said. "It's really very gratifying to have such early confirmation of one of our projections." And they nodded at each other, for all the world, Isobel thought, like a pair of well-fed penguins. The idea pleased her suddenly. Comparing them with such stupid birds made them less alarming, somehow less powerful.

"Well, come along, come along, Miss Quinn," Dr. Briant said, using the bright rallying voice he always did when speaking to her, and obediently she picked up the baby and carried him to the scales. Miss Hervey took the reading and entered it, and Isobel settled herself in the chair, the baby on her lap, and unbuttoned her blouse.

It was funny how quickly she had got used to it, sitting there with them watching her while she swabbed her nipple and lifted the baby close to her so that he could reach it. Even knowing the cameras were always working, filming every single thing she and the baby did, didn't bother her any more. At first it had been like being spied on, but now she forgot them most of the time, except when she wanted to do something she shouldn't.

Like now, wanting to hold her breast and guide it to the baby's mouth, but they wouldn't let her. Dr. Briant had said, when they taught her how to handle him at the beginning, "He must never be coerced—coaxed—to do anything. Nor helped, particularly when he is feeding. We have to see exactly what he is doing by himself, and what he learns by himself—not what you teach him, do you understand?"

Well, she didn't really see what difference it could make, but she was obedient. It was too good a job to risk doing otherwise, and besides, the cameras were always there, so she had to.

And he was already so bright, anyway. He turned his head,

mouthing eagerly, and found the nipple so fast you'd think it was made of iron and he was a magnet.

As he fed, and she sat looking down at his absorbed face and regularly pumping jaws, his eyes tight closed and his clenched fist resting lightly on her skin, she slid into the blissfully familiar peace of it, even enjoying the faint sense of shame that came with the pleasure. It was a good thing the cameras couldn't take pictures of the way she felt, she thought, and smiled inside herself. That *would* be embarrassing!

And when he'd finished and been weighed again and she'd changed his diaper and put it in the special container to go away for the chemical analysis—And a nasty old job that must be to do! Isobel thought—and he was back sleeping in his cot, it was gone twelve and time for the daily briefing. Then it would be her lunch-time, and probably another feed, and after that they'd send her for her afternoon rest, and then collect the specimens and the data from him for the next day's test session. But Isobel didn't want to think about that.

The briefing was the same as it had been every day since he was born. They talked together about the tests (and Isobel thanked God she understood so little of it; it all sounded so complicated and unfriendly), and she watched the baby on the monitor screen high on the wall and the patterns on the machines, the ones linked up to the cot with its attachments for measuring his heartbeats and his breathing and his body temperature.

And then they turned to her and reminded her again how she was to handle him, no trying to make him do as she wanted, only to do as he wanted. But there was something different today, and it pleased her.

"You are to start talking to him, Miss Quinn. Just the way any woman talks to a baby, you understand? It doesn't matter what you say—not at this stage. Later on we will modify the program—give you a list of specific sounds we want you to make—but at present you are quite free to talk as you wish. There is just one thing. I want you to wear this."

He picked up a small square object from his desk, with wires leading from it.

"It's simply a tape recorder. You'll wear the box strapped to your back, and these little microphones will rest against your throat. I'm sure you'll soon get used to it—because we need to have an accurate recording of the sounds you make to the baby, you see?" He looked closely at her and spoke in a slightly louder voice and more slowly. Just as though I were a bit daft, Isobel thought with sudden resentment.

"A child learns to speak by imitation, you see, Miss Quinn. And we need to know precisely what sort of sounds are most rapidly learned. We've already recorded all the sounds he's heard since he's been in the unit, of course, but this little gadget will help us to have an even more detailed record. You see?"

"Yes, sir," Isobel said in her usual colorless voice. "I see." As if it matters that much, she thought as she stared back at him. Scientists! Everyone knows babies learn by copying, so why all this performance to prove it?

"Well, thank you, Miss Quinn. You go and have your lunch now, and your rest. Oh, and I've changed the dosage of the red capsules. Dr. Saxby tells me you're having some discomfort, and a smaller dosage will help. You really are a most efficient milk-making machine!"

She reddened, and Briant thought, Oh, damn. I've embarrassed her, and looked away, feeling surprisingly embarrassed himself.

He had chosen this woman specifically because she was the sort she was—a simple type, immediately responsive to the baby, no outside involvements, so she was free to give her entire time to him, willing to do without time off while the baby was still on the breast, and not expecting the massive salary most women would want for a job like this. But her very virtues carried their own faults, and not the least of them was the possibility of her being upset by matters she could not understand. A woman as passive and yet responsive as she was could well suffer emotional distress which she would not overtly express. And that might affect her milk, which would be a nuisance, to put it mildly. He would have to watch more carefully the way he spoke to her.

But she seemed to have got over her momentary embarrassment, so he smiled at her as warmly as he could, and she went away to eat her solitary lunch in the small bed-sitting-room alongside the nursery, which was the only part of the Unit that wasn't monitored with cameras and tape recorders.

He had indeed upset her, but not in the way he thought. Isobel found nothing odd any more in public discussion of her breasts and the milk and the way the baby acted during feeding. But she didn't like being called a machine, even an efficient one. No one would, she told herself, no one with any feelings. If he had any, he'd know that.

And the small seed of anger against him knotted itself inside her into a hard little core of resentment.

"Have you enough data yet to offer any sort of evaluation of your early projections?" Miriam asked. "This is good coffee. The stuff they've been giving me in the ward was like a milk soup. I've been longing for something with a bit of bite to it."

She laughed then, a little awkwardly. "I'm sorry. That's a habit I seemed to have got into during the pregnancy. I'm only just realizing that I did."

"Habit?"

"Asking a question, saying something, and then veering off onto a completely different tangent. It's maddening. All that folklore about women operating on a different intellectual level because of their hormone differences would appear to have some basis in fact. I'm certainly forced to admit I've noticed it in myself—my thinking hasn't been nearly as controlled as it used to be. I imagine it's a temporary change. I certainly hope so! Grim if producing an infant damages one's thinking processes for good and all."

"I'm sure it doesn't!" Briant said. "I can think of several women who did excellent post-maternity work. Marie Curie, for example. As for going off at tangents, my dear, I do it myself, hormone balance notwithstanding. And it *is* good coffee, and the stuff they provide on Maternity *is* revolting!"

She laughed again and shook her head. "Stop humoring me. If you start that, then I'll know I'm beyond redemption. It would mean you see me as a woman who happens to be in science, and not as a scientist. And that would be depressing, to say the least."

"You're a scientist," he said. "No doubt about that. No one who can be as objective about her own thinking processes as you are could be otherwise. You're quite entitled to be . . . well, a bit off center at the moment. Anyone can experience alterations in their thought patterns under stress; I know I do. When I have problems with my wife or one of the children, I have to make considerable effort to keep my mind on work, I assure you."

He paused, a little surprised at himself. "Do you know something? I've never said that to anyone—admitted I have family problems on occasions, that is. The psychoanalysts might suggest that your own temporary alteration of intellectual function has been projected on to me."

"Analysts!" she said with a fine scorn. "Sympathetic magicians would be a better label."

"Good girl! I couldn't agree more. Though you know that."

"I'll be honest with you. It was as much to disprove some of their absurd assumptions as to help you prove your own theories that I agreed to come in on this project. They annoy me so much! A somewhat unscientific approach, perhaps—"

"Not at all! The desire to disprove a false idea is as valid a basis for a piece of research as the desire to establish the truth of a new set of ideas. Better in some ways. There's a greater danger of reaching a false conclusion when you're hell-bent on proving your own thinking. When you're trying to demolish a false promise, I suspect you are less likely to close your eyes to unacceptable facts."

"Oh, surely not! Remember Jefferson—that very bright man in my year? When he did his thesis on the portal shunt in rats, he completely ignored the work Peders had done, because it proved conclusively what *he* was trying to discredit. He made a complete idiot of himself over that, and I swear it wasn't done deliberately. He just managed to close his mind to what he didn't want to know, because it spoiled his beautiful graphs."

"A bad scientist, Jefferson."

She nodded and looked at him a little wickedly. "Maybe that's why he got such a lucrative job. I've always suspected industry prefers bad scientists."

"Cynic! But you're probably right. And how's all this for a tangent? I've quite forgotten what it was you asked."

"What? Oh, yes. I just wondered what progress you'd made so far. Or is it still too young for you to make any evaluations apart from tentative ones?"

He frowned sharply at her bent head as she poured another cup of coffee for both of them.

"That's odd," he said.

"What is?" She looked up, startled at the change in his voice.

"That you should refer to the child in the neuter. It, rather than he."

She reddened slightly and opened her mouth to speak, but they were interrupted. The medical staff dining room was almost empty, and the last group of people were just leaving. Dr. Saxby detached himself as he passed their table and put his hand on Briant's shoulder.

"Do you want to spend some time on those ECG tracings this afternoon, George? My registrar can take my clinic—it's a small one—so I could be with you from three until four-thirty if you like."

"Three? Yes, I think so. I should have the blood work through by then, and that would help. Fine. You'll come to the Unit?"

"By all means. Hello, Miss Lawton! Good to see you about again. Miss Guttner tells me you're progressing well."

"Very well, thank you. I'm returning to work next week."

"Good! No therapy like it, is there? And you can be pleased with yourself. That's a splendid infant you produced. Splendid."

"It was a team job," she said in a colorless voice.

"Oh, of course. But they couldn't have got far without you, could they?" Saxby produced his big comfortable laugh. "We haven't reached Huxley's Brave New World yet! It'll be a long time before the word 'mother' becomes as dirty a word as he suggested it would. Though the way you lot are going, George, it mayn't be *that* long. Well, I've a ward round to get through before I can come over to your unit, George, so I'd better get moving. At three then." And nodding cheerfully at them both, he went away.

There was a short silence as they both drank coffee, and then

Miriam said sharply, "Why should it be odd to refer to the infant in the neuter? It's not as though the gender were all that relevant to the work you're doing."

He moved a little uneasily. "I'm not sure. It just struck me as . . . well, odd. Perhaps I've been infected by those damned journalists."

"Journalists?"

"Oh, I had to hold a bloody press conference this morning. You know it got out—the birth? And Kegan was old-womaning around until he drove me to agreeing to talk to the wretched people. We won't know till tomorrow what sort of dog's breakfast they'll dish up out of it, but they were waffling on about the poor little guinea-pig baby. You can imagine the sort of thing. What does he look like? What does he weigh? What will his name be? It was like bathing in hot syrup."

"Perhaps you should have concerned yourself as much about avoiding emotional involvement yourself as about protecting me," she said, and her voice was still sharp. "In using the neuter term rather than the particular I display clearly my own lack of involvement, and you find it odd! Forgive me if I find *that* odd?"

"Touché!" he said and smiled awkwardly. "You're right, of course. My apologies."

"Not needed. And forget the question I asked. If you can be as . . . affected as you seem to have been by answering journalists' questions, perhaps I'd be wiser to wait for publication of results, like everyone else. Anyway, there's something else I'd like to talk about. I have an idea for a piece of work that might possibly provide a theme for my doctorate thesis. I'd like your guidance, if you can spare another few minutes."

"Of course," he said. "I'd be glad to. You need a strong piece of work. What have you thought of?"

"It's this interesting effect of hormone balance on thinking processes. Would it be possible to mount a research project into that, do you suppose? I could have access to the female population of the university, both pre and post maternity. There are plenty of students with children, after all . . ."

She lay on the narrow white bed, staring out of the window at the gray-white clouds moving heavily across the October sky, and tried to organize her thinking.

She had been so pleased when Dr. Briant had suggested she lunch with him in the medical staff dining room, aching as she was to get away for a while at least from the uncomfortable atmosphere of the Maternity Ward. The staff talked only banalities at her, until she could have screamed with irritation, and try as she might to ignore it, there was no doubt in her mind that they disliked her, these crisp women in their crisp uniforms. Well, dislike wasn't the word perhaps, disapproval was really what she felt coming from them.

And the infuriating thing was that their disapproval mattered to her. It shouldn't; she had never been a woman to give a damn about other people's opinions. She went her own way, made her own successes and failures, and cared for no opinion but her own, apart from that of people she knew to be her intellectual equals or superiors. People like Briant. So why should she care what these half-witted women thought?

Because I'm a woman, and my hormone balance is disturbed by the pregnancy—makes me respond emotionally to my biological state? An interesting hypothesis, that. She filed the thought for later use. Or is it because in a way I share their disapproval?

She swung her legs over the edge of the bed and went over to the window to look down at the courtyard. Is that it? she thought. Am I really just like every other woman down there? Do I share their prejudices and feel somewhere deep in my psyche that a woman ought to care about a baby she produces, even if she produces it under highly unnatural conditions? Do I feel anger at myself because I don't care?

But you do care. It was as though a voice had actually said the words aloud, and she moved sharply and leaned against the window to stare blankly at the room. You're having to make a conscious effort to be detached, aren't you? That's why Briant found it odd you should refer to the baby as "it"; it wasn't the use of a neuter term, but the way you sounded when you said it. Strained. Self-conscious.

"I *don't* care," she said aloud. I really don't, not in that sense. Of course I care that the project should be valid, produce worth-while results. I don't want to think I've wasted almost a year of my working life on an abort. My caring is scientific. No more and no less. I care the way Jefferson cared about his rats and their portal shunts. That's all. He didn't love his rats, and I don't love this baby. How could I?

Across the hall, someone opened the door to the nursery, and the thin wail of a baby cut across her thinking, and she raised her head sharply, feeling a sudden surge of anxiety.

And then anger took its place, and she moved sharply across to her bed and rang the bell. When the nurse came, she said crisply, "Will you ask Sister Field if I could speak to her please? As soon as possible—before Miss Guttner comes over for her ward round."

She would insist on leaving the Maternity Ward today. There was no point in staying for the next three days; her physical progress was excellent, and the proximity of these midwives and mothers and babies was having a most unfortunate effect on her. There would be much more point in spending the rest of the week working in the library, planning a project of her own. It was high time she got down to serious thought about her doctorate.

At six-thirty Kegan passed her taxi as it swung out across the courtyard. He was walking purposefully toward Dr. Briant's unit, two newspapers held firmly under his arm, and his face was set in hard lines of anger.

He'd warned the man, no one could say he hadn't warned him. If it had only been possible to hold the conference without him! But that had been out of the question, of course. It was ridiculous, really it was. To have had to practically beg the man to cooperate with him, and now be faced with the God-awful mess he'd made of it. And these were only the London evenings. Heaven help them all when the dailies came out the next day. And as for the Sundays! He felt sick as he thought about them.

And that reminded him. He'd better warn Matron to keep a

special watch on the Maternity people. The Sundays would be baying after the Lawton girl in no uncertain terms, now the evenings had led the way. Though maybe they'd turn in the other direction, looking for a different angle? It was a possibility.

He was a very confused as well as a very angry man as he pushed open the doors of Briant's unit, and hurried down the corridor toward the office.

4

Mike filed his copy at quarter past four and went back to his desk and plastic beaker of stewed tea feeling well satisfied. Four good folios there, the whole story put across clean and clear, solid with fact and not a smell of an opinion. The sort of job that pleased him most, this one. A piece of real science, worth reporting, and because of its human angle small danger of the copy being spiked in favor of something with half its intrinsic interest.

And since he'd opened it up in the first place—and he definitely owed David Dennis a drink for putting him onto it—every chance of a couple of TV spots on the strength of it. If they were the right spots, and he handled them properly, he might manage to get his foot well into that door.

He let his mind play with that again, the idea of making it on the box. It had been with him a long time, long before McLuhanism had arrived to make a lot of people cry into their beer at El Vino's and go haring after every tin-pot producer in the business.

But he wasn't going to make that mistake. With a specialty like his, he could afford to wait until a really worthwhile chance came up. Like a regular place on the *Probe* team. They didn't use a full-time science man, only that wet psychiatrist with a profile that he displayed to a damned sight better advantage than his puny little mind.

Now that was an idea. Call J. J. Gerrard direct and see if he could set up a spot on Briant for tonight's edition? He was more than the anchor man, everyone knew that, and if he wanted to put a regular science spot in the program, the producer wouldn't argue. And if Mike could set it up for tonight, and it went well, a drink with J. J. in the club afterward could pay big dividends.

He reached for his desk phone and then swore as it rang before he could pick it up.

"Mike Bridges," he said irritably. "What? Oh, yes, Graham. It's gone to the sub's desk. Yes, I'm glad you agree. I think it's a good story too. What? . . . Why? . . . Oh, all right. I'll come up."

Now why all of a sudden should Graham want him in his office? He'd liked the story well enough, admittedly, given a fairly good display to his half-dozen column inches yesterday; but when Mike had told him the press conference to which Briant had agreed could make a much better story, he hadn't seemed to think much of it. Told him not to let his report run to more than it absolutely had to, and on no account to make a feature piece out of it. Straight news was what he wanted and nothing more. And now he had sounded—how had he sounded? Irritable but excited, as though he were only just able to hold something important under control. Odd, that, Mike thought as he went up to the third floor in the rattling old lift. Graham wasn't the sort of editor to get excited easily. Maybe, just for once, he'd understood what a science story was all about? If he has, Mike thought with a familiar bitterness, the bloody millennium's arrived.

Graham was standing by his window, staring out over the roof of the Comet Building across the street, and when Mike saw who was sitting at Graham's desk, he had to make a strong effort not to show his surprise. The Old Man! Now what the hell was up?

"Ah, Mr. Bridges! Nice to see you!" Sir Daniel Sefton stood up and extended his hand across the desk, smiling the warm friendly smile that was virtually his trademark. Phony old bastard! Mike thought and shook hands with him. About as genuinely friendly as a boa constrictor, and a damned sight more dangerous. Beware him most when he smiles his widest, he told himself.

"This is quite a story you've uncovered, my boy! Mr. Moloney, can we find a drink for Mr. Bridges—for Mike?"

Mike almost grinned as Graham moved to his desk and flicked the intercom switch. It must be killing him to have the Old Man expecting him to play barman to me! He keeps his liquor just on the other side of the room, but catch him actually dishing it out himself.

There was a brief flurry as Graham's secretary came in and dispensed drinks, while the Old Man teased her kindly, and she giggled, and then they were all sitting looking at one another in silence.

After a moment the Old Man put his glass on the desk and looked at Graham, switching on his let's-get-down-to-real-business look.

"Now, Mr. Moloney—Graham. Shall I kick this one off, or would you prefer to?"

"It's up to you, Sir Daniel." Graham looked as though he would gladly kick the Old Man, Mike thought, beginning to enjoy himself. Whatever this is about, there'll be a great deal of pleasure to be got out of telling the tale around afterward.

"Right, then, Mr. Bridges. Mike. I think we can be informal, don't you? It's just this. You've uncovered a great story—a great story." He looked at Mike owlishly, and Mike murmured a swift "thank you" into his glass.

"And clearly it's going to develop. Have you seen the evenings?"

"Not yet. I've been doing my own story all afternoon, and I had to cover the opening of a new computerized diagnosis unit out at Barnet on my way back from the Sillick Memorial."

Mike was embarrassed. He should have made a point of looking at the evening coverage before doing his own piece; but he'd seen the people they'd sent to the press conference at the hospital, dismissed them as unlikely to do a decent job on it, and promptly forgotten them. Blast it! Just the sort of thing the Old Man would pick on.

But Sir Daniel was magnanimous. "Not to worry. I know you're under pressure. The *Echo*'s science man has to be, hmm? And there was nothing in the early editions, anyway. But they did a very rapid rejig, obviously, for the later editions. These went on the streets only half an hour ago. Take a look at them, will you? Then you'll be *au fait* with our . . . problem." And he glanced at Graham as he pushed copies of the two London evening papers across the desk.

Each of them had a ten- to twelve-column-inch splash on the front page, with a picture of Dr. Briant standing glowering at the desk in the board room, and each of them carried leaders about Briant and his project. One was headed "Science Goes Too Far!" and Mike skimmed swiftly through the heavy black print.

"In its search to reveal secrets of human existence," it trumpeted, "science has brought us undoubted gifts. It has, by pushing back the boundaries of human knowledge, given us much that has enriched our lives. But when science proposes to manipulate the life of a human baby, the time has come to call a halt. . . ."

It went on in the same tone for several excited paragraphs and ended in an even heavier and blacker print.

> We say that Dr. George Briant has been misguided in his attempt to delve into the mystery of human existence in the way he has. We say that he has done enough damage in bringing about the birth of this child, in giving him a father who does not know he is his father, a mother who is so ice-cold a scientist that she willingly abandons her own child to the researcher in the laboratory, where he will inevitably be regarded in the same light as any other laboratory animal. But it is not too late to undo that damage. Dr. Briant must abandon his project and restore to this unhappy baby his birthright, the chance to grow up in a real home, with real parents who will love him as he deserves to be loved. As a human being, and not as a guinea pig.

The leader in the second paper, headed "An Affront to Human Dignity," was on much the same lines, ending with a demand for a

Royal Commission to look into the "hidden and possibly evil secrets of the laboratories of Britain's universities" and an appeal to "right-thinking people" to raise their voices against this outrageous treatment of a helpless baby.

Mike pushed the papers back across the desk and looked at the Old Man, who raised his eyebrows questioningly.

"Well? What do you think of those leaders?" Sir Daniel asked.

"Not unexpected, I suppose," Mike said carefully. "With no other big news breaking, it makes a good lead item."

"Oh, come, Mike! Even if there had been another big story, it would have to be very big indeed to be bigger than this one!"

Mike couldn't resist it. "I'm not used to science stories making all that much of a splash," he said, carefully not looking at Graham sitting silently beside him. "Unless there's a big human story wrapped up in it—like the heart transplant bit—it doesn't seem to have the interest it might."

"But where's your nose, boy, where's your nose?" Sir Daniel was getting irritable. "How much more of a human angle can there be? A baby, a newborn baby, conceived in a test tube, born in a laboratory, created to be researched like a guinea pig in a cage—how much more human than that can you get?"

"But without access to the infant, it's a dead angle," Mike said. "And I can assure you there isn't a hope in hell of getting access. I've tried, believe me. I've got as good a nose as any other man on the paper, even if I do specialize in science. But I've got the sense to know what I can't do. And I can't see anyone getting past Briant to this baby, or to its mother. He's a pretty formidable man, and he's got the support of his hospital. Which is why I saw no real point in pushing the human poor-little-baby bit." He stopped then and after a pause said deliberately, "Even if I held that point of view."

"Ah!" Sir Daniel leaned forward. "You don't, I take it?"

Mike looked back at him, trying to calculate the odds, and then with a mental shrug took the risk of alienating the other man. It was a considerable risk; he knew perfectly well that Graham Moloney would certainly disagree with him with some violence.

"No, I don't. I was trained as a scientist, and there are times when science matters more than the individual. What Briant is trying to do is . . . important. More important than this baby. What he's doing might be considered unfortunate for the baby—though I'm not sure it is—but it could be of immense value to humanity as a whole."

And how does *that* grab you, chum? he thought with childish venom. Do I start tomorrow looking for a new paper, because the *Echo* can't be doing with a man who lacks the bloody human touch?

But Sir Daniel was looking at him with a satisfied expression on his face.

"I'm happy to hear it, my boy." And his voice oozed geniality. "Because it is very relevant to the dilemma in which I find myself. Now you know—everyone on the paper knows—I'm not the sort of proprietor who meddles with editorial policy." Like hell you don't, thought Mike viciously. "I hire—employ—the best brains and leave them to do their job. But sometimes—rarely, thank God—sometimes, I feel I have a moral duty to involve myself."

He seemed to savor the phrase. "Yes. A moral duty. And here is a case in point. Briant's work throws up considerable ethical problems that must be explored. Explored in the most public manner." He's beginning to address us, Mike thought. I feel like a public meeting. "The public at large must give grave consideration to a . . . a grave matter. And as a prime factor in public discussion, the *Echo* must make a decision about its own views."

He flicked a finger at the newspaper lying on the desk. "These papers have clearly made their decision. The obvious one, in my opinion. And I have no doubt that their stablemates will come out in the same vein tomorrow morning, together with the rest of them. Now, here is our dilemma—*my* dilemma. I feel the *Echo* should not be obvious. That we should take a more dispassionate view and consider the long-term effects of Briant's work. And here, I am sad to say, Mr. Moloney and I part company—in terms of points of view, that is." He smiled at Moloney, who had not moved. "Not, of course, literally! Of course not!"

Well, well, Mike thought. So that's the way it's going! Poor old

Graham! He felt himself warm toward the sullenly controlled man as he never had in the three years he had been on the paper. He had many times been reduced to helpless rage by Graham's attitude to his subjects, by his refusal to give science stories the importance Mike believed they had, but at least he was consistent in his attitudes. If he was prepared to fight the Old Man on it as well as one of his juniors, then there was muscle in the man he had never before recognized. Good for Graham. To risk his job—and Sir Daniel had made it very clear that he did risk it—was a courageous thing to do when you considered how few editors' chairs there were on the Street.

Graham stirred and spoke with a careful lack of emphasis.

"I would be prepared to write a leader on this project, but I would find it difficult to take the opposing point of view to that given in those two leaders. I've read Mike's copy carefully, and as he tells the story of Briant's explanation of what he's doing, I can't see any other way to treat it. He is using a human child as research material, removing him from what everybody—our readers—must regard as a normal human life. And that . . . that is not good. And quite apart from my own views, I think we are in real danger of losing readership if we don't reflect what I am convinced will be the general tenor of public opinion. And I am not here to lose you readers."

Oh, well played, Graham, Mike thought. That'll get him where he lives.

"I take your points, and they do you credit," Sir Daniel said smoothly. "But we don't only reflect public opinion, you know. We guide it. And anyway, there will be enough public opinion in line with mine and Mike's here"—he threw a brilliant smile at Mike—"to protect us from too great a loss of circulation. Especially if we are the only paper to reflect the other side of the question. And if we project this other point of view with enough . . . skill, we may indeed build our figures."

A nice volley shot, Mike applauded silently. I'm enjoying this. Over to you, Graham.

But Sir Daniel was speaking again. "I would not, quite frankly, have involved you in this policy disagreement between us, Mike, had it been possible to avoid doing so. But I have put to Graham a way round our dilemma which *does* involve you. He has accepted it in principle, which does him great credit. A man of lesser integrity and lesser . . . care for the welfare of this paper might have been stubborn and even resigned because of so divergent a set of opinions between himself and his proprietor. But Graham is a better man than that, and can recognize an acceptable compromise when he sees one."

Oh, you bastard, Mike thought, staring at Sir Daniel's sleek expression. The sooner I get off this Street and onto the box the better.

He glanced for a brief moment at Graham's heavy body and closed face, and looked away, feeling a little sick. Graham, well past fifty, with three children still at school, and younger men baying at his heels, pushed into a corner like this. It was obscene.

"What we would suggest is this, Mike," Sir Daniel went on. "We will use the leader column tomorrow to discuss the question of financing scientific research in this country. I understand Briant has problems in this area, and it will be perfectly possible for Graham to prepare a strong piece on this shocking insufficiency of government support for science, without discussing the pros and cons of this particular piece of science. And you"—he paused, looked at Mike with great solemnity, and then went on weightily—"you will write a feature article which will put the point of view you so fortunately genuinely hold, that the legitimate demands of science must sometimes supersede the welfare of the individual. And I know you will give us an excellent piece."

I ought to throw it in his teeth. I ought to stand up and shout, My editor, right or wrong, and sod you. Graham sitting there waiting for me to kick him in the teeth. I ought to tell him what to do with his feature article.

Mike rubbed the back of his neck, and the silence dropped clammily on him as he tried to think it through properly. The Old Man's right, of course. The others *will* come out tomorrow shrieking for Briant's blood, just as these two have this evening. And I know what Briant is doing, and why, and though I don't go all the way with him, I go far enough to want to come in on his side. And there is the money angle, of course. If Graham can write something solid about the lousy deal research gets in this country, it can do nothing but good. And Christ, but it's an opportunity! A big lead feature with a strong by-line—if that doesn't get J. J. Gerrard and *Probe* for me, nothing will. Oh, Christ, why did I ever get into this business? Even teaching Boyle's Law to snotty kids in a secondary modern would be better than this. Wouldn't it?

"Well?" Sir Daniel's voice carried a faint rasp of impatience, a hint of warning that Mike heard very clearly, and he raised his head and looked at Graham.

"You're quite sure that's the way you want it, Graham? You could square it with yourself?"

Graham looked back at him, and for a moment they sat and stared at each other. Then Graham said, "It's all right. I can live with it. As long as I don't have to use my leader column to support Briant, and any *Echo* support for him goes out under your by-line —now and in the future—I can live with it."

He looked then at Sir Daniel. "But I must stick at that. It's my right as an editor. You have yours as a proprietor, but I have mine too. As long as you leave me my leader column, I . . . I'll be happy enough."

"Splendid!" Sir Daniel stood up and looked at his watch with some ostentation. "I'm delighted that we've settled the matter. For the present."

Was he still threatening Graham? Mike, beginning to feel some exhilaration as he thought about the piece he would now have to write, and write bloody fast, pushed the thought away. If he does lean on Graham again after tomorrow, then I'll stand up and be counted. After tomorrow. If necessary.

"I'm late for a meeting at the House now, Mike, so I can't wait to see your copy. Send it round to me, will you? I'm dining at Stone's."

"There won't be time, sir." Graham's voice sounded very loud, contrasting sharply with the heaviness it had held all through the conversation so far. "I'll have to lock up the pages before seven, and I doubt Mike will be able to do more than meet the deadline. Will you?"

"What? Oh, Lord, I doubt it. A big feature—no. I'm sorry, I'll need every minute I've got." It was something to be able to make this much of a gesture of loyalty.

Sir Daniel was already at the door, shrugging into his heavy black overcoat with its expensive sheen and elegantly cut lines, and he looked at them both with only the faintest narrowing of his eyes altering his expression of bland good will.

"Oh. Yes. I see. Well, so be it. I am sure I can rely on you both to carry out my instructions—my wishes. I shall look forward to seeing the first edition, then. You'll send a copy round by hand to Eaton Square, Moloney? I'll be home by midnight and eager to see what you produce for me. Good evening, gentlemen—oh, and get your secretary to tell the doorman to make sure my car is waiting, will you? I have to stop off in Personnel on my way down. I'll be ready in five minutes." And he went, the door swinging behind him, leaving an embarrassed silence between the two men.

Then Graham switched on his intercom and snapped, "Tell Sam Sir Daniel's on his way down, wants his car at the front," before sitting down heavily and sweeping the two newspapers on his blotter into the wastepaper basket beside his desk.

"Look, Graham, I'm bloody sorry," Mike said awkwardly.

Graham didn't look up. "Whether that's an apology or an expression of sympathy, I don't want it. And you'd better get moving if you're going to meet the deadline. I want your copy up here by six-thirty at the latest. You can have five ten-inch sticks, and no more, understand? Now get the hell out of here."

Mike shrugged and moved to the door, and then Graham's voice pulled him back. "And keep your mouth shut about this, do you understand? It's my business and no one else's. Not even yours. Just remember that."

Mike looked at him silently, and Graham raised his head and stared back. His expression was harsh and defiant, but Mike recognized the appeal the older man was making, and he nodded.

"Sure," he said and ran down the stairs, back to the newsroom and his desk. The thought of getting into the small shaky enclosure of plaited metal strips which was the lift was suddenly more than he could contemplate.

5

Isobel stood quietly in front of the cupboard door, her hands clasped on her beige overall, almost melting into her background of buff paint. There was no readable expression on her face, but Marjorie felt an unease as she looked at her, as though the woman were watching her through narrowed lids. Which was a curious sensation, since in fact her eyes were downcast, apparently studying the vinyl squares of the floor.

"Hello! I'm Mrs. Briant. You must be Miss Quinn?" Marjorie said, with all the warm friendliness she could project. "It's a foul morning, isn't it? I'm drenched, just running from the car to the door!"

Isobel looked up, and her glance slid across Majorie to the window.

"How do you do, Mrs. Briant," she said in a voice as neutral as her appearance. "Yes, it is raining a lot."

"Now, let me see." Marjorie cocked her head to one side and

smiled with a brightness she didn't feel. It was most odd the way this woman had immediately made her feel as though she had to be conciliating. It was like interviewing someone who had answered one of her frequent advertisements for a daily maid, trying to create a spurious atmosphere of equality and friendship that would compensate for the low pay she had to offer. "You're from . . . Scotland! But you had an Irish mother or father. Am I right?" She produced a tinkly little laugh. "I do rather a lot of amateur acting, you know, and I'm supposed to be rather good at accents."

"I was born in Liverpool."

"Oh! Oh, dear. Not so good after all, then! Though I don't know. There is a strong Irish and Scottish element in the city, isn't there? Whatever it is, it's left a pretty burr in your voice."

"It's nice of you to say so, Mrs. Briant." Still Isobel gave back no warmth at all, and Marjorie felt a stab of irritation. She was doing her best to be friendly, damn it, and she didn't have to.

"Well, now, where's the baby? I—"

The door opened, and George followed Barbara Hervey into the room. Marjorie turned to them with relief.

"Good morning, Barbara! How nice to see you again. Are you keeping well?"

"Very well, thank you, Mrs. Briant. And you?"

"Oh, I rub along, you know! It doesn't do to worry about oneself, does it? Well, George? Do I have to put on a special overall or something? You all look so . . . well, *hospitally,* in those coats of yours! I feel the complete outsider!"

"There's no need," George said. "We don't particularly want to protect him from infection. In fact, it's quite useful to expose him to people from outside the Unit, within reason. He has to build his own resistance to infections and he can't do that if he never meets them. But take your coat off, Marjorie. It's warm in the nursery, and you'll be uncomfortable. And it's damp too, I imagine."

"What's this room for, George?" Marjorie turned her back to him so that he could help her out of her coat. "It all looks very intriguing! This is the first time I've come into the Unit, you know, Barbara! I feel rather like a visitor to a Stately Home who's been allowed to peep into the Duke's private apartments." And she looked over her shoulder at her husband. But he was hanging up her coat and appeared not to notice the edge on her voice.

Barbara became suddenly animated. "Oh, you should have come before, Mrs. Briant. We're really very lucky in our equipment. George had to coax and nag and beg and borrow and almost steal to get most of it! He really has had to struggle to get this project under way. Though, of course, you know that as well as I do! Well, this is the main monitoring system. These screens are linked to the cot, which has a series of receptor units built into it. They pick up the infant's heartbeat, respiration rate, body temperature, and so on. And this one is for the electroencephalogram, which records his brain impulses. The electrodes for that are only linked up at intervals, of course, since they have to be directly attached to his scalp. It was simpler to leave those *in situ*, as you'll see. And this screen here, you see? This one links to the TV cameras. They're really splendid. George got those from a commercial company, you know, in Germany. There wasn't a single British company that would cooperate. They're the last word in this sort of equipment. The screen's dead at the moment, but the cameras are still operating, of course. But they're taking a video tape—rather like a film, you know. We can rerun them whenever we want to. We only have this screen operating when we're all in here and want to observe him directly—"

"Oh, my dear, stop!" Marjorie shuddered delicately. "It's all too much for me to take in! It's like one of those awful science-fiction films they do on television, too complicated for words. You've got everything but those great bubbling glass things they always have for the mad scientist!"

"We do all the chemical work in another part of the Unit," Barbara said. "Not that we've got any retorts of that sort there! They're not true at all, you know, those absurd laboratories you see in popular films. But it isn't all that complicated, you know, really. Not like the computer unit we use at the university." She seemed a little hurt suddenly. "I thought you wanted the equipment explained—"

"Well, I thought I did too, but I'm just not bright enough to cope with it, am I, George? Poor George gave up trying to explain to me years ago! I'm just too simple a soul altogether, really. I'm interested in the *baby*, of course, but then, what woman wouldn't be?"

Barbara pushed her hands into her overall pocket and flushed slightly, and Marjorie smiled kindly at her and turned to George again.

"I've already introduced myself to Miss Quinn, George. If you're too busy with all your equipment, I'm sure she can take me to see the baby. And she won't bewilder me with all sorts of complicated science. I'm sure—"

"I want to come up anyway. I see him every morning," George said. "Not that Miss Quinn couldn't take you, of course. I've explained why you're here this morning, Marjorie."

"Oh, have you?" Marjorie turned back to Isobel. "I'm really quite privileged, aren't I, Miss Quinn? After all the fuss in the papers this morning, I feel positively part of this project! To be the legal mother of so important a baby—it'll be quite something, don't you think?"

"Yes, Mrs. Briant," Isobel said, and again Marjorie felt the chill of the rejection in her voice.

"I'll start the collation of yesterday's material, George," Barbara said. "Mr. Kegan phoned over at nine to say he wanted to talk to you as soon as possible, and you won't have time to do it yourself before he comes."

"Mmm? Oh, yes. Get Peter in from Histology to help you. He should have finished matching the chromosome analyses with the projections by now. And Davis can help too. He finished the metabolism checks early yesterday evening. Elsa and Vernon can get on with checking the endocrine levels this morning, and that will leave young Isaacs to monitor today's stuff. Can you all cope without me? With all this flap going on, it's very unlikely I'll get much peace to do any real work today."

Barbara's rather narrow cheeks reddened with pleasure. "Of course, George. And I hope it won't be too grim."

"So do I, but I'm not very sanguine. It'll probably be God-awful."

Marjorie moved edgily. That's the worst thing about being so perceptive, she thought. It makes me a good actress, but I'm too sensitive to atmosphere. That dried-up Hervey creature throwing her brain at George the way any other woman worth her salt'd throw her looks, and this Quinn woman glowering. What the hell have I done to upset her? She's sending out great waves of nastiness. I wonder if Ian's heard yet? He said they'd call at eleven if they were going to call him at all. I want to get home.

"Shall we go, then, George?" she said and opened the door.

"Yes, yes. And thank you, Barbara."

They went up the stairs in a little procession, Marjorie following George, very aware of Isobel behind her. She moves very lightly for someone of her size, Marjorie thought. What *have* I done to make her so chilly? Or is it that she's like Barbara Hervey? I swear that woman has a *tendre* for George, not that she'd know it, bloodless creature. And not that George would know it either. I almost wish he would. I'd know what I was dealing with then. Oh, God, I wish—

"This way, Marjorie." George pushed a door open and stood back, and she walked into the room and stood in the center of it looking around with curiosity.

"How odd! I suppose I thought it would be like a hospital ward, but it's quite like an ordinary nursery, really, except it's so dull. I'll have a look in the loft, shall I, for those little Kate Greenaway pictures that used to be in Hilary's room? Or are they too girlish? Ian had some rather nice animal ones—"

"We don't want to provide anything of that sort just yet. We have to take great care to select the visual environment so that its effect can be measured. Thank you for thinking of it, though—"

"Oh, dear! Poor little scrap." Marjorie made a *moue* at Isobel, who had walked over to the cot in the far corner of the room and was standing in the same apparently relaxed but watchful posture she had displayed downstairs. "Isn't that just like a man?" And for the first time, she got a response, for Isobel bobbed her head slightly and then looked down at the infant in the cot.

Marjorie went over too and stood looking at the baby. He was asleep, lying on his front with his head turned to one side.

She frowned sharply. "What are those things on his head?"

"Electrodes. For the electroencephalograms."

"But don't they hurt him? They look as though they're . . . embedded in his scalp!"

"They are. But they don't perturb him in the least." George had come to stand beside her, also looking down at the baby. "As you can see, he is sleeping perfectly well."

Marjorie shuddered slightly. "All the same, they look—I don't know. If I really were his mother, I'd hate to see them there. How long must they stay there?"

"We haven't yet decided." George sounded irritable suddenly. "Really, Marjorie, you mustn't let yourself be infected by the hysterical nonsense in this morning's papers. He is not being treated in any way that need worry you. We are simply observing him, which is a very different thing from actually doing anything *to* him. He lives and feeds and is handled just like any other baby. Such specimens as we collect are obtained without bothering him in the slightest—smears for chromosome checks, the occasional blood sample, and so on, that's all. There's no element of vivisection in the work, no matter what those overemotional reports may suggest."

Marjorie looked up at Isobel and, surprisingly, she nodded. "He's a very good baby, Mrs. Briant," she said. "He takes his feeds very well, not like a fretful one would."

"Ian was a very fretful baby." Marjorie looked at the sleeping infant again. "I had a frightful time with him. Not like Hilary. She was very placid."

She shrugged then. "Well, I've seen him. Will that satisfy these various people on the adoption question? I told you last night, George, I can't do more than merely agree. I've done my share of baby care. I really can't start again. Not at my age." And she looked at Isobel, almost defiantly. "It's not that I don't care. I was devoted to my own two, you know. But they were my own. I'm not really cut out for adoption. I'm past forty, after all." She laughed a little tinkling laugh again. "Even if I do play girls in their twenties, and just about get away with it."

"Your age has nothing to do with it," George said, and then remembered to add, "Not that you look it."

"Maybe, but I haven't the patience any more. Besides, I couldn't cope with all this . . . science." She waved her hand comprehensively, as though to take in the room downstairs with its monitor screens, as well as the cameras built unobstrusively into the walls around them.

"Well, the question doesn't arise. All we need from you is your token consent to the legalities. Miss Quinn is here to look after him. Which she is doing very well indeed."

"I'm sure she is." Marjorie smiled again at the other woman. "It's a big job you've taken on, isn't it? Looking after someone else's child can't be easy."

"I never think about it," Isobel said. "A baby is a baby. And he's very easy."

"All the same, sooner you than me! Though he's a nice baby, to look at, I mean. So often very young babies are perfectly hideous, aren't they? I know Ian was! He looks very handsome now. He's an actor, you know."

"His eyes are a very nice color," Isobel said, still staring at the sleeping baby. "A real blue."

"They will lighten, of course," George said. "As his hair will. By the end of his first year he'll be light-haired, but it will change again so that in maturity he'll be quite definitely dark. We have an artist's projection made on the basis of our early work, and from the results we've had so far, I have every reason to hope we've pulled it off. We could have been very mistaken in our early extrapolations, you know. Working on so small a piece of basic material, it was remarkably difficult to be sure we had correctly identified the genes. I'm beginning to be quite confident that we were right, though it will be some years before we can be really certain we've made the breakthrough. If you'd care to see some of the early results, Marjorie, I could explain them."

"Would there be much point?"

"What? Oh. Well, perhaps . . . it is complex material, of course."

The sudden surge of enthusiasm which had given his words a clipped speed subsided, and he turned toward the door.

"And time is pressing. Kegan will be waiting for me downstairs. Miss Quinn, Miss Hervey will deal with all today's work."

"Yes, Dr. Briant."

"And I must hurry too. Ian will be waiting for me," Marjorie said. "He's waiting to hear whether or not he's been cast, and he'll be feeling like a caged bear, poor darling. I'd like to take the car, George."

At the door Marjorie looked back over her shoulder at Isobel. "Goodbye, Miss Quinn. Thank you. I hope he'll go on being easy."

And for the first time, Isobel smiled at her. "Goodbye Mrs. Briant. I expect he will. Dr. Briant says he was born to have a nice way with him."

As they went downstairs, Marjorie said thoughtfully, "I think I know why, now."

"What?"

"Why she seemed to dislike me the moment she set eyes on me."

"Who? Miss Quinn? Oh, really, Marjorie! How can you say that? Was she impertinent?"

"No, of course not. But she did dislike me, really she did. And it was because you told her I was to be the baby's legal mother when the adoption went through."

He stopped at the foot of the stairs and stared at her. "What possible reason would that be for disliking you? Really, Marjorie, you do take great leaps when you jump to your conclusions."

"So you always say. But I'm right," she said insistently. "She was scared I'd interfere with her baby. And once she was sure I wouldn't—because I did make it clear, you know, that I had no intention of doing more than agreeing to the legal business—she felt safe again."

"Marjorie, you must stop seeing things in terms of—like a play! Such subtleties are hardly within her grasp. She was selected most carefully, you know. Most carefully indeed. She has a job to do, and she's doing it quite well. And that's as far as it goes."

"I wouldn't be too sure. The job consists of giving him loving care, doesn't it? And she loves him, I promise you. She was like a threatened mother bear up there."

"If the child were a little older, you might have a point. But he's only just over a week, remember. But I'll talk to Saxby. There may be a case for replacing her with someone else later, having a series of nurses rather than a permanent one, in case she becomes over-emotionally involved. As long as that doesn't disturb him. But I needn't worry about it yet, I'm quite sure."

"Well, it's up to you. If you're sure. But I'm glad to have worked out why she was so—" She gave a little shrug of distaste. "I know it's vanity, but I need to know why people react to me in different ways. I need to be liked. Not that you'd know about that sort of feeling, would you? You never have it."

"Marjorie, I really must go." He looked at his watch. "I hope to get home at a reasonable time tonight, but it rather depends on what Kegan wants. More newspaper problems, I imagine, which are a bloody nuisance, but I'll have to deal with him. You want the car, you say?"

"Yes, please. And I'll expect you when I see you. As usual. May I have my coat?"

He went into the monitoring room, and as the door swung open she could see Mr. Kegan and Miss Hervey talking over the banks of monitor screens, and she stepped back out of their sight. She wasn't in the mood to cope with Kegan's heavy playfulness, the sort of labored gallantry he produced whenever they met at official hospital functions. And as for Barbara Hervey—she was a bore of the first water.

George came back with her coat, and as she put it on, grimacing at the discomfort of its dampness, he said a little awkwardly, "Anyway, thank you, Marjorie. You can see now how important your cooperation is on this adoption question? Without control of the baby, the whole Unit is wasted. And it took a great deal of effort to set up, a lot of work already done. I . . . I really don't think I could tolerate the loss of it all."

"It was the least I could do, I suppose. I could hardly refuse, could I? Though I wish you'd given him a different name. I suppose it's too late to alter that now."

"It was worth doing, or so I thought at the time. I'd hoped to gain sympathy from those idiotic journalists. They go in for the emotional point of view, and I thought it would help them see me in a fatherly light, giving him my own name. Anyway, he's got to be called something."

"Yes. But all those reports about Baby George Briant—they made me feel, oh, I don't know. I didn't like it. But I'll get used to it. One gets used to everything sooner or later."

He kissed her cheek and put one arm around her shoulders and hugged her. "You'd better hurry home and out of that damp coat. Goodbye, my dear, and thank you again. Do you mind seeing yourself out? The keys are in the ignition." And he went, the door swinging behind him, leaving her pulling on her gloves in the narrow hallway.

"Television? Tonight? Oh, for Christ's sake, Kegan, leave me alone, will you? You got your press conference, and much good it's done! You have seen this morning's papers, I imagine?"

"I told you last night when I brought the evenings over how it would be. And you'll have to admit you . . . well, you lost your temper, and you put their backs up. I can't be blamed for that. All I know is that I'm almost at my wits' ends trying to cope with the demands for access to you—the television people, radio, and there's all the foreign press agency people too. I've done nothing but deal with the Briant project for days, it seems to me! And I have a responsibility to the Committee, you know, and they have to the Regional Board, even though you're working in a section of the hospital that's outside the NHS establishment, and not using Ministry money. Because you are using some hospital staff, remember."

He moved agitatedly across the room and then turned and came back to stand over Briant's chair. "Look, Dr. Briant, I've been with you on this from the word go, you know I have. Who first got the use of this building for you? Who soothed the finance people when you annexed the equipment you needed? Who keeps on trying to raise money for you, got you your first grant? I know I wasn't the only one who saw your work was important enough to be worth backing, but you must admit you owe me something! And all I'm asking of you now is your cooperation in dealing with all this publicity, that's all."

"My dear Kegan, you know as well as I do that you came in on my side of the fence not out of some great disinterested love of science—you don't know what science is all about!—but because you saw a hope of personal glory in it! And something more, I suspect. I haven't forgotten the way you talked about taking out patents on some of the techniques I developed here. That was an obscenity, if you like. Oh, no, Kegan. Don't try the gratitude line with me. Whatever you've done you've done for science and not for me personally, whether you see it that way or not. I owe nothing to anybody, not gratitude or anything else, do you understand me? I'm a scientist, a *scientist,* God damn it all! Do you have any conception of what that means? Science is entitled to all the support it can get, to all it needs. It *demands,* it doesn't come cap in hand asking for favors and groveling its gratitude!"

He stood up and in his turn moved sharply from one side of the room to the other. His face was red, and his shoulders hunched over his chest as he marched, hands in pockets. "When will you get it into your head that this project is what matters, not me, not you, not the bloody hospital, or the newspapers, or your bleating television people! The *project* and nothing else!"

"And when will you get it into *your* head that it's the project I'm trying to keep in mind? Though you're doing your best to make me forget it! I've got some power in this place, Dr. Briant, even though I'm not a doctor or a great scientist! And if you push me much harder, I'll wash my hands of the whole thing and tell the Committee I can't cope, and make it clear I want you out—out, do you understand? And out you'll go, take it from me, especially after the fiasco you made of the press conference and the results of it spread all over the papers this morning!"

Kegan breathed deeply, suddenly aware that he was shouting, and went on more quietly. "You may see science as the great God we've all got to worship, but if we don't see it that way, and not many do, take it from me, you'll have nothing to do your worshipping with. I don't understand you, I really don't. You say this project is the only thing that matters, and yet you do your best to scuttle it by refusing to cooperate with what is necessary to keep it going!"

Briant stood still, staring at him from under his brows, and Kegan stared back, his heavy face gleaming slightly with sweat.

"George." Barbara Hervey stirred nervously. "George, may I?"

"What?" He turned to look at her.

She took a deep and slightly tremulous breath. "Look, I know it isn't really my business, but I know what you mean. Better than anyone else could. I'm your senior assistant, and I do understand, you know? But he's right. He really is."

She leaned forward on her elbows and looked up at Briant with an expression of almost ludicrous earnestness on her face. "People outside our field, they can't understand. They haven't the training, the intellectual equipment. And it's all been thrown at them so suddenly, hasn't it? I mean, we've been working towards all this for years, you know? Haven't we? So we're accustomed to the idea of what we're doing. But the newspaper people—and the people who read them, which is pretty well everybody—they've had no chance to think the thing through. All they see is a baby, a newborn baby, a symbol of all people care about. And he's in a special unit, you know, had a very unusual start to his life. It's perfectly reasonable that they can't understand."

"It's a valid point," Briant said after a moment. "I suppose it's a valid point. But what can *I* do about it? Ever since . . . since before Galileo scientists have had to accept that the idiot mass doesn't comprehend, can't see what good science can do. So they vilify it. And I'm no politician, Barbara—no politician! I've got vital work to do, absolutely vital work to do, and I know it if they don't. I tried to explain at that press conference and the only one who understood was Bridges, the only one. He wrote the only intelligent thing that appeared this morning. All I ask is to be left to get on with my work, and enough support to make it possible. Is it so much to ask?"

"No, of course it isn't. But you've got to convince everybody, not just me and people like Bridges, people who've had a scientific training. You're preaching to the converted in us, but you've got to get at everyone else. So Mr. Kegan is right. You'll *have* to cooperate and answer their questions and explain. Even if it wastes your time. It won't really be wasting it, you know. And I can hold things here, really I can. The work will get done, even if you miss the doing of it. And I know that's miserable for you, but what else can you do?"

"I seem to have been here so often before," Briant said heavily and moved wearily back to his chair. "First trying to convince you, Kegan, and then those journalists, and Marjorie—and now again. And you beat me every time, don't you, you and all the people like you, Kegan? The blind ones."

He rubbed his face then. "Oh, God, I'm sorry. That was bloody offensive, and I didn't mean it to be. But you are blind, you know."

"You certainly make me feel so," Kegan said, and anger was still simmering in him. "And stupid into the bargain. And I know I'm *not* stupid, any more than the next person is. I care about what you're doing, even if I'm not as head over ears in love with it as you are. But you do your best to make me stop caring. I'll tell you something, Dr. Briant, I don't know why I put up with you and your arrogant ways, that I don't! It says a lot for me, it really does."

"Yes. Yes. I'm sorry, Kegan. You're right, of course. I was abominably ill-mannered, and I apologize. I've had—it hasn't been easy, this past week. And the papers this morning—I say I don't care, but I suppose I do. It stung, that eruption of uncomprehending idiocy. It shouldn't, but—"

"Of course it stung!" Barbara said and leaned over to rest a hand on Briant's arm. "It hurt me, I know that! I could have wept this morning when I opened the papers, I really could. But you can make it different, George, if you'll only cooperate with this television thing. It's an important program, you know. Virtually everyone watches *Probe* and that Gerrard man—even I do! You could make them see it so clearly if only you'd try."

"And manage to avoid losing your temper," Kegan said. "If you can. Because I promise you, if you do that, on a live transmission like this has to be, you really will scupper yourself. And then I'll be past caring. It's up to you now. I'm certainly not going to say another word about it. Just make up your mind, one way or the other, and let me know your decision. And within the next half-hour, because I can't and won't hold these people off any longer than that. You'll find me in *my* office, trying to get on with *my* job, when you're ready to talk. Good morning!"

And the door slammed behind him.

6

"In many ways, I remain a child at heart, Graham," Sir Daniel said. "No, not whisky. A most uncivilized drink at this hour. Brandy, if you have it? Thank you. Yes, indeed, a child at heart. I still find the ability of television to enter the minds of millions a remarkable thing. What? Oh. Let me see the label. Hmm. Yes, perhaps a little soda would be as well. Yes, millions. With the Eurovision linkup, and the satellite feeding the United States and Canada, the mind boggles. And J. J. told me there will be tape recordings of the program going out in Australia and New Zealand. Quite a remarkable degree of coverage, remarkable. Indeed a pervasive medium."

He drank some brandy and then added sharply, "I take it young Bridges has been well briefed?"

"He'll mention the *Echo* as often as he possibly can," Graham said dryly, and defiantly filled his glass with whisky for the second time. "Of course, if you'd accepted the invitation to take part yourself—"

"Oh, no, no, my dear chap, no. I'm only a proprietor, after all. People know that the real power in a newspaper lies with the editorial staff. I would have had no value at all. None at all. No, no more brandy, thank you. I try to be a reasonably abstemious individual. Perhaps you had better switch the set on? It's almost nine o'clock, and I don't think we should miss any of the program. And the other members of the staff who are joining us had better put in an appearance soon, don't you think?"

"Most of them preferred to see it at home. With their families."

"Really! How little interest people take in their jobs these days. One would have thought discussion with one's working colleagues, after so important a transmission, would have superseded all else, wouldn't one?"

"Yes. One would," Graham said savagely. "But it all depends on the pressures, doesn't it?" And he switched on the set and went back to his desk, putting as much physical space as possible between himself and his employer.

Bodily discomfort, added to the anger that still bubbled unpleasantly inside him, had the effect of clarifying his mind, just as it had on the day of the press conference. What right had they to make a panel discussion out of this? And what a panel! A journalist and an MP, as well as J. J. Gerrard himself, and what was he? Just another bloody journalist, a dilettante with a ragbag mind, who thought that because he had a smattering of scientific language, which he produced with a glib assurance that made George want to choke him, he was qualified to question *him*, a serious scientist with an intellectual grasp that Gerrard could never understand, let alone achieve.

And this physical discomfort! Did they have to use these foul lights that blistered the back of his neck with heat and almost blinded him, making his eyes water with their stabbing? Did they have to sit him in a swivel chair that swung sideways with every movement of his body? Did they have to have so tight-packed an audience, with the front row so close to the dais on which he was sitting that he could positively feel their stupid gawping eyes on him?

And the place smelled too, of hot bodies, hot electrical equipment, and the fumes of whisky; not surprising that, considering the amount of the stuff they swallowed during the half-hour he had spent in that crowded room full of people who talked to one another in an incomprehensible private language, and at him as though he were a stupid child when they explained how the program would run.

He should never have agreed to take part in this charade, should have adhered to his first decision to refuse. Bloody Kegan. He sat and thought somberly about Kegan, keeping his chin tucked into his neck and his eyes on the toes of his outstretched feet, as people clutching clipboards bustled about, and men wearing earphones and pulling the attached wires behind them moved importantly from place to place and shouted at the invisible listeners who spoke to them through the earphones.

And then, suddenly, the big studio hushed expectantly as one of the earphoned men shouted, "All right, studio, a minute from the top. Counting now. Audience, remember, start your applause when I signal. Forty-five. Ready on opening captions. Thirty. Camera three, clear that shot on J. J.'s entrance. Twenty. fifteen. OK, start your applause, *now*. Ten, nine, eight, seven, six, five . . ."

The applause, scattered at first, thickened, took on a note of real enthusiasm, and tinny music could be heard threading through it, and then J. J. Gerrard was coming through the wide entrance at the back of the dais, his rather fat face heavily serious over his pink shirt, walking purposefully to the chair in the center. George felt rather than saw the swing of the camera that was aiming over his own left shoulder at Gerrard, felt it move backward, and then a great surge of apprehension came up into his chest, drying his mouth and clogging his throat. Christ! What was he doing sitting here? He ought to get up and go, just like that, and to hell with the lot of them.

". . . a matter which concerns all of us, very deeply," Gerrard was saying. "That, for all its surface appearance of mysterious and complex scientific endeavor beyond the ordinary man's comprehension, carries implications which must affect all of us, now and in the future. A matter with which I believe everyone, the studio audience here, the millions watching tonight in this country and all over the world, should be fully aware. And that is why we are here. Michael Bridges, the scientific journalist who first revealed to the public at large that this project existed—and we all owe him a great debt . . ."

A camera on the far side moved, swung in to stare at Michael Bridges, sitting on George's right, and came so close that George could see inside its Cyclops eye to the movement of the focusing mechanism.

"Kenneth Gurney, MP, a backbencher with no governmental or party axe to grind, but a keen awareness of the rights of the man in the street, here to ask questions on behalf of the watching millions. . . ."

George looked with distaste at the man sitting on Gerrard's other side, at the shining dapper head, the pin-striped suit with a white carnation in the buttonhole, and the sleek self-satisfied smirk on his face, and thought, *He's* enjoying this, pompous bastard.

"And of course, the man who knows most about it, the scientist who designed this project, set it up, launched it on an unknowing world. Dr. George Briant . . ."

The camera swung again, but this time George looked above it, to a monitor screen hung on a metal rafter above the audience, to see his own face in close-up, the eyes staring upward in a way that gave him an absurdly soulful look. Immediately he looked away and stared instead at J. J. Gerrard, not caring whether or not he showed his dislike for the situation he was in.

"Dr. Briant, let me tell you here and now that we are not here to make judgments. We are all"—he swung his hand comprehensively, to take in the audience, the studio staff, somehow implying he took in the watching millions too—"we are all worried by what we have heard of your work. We can't deny that. But we are not going to condemn merely because we don't understand. It is because we need to understand that we have asked you to come here tonight. I for one am making a disinterested search for information. No more and no less. You would agree that we have a right to seek this information?"

"If you feel you need it," George said dryly.

"Indeed, we do! So far all we know is what has appeared in the newspapers, that you have, shall we say, brought into life a baby—a human baby just like any one of the infants sleeping in their mothers' arms all over the world—in a way that is to say the least unusual. That you propose to keep this baby in your laboratories and investigate him—"

"*Not* in a laboratory, if you use the word to mean a place full of test tubes and retorts and animals in cages. In a well-equipped nursery where he can be observed with no distress to himself—that is all."

"Ah! Thank you for the definition. Very well, in a special nursery where he can be observed. As we understand it, he will live what you must admit is an . . . unnatural life? until he reaches maturity. And we want to know the hows and whys, the purposes of this project. Why you should feel it reasonable to subject a human baby to this distasteful experience—"

George moved sharply. "For someone who started out by stating he was not here to make judgments, you would appear to have a few already to hand," he said acidly. "Unnatural, distasteful—all words that apply to value judgments, wouldn't you say?"

"I stand rebuked," J. J. Gerrard said smoothly and swung his chair to face the audience. "Not for the first time, hmm?" And the audience responded with a soft wave of laughter, approving his modest admission of fallibility.

He turned back to George. "I apologize. But let us go on. And just to sketch in the background, could you recapitulate for us? For the benefit of those who have somehow failed to read the widespread newspaper accounts?"

George inclined his head and took from his pocket the folded paper that carried the statement he had read at his press conference.

"I can only repeat what I have already said to other journalists," he said and began to read. When he reached the end and put the paper back in his pocket, the audience shifted and swayed slightly, making him realize just how raptly they had listened to him.

After a momentary pause, Gerrard swung his chair again and

said to the audience, "I hope you all understood all that. I can't deny a lot of it was way over *my* head."

And the audience laughed, with relief rather than humor, and from somewhere at the back someone clapped loudly, making the laughter rise again before it subsided into silence.

But by then Gerrard was facing George again, an expression of great seriousness replacing the wry look he had produced for the audience.

"Clearly, we need a little more detail, Dr. Briant, if we are fully to understand. Could you tell us more about these extrapolations—or predictions—you were able to make from your study of the newly fertilized egg cell? And then can you give us an account of how far they have proved accurate? And a brief account of the investigations you have made since the child's birth?"

"It'll have to be brief," George said dryly. "You've asked enough to keep me talking for a month. All right. The extrapolations. On the basis of the work done by other researchers on the structure of DNA strands, and my own identification of Briant Bodies Alpha and Beta, I was able to choose a conception that would produce certain clearly defined physical characteristics. Sex, hair, eye and skin color, physique. These were very easily identifiable. Less easy to identify were personality traits which I believe are carried by Briant Bodies Gamma and Delta. As you may know, there has been much scientific argument about the ways such traits appear. Are they inborn, or are they created by the action of environmental influences?"

As he warmed to his theme, George forgot he was talking to one individual, and through him to a huge lay audience. It was as though he were dictating material for a paper in one of the journals or addressing a class of senior students.

"I believe the importance of genetic influences has been diminished in the amount of work that has been done on environmental influences. Some sociologists and to a lesser degree some psychoanalysts seem to assume they are working on pieces of wax, that a baby takes on all its imprints from outside. Yet in all logic, how can this be so? No amount of stimulation from the environment can, for example, increase the intelligence quotient of a known mongol. I don't deny that very often a potential for intelligence is underdeveloped because the environment lacks sufficient stimuli; but however much the environment is manipulated, unless the genetic material is good, there is a point beyond which such manipulation cannot have an effect."

"Do you mean that your researches will actually be able to define exactly what the full intelligence potential of the individual is?" Gerrard cut in. "I thought the idea of a fixed IQ rating was out of date now, that the latest reports from educationists say you can't measure it exactly."

George frowned sharply, irritated at being stopped just as he was getting well into his stride. "Educationists, as you call them, can't measure the full potential because they have such primitive tools and methods of assessment. What I am trying to do is identify *genetic* potential long before the birth of the infant, and therefore long before he has been affected by his environment. And if you will be good enough to let me go on, you will see how I am monitoring the environment of the infant in order to see precisely what effect it has. May I therefore continue?"

Gerrard blinked and then folded his arms and leaned back in his chair. "By all means," he said, a little stiffly.

"Thank you. Now, as I said, my own investigation of DNA strands revealed what I believe to be specific intelligence and personality factors in Briant Bodies Gamma and Delta. I started by looking at the chromosome patterns, of course—remember the men who are born with an extra Y chromosome, who show aggressive behavior and antisocial tendencies. It would take far too long to tell you in detail how I identified the specific genetic patterns of these chromosomes; you'll have to accept my assurance that I believe I did identify them."

"Ah! That sounds very—" Gerrard leaned forward again.

"Mr. Gerrard!" George stood up so sharply that his swivel chair swung half around. "Did you or did you not say that the purpose of my presence here this evening was to give you information about my work?"

"What? Well, of course, Dr. Briant! But—"

"Then will you be good enough to permit me to do just that? If you persist in interrupting me, it is unlikely in the extreme that I will have sufficient time to give you the complete picture which you say you are so anxious to get! I am a logical man, Mr. Gerrard, accustomed to presenting material in a concise, ordered and intelligible manner. *Ordered.* And that means that all these questions you are jumping in with will be answered as part of the statement I am here to make. If you will contain yourself in reasonable patience, and permit me to do what I came here to do, we will all be better off! Do I make myself clear?"

There was a rustle from the audience as George sat down again, but he ignored it. Let them think him high-handed; he was damned if he was going to let this greasy television pundit push him about.

Gerrard was looking at him with his eyebrows slightly raised. "Indeed you do! But may I point out to you, Dr. Briant, that I for one—and I think it likely that the audience feels much as I do—find the material you are giving us in so admirably *concise* and *ordered* a manner is not as intelligible as it might be, since we are ordinary simple souls? The language you speak is somewhat above our heads. So while I take your point that you are prepared to give us all the information we seek, may I reserve the right to interrupt when it is absolutely necessary to do so? For example, to ask for definitions of some of the words you use?" He turned to the audience. "That *is* fair enough, wouldn't you say?"

A murmur of assent went up as the audience shifted and rustled again, and Gerrard turned back to Briant. "Will you accept the need for *this* much interruption, Dr. Briant?"

"For definitions of terms, by all means. But I insist, no more of these attempts to anticipate. At the end, if there are any gaps, then by all means. But now, may I continue?"

Gerrard inclined his head with exaggerated courtesy, and George leaned back and went on.

"Where was I, then? Ah, yes. I was able to identify specific gene factors which carry personality traits. And I chose a conception that promised me a child of certain defined personality characteristics as well as physical ones. If our predictions are correct, he was born with an even temperament, high intelligence, a low aggression response. And we have in fact been able to demonstrate already that this is so. His responses to his environment have been measured in detail from his birth. Oh, and incidentally, I must tell you at this point that his pre-birth environment was most carefully handled. The mother was as perfect a physical specimen as we could find. Throughout the pregnancy, we used vacuum decompression to ensure that the infant's blood and therefore oxygen and food supplies were maximal."

"Vacuum decompression?" Gerrard asked quickly, wrinkling his brows with a neatly sketched-in expression of intelligent inquiry.

"An acceptable question," George said dryly. "Very well. This is a device we used that created a vacuum over the mother's abdomen for regular periods during the pregnancy. It was derived from an ordinary domestic vacuum cleaner. She sat in an envelope from which air was removed. This lifted the atmospheric pressure—fifteen pounds per square inch, as you may know—from the walls of the uterus and thus allowed the maximum free passage of blood through the maternal and infant blood vessels. So, we could be sure the unborn child was given a full and more than adequate food and oxygen supply throughout.

"Now, where was I? Oh, yes. The investigations we have made. Well, we have measured the child's responses from birth. His high intelligence has been early manifested. He has modified his inherent reflexes according to the type of stimuli he gets. For example, all babies turn the head and the mouth towards a touch on the cheek, seeking the nipple. This 'rooting' reflex is quite outside the infant's conscious control. Now, when I touch his cheek with my finger, he responds normally, but not as quickly as he responds when he is held to the breast. Within this first week he has learned the difference between the touch of a finger and the touch of his nurse's body. I must tell you, if you don't already know from the newspapers, that he is cared for by a most responsive nurse who has been enabled by hormone therapy to breast feed him.

"He has also responded with increasing rapidity to other stimuli, particularly sound. When I speak to him he responds; but not with the same speed with which he responds to his nurse, from whom of course he obtains satisfaction of his physical needs. We know too that he more than normally rapidly recognizes differences in temperature as well as differences in individual voices. All this points to a higher than usual intelligence quotient."

For the first time Michael Bridges stirred, and George looked at him over his shoulder, momentarily surprised. "There is one point, Dr. Briant," he said. "Controls. You can't measure any response without something against which to measure it. You've got to have a yardstick of some sort—"

"Oh, I know! That was one of my greatest initial problems," George said approvingly. "You clearly see the importance of this point. It does you credit. But I couldn't set up an ideal control system. I had considered selecting a twinning conception, and using the other infant as a control. But this would have been difficult because of the problem of creating the ideal pre-birth environment. Twins have a lesser chance of good pre-birth life since they must share the available food and oxygen supplies. And anyway, if I monitored two babies, I would be creating the same environment for both of them, wouldn't I? No, I got over this problem by collecting data on a large series of babies to whom I had access during the preliminary work on this project. A pediatrician at my hospital —the same one now supervising the infant's general health—gave me enormous help, enormous. I have a great deal of essential data on infant behavior that I am using as control material. And there is no doubt in my mind that this infant is of higher than average intelligence.

"Now, this infant has been put in a perfect environment. He is being so carefully nurtured that never yet has he suffered any frustration. In normal situations, babies experience frequent frustration from birth. They want food, and the only way they can express their desire for it is to cry. This is their signaling method. But the moment a baby cries for food he is frustrated in his desire. He cannot understand that he is waiting only a matter of moments before his desire will be satisfied. He just feels the desperation of hunger that is not being dealt with. And one thing we do know from the work of really scientific psychologists—those of the behaviorist school—is that frustration creates an aggressive response, anger.

"We have trained the nurse caring for this infant to recognize the first signs of desire for food. He has never—never since his birth—cried to be fed. As soon as he shows the slight movements that herald developing hunger, he is put to the breast. Similarly, as soon as he shows the smallest sign of being too cold, or too warm, his environment is manipulated to create the conditions of maximum comfort. I must tell you that this infant has never cried *at all* apart from at the moment of birth when he took his first breath—and that must be accepted as an unavoidable demand for satisfaction of an impossible desire. He could not be returned, as he would have wished, to his pre-birth environment, but he was put into a close facsimile of it immediately. He lies in a cot equipped with a special mattress which is filled with liquid; he lies on so resilient a surface that it is very close to actually lying in liquid, as of course the unborn infant does. His cot pulses gently too with a rhythm matched to that of his mother's average pulse rate during pregnancy.

"He has never suffered discomfort or pain, either. When blood tests are taken, we use local anesthesia, sprayed on the skin. The electrodes permanently attached to his scalp—we need those to take the frequent and essential measurements of electric impulses produced by his brain—are also imperceptible to him, since the resilience of his mattress ensures he feels no pressure from them at all.

"So, as I say, this child has been given the most perfect environment possible. And already he has shown some most interesting behavior, apart from the signs of his intelligence I have already described for you. For example, he has a waking and sleeping pattern that follows closely the one regarded as normal—sleeps most at night, feeds at four regular intervals during the day even though he is so young. Which suggests that the life patterns imposed on infants in fact derive from biological need. The difference with this baby is that he himself has selected the time at which he will display the pattern, rather than having it imposed on him by a mother's pattern of giving care. That completes my statement. You may now question and comment if you choose."

There was another brief silence, and then Bridges said softly, "A baby who never cries, because he never needs to."

He raised his head and looked very directly at J. J. Gerrard. "He sounds a most fortunate baby," he said loudly. "How many infants can be as free from distress as that? I've always thought babies have a pretty rotten life, completely under the control of people who don't have any idea of what goes on inside a baby's mind—"

"A fair point, and a very reassuring one," Gerrard said with a fine judicial air. "All right. The baby, despite the fact that he has been denied his birthright of the care of deeply loving parents who created him in love, is as well cared for—"

"Now, let's stop right there," George said sharply, and his voice was louder than he meant it to be. "Let's get this business of birthrights and loving parents in some sort of perspective. You labor under the idea that the best people to care for a child are the people who conceived and bore him. Human society has always operated this way. And in my opinion the results of this method of child rearing show what an inefficient method it is. We live in a world that operates on greed, on aggression, on violence and cruelty. We are faced with one of the unhappiest young generations we have ever had—antisocial, with juvenile delinquency causing immense distress, not least to the young themselves. And on the physical health side, enormous numbers of children are badly fed, physically neglected, by the loving parents who bore them! Is that the system you want to maintain? Do you want to see humanity kill itself off because of its inability to rear improved generations to follow on?"

"Is that what you're trying to do then? Take our kids away from us because you reckon you know what's good for them better than what we do? You're no better than a Hitler."

Startled, George turned his head to stare at a woman who was standing up somewhere in the middle of the tight-packed rows of the audience. Her face was red with emotion and she was standing with her head poked angrily forward.

"Who do you think you are, you scientists?" she cried shrilly.

"Didn't you have a mother that loved you? And haven't you got kids of your own? Would you let someone take *your* kids away? Or is it all right for you to keep your own kids, but the likes of us, ordinary people, who've got to give up—"

"Madam, I wish you would listen instead of jumping to ridiculous conclusions!" George shouted above her voice. "I have not for a moment suggested that children should be removed from the care of their parents. And I have *no* political motives! If you will wait with reasonable patience, I will explain—"

"You'll get your chance in a moment," Gerrard called, equally loudly. "We must give Dr. Briant a fair hearing first, please, but since the point has been raised—Dr. Briant?"

Unwillingly the woman sat down, and George said acidly, "Thank you. Very well. I do *not* propose that children be removed from their parents' care. I *do* propose to seek information that will help them to make a better job of rearing those children. Love sounds like an important word, but it is shapeless, it can't be defined. And it can't replace knowledge. However deeply you care for your children, without knowledge of how they develop, how their experiences affect their personalities, you can't give them this . . . this *birthright* you talk about so glibly. It is precisely because I care about the future of humanity that I am undertaking this work."

"All right, Dr. Briant." For the first time the man on Gerrard's other side spoke, and his voice was smooth and the accent very carefully cultured. "If we accept this—that you can give us information that will help us to rear better offspring—how do you propose this information be used?"

"How do you mean, be used? How is any information used? We have information about methods of curing disease, for example, and apply them. It's as simple as that."

"Is it? I'm not so sure. It seems to me that you propose to tell us, on the basis of your researches, the right way to create super children, and then the right way to bring them up. But how is it to be done? Will the whole population have to submit itself to tests of their suitability to have children? And if you had to seek through two thousand people to find your pair of suitable parents, does that mean that—let me see—only point naught naught one of the population will be considered fit for parenthood? And once they are permitted to produce their babies, will they have to accept constant control over the way they care for them? I'm not afraid to make judgments, Mr. Gerrard. And I tell you here and now, I find this whole idea utterly revolting."

Immediately a great roar of applause broke out, and Gurney looked at the audience, and this time his self-satisfied smirk seemed to be so obvious, to George at any rate, that he could not understand how the audience too could fail to see it. But clearly they didn't. Their approval was so strong it was almost tangible, filling the big cluttered studio with sound.

Gerrard was waving his hands from side to side, and gradually the noise diminished, and he turned to George and raised his eyebrows.

"Well, Dr. Briant? Can you answer that?"

"I can answer it only as any other scientist would," George said, and anger clipped his words. "By asking *you* for the answer. My goals are clear-cut. I must seek knowledge, the truth that derives from knowledge. I am trying to give you hard facts, tell you how the traits of human personality are carried from parents to offspring, tell you accurately how the environment modifies inherited characteristics. When this child involved in my project reaches maturity, I will have amassed a body of immensely valuable knowledge, but what you, what humanity as a whole does with it, is out of my hands. I must repeat, I have no political motives, I'm not in the least interested in the dismal machinations of politicians. It is *you* who must concern yourself with the . . . the ethical problems involved. You who must decide whether you are prepared to go on allowing dangerous aggression to mar life for all of us. If you are happy to go on living under the constant threat of war, if you are prepared to see the discoveries of science perverted by inadequate people to the creation of foul weapons, what can I do? What can any scientist do? I know perfectly well that certain of my colleagues have made some attempt to concern themselves with these questions. No doubt you have heard of the Pugwash conferences. But they concern themselves primarily with discussing the application of nuclear physics, and I cannot see that the work of a biologist could profitably be discussed at such a conference, and certainly not by me. I can only repeat, I have no involvement with political ideas or so-called social ethics. I can only give you a tool for good. It is up to you whether you use it or not."

"You say it is a good tool, sir!" This time the interruption came from a man in the front row of the audience, a tall man who was leaning forward, and George looked at him, feeling less hostility than the woman who had shouted at him earlier had created; and then he realized it was because he spoke in an educated voice.

"But as you so clearly realize, scientists have many times created tools that can be used for good, but which have then been perverted to evil use. Now tell me the answers to two points. One, is there not a way in which *your* good tool could be perverted, and two, since this tool must inevitably be given into the hands of the people you despise for their aggressiveness and bad inheritance and rearing, how do you expect them to use it? Isn't this a self-defeating exercise upon which you are engaged?"

George leaned back and stared consideringly at the questioner. He had been right in his snap judgment—indeed an intelligent, educated individual.

"I'd like to discuss that first point, if I may, Dr. Briant," Gerrard cut in. "Because although I don't entirely share with you your view of the essential rottenness of all humanity as it exists today, I can see there are sections of it that are dangerous—"

"I have not suggested for a moment that I regard all humanity as rotten," George said icily. "That is a most unjust and . . . and . . . absurd generalization." He had nearly said stupid and stopped himself in time. No need, in so public a setting, to show his true opinion of the man's shallowness. He had already diminished the man in his audience's eyes by refusing to accept his interruptions. No need for more.

"All right, but to return to the point. I can see how your good tool, as you call it, could be used. I will accept that you are designing it to enable humanity to select and rear a future generation that is peaceful and creative rather than aggressive and destructive, that your personal motives are good. But can't you see that there is an obverse to everything? That just as you are making it possible to select conceptions that will result in the right sort of people, as you define them, and reject the potentially bad ones, so it would be possible to reject the good and retain the bad. I can see a situation in which a government made up of aggressive men, their minds set on world domination achieved through war, could seize on your researches to create the most warlike and dangerous nation that has ever existed, which links with this gentleman's second point." He whirled and pointed at the man in the front row. "In you, sir, we hear the voice of cool reason, of the natural fears of good men."

He turned back to George. "We are afraid you are taking upon yourself the creation of a tool that has an even greater potential for evil than for good. And we have a right to ask you, as the creator of the tool, not only whether the way you are forging it is acceptable to the dignity of man, but whether the results can be safely presented to the world."

"And there's something else too!" Now several people in the audience were on their feet and waving in an attempt to attract the attention of Gerrard, who left the dais and walked up the narrow central aisle, holding a hand microphone high in the air. It was a man wearing an overcoat pulled high around his neck who succeeded in getting the chance to speak as Gerrard thrust the microphone at him.

"Something else too!" the man repeated. "All this talk about bodies and minds—what about man's soul, sir! His soul! We are more than mere animals, remember! God created us for His own purposes, gave us free will to decide between good and evil, but retained unto Himself the ultimate decisions about the creation of life. To do as you are doing, to take to yourself the right to decide who shall and who shall not be born, is to set yourself up above God—"

"And God shall not be mocked!" A woman sitting beside him leapt to her feet and seized the microphone from Gerrard's hand. "You're evil, you scientists, evil, that's what you are! Mocking God, stealing babies from their mothers. You're a Herod, a wicked, evil—"

"Thank you. And someone else now." Skillfully, Gerrard maneuvered the microphone away from her and moved quickly up the aisle to the back of the audience; and the camera, pushed by a sweating man in a stained white shirt, followed him. "You, the lady at the end there. You look very anxious to say something."

"I am, oh, I am! I've got a baby. He's three months old and I love him and I wouldn't do a thing to harm him. And it's wicked, wicked what you're doing to this poor little baby you've got locked up in your laboratory! I'm not all that religious, I reckon you can be good without goin' to Church, and that, but I know wickedness when I see it, and it ought to be put a stop to."

"And who's going to put a stop to it? That's what I want to know!" A man behind the young mother reached for the microphone, but this time Gerrard held on firmly. "You've got an MP up there. What does he say is to be done about it? Eh? If we all want it put a stop to, will the government do something about it, or will it be like you said, Mr. Gerrard? Will they see they can use this . . . this *science* for their own political ideas? Eh? What do you say to that?"

By now, other men with microphones were moving among the audience, and so many people were shouting to be heard that George could no longer identify individual speakers as words overleaped one another and blended together into a great cry of confused and frightened protest.

". . . and the next thing, you'll be choosing only the types you want, and breeding out the minority groups you and your like have always hated. You'll carry on where Hitler left off, if they let you, getting rid of Jews and Gypsies and colored people and . . ."

". . . what about the people who won't do what you scientists tell them and get pregnant anyway. Will the next thing be abortions for people who don't want them, and forced sterilization for them afterwards, and . . ."

". . . you and all your fancy long words. It's a bloody con, that's what it is. You're trying to blind us with all your scientific talk, so that we don't see what you're getting at, and leave you alone till it's too late . . ."

". . . you're a wicked, evil man, like that other woman said, flying in the face of Nature and God . . ."

". . . and what about Einstein? They said he was mentally deficient, and if people like you get your way, they'll kill off children like he was, and then . . ."

". . . you're trying to make science into the new religion, that's what you're doing, and it's a . . ."

". . . and who's paying for your filthy experiments? That's what I'd like to know. It's coming out of our taxes, that's where, and we ought to put a stop to it. It's our money, that's what you lot ought to remember, and we ought to have a say in . . ."

". . . all your rubbishing talk about the future of mankind—it's a load of crap—like this nonsense about the population explosion. There's plenty of food for the world however many people there are in it, because no one's started farming the seas yet, have they? That's what you scientists ought to be doing, improving food production, and finding ways to colonize the planets and the moon, instead of messing about with people and the children they have. Mankind is a dominant species because it's adaptable, and you're trying to stop the natural methods of evolution for your own rotten reasons and . . ."

Above the uproar, Gerrard signaled furiously at the men with the microphones, and they fell back to the sides of the studio, pulling the microphones away from eagerly reaching hands, and Gerrard began to walk backward toward the dais, looking from side to side as he went.

"All right, all right!" he shouted, and the audience began gradually to quieten. "All right! We're not getting anywhere like this. Let's get a majority opinion on this. Let's have a show of hands. How many people think this project ought to be stopped right now before it goes any further?"

Immediately a sea of hands shot up, waving, and Gerrard nodded and cried, "And let's get the other side. Anyone think it's a good thing?"

And this time other hands went up, and Gerrard craned to see.

"So it's not unanimous! Right. Let's hear the other side. You, sir, what reason do you have for seeing this project as worth following through?"

A young man wearing a brightly colored college scarf pushed his way to the end of the row to get within reach of the microphone.

"Look, this opposition is to be expected." He spoke in a surprisingly deep voice. "People are always scared of what they don't understand, but you can't stop progress, can you? We'd still be living in caves like the half-apes we sprang from if the frightened little people had their way. Dr. Briant is right. He can give us a wonderful tool, a wonderful one. We, the people who'll have the next generation of children, we want a better world than the one we've got from all of you! None of this will affect you, anyway. It's *us* who'll have the next lot of babies, not you. You've had your chance and made a rotten mess of it. And you can't stop science from helping us to make a better job of things. People with education won't misuse what Dr. Briant discovers. And we're the best-educated generation ever—"

"You kids think you know it all," a woman shouted from the front of the now thoroughly stirred-up audience. "Wait until they try to take your babies off you, then you'll change your tune, you—"

"Now, madam, let's give both sides a fair hearing," Gerrard called. "Anyone else with this young man?"

"Yes! He's right! All this stupid talk about God and men's souls—what we need is real education, not the prejudices of superstitious religion mongers like that man up the front," a voice called. And then, quite suddenly, there was uproar again, with the audience almost entirely on its feet and shouting and milling about, completely out of Gerrard's control.

Above his head, George saw the monitor black out, and then a few words faded in. "Normal service will be resumed." And he looked away at the crowd so near to him and felt a stab of real fear. These people were dangerous in their fury, and for a brief moment he knew the terror of the threat of physical attack, and he looked over his shoulder for an escape route.

But already the noise was diminishing, the violence of the anger subsiding as rapidly as it had built up, and he looked back at the audience to see people taking their places again, Gerrard and the earphoned men in shirtsleeves moving quickly and purposefully among them, urging them into seats.

Gerrard came back to the dais and held his hands up for silence, and though there was still a good deal of noise he made himself heard above it.

"Now, come on, come on. Where's your sense, all of you? This program is being seen all over the world! Do you want the rest of the world to say the British are so aggressive that they *need* the sort of controls we've been talking about? Come on now, cool it, cool it."

"Nothing like a little chauvinism, is there?" George turned and looked in surprise at the source of the murmured comment; and he saw Michael Bridges close beside him, surprised because he'd forgotten he was there.

"If ever there were an indictment of uncontrolled human responses, here it is," George said bitterly. "I can't imagine even the most rabid antiscience types not seeing that—"

"Can't you?" Bridges grinned and then laughed equally bitterly. "For a brilliant man, you can be very naïve, Dr. Briant. Don't make the fatal mistake of assuming other people think as logically as you do, or even hear what's said to them. No matter how often you tell 'em you haven't got this infant in a laboratory cage, for example, they'll still believe that's where he is, with a chain round his neck very likely. You've frightened them sick—"

"All right, Julian, back on camera four," Gerrard was shouting, and then the monitor lit up again, and Gerrard said smoothly, "Well, sorry for that momentary interruption, ladies and gentlemen. Due to factors beyond our control, and all that! Now, let's see where we were. Dr. Briant has told us how his project is operating, and what he expects to discover from it. Mr. Gurney has voiced the fears of many in his questions on the way Dr. Briant's discoveries may be used. Mr. Bridges has asked a couple of pertinent scientific questions—but let's hear more from him before, perhaps, returning to the audience here in the studio for some more of their opinion."

Mike leaned forward obediently. "My function, Mr. Gerrard, is to report facts as I find them. I believe—as my paper, the *Echo*, believes—that the greatest danger to mankind is not science and its discoveries, but ignorance. For this reason we support Dr. Briant in his efforts to combat ignorance, by reporting every piece of information about his work that we can. I'm not sure newspapers should do more than this—inform and then reflect public opinion. Whether we ought to set ourselves up as molders of it is another question."

He stopped, seeming to collect himself. Careful, careful, he was thinking. Don't go on too long about the paper, or you'll put your foot right in it with Sefton, one way or another. Speak for yourself now.

He looked at the audience and bit his lip. "Look," he said, a little awkwardly. "I'm like the rest of you. I don't know where the work of people like Dr. Briant is leading us. Maybe it'll be a better world we'll have, maybe not. But I have enough scientific training myself to know what a hell of a dilemma he's in. Science has *got* to go on looking for knowledge. That's what it's all about. It's above —no, not above—*beyond* politics, beyond such things as ideas about religion, and the uses to which its discoveries are put. If scientists had to think always about what might happen politically or socially because of their work, they'd never get the work done. There wouldn't be any ethical problems to worry about, because as that young man in the audience said, we'd still be living in caves or the trees.

"I tell you flatly, the sort of scientists you should be frightened of aren't the ones like Dr. Briant, who . . . well, opt out of the ethical questions. The really dangerous scientists are those who *do* have political and moral ideas and set out to use their science to further their own ideological ends. Can't you see that? Dr. Briant is doing the right thing—doing his own job to the best of his ability and leaving the rest of it to the people he's doing it for—you."

He stopped, and there was a pause, and then someone started to clap at the back of the studio, and George, who had been sitting with his chin on his chest, impassively listening, looked up.

The solitary applauder was the young man in the scarf, but even as George looked at him, another man joined in, then a woman, and gradually the sound built up until several hands were clapping, but not loudly enough to drown the boos and shouts other members of the audience were producing.

Gerrard raised his hands again, and this time his control over them was so complete that the applause stopped and there was silence.

"A very reasonable argument, Mr. Bridges, very reasonable. It makes some sense to me, and clearly to some of the audience here tonight. But not enough sense. You say—and so does Dr. Briant—that the '*safe*' scientists are the ones who don't concern themselves with ideological issues. Are you sure? Look, who should be the leaders, the individuals who make the decisions that affect the lives of ordinary people? Shouldn't it be the thinkers, the creators of ideas? Shouldn't it be the people who have as their driving force the desire to reveal truths about human life? Of course it should. But they won't. They discover things that because they have a power for good have an equal power for bad—one can't exist without the other—and then say, 'Here it is, do what you like with it. It's none of our business. We're too busy looking for more truths.' And what happens? Their dangerous truths are left in the hands of politicians, some of them people who are driven by little things, like the desire for personal power, and who don't understand the explosive possibilities of what they have been given; or if they understand, don't care. The scientists and philosophers—and I think it's significant that scientific study used to be called natural philosophy—they think in a big way, about yesterday and tomorrow, about the whole great sweep of mankind in the world. But politicians don't. By definition, they are concerned only with the here and now. They don't think in any sort of . . . of historical context. That's why I worry about Dr. Briant and his work."

He whirled in his chair and looked at the audience. "I said I wasn't here to make moral judgments, that all we wanted was to understand what this project was all about and where it is leading. Well, I'm going to break my word. I *am* going to make moral judgments. I'm going to say what I believe, and what I'm convinced the vast majority of caring people believe. That science can be dangerous because people are imperfect and can't be trusted with the weapons science creates. That there is a power beyond mankind itself—and I'm not ashamed to say I trust in the existence and loving-kindness of God—that should be accepted, just as our own imperfections should be accepted. That when someone—

one man like Dr. Briant—starts to meddle with the functions of the power that is God, disaster stares us in the face. That our instinctive loathing for the way Dr. Briant is manipulating human life, is using a human child as a lever to open the box that holds God's secrets about life, our response, I say, is not reactionary, not the stupid fears of little men, but is born of our awareness of the dangers of knowing too much, is a God-given warning, if you like. There must come a point at which man must stop trying to decide his own destiny, and I believe that point has come now, in our time. But I am not saying that Dr. Briant should necessarily be stopped from making his scientific searches, for his ability to do so is as God-given as that warning. But I do say that we, the ordinary man, must either insist he takes responsibility for what he discovers, and *does* concern himself with the ethics of its methods and application, or accept the responsibility to ourselves, and make our own decisions about how science is used. We dare not shrug our shoulders and leave a great chasm into which cynical politicians might leap, and take us all to perdition with them."

He stopped, quite sharply, staring at the audience, which stared back in dumfounded silence. Then he rubbed his sweating face and said huskily, "I'm sorry. I am here to act as a . . . a chairman, an impartial chairman, and I've let myself be carried away. I'm sorry."

And then the applause leapt into existence like a great roaring animal as people jumped up, shouting, clapping, screaming their agreement and their opposition, moving in a heaving mass. And above their heads the monitors showed captions rolling, and the faint tinny music entwined itself into the noise, and the screens blacked.

Through the uproar Briant moved toward Gerrard and touched his shoulder, and Gerrard turned his fat gleaming face toward him.

"Gerrard," George shouted above the din. "You're wrong, you couldn't be more wrong, but you said that with so much . . . with such intelligence that I must both apologize to you and compliment you. I thought you were a . . . a shallow man, incapable of producing a logical argument. But you *are* a thinker, even if a wrong-headed one, and I compliment you because . . ."

Gerrard had been looking at him with a gradually spreading grin on his face, and now he thumped George on the back with great bonhomie and beamed with immense satisfaction.

"That's very big of you, old man, considering I made mincemeat of you. And it *was* bloody good television, wasn't it? Christ, if that doesn't keep 'em watching, nothing will." And he turned and moved across the dais and out of the studio, followed by his cohort of technicians and production assistants, who thumped him on the back and shouted their own compliments into his receptive ears.

And George stepped back and stared after him, feeling as though he had been slapped, and behind him Mike murmured, "I told you, Dr. Briant. For a brilliant man, you can be very naïve. J. J. has just shown you his one real skill—the way he can judge the mood of an audience and play it like a violin. And if you, an intelligent man who can think, can be swept away by him, how do you think *they've* been affected? I tell you, Dr. Briant, you've unleashed a hell of a lot more than you realize with this project of yours. A hell of a lot more."

7

"I've got to go home," Hilary said again and set her mouth stubbornly. "I've got to. You can phone them first if you like, but I've got to go."

"But what good will it do, my dear?" Miss Schofield said helplessly. "You'll only be exposing yourself to more distress. I do understand how upset you are—"

"Miss Schofield." Matron spoke from her place by the door of the headmistress's study. "May I speak to you privately for a moment? If Hilary could wait outside just for a second or two, dear?"

Sulkily, Hilary went, moving with even more than her usual lumpishness, and as the door closed behind her, Matron said urgently, "It will be better if she goes, believes me. I told you there'd be trouble if you let the seniors see this wretched program, and there will be, and even more if Hilary stays. All this talk about religion, it's not nice, you know. There's enough unhealthy religious excitement as it is, with that girl Elliot and her Evangelistic nonsense. You didn't see what happened. I saw it with them, remember that, I saw the effect it had. Elliot got so excited, I thought she was going to pass out. I swear that girl's a petit mal subject, and when she started shouting at Hilary Briant as she did —I really think you should send the girl home. And Margaret Elliot too, if you can. It's not healthy."

"Oh, really, Miss Buck! If we can't cope with an adolescent upheaval of this sort without sending girls home, we have no right to be running a progressive school. And as for Margaret Elliot . . ."

By the time they had come to the end of their argument and Matron had opened the door again, fixing a bright smile on her face for Hilary's benefit, the problem had been solved. Hilary had gone, leaving the back door of the Head's house swinging wide. And by the time Miss Schofield had made her agitated call to her home, Hilary had picked up her first lift.

"I had to come home, Daddy," Hilary said again. "I just had to. If you'd have *seen*—they were hateful, they really were. One of the girls in the Sixth said you were no better than a Hitler, she did! And I wanted to die, I really did. I had to come home. It's not long to end of term, and I could do my A levels somewhere else, couldn't I? I can't go back, I truly can't. Daddy, you do see, don't you?"

"Oh, for crying out loud, Hilary," Ian said, "turn it off, will you? I never heard such a load of crap in my life. Oh, all right, Rusty. I'm sorry. Rubbish, then. Who do you think gives a damn about you? And even if your stupid girls do have a go at you because of the Prof's work, what's the odds? You'll get something out of it if you've got any sense."

He grinned across at his mother. "Like me, eh, Rusty? You've done a great job for me, Prof—Dad. A great job. You've turned out to be a great show-biz contact. Get you!" And he laughed loudly and swung his legs back over the arm of his chair so that he could reach the sherry decanter.

"What are you talking about?" George was quite incredibly tired; his whole body seemed to ache with fatigue, and his mind seemed to operate dully, as though there were a film over it. "And leave that sherry alone. You've had more than enough, and that's all there is. What are you talking about, a contact?"

"You've been too wrapped up in yourself to hear anything anyone says to you tonight," Marjorie said sharply. "And let him have his sherry. He's entitled to celebrate."

"Celebrate what? For Christ's sake, haven't I had enough to put up with today without you all starting on me? I'm tired! It's late, and I'm bloody *tired*—"

"My job, Prof, my job!" Ian said and laughed again. "I told you he wouldn't take it in, Rusty, didn't I?"

"Take in what?" George shouted, and Hilary winced and then moved closer to him on the sofa they were sharing beside the dying fire.

"The producer phoned him as soon as your program went off the air. He's got the part after all. They start rehearsing next week. I told you as soon as you came in. Or weren't you listening to a word I said?"

"And I've no illusions, Prof, none at all. In this business it isn't talent that matters. It's who you know. And I know *you*! They'll make a great splash out of it, and I couldn't care less. If they want to make publicity out of my being your son, it's great by me. Great, great, great! As long as I get in, who cares how the door gets opened? Not this baby! Once I've had a couple of decent jobs, I'll be a name in my own right. But till then I'll gladly use yours. And if Hilary can't get something out of it too, she's a bloody sight more of a fool than she looks, if that's possible."

"Oh, leave her alone, Ian. She's overwrought. She'll go back to school in the morning when she feels better," Marjorie said. But she didn't look at Hilary.

"No she won't!" George was on his feet, and his face was blazing with anger. "If you can't recognize her integrity, I can! As for you—" He looked at Ian, sprawled in his armchair, with an expression of plain dislike on his face. "As for you, Ian, you can forget it. If you've been given a . . . a . . . job on the strength of my project, you can forget it. I will not on any account have any member of my family make such corrupt use of what I'm doing, do you understand? If you don't refuse this job yourself, then by God I'll do it for you. And the way I'll do it won't be pleasant for you, and well you know it. Do you hear me?"

"Dad!" Ian almost wailed the word, and the expression of disbelief on his face was absurd in its intensity. "Dad, you can't mean that! I've been trying for almost a year to get in, and now I'm in you can't kill it for me! What harm can it do you? All I want from your name is a bit of a leg-up, that's all! I told you, they'll soon forget I'm your son, and I'll get on on my own. But in show business you've got to make the best of every trick in the book. Please, Dad—"

"No!" George rubbed his face wearily and then went on in a more reasonable voice. "For God's sake, Ian, you must surely see why you can't use your connection with me in this way! To get a job in a—what is it?—a protest musical with everyone standing around nude? It's obscene! I'm trying to do a piece of honest research and you want to use it for a purpose like this one? Have you no sense of dignity?"

"You didn't look all that dignified tonight!" Marjorie was on her feet too, clutching her dressing gown to her chest with her knuckles showing white with anger. "Sitting there, being bawled at by every Tom, Dick and Harry! Very dignified, that was! You've no right to treat Ian this way! You've done little enough for him, God knows, all these years. The cheapest school you could find—a bloody sight cheaper than Hilary's and don't you forget it!—just because he had the guts to tell you right from the start he didn't give a rotten damn for your stinking lousy science! Just because your precious daughter sucks round you and bleats her half-baked science at you, she's the only one you care about! Well, Ian's entitled to your interest too. He's *entitled* to it, you hear me? We've had nothing out of our lives with you, nothing at all, and I'm not standing by and letting you ruin the only chance you've ever given him, and that without intending to. Don't push me too far, George, don't push me too far."

"Don't push *you* too far! Christ almighty! You say that to me? You say that Ian's entitled to—listen, Marjorie, and you too."

With a sudden new access of rage George turned on Ian, who

shrank back in his chair, fear making his face sag for a moment.

"Yes, *you*, you with your stupid little mind and your stupid little ambitions and your revolting talk! You make me sick, physically sick! I've tried with you, God knows I've tried! From the time you were old enough to be interesting, from the time you started to talk intelligibly, I've tried to make something out of you! I've tried to instill into you a little—just a very little of what thinking is all about. I've done my damnedest to give you the sort of background, the sort of training that would help you make something of yourself! And where have my efforts got me? Where? You never tried, never made the least shift to take what I had to give you. You went whining and mewing to your mother, grizzling your stupidities, rejecting everything that—"

"Just you wait a minute!" Ian was on his feet too, and his face was as white as his father's. For a brief moment they looked quite remarkably alike as they stood facing each other with their heads poked forward and their shoulders rigid, for all the world like a pair of rutting stags. "Just let me say something while we're at it! *You've* given me? *You've* tried? *You've* been rejected? Jesus wept, you don't know which way is up! You made up some fancy picture in your head of what your son ought to be, and you set about making it real. *You* decided that I had to be a carbon copy of you, another little George Briant. Well, I'm not! I never was and I never will be! I'm Ian, *Ian*, do you hear me? I'm myself, and I'll do my own thing because it's what I want to do, and I've as much right as you or anyone else to live my life the way I want to! I don't owe you a bloody thing not one bloody thing. It's you that owe me, and never paid your whack! If you'd cared about me as a person, as Ian, and not just as your stinking lousy son, you'd have cared for me for what I am, and not for what I might turn into, not because I might bring a bit of glory onto your head! There's not a thing about me that you don't despise, and haven't despised for as long as I can remember. You don't like the way I talk? Bloody hard luck! I don't like the way *you* talk, never have, not since I sat and tried to understand what the hell it was you were talking about. I'll talk *my* way, I'll dress *my* way, I'll wear my hair the length *I* want it. I'll do anything that'll make me different from you and everything you stand for! And if it annoys you, well, hard luck again, chum! What Rusty said is dead right. You've never given me one lousy thing that mattered to me—to *me*, and not to you—except now, by accident. And if you take that away from me, I'll, I'll . . ."

He stopped, as suddenly as he had started, and stared at his father with his jaw moving spasmodically, looking as though he were on the edge of tears. And then he shrugged and turned away and muttered, "Ah, what's the use? I've said it all before, and it's like throwing arrows at a bulldozer. You've never had any time for me. It's all for Hilary, always has been."

"You see, George?" Marjorie's voice was high and thin. "You see what you've done? It's true, every word of it, and it always has been. Hilary's had the best school, the best of everything, just because she's like you and interested in your things, but Ian—me and Ian—we . . ."

And she too stopped and shook her head and then turned away from George's bleak silence to stand beside Ian.

Hilary was crying, sniffing and gulping unappetizingly on the sofa, and Ian moved closer to his mother to stand with as arm across her shoulders, looking at George with an anxious mixture of sulky antagonism and pleading on his face. And George stood almost swaying with weariness and tried to think clearly.

"That's not true and you know it. I gave both of them the same, as much as I could afford at the time. However little it was, it was the best I could do. But for God's sake, leave it till tomorrow. I've had enough for one day, and I can't stand any more. Leave it till tomorrow—"

"No! We'll settle it here and now. Right here and now," Marjorie cried, and then the telephone shrilled sharply and she stopped and stood blinking stupidly in surprise.

It was Ian who moved first to pick up the telephone and still its insistent nagging.

"Yes, he's here. Who?" He covered the mouthpiece with one hand. "It's the TV studio. Do they work all night, for Christ's sake? They want you." And he looked across at George with a defiant sneer on his face. "Nice somebody does, I suppose."

George turned his back and sat down on the sofa again and shook his head. "Tell them I won't talk to them. Not at this hour. They've had their circus, and they can leave me alone."

"He's, er, not available," Ian said into the telephone, sounding ridiculously pompous. "Can I help you? I'm Ian Briant if it matters. Yes. What? Oh. Just a minute. I'll see if I can speak to him. Hold on."

He turned to George with his face suddenly bright with excitement, his anger apparently evaporating instantly. "Dad! There's a call from America! For you. Someone from New York wants to talk to you urgently. They're holding on to another line to the studios, and this bloke says should he pass on your phone number? Shall I say yes?"

"No." George started to speak, but Marjorie swept across the room and pulled the phone from Ian's hand.

"This is Mrs. Briant speaking. I hope you will forgive my husband. As you can imagine, he is extremely tired. Now, what do these American people want? Yes, I'll hold."

"Marjorie, I told you I won't speak to anyone, no one at all. I don't care who it is! Not now or—"

"Sssh! I'm trying to hear what he's saying on the other line." Marjorie put her other hand over her ear and turned her back on him, her face tense with the effort to hear.

"Yes? Oh. Oh, I see. Yes. Yes. I see! Well, look, tell them they can call here right away. Yes, we'll speak to them, yes." And she hung up and turned to look at George with her face suddenly gleaming with suppressed excitement.

"George! Don't be a fool, you hear me? This call, it's important, terribly important. I know you're tired, but you've got to take it."

"No," George said again, mechanically, and Hilary put her hand out protectively and covered his and looked at her mother with clear dislike in her eyes.

"Leave him alone, Mummy."

"You mind your own damned business, Hilary! And get out of here and go to bed! You've caused enough upset for one night, running off from school in that stupid fashion. This is nothing to do with you."

"Let her be," George said, and his voice was blurred with exhaustion. "Let her be. Bad enough she heard the start of this argument. She'll have to see the end of it. What's so vital about this call?"

"It's an American science foundation!" Marjorie seemed to push Hilary out of her mind completely. "That was the producer's assistant, and he said these people phoned because they want to offer you a research fellowship, and they want to get at you before anyone else does, because they know there'll be people all over the world who'll try to grab you. And they told him you can have anything you want, anything at all! Laboratories, money, name your own price, he said they said! Do you hear me, George? Name your own price."

Again the telephone shrilled, and she grabbed at it and said breathlessly, "Yes? Yes, this is Mrs. George Briant. No Dr. Briant can't speak now, I don't think he can." She looked over her shoulder at George, who was sitting stretched out on the sofa with his head thrown back against the cushions, his eyes closed. "No, he can't, but I can take any essential messages. Yes, all right, I'll hold."

She held the phone against her chest and looked at George with anguish on her face. "George! George, for God's sake! Don't be so stubborn! I know you're tired, but—"

"Marjorie, I'm going to bed. I've had more than enough, and I'm going to bed." George dragged himself to his feet. "I don't care what you do or what you say to these people, I'm past caring. I'll deal with it in the morning, if they want to call again. But it won't do them any good, and you might as well know it now. If you think I'm going to walk out on this project now, for the best laboratory in the world or all the dollars ever printed, you're out of your mind. Come on, Hilary. It's late. You need your sleep too."

They went up the stairs together, Hilary pressing close behind her father, leaving Marjorie and Ian staring after them.

Kenneth Gurney left the studios as soon as he decently could after the program came off the air, this time prepared to forfeit the hour of drinking that was rich with opportunities to talk himself into another appearance soon. Quite apart from anything else, he hadn't made much of a showing on the program, and although there had been good reasons for his uncharacteristic willingness to say so little, there was no need to remind them, by his continued presence, that his contribution had been so small.

He smiled slightly as he thought of those good reasons. As he had listened to Briant, it had hit him so suddenly that he could think of little else. The man was sitting there, putting an opportunity in a million on a plate for him. Thinking about that was more important than making a good personal showing on the program. If things worked out well, there would be plenty more television opportunities where this one had come from. And now there were important things to do.

But he paused as he came out into the street through the heavy double glass doors, partly from interest and partly because the milling crowd on the pavement forced him to do so.

There was a good deal of noise, voices shouting and shrilling, and it was centered on the figure of a big woman standing at the edge of the curb. She was clutching a handbag close to her chest and peering over it at the crowd that was clustering close to her, but her posture, defensive though it appeared at first glance, had no real fear in it, despite the pushing and shoving that threatened to topple her into the roadway.

Her face looks odd, Gurney thought, as though the flesh were melting and falling off the bones; and then he saw it was because of the mixture of light on her, the bright fluorescence pouring from the studio entrance, and the yellow sodium glare from the lamp under which she stood.

"It is true! It is true! The Lord shall not be mocked!" she cried, and her voice had a thick grating quality. "We are standing at the edge of the Pit! The wicked scientists are leading us all to perdition! We have turned away from Him who is our redeemer and worship the golden calf that is science, and woe, woe unto the nations that we are fallen into the hands of Herod and the Antichrist! We must step back while there is time, come back to God in repentance, and no more listen to the evil whispers of the Satan worshipers, the scientists who seek to destroy us all."

And then suddenly she blinked and spoke in a perfectly ordinary voice. "We can't let them do it. That poor little baby, all locked up in a laboratory. It's a sin and a crime, that's what it is, poor little thing." And then she raised her head again and with her eyes closed wailed shrilly, "The nations shall save the little ones, the nations shall seize the Antichrist and destroy him that we may be saved again from our sinfulness! God is speaking to us, He is come again into our midst—"

"He's not comin'. He's just breathin' heavy!" a man shouted suddenly and grinned proudly at the burst of laughter that greeted his cry. Another man called raucously, "Here come de Lawd, here come de Lawd. Never mind de judge, folks, here come de Lawd."

"Shut up! Shut up, you horrible creatures!" a woman shouted and pushed against the man next to her, the one who had made the first jeer. "You're wicked, wicked! She's upset, but she shouldn't be tormented, poor soul. And she's talking sense too, more than you know." And a murmur of agreement rose, and another woman pushed through the crowd to the figure beneath the lamppost and put a protective hand on her arm.

"Never mind, dearie, never you mind them. You say what you want to say. You've got the right like anyone else."

And the big woman raised her head again and intoned, "We are on the edge of the Pit! The fires shall engulf us all unless we return to God in penitence and true humility and beg His forgiveness. And He shall visit his vengeance and His wrath upon the Herod who destroys the little children, who mocks the power that is God's and God's alone, and brings destruction to God's children."

And then a man pushed through the crowd, a tall man in a heavy overcoat, and he took the woman's arm gently and leaned over and spoke softly but with such authority that the crowd hushed and his words could be clearly heard.

"Come, my dear. You must not upset yourself so. I do understand your distress, indeed I do. But let me take you home. You can trust me. I am a minister of the Church, you see?" And he pulled his scarf aside so that his clerical collar showed. "Let me take you home and you can talk to me of your distress and feel better."

"What sort of minister?" The woman again spoke in an ordinary voice, but now it was heavy with suspicion.

He smiled. "Oh, don't be afraid. I'm a Free Church man. You're safe with me."

She blinked at him and then nodded. "I'm tired," she said, suddenly sounding pitiful. "I'm so tired. But God spoke to me. I had to tell them, didn't I? I had to tell them?"

"Is she talking sense, Padre?" a man dressed in a neat but shabby blue suit called from the back of the crowd. "Is she? I mean, about this scientist being against God and all? Women, they get excited, but they talk sense sometimes all the same. Is *she* talking any sense?"

The tall man looked up, hesitated, and then spoke with a careful deliberation. "I cannot say. It would be a braver man than I who would dare to say that God could not work through any channel He chose. As this unhappy lady said, God shall not be mocked. He has infinite patience, infinite love, but man has turned away from God before, and God has needed to bring him back from his sinfulness, and it may be, it may be such a time has come again. I cannot say. You must ask your own souls such questions. And"—he smiled suddenly—"ask your ministers, if you are believers. The mockers tell us that religion is dead in the world, but yet you all stand here to listen to the cries of a religious soul in distress. I have always the hope that religion and love of God are with us still. And God works in a mysterious way—as much through people like this lady as through me and men of the Church like me. So ask your ministers and seek in your own hearts. But let me take this lady home now, she needs my care. Has anyone here transport? She is not really fit to walk very far."

Acting on one of his rare impulses, Kenneth Gurney called loudly from his place on the steps, "Er, Padre!"

Heads turned, and someone said, "It's that MP, the one who was on the program."

"Let me pay for her taxi fare to her home. I'd be happy to." Gurney pulled his wallet from his pocket, took out a note, and pushed through the crowd toward the lamppost.

"Thank you, sir, thank you," the tall man said and took it, and then with his arm around the shoulder of the big woman, gently urged her off the pavement and across the road toward the cab rank on the other side. She sagged against him, suddenly seeming bewildered yet apathetic, and dragging her feet a little on the asphalt, let him take her away.

"Here, mister," the man in the blue suit called, waving his arm to attract Gurney's attention. "What do you think? Was she talkin' any sense?"

Gurney smiled and automatically straightened his tie.

"Really, sir, I am hardly in a position to say. I'm just a simple member of Parliament! Questions of religion are too abstruse—complicated—for me."

"The government ought to do somethin' about it, I tell you that!" This came from the woman who had earlier shouted down the men who had jeered. "Religion or not, the government ought to put a stop to such things. Muckin' about with nature like they do, it ought to be put a stop to. It's not right, a poor baby, and that woman what had him, she's not in her right mind, if you ask me, lettin' scientists mess about with her in that fashion!"

"And it's right what J. J. Gerrard said," a woman who hadn't yet spoken called out. "If we don't watch out, the government'll start saying who can have babies and who can't, and then the next thing, they'll take the babies right away from us."

"Actually, it was I who—well, never mind," Gurney said. "And now, if you don't mind, I really must go." And he tried to move away. But one of the women in the crowd pulled at his shoulder and turned him back to face her.

"Here, we got a right to know what you lot are goin' to do about it! Are you goin' to let this scientist go on experimenting on babies, and then take our kids away from us? It's all wrong! He ought to be put a stop to, like that lady said. The government ought to do something about it. What are you going to do? You're in the government!" And she moved closer to him, edging other people away with a thrusting shoulder.

Gurney turned, about to try again to get away, and then stopped. He could see, over the heads of the people looking at him, a cameraman on the studio steps, with a technician standing beside him with a microphone held high. Immediately, Gurney raised his head and spoke as loudly and clearly as he could.

"I am not a member of the government, Madam, just a simple backbencher. But I can tell you this. I share your concern about this child, and about the work of Dr. Briant. I am not at all happy about the way in which scientists like him can so easily embark on experiments which involve human beings. And it is my firm intention to raise the matter in the House at the earliest opportunity. I"—he paused, and then went on more portentously—"I should not perhaps at this point say exactly how I shall raise the matter, but some of you may have heard that in the recent ballot for the presentation of private members' bills I drew an advantageous place. I think it is reasonable to say that you may expect soon to hear reports of my efforts. And now I must ask you to let me through. I have an important evening's work ahead of me, late as it is."

As his taxi pulled away, he looked back at the crowd, still clustering on the pavement, talking and arguing with great animation. He smiled. He'd put in an excellent ten minutes there, and as he settled back into the comfort of the seat and crossed his legs, taking care not to spoil the crease of his trousers, he told himself, Ten weeks from now, I'll be able to assess just how useful that ten minutes was. Ten weeks to get it drafted and get the support lined up. I can do it. With luck and a great deal of judgment.

Miriam hadn't wanted to see the program. She had told herself so over and over again. It had been bad enough reading the newspaper comments about her "callous scientific" approach, the statements Briant had made about her personality, her cool intellectualism. It shouldn't have bothered her, not in the least. It was all true, after all, she told herself, as she switched off the set in her sitting room and went to get the coffee that was percolating in the small kitchenette. She *was* a cool individual, had always prided herself on her ability to divorce her mind from her feelings. And yet, it had hurt. And, oddly, the program had hurt too, even though her own involvement in the project had hardly been mentioned.

Perhaps if she hadn't been so tired she would have been better able to assess the program's content with more logic. As it was, she had felt herself swept by the mood of the crowd in the studio, had been swayed from one side of the argument to the other, like any half-educated layman.

She stood and stared at the coffee spurting into the glass-bubbled lid of the percolator, and then with a sharp movement she turned off the gas and went back to the sitting room. Coffee was the last thing she ought to be drinking with a sleep problem hanging over her. A stimulant drug at this hour of the night—

And then she put her hands to her head and murmured aloud, "Oh, God."

How mixed up can my thinking get? I don't just have to sit around and tolerate this wretched insomnia and the effect it has on me. There's a simple answer staring me in the face, and it takes this long to see it.

"Norma Gould," she muttered aloud. "Norma Gould. Where's her number? It's been almost a year, but she must be still there."

That's something else, she thought as she riffled through the telephone directory. The way I keep talking to myself, aloud. It's incredible, the effect lack of sleep can have. That's another area of research I might consider sometime.

The dull burring in her ear stopped with a click, and a voice said sharply, "Yes?"

"Oh, er, is that Dr. Gould's surgery? Could I speak to her, please?"

"Who wants her?" snapped the voice irritably.

"Miss Lawton, Miriam Lawton."

"Miss—ye gods, Miriam! Well, of all things! I was thinking about you only a few days ago—well, a few weeks ago really—and I said to Joe, 'What ever happened to Miriam? I haven't heard from her in I don't know how long.' My dear girl, how *are* you? And why in the name of all that's holy have you been hiding yourself all this time? No one's seen hide nor hair of you in months."

Wincing slightly, Miriam held the phone away from her ear. Norma had always been a talker, she'd forgotten that. But an essentially kind person, for all her chatter and her rather flibberty mind.

"I know. I'm sorry, Norma. I've been . . . well, tied up with work. You know how it is."

"I know how it is with *you*. I always said you worked too hard. Remember? I used to tell you there's more to living than work, however interesting the work is. Like keeping up with your friends, you wretch."

"Yes. I'm sorry, Norma. But as you say, I've always been the same, er, how are you all? How're Joe and the children? And the practice?"

"Oh, Joe's fine! He's got a senior registrarship, you know? And one of his consultants should retire next year, if he doesn't die of a stroke first—and he deserves to, he's a horrible old man—and Joe should get the appointment. As for the kids, thriving, the little tearaways. Jeremy's started nursery school now, the complete three-year-old. And as for me, my dear, I'm pregnant again! Joe keeps muttering darkly that it's a mistake to let them outnumber us, but I'm thrilled to bits about it. I think he is too, if he were to tell the truth. Founding the Gould dynasty, and all that. As for the practice, well, I'm overworked and underpaid like every GP these days. You had more sense than I did, that's for sure. I should have stuck to science like you, instead of going to medical school."

"Oh, I don't know," Miriam said and then almost desperately went on. "Look, Norma, I must be honest. One of the reasons I called you is that you did go to medical school. I mean, I'd like some professional assistance."

"I might have known it! So much for the ties of friendship! Wretch! But it's all right. I'm used to it. Everyone I know picks my brains till they bleed. What do you want? If it's to get me to collect data from the practice for one of your research projects, I must be honest. What with the pregnancy—and I have been rather tired —and the half-witted assistant I'm lumbered with—"

"No, it's nothing like that. I, well, I've been working too hard or something. Not feeling very good. It's mainly because I'm not sleeping too well, and if I could ask your help with that, I'd be most grateful."

"Not sleeping? Oh? That can be grim! What sort of not sleeping?"

"What?"

"I mean, do you have trouble getting off to sleep, or what?"

"No, not that. I fall asleep all right, but I wake up after a while and then just can't get off again. It's, well, I'm tired of it. One can't work well if one's tired, so I—look, could you let me have a prescription for a barbiturate of some sort? Just to get me back into a proper sleep rhythm."

There was a short silence, and then the thin voice said slowly, "You never did do any clinical medicine, did you?"

"Mmm? No, of course I didn't. I've always been in biology."

"Yes, well, look, Miriam, I'll be glad to help you. But not by just dishing out a handful of barbiturates. That wouldn't be any help, anyway. Come and see me. Tomorrow, after surgery."

"Oh, Norma, surely that isn't necessary? I mean, I'd love to see you sometime, socially, because it *has* been far too long I know, but not as a patient. Couldn't you just put a script in the post for me? If—if you wouldn't mind sending it off tonight, I'd get it first post tomorrow, and—"

"If it's that urgent to you, then I'm even more sure I ought to examine you properly." The clacking voice at the end of the telephone had taken on an authoritative note. "I've known you a long time, Miriam, and I know you take about as much care of yourself as a babe in arms. And insomnia is not a symptom I would ever agree to treat in isolation, and most certainly not on the phone."

"Oh, well, look, forget it, Norma. I shouldn't have bothered you. I'll be in touch again, sometime soon, and we'll arrange—"

"Oh, no you don't, Miriam Lawton! I won't be put off as easily as that! I'm too old a friend to let you be so foolish. And if you won't come to me, then I'll come and see you. You're still living in Camden Town? Albert Street? The Regents Park end?"

"What? Oh, yes, but really, Norma, there isn't the least need to—"

"I happen to think there is. Don't you dare to question my clinical judgment, madam!" The voice dropped its bantering tone then and went on more gently. "Really, Miriam, I mean it. The sort of insomnia you have may be important. And it needs treatment. Please, do come and see me." There was a pause. "And maybe I can help with the other problems too."

"What other problems?" Miriam said sharply.

"The trouble you're having in concentrating on work? The loss of appetite? The confused feelings you get? Am I right?"

There was a long silence, and the little tinny voice said, "Miriam? Are you still there?"

"Yes, I'm still here. All right, Norma. Tomorrow morning after surgery. About half past eleven?"

"Yes. I'll be waiting for you. And I promise you, this is the last bad night you'll have. Good night, Miriam. I'm very glad you called."

And after she had put the phone back on its rest, Miriam sat and stared at it, thinking over and over again, I wish I hadn't. I wish I hadn't.

8

"I don't see why you want to send me on it," Mike said again and stared stubbornly at Sir Daniel. "I'm a science writer, not a woman's page feature type. One of the women would make a much better job of it."

"You are being remarkably obtuse, Bridges," Sir Daniel snapped. "It isn't a woman's page feature I want. I want a hard factual story about the way the girl feels about her part in the project, her views on last night's program and the arguments it's thrown up. I want a piece that shows some insight into her psychology. And you will do a better job of it than anyone else because you've got the whole thing at your fingers' ends."

"I don't like it. According to Briant, she's a chilly piece, couldn't care less about the baby as a baby. She was only concerned with the success of the project. If that's the sort she is, that's what I'll have to write. And isn't there enough public alienation over the whole thing already? After last night's performance, with Gerrard setting himself up as the soul of the people, it'll just add fuel to the—have you *seen* what's going on in Trafalgar Square this morning? There are hordes of women there, babies in prams and pushchairs, hot gospelers milling around, placards about the evils of science and repent-for-the-end-is-nigh stuff, and it's obviously spontaneous. There hasn't been time for any formal organization to go into it. And if we go on coming out on Briant's side, *and* run a piece about the girl, who isn't all that sympathetic, to say the least, well, it won't make the *Echo* very popular. And anyway, you've already made it pretty clear that you weren't impressed with the showing I put up last night. I should have said more than I did, you were right." He let some of his own annoyance with himself leak into his voice. "I just didn't have the . . . the attack I should have had. Put it down to inexperience, maybe, if you want to be charitable. But it could be I'm just not up to the job. Maybe I don't want to do the story because I . . . I'm not sure I can do it well enough."

"That's for me to worry about, Graham and I, that is." Sir Daniel shot a glance at Graham, sitting heavily silent behind his desk. "I've been in this business a long time, Bridges—Mike. I can assure you that you can do it, as I—we—want it. A little humility isn't a bad thing in a journalist. And I can also assure you that for all the hysterical people mobbing the Square—and of course I saw them—there's plenty of the other sort of opinion. For heaven's sake, man, can't you see? The more hysterical one side gets, the more appreciation the other will have of hard-hitting factual reporting! Now, will you stop arguing and go and get me a story?"

"If you're absolutely determined—"

"I am. And much as I respect and admire your scruples, I must override them this time. I know best what's right for this paper, you'll grant me that. And wouldn't you prefer that *we* should run a piece of yours on her rather than let anyone else? You've got the most direct lead to her, and you can get at her before the others if you get a move on. Do you want to see the opposition crucify her? Because they would, I promise you."

"Yes. I suppose that's true. Oh, all right. I'll see if I can find her. I'd better start with the woman who wrote to that auntie page. She should be able to put me onto the girl's name, and once I've got that, it shouldn't be difficult to find where she lives. I'll need some money."

"Of course. But don't spend too much on it. From what you found out about that orderly female, you should get what you want out of her for the price of a meal. I'd like to see your copy filed within a week."

"I can't guarantee that! The only thing I can promise is if I get to her first, I'll keep everyone else off. But that's all. To get the piece you want, I'll need to get to know her. It may take a lot of time." Mike stood up and moved over to the door.

"If I get a good piece, then I'm prepared to wait," Sir Daniel said. "But it had better be good, remember that. And . . ."

Mike looked back at Sir Daniel's heavy figure silhouetted against the big window.

". . . and it will be worth your while. I'm not niggardly when it comes to recognizing achievement. And you can achieve."

"That's good to know," Mike said harshly, carefully not looking at Graham, and closed the door behind him with a savage tug.

Miriam sat rigidly in a corner of the shabby waiting room, her head aching with a sick throb, her eyes hot and sandy. Last night had been the worst ever; if she'd had as much as two hours' sleep, she'd be surprised. A horrible night. The thoughts had come to overtake her again, the sick imaginings she couldn't control, that swept her mind away in a revolting welter of feeling; the thoughts that filled not only her mind but her whole body, until she had been unable to stop it happening, that childish behavior that should have been left behind with the other miseries of adolescence, and even that hadn't brought the comfort of sleep.

She tried to wrench her thinking straight, to stop the treadmill progression of memory and shame, looking at the other people in the room with her. A slatternly woman in a shabby blue coat, holding a baby on her lap, bouncing it from side to side and talking at it in strings of babbling syllables, trying to make it repeat them. "Da, da, da, den. Kutchie, kutchie, kutchie. Da, da, da."

Even from her place in the corner, Miriam could smell the child, the thick sour milkiness of it, the heavy miasma of urine-soaked diapers, and her stomach heaved and tightened. It's just as well I couldn't eat breakfast. If I had, I'd be sick.

The receptionist on the other side of the scarred desk in the corner had her head down over a pile of buff-colored cards, radiating dislike at Miriam from every line of her posture. I shouldn't have been so unpleasant to her, Miriam thought. She wasn't to know I wasn't one of the ordinary patients. I made her look a fool in front of other people, it wasn't right of me. Not like me, really. God, I feel rotten.

The woman with the baby heaved to her feet in response to a pealing bell, collected a couple of bags and paper-wrapped parcels and went out, talking to the baby as she moved. "Come on then, my lovey, Doctor's ready for you now. Come on then."

Outside, Miriam could hear the rumbling traffic, and she began to count each extra crescendo of sound that came as individual vehicles passed the tall windows of the waiting room. Three, four, five—that was a big one, a lorry, count it as two—eight, nine. God, why am I sitting here? I should have told her I'd moved and then hung up—eleven, twelve . . .

The woman behind the desk stood up and, pointedly ignoring Miriam in her corner, went out, slamming the door behind her, and Miriam sat on, alone in the room, still counting. Anything to keep her mind occupied. She closed her eyes and counted on in a sort of desperation: seventeen, eighteen . . .

"Miriam! Come on in and sit down. My girl's making us some tea. I hope she won't be too long. She's got the sulks over something this morning."

Miriam opened her eyes and stared at the figure by the door, a square figure with short curly hair standing up untidily over a smoothly plump face, a white coat buttoned strainingly over the big abdomen. My God, did I look like that when I was pregnant? I hope not. Why not? What would it matter if I had?

"Hello, Norma," she said, her voice surprisingly even. The way she was feeling, it should have sounded different. "You look . . . very well."

"More than I can say for you," Norma said bluntly. "I'm glad you came. You obviously need to."

"Do I?" Miriam essayed and managed a light laugh. "You always did jump to conclusions, Norma. It must make you a great diagnostician sometimes. This time, though, you're wrong. I'm not in the least ill, I promise you."

"No? Then why aren't you sleeping?" Norma led the way out of the room and into the cluttered overheated surgery next door to it. She pulled a chair forward for Miriam and sat herself in the shabbily cushioned one in front of an old roll-top desk. "People who are well sleep well. I do."

Miriam shrugged. "I'm working hard, that's all. On a thesis for my doctorate. I've a lot of complex material to think about."

"Meaning I haven't? Don't you believe it. When you've got a three thousand GP list heavily overloaded with children and geriatrics, a house to run, a difficult husband and a couple of energetic kids, *and* you're pregnant into the bargain, you'll see how complex thinking can get." But her voice was equable. "No, my dear girl. There's more to this problem of yours than you realize. Now don't sit there looking so buttoned up! This is Norma, remember? We've known each other since we were in third form together. I know more about you than you know yourself, in some ways. So don't come the dignified iceberg over me. I won't wear it. Now, we'll start at the beginning, shall we? When did the sleeplessness start?"

Miriam sat staring at her hands in her lap, the fingers interlocked in an intricate pattern.

"It is a long time, isn't it?" she said abruptly. "Third form. I'd forgotten."

"I haven't." Norma leaned back in her chair and looked at her with her face twisted in a half-grin. "I thought the sun shone out of you, do you know that?"

Miriam looked up at her and frowned. "What?"

"I did. You were so bloody clever, and so gorgeous to look at. I envied you like hell. Until we got to college. Then I felt sorry for you."

"Oh?"

"Perhaps I shouldn't say it, but"—Norma shook her head—"oh, it was an odd life, yours. Just you and your father. And after he died, just after we started at college, I remember it so well. I cried more than you did. You seemed to get even more brilliant, even more gorgeous. And even more shut up inside yourself. Plain run-of-the-mill me went to the parties, had all the fun, and you sat in your room—"

"I was concentrating on work, at college," Miriam said stiffly. "And really, Norma, I don't see that—"

"This has anything to do with me? That I have any right to dig out past history? But I think it may be relevant, in fact, to the reason you're here this morning. But we'll get back to that—oh, tea. Thanks a lot, m'dear."

With a cup of tea steaming beside her, Miriam found it easier to answer Norma's questions, and as the other woman scribbled busily on a buff card, she gradually relaxed and answered her questions almost without thinking.

"It started about, about a fortnight ago. But it's been very marked. I estimate I get about, oh, three hours' sleep a night, at most. And it's very restless sleep."

"Appetite?"

"I don't really care much about food at the best of times, but I suppose it is less."

"Menstrual pattern?"

"What?"

Norma looked up and said patiently, "Your menstrual cycle. Have you noticed any changes?"

Miriam felt her face redden, and as she saw the faint surprise and then the look of sudden comprehension on the other's face, reddened even more.

"I, I don't . . . I can't, I . . ." she floundered and then stopped.

"Oh, my dear girl!" Norma put down her pen. "Why on earth didn't you tell me sooner? Knowing you, it never entered my head that—for heaven's sake, I was convinced you were in the middle of a clinical endogenous depression! The more I looked back on the way I remembered you, the more likely it seemed. And all the time

—you silly girl! Honestly, you make me feel like your grandmother, for all we're the same age. How far on are you?"

"What?" Miriam was bewildered. She hadn't expected any questioning that might, in the answering, reveal her involvement in the Briant project, hadn't expected to be asked to give any sort of medical history, and in trying to sort out an answer had lost the thread of what Norma was saying. "What do you mean?"

"Look, Miriam," Norma said patiently, "are you or are you not pregnant? Is that really what you want my help with?"

Miriam stared at her for a long moment and then shakily started to laugh, and went on laughing until her hot eyes ran tears.

"Oh, my God. Oh, my God! Is that what—" She shook her head and scrubbed at her face with shaking fingers. And then she took a deep breath.

"I am not pregnant. Very far from it. I can assure you that . . . that there is not the remotest possibility of it. I am simply sleeping very badly at present and need some help to get over it. That's all. As for depresssion, why on earth should you think that? Did I sound depressed on the telephone?"

"I wasn't using the word to describe a change in mood." Norma spoke almost absently, staring at her under faintly frowning brows. "Clinical depression is a mental illness, and I thought, if you're not pregnant, why the confusion when I asked about your menstrual cycle?"

"Why should you think I had a mental illness? After five minutes' talk on the phone?"

"Waking in the early hours, and not sleeping again—almost specifically diagnostic. And you didn't deny the other symptoms—inability to concentrate, loss of appetite, confused thinking. Miriam, *why* did you get so bothered when I asked about your menstrual cycle? I can't possibly understand what's the matter with you if you aren't honest with me."

"There's nothing the matter with me." Miriam stood up and started to pull on her gloves with sharp angry tugs. "Except I was stupid enough to ask you to help me with a script for sleeping pills. I should have known you wouldn't be able to resist probing at me."

"It's all so *uncharacteristic*," Norma said, seeming unaware of the insulting tone in Miriam's voice. "I've known you since we were twelve-year-olds—more than half our lifetimes—and in less than a year you've changed so much you look awful. You're—"

"I have not changed! I'm just not sleeping well, that's all! How often must I—" And to her own horror, Miriam felt her eyes fill with tears, her throat constrict with them, and stopped.

"But you have! Look at you now! You're shaking, and crying. Ye gods, Miriam, you *never* cried! Oh, look, come over here."

She pulled Miriam by the arm over to the red-blanketed couch in the corner and, grunting a little with the effort, pushed her onto it and made her swing her legs up until she was lying down, and then she sat on the edge of it beside her.

"Look, you'll have to do something about the state you're in, can't you see that? You're an intelligent girl, a brilliant one, but you don't seem able to understand that there is something more the matter with you than mere insomnia. Won't you try and tell me? Just talking it out will help."

"Oh, Norma, do stop all this amateur psychiatry, will you? I've little enough use for the people who are supposed to be good at it, but when GPs start—"

"I've got a thick skin. And the more aggressive you are towards the idea, the more convinced I am you need help. I wonder." She looked consideringly at the face on the pillow and then said slowly, "Miriam, look at me. I'm pregnant, you see? Very obvious, isn't it? How does it make you feel, seeing me like this?"

"Feel? Indifferent. What concern is it of mine?"

"No jealousy? Or disgust?"

There was a short silence and then Miriam said, "Why should I feel either? I told you, it's no concern of mine."

"But of course it is! You're a women too. You're capable of being pregnant, just as I am. And the way you respond to the fact of pregnancy reveals a lot about the way you feel about your own femininity."

"Femininity, femininity?" Miriam sat up so suddenly that she almost toppled Norma off the edge of the couch. "I'll tell you this much, I hate it. Hate it, you hear me? All I want is to do a worthwhile job of work without any of this—this *boring* business about being a woman. Who cares what my sex is? Where do you get the crazy idea that I'm sleeping badly because of the way I feel about your blasted pregnancy! I'm sick to death of pregnancy and women and . . . and . . ."

She put her hands to her face and took a deep breath and said, "I'm sorry. I didn't mean to—look, maybe you're right. I mean, maybe this, the way I'm not sleeping, has something to do with . . . with my . . . with being a female. I'm researching hormone balances for my thesis, you know? And, er . . ." She began to improvise wildly. "I've been experimenting with myself. Taking various hormone preparations to see what sort of effect they'd have. I, well, I've obviously got some results. I mean, I've got myself so unbalanced it's not only interfering with my sleep, it's interfering with my general, my general ability to think clearly. You see? But if I could have some help with sleep, I could complete my investigations and then I'll be fine again. And, er, that's why I got so bothered when you asked about my menstrual pattern, because of course I've made it go haywire."

Norma was looking at her with her face creased with indecision. "Oh, Lord. I don't know. If you are doing something so, so stupid—and it *is* stupid to use yourself for experimental material—it might account for, oh, I don't *know*. Look, I'm not calling you a liar, Miriam, but *do* people use themselves to get data for theses? It's a while since I did any real science, but it seems to me unusual?"

"Oh, yes, yes," Miriam said swiftly. "People working on antibiotics have given themselves injections of strains of certain pathogens, and—"

"Yes, that's true, but isn't that because it's a dangerous thing to do to anyone else? Hormone balances—surely you can get all the material you want from working on menstruating women, or postpartum ones? Why mess about with your own health? I can't help feeling, still, that there's more than you've told me. I've known you so long, you see."

For a moment Miriam felt an intense desire to tell her the whole story, to pour out into this familiar ear a full account of the way she had spent the past year, to ask whether the way she was feeling was a normal response to having a baby. After all, Norma had had two.

But how could she? One of the reasons Briant had found her of such value to the project was her freedom from personal ties. "With no one to question what you're doing," he'd said, "it will obviously be much easier to maintain your anonymity, and that is ideal for many reasons. Not least because you'll be left in peace if no one apart from myself and of course one or two other people concerned with your care during pregnancy and confinement know your identity."

And with last night's television program added to the massive newspaper comment, she could imagine just how much badgering she would get if her involvement with the project became known. The thought of suffering the sort of onslaught George was suffering made her shrink. No, she couldn't possibly tell Norma, of all people, Norma who was about as discreet as a public address system.

"Truly, you're worrying unnecessarily," she said now and looked at Norma with as limpidly honest a gaze as she could manage. "I've just got a sleep problem."

"Well, it's against my better judgment, but I'll do it. Soneryl—nothing heftier than that. And not much of it. Try to stop using them as soon as you possibly can."

She turned in her chair and looked at Miriam, now sitting on the edge of the couch, and smiled at her a little tentatively.

"But, look, Miriam, will you let me talk to you about something now I've got you here? No matter what effect your performances with hormones may be having on you, you must admit you did respond rather, well, *violently*, when I asked you how you felt about my pregnancy. And I'm really very fond of you, as fond of you as you'll let me be. And I'd like to see you happy."

"I'm perfectly happy," Miriam said, trying not to sound repressive. All she wanted was to get that prescription into her hands and go. But she hadn't got it yet.

"Oh, I daresay you think you are, but you could be so much happier. I said before, you're a woman. And I never yet met a woman, no matter how bright, no matter how ambitious, who didn't need some sort of emotional involvement. I know it sounds corny, but love is important to women—"

"Oh, Norma, for heaven's sake! Don't start on that! You used to go on and on about it and it made me irritable then. You seemed to think the most interesting thing about a lecturer wasn't what he had to teach us, but what he looked like. And I told you then, *you* may have this starry-eyed thing about love and marriage, but that doesn't mean every other woman has—"

"Oh, I know, I know. I was a bit sloppy in the old days, but then, that's part of adolescence. Perhaps I did go to extremes, falling in and out of love like a yo-yo." She laughed reminiscently. "And it was fun. But you went to the other extreme, denying any need at all for emotional involvement. And—look, Miriam, you're a biologist, right?"

"Yes, and my work is all I want to—"

"Let me finish. If you won't accept my word for it, try and work it out for yourself, in your own way. You're a biologist, so I'll put it to you in biological terms. One of the strongest drives of any organism is to reproduce, right? Salmon go leaping up rivers against incredible odds just to deposit their spawn at the right place. Dogs cover great distances to track down bitches in heat—there's a great range of intense animal behavior that derives directly from this urgent need to mate. Right?"

"So?"

"So people are animals too, in a biological sense. We have just as intense a drive to reproduce ourselves. No matter how much individual intellectual processes attempt to control this basic drive, no matter how important other aspects of living become, the drive is there. Am I still right?"

"Well, I suppose—"

"Oh, of course I am! I'm pointing out facts here, not surmise. All right. The drive is there. Now, let's look at the difference in the drive between men and women, OK? Men have only one biological function, in a reproductive sense. They simply want—and want pretty urgently—to impregnate a female. And they can do it without being emotionally involved with the female in question. But women are different. As I see it, women not only have the same intense biological need to reproduce, it's greater than men's, in some ways. And because her part in reproduction takes so long—more than a year, when you add on the feeding period—there is a biological mechanism that—"

"Norma, I just don't see what you're getting at."

"Wait a minute, will you? And listen. I'm speaking your language now, not my own. And I may be only a tuppenny-ha'penny GP, but I did have a basic scientific training before I went to medical school, so I know what I'm talking about. What was I saying? Oh, I know. The biological mechanism. It makes a woman need to *love* a man. She has to love him to assure herself she can produce a good infant, and love him to ensure she and her infant will be protected when they need to be. And if you can't see that, you're committing the great scientific sin. Refusing to accept a piece of evidence because it doesn't happen to fit into your own theorizing. I mean it. Love is important to women, vital to them. You're a woman. If you don't allow your biology to fulfill itself, you can't be completely happy. You need some sort of emotional involvement. Q.E.D."

Miriam sat and stared at the round smooth face for a long moment. Then she said slowly, "You're saying that the woman who does not have babies is running directly counter to her own deepest biological drives. That childlessness indicates an unfulfilled and therefore unhealthy and distressed individual?"

"Yes."

"But there are millions of childless women. Are they all so unhappy?"

"Lots of them are. Of course, it's possible for them to redirect their drives. Nuns do that, I suppose, and some nurses and schoolteachers."

"And people like me!" Miriam felt an odd surge of triumph, as though she had succeeded in making a victory over the thinking processes of an intellect far superior to her own; which was absurd because however pleasant a person Norma was she was far from being one of the world's great brains. "I'm perfectly well able to redirect my drives, which I must accept exist in a purely biological sense, into the work I do."

"But in the name of all that's holy, Miriam, why *should* you? You can do both! There is no earthly reason why you shouldn't have all the satisfaction of a complete sex life as well as an intellectual one! And when you have that, oh boy, have you got something! You mayn't think very highly of the work I do, because you've always been able to run rings round me, mentally speaking. But it's right for me. I'm a good doctor—a bloody good doctor—and I'm doing immensely worthwhile work in my own way, even if I'm not doing much about shoving forward the frontiers of knowledge and all that. It takes up an enormous amount of energy, physically, intellectually, emotionally, but I still have a husband I love, and kids I love, and I'm going to have more after this one—four or five, who knows? And all the time I'll still be a doctor with a mind I use. I'll be using and enjoying my body, and my mind, and—don't you see what I'm trying to tell you? You could do the same! It may be true what you told me, that the state you're in now is due directly to the hormones you've been pumping into yourself. But I take leave to doubt whether that's the whole story. I think the way you've responded to this hormone thing indicates an . . . an underlying problem. I think you're heading full tilt for a frank mental illness—clinical depression, maybe a tension state of some sort—because you're not giving yourself a chance. I know you had a crippling childhood in many ways—"

"Crippling? What on earth do you mean?"

"What I say. You had a really awful time, didn't you? A mother who died when you were a tiny kid, and then brought up by a man who was so turned in on himself he couldn't possibly give a girl the sort of love she needed—"

"Oh, Norma, that's parlor psychology of the most sickly sort! I will not accept this unsubstantiated theorizing about the effects of young experience on adult behavior! It sounds seductively appealing, I grant you, and it's a very useful escape route. Mrs. X shows obsessional behavior? Ah, that's because she was put on a pot at the age of two. Mrs. Y shows obsessional behavior? Ah, that's because she *wasn't* put on a pot at the age of two. Up to now, you've made some sort of sense. But when you start on this Freudian stuff, I lose patience. Show me facts to prove the effects of environmental experiences, and I'll listen, but this—look, let me put a point to you. You're suggesting that because my father was an . . . an unloving undemonstrative man I've learned the same responses by being exposed to him?"

"Exactly."

"But isn't it just as possible that I am genetically lacking this response? That he carried in his genes a personality trait that created emotionally unresponsive behavior in him, and passed the genes on to me? If that were so, your whole theory falls down. I don't have this great urgent need for love and whatever battened down under hatches built by my life with my father. I just don't have it, period."

"Oh, Lord, you sound like that Briant man on television last night. The sickest thing I ever heard—"

"Sick? What's sick about it? He's trying to bring some order, some factual sense into this whole confused area of human behavior and its motivating drives. How can that be sick? It's a lot less sick than the fantasies your woolly-minded psychoanalytical school spins. That's all they are. Fantasies—unprovable and largely inapplicable."

"You look better. Getting annoyed with me has put some color back in your face. You looked like a piece of bad cheese when you came in here. And you can say what you like. The strength of your responses to my suggestions makes it clear that I've touched on something in your psyche that's very real to you—"

"Oh, Norma, for God's sake! Are you quite inaccessible to plain logic? I came here to see you because I had a symptom that . . . that is due entirely to my disturbed hormone balance—"

"So you say—"

"—*entirely* to my disturbed hormone balance, and you start on the fabrication of an involved story about my infant experiences. And you're weaving it on an almost nonexistent thread." She stopped and then said slowly, "Look, let me put something to *you*. You've been following the news about this Briant project?"

"Who hasn't? You'd have to be blind, deaf and buried in idiocy not to."

"All right. Now, this, er, this woman who was used to produce the baby."

Norma grimaced. "Honestly, Miriam, doesn't *that* make you feel —oh, I don't know—repelled? Even someone as dedicated to science as you are must see—"

"Forget the value judgments. They're irrelevent. Now, according to the newspaper reports, the woman, er, has had no contact at all with the natural father of the infant. No physical contact, let alone any emotional contact. But she has fulfilled her biological function, she's had a baby. And I would suggest that she should be, well, more satisfied with herself than she was before, if your theory stands up. But suppose she isn't? Suppose, for hypothesis' sake, that in fact she has been made . . . in some way unhappy by her experience. She, er, she's an intellectual type, emotionally unresponsive, according to the papers."

Should she risk it? Would Norma jump to one of her conclusions and this time with deadly accuracy? But having gone this far . . .

"Much the same sort of person as I am myself," she went on deliberately. "If she has been, well, distressed by having this baby, wouldn't it mean that in fact she was genetically designed, as it were, *not* to need to a marked degree the satisfaction of this basic drive to reproduce? In which case, your whole theory about my need to have some sort of emotional involvement with someone falls flat on its face. Because if one woman is genetically structured in this way, so could I be."

"I'll bet my bottom dollar she *is* distressed by her experience, and I'd dearly like to know how she's feeling right now. There's been nothing much about her in the papers, has there? They're certainly keeping her well hidden."

"Why are you so sure she's distressed? I was only hypothesizing for the purposes of this, er, argument."

"But she must be!" Norma said, showing a sudden spark of irritation. "Didn't you listen to what I tried to explain? It isn't *reproduction* that drives women. It's a need to love a man! The reproduction bit comes later, depends for its success in terms of feminine satisfaction on the existence of a viable and enjoyable man-woman relationship! This woman who produced this baby has run directly counter to her own deepest needs, don't you see? She's never loved, never made love! How can she feel anything but distress because of having had that baby? Especially when you remember the poor devil had it taken away from her at birth."

The telephone rang sharply, and Norma made a face and turned around to her desk to pick it up.

"Dr. Gould. What? Oh, Mrs. Giannotti, what's the trouble? Oh. Has he a temperature?"

Miriam stared at the broad white expanse of Norma's back, her mind whirling, trying to think clearly through the sound of Norma's voice chattering about aspirin and bed rest and when she could visit the patient.

Was that the trouble? Could there be some really logical sense in what Norma had said? After all, she had had a baby, two babies. She should know.

Was this why it had kept happening, this awful pubertal behavior that had so bedeviled and bewildered her these past days and most of all nights? Had producing the baby mobilized in her a whole mass of primitive drives and desires that because of the hormonal changes of the pregnancy were no longer amenable to intellectual control?

She closed her eyes for a moment, trying to arrange her thoughts methodically. If the way she was feeling now, the undoubted stress she was suffering, was due to the existence of these drives—or rather, their sudden clamoring demands for satisfaction—would patiently waiting for her hormone balance to be restored to normal solve her problem? No, it would not. Would it? Once she faced up to the fact that she had them—and Norma's explanation of their existence held water, it couldn't be denied—they were there. They couldn't just be damped down again.

All right, she told herself. I have a drive toward satisfaction of a sexual need, a drive that has been in part created by producing the baby. I have to face the fact that this is so. This is why I've been feeling so miserable. Because I've been trying to satisfy it—

Trying to satisfy it in a way that fills me with revulsion. Face it, face it. You've suffered most of this distress because of the way you've been forced against your conscious will to cope with this need.

So what's the answer? I can't go on like this, and clearly unless I do something—something positive—I'm going to go on suffering the whole bloody situation. What's the answer?

But she couldn't think clearly beyond that point. She opened her eyes again and stared at the whiteness of Norma's back, the words running in circles in her mind.

Norma cradled the phone with a clatter and turned back to her.

"Sorry about that. I should be grateful we weren't interrupted before. This wretched phone never stops."

Miriam slid off the couch and straightened her coat, keeping her head down. She didn't want to look at Norma. "I must let you get on," she said, keeping her voice light. "It's been very nice seeing you again, and most interesting to talk. And thank you for the script."

"Oh, yes, it's here." Norma held out the scribbled prescription, and Miriam let her eyes move swiftly up to her face as she took it. "But, look, don't be furious with me, will you, for talking as I did? I told you, I'm fond of you, and I've thought for years I ought to say to you the sort of things I did this morning, but somehow it wasn't ever possible. You've always worn a sort . . . a sort of carapace. I don't know, you made it impossible for anyone, even me, to get near you. Well, I've said it, and I hope you won't take it unkindly. It wasn't meant that way. I truly think you need to face up to the fact that you're as much a woman as anyone else, and that you need loving."

"Oh, my dear Norma, start on that again, and we'll be here arguing till doomsday! Let's face it, you married women are incorrigible matchmakers. You want to convert everyone to your way of life," Miriam said and laughed lightly, aware of the brittle falsity in her tone, but knowing herself unable to do anything about it. "I must go, really."

"Well, we know the good of it, and—"

"And thanks again," Miriam said quickly.

She moved to the door, and Norma followed her eagerly.

"You'll keep in touch, now? Come and have dinner with us soon? Joe'd love to see you. He always said you had the best mind of any woman he'd ever met. Next week, perhaps? We could make a date now."

"I, I'd love to, really, Norma, but I haven't got my diary with me. I'll phone you, yes. Soon. Really I will."

She was out of the front door, poised on the cracked concrete steps, aching to get away and think, somewhere quiet and peaceful. And to get this prescription filled and get some sleep, some real uninterrupted sleep. "I'll phone you," she said again. "And thanks so much. I'm really grateful."

Norma watched her as she walked quickly up the road toward the underground station at the far end, frowning slightly. Should she have let her have that script? Was it in fact as she had first thought, a case of depression? But if she *had* been taking hormones it could account for it.

The baby moved inside her with a sudden thump, and she put her hand on her belly and relaxed. Lovely feeling, that. Poor Miriam, she thought. Brilliant and so stupid.

9

On the evening George Briant was to dine with Sir Daniel Sefton, he used the Nurses' Home way out. At first he had found it an almost intolerable situation, having to sneak in and out of his own hospital by devious routes. But after almost three weeks of it, he took an almost schoolboyish pleasure in evading the idiots; schoolboyish because they really were such idiots, and no intelligent man, he thought, with a faint sense of shame, should gain pleasure from pitting his wits against such people.

He stood for a moment on the Nurses' Home steps, pulling on his gloves and looking along the road toward the hospital's main entrance. They were there, of course. The couple of newspapermen leaning against the railings of the public library opposite, the knot of people carrying banners and placards, the watchful policeman standing stolidly in front of the hospital's double doors.

He narrowed his eyes against the deepening twilight, trying to read some of the placards; perhaps there might be a new one. But they were the same old statements. "For God so loves the world that He forgives those who repent, but His wrath shall be visited upon the sinners"; "A little child suffers for us"; "Briant is the Antichrist." A position of greater importance than most men are offered, he thought sardonically. And there was the skinny woman with her now rather tattered "Support the Association for Abolishing Cruelty to Children" and the ugly one with her "Care for sick children comes before creating super children" and the little bowler-hatted man with his "Science shatters. It's people that matters." Briant rather liked that one. What it lacked in grammar, he thought, it made up for in pith. The man might hold crazy notions in his head, but he at least knew how to put them across.

He thrust his hands deep into his overcoat pockets and turned away to walk briskly down the street toward the tube station. It was getting late, and with the rush hour still filling the trains, he might be held up. This was one of the occasions when he missed the car, but it couldn't be helped. He had been forced to swallow with what grace he could the demands that Marjorie had made when the break came. And at the time he had been so angrily unhappy that he could not have argued with her anyway.

He still could not really understand why she had chosen that issue on which to finally put an end to their life together. Had it been because of his flat refusal to allow Ian to accept the job in that ghastly musical, or his insistence that Hilary be allowed to leave school and work with him for a year in the Unit before taking her A levels at a polytechnic, he would have understood. But it was because of his refusal to accept either the first American offer or any of the others that came after it.

Her inability to realize the impossibility of leaving the project, after the years of effort that had gone into setting it up, was extraordinary in George's eyes. After eighteen years during which he had been utterly devoted to his work, and had shown never the least interest in making money for its own sake, why did she find it so odd that he should be consistent?

But she had completely blocked any of his attempts to have rational discussions of the situation, had just repeated drearily, "This is the end. And I'm not going to go out into the street with nothing to show for eighteen years of hell. You can get out." And he had had to go, had to agree to send her money regularly, to let her have the car, because she had made it very clear indeed that if he refused her terms, she would go to court and make sure the adoption proceedings were ruined. And torn between keeping his wife and son, or keeping the project, he had made the only possible choice.

But he missed her. As he pushed his way into a southbound train, keeping his head bent as usual, his face shaded by his hat in case someone recognized him, he was suddenly swept by a wave of urgent need for her, an intensely sensual memory of the warmth of her beside him in bed that was so vivid it was as though he were actually there, reaching out to touch her familiar scented body. And even as he felt desire wash over him, he realized why. The woman standing close beside him was wearing the perfume Marjorie always wore, a musky sexual smell that once he had disliked; it was extraordinary how the heaviness of it created a clamoring need for her.

At the risk of drawing unwanted attention to himself, he pushed farther into the train, thrusting people aside, to get away from the smell, to stand holding on to a swaying strap and stare unseeingly at the pipes and wires swooping past the black windows as the train bucketed on its way.

He would have to do something about this. It was happening too often. For the first week or so he hadn't been aware of his need, but now he had to face it. He had never been a man with a great interest in sex, never thought of himself as a particularly—what was it? yes—virile man. But clearly he needed a woman more than he had suspected he could. At the age of forty-five he should surely be able to come to terms with his own body, but since he apparently was not as able as he might be, he would have to do something about it.

But one thing was sure. He would replace Marjorie with someone he liked and didn't merely desire. He wouldn't make the same mistake twice, loving a woman as he had loved Marjorie in spite of her shallowness, her stupid adoration of Ian, her rejection of Hilary.

Ian and Hilary. He had that much to be grateful for, anyway. To be relieved of Ian, with his nasty little mind, his puny show business ambitions, his slyness, his totally intolerable personality, yet still to have Hilary with her unquestioning acceptance of him as a scientist first and foremost, her razor sharp comprehension of the way his mind worked—that was indeed something to be grateful for. She didn't seem to notice the discomfort of their life now, didn't seem to mind in the least having so tiny a room at the top of the Unit, or having to cook their dull little meals in the dingy kitchen cluttered with laboratory equipment. She worked hard too, dealing with all the tedious little jobs in the Unit that would waste the time of the trained staff, yet expecting no payment, none of the fripperies most girls of her age seemed to care about. Hilary more than made up for everything else that had gone so wrong in his personal life. If the family had to split down the middle, at least it had split the right way.

Sir Daniel was waiting for him in the leathery sporting-printed bar of the restaurant and greeted him with a bland friendliness that went a little way toward allaying George's suspicions. He had been very suspicious indeed when two days after that disastrous *Probe* program he had received the invitation written on expensive stationery bearing an Eaton Square address, even more suspicious at the way the man had written again and again and eventually managed to reach him on the telephone, making his determination very plain.

"I would prefer not to commit to paper at this stage my reasons for wanting so much to talk to you, nor to discuss them on the telephone," Sir Daniel had said. "May I simply say that I have the welfare of your project deeply at heart, and can make what I am sure you will see as a most advantageous proposal? I do most earnestly advise you to agree to this meeting."

And with both Hilary and Barbara Hervey reminding him that the *Echo* had consistently applauded the project, still ran frequent leaders castigating the government for its lack of support for science, he had given in.

"I took the liberty of ordering our meal in advance, Dr. Briant," Sir Daniel said. "I know this place very well, and know which of their offerings are best. A few native oysters, some of their truly excellent saddle of mutton, and a most interesting couple of wines. But if you would prefer something different?"

"Thank you, no. Whatever you suggest. I am not particularly interested in food."

"My dear man, how could you be? I know all too well that such an interest can be . . . costly. And in your position, you could hardly indulge yourself in any way."

"If you mean I have no money, you're right. Is that your reason for this invitation? To feed one of the starving?"

"Oh, please, you mustn't be offended! I merely wanted to make it clear from the outset that I am aware of what is your most pressing problem. Financing your exciting work. But we really must not get down to cases quite so abruptly. I suggest we eat and then relax and talk. An aperitif? No? Then we'll go in." And he crooked an imperious finger at the headwaiter and led the way to a table in the corner of the big main room.

They ate to the company of desultory conversation on general subjects, in part because the waiters were so attentive that it would not have been possible to do otherwise, but also because Sir Daniel made it quite clear that he had no intention of being hurried. Not that George minded. He was hungrier than he had thought and, despite his denial of interest in food, thoroughly enjoyed the excellence of what he was given.

But all through the meal he was aware of still holding a deep suspicion, particularly as he didn't like his host, finding his smooth talk rather repellent, and some embarrassment in his arrogant way of dealing with the waiters. But he controlled his suspicion, tried to show a relaxation he didn't feel as coffee cups were put before them and Sir Daniel leaned back in his chair to look consideringly at him.

"Well, now, Dr. Briant. Shall we settle to some practical talk? You want to know why I suggested this meeting?"

"I'm interested, yes."

"You appreciate that my newspaper, the *Echo*, has from the start consistently supported you, in spite of an almost general outcry against you?"

"Oh! Am I supposed to appreciate it? I regarded the paper's attitude as the only intelligent one. Or should I be appreciative because intelligent reporting is so rare?"

"I used the word in a different sense. I meant to make it clear that you had no need to fear my paper. Of course, I ask no appreciation, although I might perhaps point out that I had to overcome considerable editorial diffidence to ensure the *Echo* would take the line it did." He smiled. "Newspaper proprietors have remarkably little power, you know. I for one am constantly bullied by my editors. But on this issue I felt so deeply that I made a stand. And I am happy to say that my senior editorial people have come round completely to my way of thinking. So much so that"—he paused—"so much so that I am here to make to you an offer that I am convinced will be of great attraction to you."

"An offer? What of? What can your newspaper offer me apart from the type of support it already gives?"

"Money."

George raised his eyebrows. "Oh? Do you propose to run an appeal on behalf of the project? I doubt there'd be much point in it if you did. From all accounts, the publicity about it has only had the effect of making large numbers of people send donations to children's charities, and provide this absurd religious revival cult with considerable funds. But not one solitary donation has come my way. Not one."

He laughed a little bitterly. "It's ironic, you know. The only reason I consented to give a press conference in the first place was because I had been led to believe I would gain public sympathy for my work and thus be able to finance it. In the event—"

"In the event, you are almost at the end of your resources. Your staff have agreed to work at half salary—most devoted of them—you and your daughter are living in difficult straits since you left your wife, and unless something is done soon, there is a real danger the project will founder by the end of the year."

George's cup clattered into its saucer. "How in hell's name—"

"Do I know all that?" Sir Daniel leaned back in his chair and produced a bland smile. "I am a newspaperman, Dr. Briant. It is my business to know. I know one or two other things too. Such as that your son appeared at Bow Street the other day on a charge of possessing cannabis—oh, *you* were unaware of that fact? Well, well. It wasn't reported, of course. The *Echo* was the only paper to discover that Ian Webb and Ian Briant were the same person. Your wife's name, was it not? And I made a point of keeping that information out of our news columns."

"That stupid—my God, how could even *he* be so stupid? If he wants to behave in so, so lunatic a fashion, it's his concern. But to risk—"

"Bad publicity for you? May I tell you something, Dr. Briant? Your son actively *wants* bad publicity for you. He is a very bitter young man. Extremely bitter. And very voluble about his feelings. I may say it is costing the *Echo* quite a sum to ensure he controls that volubility. And only as long as we—I am willing to maintain the control at the level he demands will his urge to talk be held in check. I wonder if you are beginning to understand why I was so anxious to arrange this meeting?"

The attempt to disguise suspicion was abandoned. George sat very erect in his chair, staring at the man opposite him.

"Sir Daniel, I am a practical man. Not in the least devious. I must ask you to what all this is leading, and ask you to tell me in direct terms. Otherwise, I must go. I am not prepared to sit here and be threatened."

"My dear Dr. Briant! I am not threatening you! I told you, I am here to offer you the money you so desperately need. All the rest of our talk was designed to sketch in some of the background! No more than that."

"Why?"

"Why what?"

"Why are you offering me money? What is it you want to get out of me? Because it's bloody clear you want something! You tell me you've used your money already to keep my son quiet, offer me more. I may be a practical man, Sir Daniel, and unskilled in the maneuverings you appear to find so enthralling, but I'm not such a fool as to be unable to recognize manipulation when I meet it."

"Manipulation? Oh, come, Dr. Briant! You're most unjust! I am prepared to offer you a straightforward businesslike arrangement, and you virtually accuse me of chicanery! Let me point out that I made my first approach to you before your son was so . . . indiscreet. I merely added his, um, involvement to my list of reasons for persuading you to consider my proposition. Any man would be entitled to feel hurt, even offended, at your cavalier response!" But he didn't look at all hurt or offended; he was patently enjoying himself.

"Ah! We begin to get to the point! Businesslike, you say? Proposition? What is it you want to buy, what have I got that could be of any use to you?"

"Baby George Briant," Sir Daniel said softly.

"What? The baby? You want to buy the *baby*?"

"Precisely. Or, rather, world rights in him. I want to obtain for the *Echo* full reporting rights on his life, his progress, everything about him, and also all the pictures of him we can get. And I mean full *world* rights, in newspapers, magazines, television, advertising—"

"*Advertising?* Are you out of your mind?" And George suddenly threw back his head and laughed.

"Does that seem absurd to you? I can assure you that baby is worth a good deal of money, properly exploited. The way he's fed, dressed, the equipment used for him—all this will have a powerful effect on the marketing of such goods. And, of course, the reporting of his story will have enormous appeal, for years and years to come. Oh, come on, Dr. Briant! Don't try to tell me the possibility hadn't entered your mind? Why else were you so adamant that no one should have access to the child? Because you realized the immense commercial value he has, surely! You insist you're a straightforward man, lacking in deviousness, but you can't be *that* simple!"

George was no longer laughing. "Perhaps I am simple. I refused access to him for one reason only—to protect the project. To expose the child to outside influences could damage the work irreparably. For Christ's sake, your articles about my work—the things your man Bridges wrote—they made it clear to the public that this was why he had to be protected! Don't you believe what you publish?"

"Of course! But one can publish the truth without publishing every part of it! All right, I'll accept that you never recognized the commercial possibilities of your project. May I suggest you recognize them now? I am prepared to pay you fifteen thousand pounds a year for the next five years, with an option on the following five, and so on until the child reaches his majority, in exchange for world rights in the story. It's a fair offer. We'll make a reasonable profit out of it, and you'll be able to keep going. No one will be harmed. Indeed, the very opposite. It's clear to me that without an injection of real money soon your work will founder. Remember, Gurney is hot on your tail! If this bill he's announced gets through, then the chances are the little you get in grants from the sources which support you now will dry up completely. And you can be certain the hospital will have to close your unit. But I'm offering you enough money to equip a new unit, or at least keep the existing one alive. Come on, man! Use your head!"

There was a long pause, and George sat staring into the dregs of his coffee, trying to think. Then he looked up and said dully, "And if I refuse, take my chances on the bill being defeated? Its passage is far from being a foregone conclusion. I'm all right for the next six months, poverty-stricken though I may be, and by then I'll be able to get more money, somehow. I always have before, and I can do it again."

"If it becomes public knowledge that your own son is a delinquent? A junkie? That you haven't been able to rear your own child successfully? Are you sure?" Sir Daniel said softly.

George nodded heavily. "Yes. Yes. I expected that. I can see now why—oh, ye gods, why is it? Why does a piece of honest science create such situations? I'm trying to show how to make better, more valuable people. I'm trying to pull humanity out of the mud of its own past, help it to leap into a future that— And I have to tolerate this sort of— *Why?*"

His voice began to rise and his face flushed as he banged his clenched fist on the table so that the cups rattled, and the people at the next table looked at them curiously. "Why, in the name of good sense, does it have to be like this?"

"Because we are still in the present, Dr. Briant," Sir Daniel said crisply. "You promise a future world inhabited by people bred and reared to be perfectly intelligent, perfectly in harmony with each other, perfectly beautiful. Well, that's as it may be. But I won't be here to see it, any more than you will, and I've more sense than to live totally on the hopes of the future, even if you're prepared to. All I can tell you is that I see a way to make a practical deal, right here and now, in the present. If you can't see that your picture of the future hasn't a hope of becoming real without the help of people like me, then you really are a fool. And I gave you more credit than that."

He leaned back in his chair and beckoned the waiter. "Perhaps you need a little time to think. A little more brandy and some hot coffee to replace this will bridge the time most agreebly. The Napoleon, and for heaven's sake don't warm the glass. Barbaric trick."

The baby was lying on his back, his eyes fixed on the brightly colored fish of the mobile fixed above his cot, dribbling a little as he spasmodically moved his hands toward it. The diffused light from the concealed fitting around the head of the cot shone on his hair, and Isobel's lips curved as she looked at the curls that were already visible on his round head.

He's come on a treat this past few weeks, she thought. Dr. Briant says he's the most advanced baby he's ever seen, and he's right. He really is.

As she thought about Dr. Briant, she frowned slightly. He'd been so—what was it?—far away this past couple of weeks or so when she talked to him. From the day he and his daughter had moved into the rooms at the top of the Unit, he'd been more distant, even though she'd seen much more of him than she had during that very first week.

I wonder why, Georgie boy. She began one of her silent conversations with the baby in the cot beside her, her head bent over the rompers she was sewing for him. He didn't need them, but she liked to make things for him, and Miss Hervey had shrugged unconcernedly when she'd asked if she could. It would have been much nicer to be able to talk out loud to the baby, but she couldn't do that, not with that tape recorder stuck on her back all the time.

But a silent conversation was almost as good, the way he would turn his head toward her when she looked at him, would give her one of his wide pink smiles, and make his funny bubbly noises. Smiling, at a month old! A marvelous baby.

I wonder why, Georgie boy. Why he moved in, I mean. He's got a proper home, after all. But that wife of his—hard, she looked, didn't you think so, Georgie? But she's keeping her promise, never comes messing around even if she is supposed to be your legal mother.

She dropped her sewing on her lap and looked at the baby, and he turned his head and looked back at her intently, his blue eyes milky and considering, and then he smiled, his mouth opening wide.

"Who's a lovely boy, then? Who's the best boy in the world, then?" Isobel murmured aloud. It was all right to talk like that into the tape recorder. Part of the job. It was only her private thinking that had to be kept a secret between herself and Georgie.

All the fuss there had been when that adoption went through. She'd caught the worry from everyone else, that week. They'd been sure the thing would fail, that the court would say no, what with all the fuss in the papers and on the television about the project, and Georgie being too young to be legally adopted yet. But there were ways around everything, it seemed, and Dr. Briant had managed it, somehow. He'd found some lawyers to work on his side, and they'd got it through.

It's silly, Georgie, isn't it? The way people go on and on about it, taking sides? One paper says about how wicked it is, you being here. And then that other one gets all excited and calls you the hope of mankind. I ask you! You're just little Georgie, aren't you? My little Georgie. All this taking sides! If they could only see you, the ones who keep on about how wicked it is to keep you here, they'd soon know there was nothing to worry about.

And for Isobel there was nothing to worry about in that sense. She read the papers regularly, saw the many television news programs about what was being said in the world outside the safe cocoon of the Unit, where she lived wrapped up in the baby and her fierce secret love for him, yet none of it really impinged on her consciousness. Her only concern was the baby, and the importance of not upsetting anyone, in case they tried to send her away.

It was an always present concern that, the need to cover up the way she felt about him. She could not have explained even to herself why it was necessary to hide it. She simply had an instinctive certainty that any obvious display of her attachment would be dangerous.

There had been a few times, during the week after the *Probe* program, when she had been marginally affected by the reported fuss and discussion. Was what Dr. Briant was doing with the baby a wicked thing, as some people said? she had wondered. And then there had been the announcement of Kenneth Gurney's private member's bill—the Scientific Research and Human Experimentation Control Bill—and she had gratefully dismissed the question from her mind. If it was politics that was at the root of the fuss, it had no relevance for her. She didn't care about Dr. Briant's involvement with ideas, or lack of it, or possible political uses of his work. As long as the papers went on about dreary politics, she could not take their excited leader articles seriously.

As for the religious aspect, she had first been a little amused and then scandalized by the reports she read about that. She had long ago abandoned the little religion she had been taught in her childhood, clinging only to a vague acceptance of the existence of God as a beneficent creature who sometimes—just sometimes—involved Himself in her life, as He had when she had got the job looking after the baby. But she looked upon posturings and rituals of orthodox religious practice much as she would regard the games of children, with an indulgent attitude of "If it pleases them it's harmless enough."

But as the get-back-to-God cult took root, and more and more newspaper reports appeared on the meetings in Trafalgar Square, the rallies and marches, she had been shocked. Although she had no use for the practices of orthodox religion, she had a definite dislike of primitive evangelism. Her parents, halfhearted though they had been in their Catholicism, had at least ingrained that deeply into her.

And when she looked at the baby in his cot, after reading of the hysterical assertions about his suffering at Dr. Briant's hands, the spreading cult seemed to her to be such obvious nonsense anyway. How could he be the instrument that would bring sinful mankind back to God, as the evangelists said, this baby she fed, changed, bathed, and loved? To suggest so was ridiculous in Isobel's eyes. It was easy, then, to dismiss the whole thing from her mind as an irrelevance.

And so for the past weeks she had gone on simply living from day to day, glorying in the baby's developing attachment to her, the way he responded to her far more rapidly than to anyone else in the Unit, even though he saw them all so frequently. And as they came more and more to take her for granted, talking in front of her as freely as if she were as much a part of the research team as they were, she gained assurance. She let herself think about them as individuals and not just in relation to the baby.

She thought about Dr. Briant and his behavior, about the way Miss Hervey looked at him, the way they, together with Hilary Briant, would sit working and talking together for hours on end. She let herself wonder about them. Surmising about the people in the Unit brought an added interest to what was an undoubtedly circumscribed life.

But she never allowed herself to think about the work they were doing. If she had considered it at all, she would have expected to have become accustomed to the tests the baby underwent, the electroencephalograms, the blood tests, the collection of smears from his mouth, and the other tests she didn't understand. In fact, each time one of the researchers arrived with a covered tray of equipment, she had to make an intense effort to maintain her quiet front, to appear as calm and unconcerned as she believed it essential to appear, though she ached to pull the syringes from their hands, and hold him close to her, defying them, refusing to allow them to touch him.

Yet despite her growing hatred of the things they did, she continued to keep her feelings in close check, living from four o'clock each day to three o'clock the next, steeling herself to accept what happened during that one hateful hour every afternoon.

And today, at five o'clock, the long safe hours of contentment stretched before her, hours in which she could safely love her baby and talk to him inside her head. She could sit in this warm quiet room, encapsulated away from the arguing people and the dingy gray skies she could see from the nursery window, happy until tomorrow afternoon at three o'clock.

Hilary looked at the grayness of the cold sky outside the window and then at Barbara Hervey's bent head and wondered whether it was worth pretending there was a draft that made it necessary for her to shift her chair. Then she could sit at the same side of the table. But that would mean she wouldn't be able to look at her so easily without being noticed; and anyway, the last thing she wanted to do was give Barbara the idea that she, Hilary, was one of those silly types who fussed over physical discomfort.

It was lovely, the way the light lit the curve of her cheek, showing the faint downiness on her upper lip. She could see the tip of Barbara's tongue at the corner of her mouth, and she shivered with a little frisson of pleasure; it made her look so defenseless, so very *real*, the way she did that, like a child just learning to write.

Barbara looked up and caught her eye and smiled, and Hilary felt herself redden and hated her own inability to control it.

"Bogged down? It's not easy stuff, that. Do you need any help?"

"Oh, no! I'm . . . well, actually, there is a small thing." She'd nearly missed an opportunity there. "I'm sorry to bother you. I mean, I can manage, I think, if you're busy."

"Oh, not to worry." Barbara stretched her neck. "I'll finish this today quite easily. Let's see, then. Is it the graph or the readings?"

"Er, I'm not sure." Hilary picked up her papers and came eagerly around the table to put them in front of Barbara. "Does this look right to you?"

Barbara took the graph and studied it for a moment. "Oh, this is lovely, Hilary! Really lovely. You make such a clean job of the things you do. Don't tell him I said so, but Vernon's graphs look like spiderwebs compared with these."

"I'll copy them if you like," Hilary said quickly. "I like doing graphs like this—making them neat, I mean. I . . . I'm awfully glad you like the way I do it."

"Heavens, no! If we let you start going over other people's work, there'll be all hell to pay! And the last thing we dare do is upset people, the way things are. Half-pay is bad enough."

She looked up and smiled as she saw the crestfallen look on Hilary's face. "Oh, look, don't be upset! It was sweet of you to offer. You weren't to know that Vernon is the sort to get uppity about things. Now, don't *you* go getting uppity too, will you?"

"Oh, of course not! I . . . I just want to be useful," Hilary said and reddened again. "It . . . it's so marvelous, working here with you like this."

"It must be. It's a great project," Barbara said. "At your age I'd have given—oh, anything to work with someone like your father on such a project. He's a great man, you know. You're a very lucky girl."

"Oh, I know. And it's not just Daddy. I mean, I think . . . I think you're all marvelous. You, specially. You work harder than anyone." And then, with a daring of which she wouldn't have thought herself capable, she added, "I worry about you sometimes."

"Worry? About me? My dear Hilary! Whatever for? I've never been happier in a job before!"

"Well, you work so hard. You're here to all hours every night. I can't think how Daddy would get through it all without you."

Barbara looked up at her sharply and then away. "Oh?" she said with a casual air. "Has has he remarked on it?"

"Oh, yes!" It's not really a lie, she thought. If I asked him, he'd say it, I'm sure he would. "He thinks you—he really appreciates the things you do."

"I . . . I don't want appreciation. It's such a vital piece of research, you know, I'm just happy to be able to work with—to work on it. But I'm glad your father is pleased."

She stood up and moved away toward the window.

"Er, I don't want to pry, Hilary, believe me, but, er, I worry too. About you and your father. It's . . . I know a little about what happened, of course, why you're living here. I just wondered, how is your father feeling about things? He's working much too hard. Never seems to relax, you know? Nor do you, of course. You could say *I've* been worrying about the Briants!" And she looked sideways at Hilary and laughed lightly. "All of us worrying about each other! Sounds like a television soap opera, doesn't it?"

"Oh, no! It sounds nice," Hilary said, and again the ready flush covered her cheeks. "When people worry about you it means they like you."

"Of course I like you! When you work really closely with people you either like them or loathe them. You can't be indifferent. And for me, well, I can't work well if I'm not on good terms with my colleagues. That's why I'm pleased your father likes . . . likes my work, you know? And why I've been concerned about him, about both of you."

"Please, don't be anxious," Hilary said earnestly. "There's no need. I've never been happier in all my life. Away from school—it was dismal, school—and doing real work, and having my father to look after, it's marvelous. I . . . it was rather awful when—I mean, my mother and Ian—but it's over now and, really, there's no need to worry about us."

"Your father too? I mean, you know, he's not upset by—well, family problems can be depressing. Though he's working better than ever, if that were possible. But he doesn't say much about how he feels."

"He never does. Except when he's angry about something." Hilary's voice took on a tinge of pride. "He's rather grim when he's angry, isn't he? Quite frightening, really."

"Yes. I know what you mean. Though he only gets angry about important things. But I was wondering about . . . whether he misses your mother and brother. It can't be easy for him."

"No one could miss Ian!" Hilary said with sudden bitterness. "He gave Daddy a ghastly time. I know it sounds awful, but not having to put up with Ian is almost the best thing about it all." Even to Barbara, Hilary couldn't talk about her mother. She couldn't even think about her; it had been easier to close her mind tightly into a box inside which her mother was locked.

"Brothers can be pretty ghastly," Barbara said almost absently. "Teenage boys. Though I imagine your father is a bit—well, lonely sometimes?"

"I don't think so. We're very close, you know, Daddy and I. We can talk about the project, and that's super. He needs to talk about work, and he couldn't before, when I was at school. And at home it was—oh, you know. Not everyone is as interested in science as we are."

"No. I know. Yes, I imagine you're a great comfort to him. A great comfort."

Barbara moved restlessly and went back to her chair and sat down again, and then she looked up at Hilary with a rather over-bright smile on her face. "But all the same, it's a bit dreary for you both, just being tied to the Unit. I was wondering, er, I'd so much like you both to come and have dinner with me one evening. My flat's not very big, but I've room for a small dinner party. Do you think your father would, er, like that?"

"Oh, that would be *super!*" Hilary was scarlet with pleasure. "I'm sure he would. I mean, apart from anything else, he must be sick of my awful cooking! Not that that would be the reason, I mean. Oh, I am awful! That sounded so greedy."

Barbara laughed. "Not in the least! I know exactly what you meant! Well, I'll leave it with you to talk to him about it. Next Saturday—would that be all right?"

They spent the remainder of the dwindling afternoon ostensibly working on the graphs. But Hilary was anxiously considering whether she could stretch her small budget to buy flowers to take to the dinner party, and Barbara was equally anxiously planning a menu designed to show George Briant that she was as good a cook as she was a biologist.

10

Gurney left the House by the St. Stephen's Hall entrance, for once forgoing the pleasure of using a members-only way out; there was no point in seeking the stab of pleasure he got from being recognized as an MP by the people who hung about staring, not today. It wouldn't help him feel any better.

How could Davidson be so stupid? Couldn't he see that the mere fact that public opinion was strongly against Briant should be enough to carry it through without trouble? But he had just sat there muttering about proof of the man's lack of financial integrity. As if that mattered! Gurney had tried as patiently as he could, to get the thing across to him. "It's what he's doing that's the real point at issue," he'd said, "not where he gets the money from. People are unhappy about it—using a human child for his experiments. You've heard enough to know that, surely. But you know as well as I do that it just isn't possible to legislate controls of scientific experiments in blanket fashion. You'd have to build in so many protections for acceptable work that the unacceptable would slide through. The only possible way is to go back to square one and control the selection of experimental material. That's why I've named the bill as I have, the Scientific Research and *Human Experimentation* Control Bill, remember. It doesn't mean I've got to prove there's any dirty work going on in a financial sense—and you know no private member's bill can discuss finance, anyway."

"Nay, lad, you'll 'ave to do better nor that," Davidson had coughed through his cigarette, splattering his huge belly with ash. "I'm as 'uman as the next feller, but I know what I don't know. And I don't know enough about science to try to stop progress just because I don't fancy the way they 'ave to make their progress. Folks didn't fancy the way the chap who started vaccination did 'is job, but if 'e'd been stopped just because of their squeamishness, we'd still be dyin' of smallpox. I reckon it's the way they get their money that matters. Whether it comes into the wording of the bill or not—and o' course I know it can't be part of the structure—isn't relevant. But if this Briant bloke or scientists like 'im could be shown to be playin' about wi' other people's cash, then I'll support your bill. But not otherwise. I'm a practical feller, Gurney. An' I've been around politics a sight longer nor you. Folks'll get over the way they feel now about this baby. This time next year, they'll've forgotten all about it. But money, that's somethin' else again. They never forget that. So I don't neither. You show me someone finaglin', and I'll be down like a ton o' bricks. But if Briant's straight—and I'll tell you flat, I've no reason to think otherwise—I'm all for leavin' 'im be, no matter 'ow many babies he gets involved with. And from all accounts, the kid's not comin' to any harm. Clean opposite, if anything. Wish I'd 'ad that sort o' care as a nipper. Would 'ave been a sight better than growin' up in the slag heaps I called home, I can tell yer."

He'd hauled his great bulk up out of his chair then and looked down at Gurney. "I know 'ow you feel, lad. You've got a chance to do a bit of good for yourself wi' your bill, and you're as entitled as the next feller to drum up all the support you can get. I'll do this much for you. I'll not say owt against your bill—yet. But unless you can give me some o' my sort of real solid reasons to support you, I'll 'ave to stand against you. You see that? I'm not one for abstainin' on important issues, and this is important, I'll grant you. You find some ugly facts—if there are any—an' I'll stand be'ind you. But wi'out 'em, no go."

"And your . . . coterie?"

"Nay, lad," Davidson had laughed with fat complacency. "You've been listenin' to too much lobby gossip. I'm not that strong! I've me friends, I don't deny, and they credit me wi' some sense and take some guidance from me long experience. But they're not in m' pocket, you know. Minds of their own, the lads 'ave." And he'd gone lumbering out of the bar, leaving Gurney seething with impotent rage.

Like hell they aren't in his pocket! he thought now as he walked quickly up Whitehall. If he stands up in debate and comes out against me, more than half the northern members will march right after him into the noes' lobby. And if they go, what hope of hanging on to the support I've already got? It was too chancy. Davidson had him in a cleft stick and knew it.

Davidson hadn't liked Gurney from the start. He had too many important ears in the House, and it had been an error of judgment on Gurney's part to go against him on that bloody cotton mill issue in his first year. Well, he'd paid for that. Two possible plums had been lost to him because of that—the place on the Education Bill Committee, the undersecretaryship Davidson had grabbed for his own protégés—but he'd swallowed that, and over the past few months had built some sort of relationship with the man. Not much of a one, but enough, he'd thought, to risk canvassing his support for his bill. And he'd been wrong again. Or had he?

He reached Trafalgar Square and stood on the edge of the pavement, thinking, letting the crowds surge around him. Or had he? Davidson hadn't said he'd fight him. Yet. He'd shown there was a way to get his support, and with it that of his tribe of camp followers. Find facts that prove Briant is financially unreliable, and you're on your way, he told himself. Dig out some facts. Now, that shouldn't be too difficult. Should it?

He was still thinking about ways and means when he reached the restaurant. He could see Cora's back against the glass and felt a sudden surge of anger. Bloody woman! What the hell was the point of using such a dismal place to meet if it weren't that they were safe from possible observation? She knew that and yet plumped herself at a table in the window for all the world to see her. No doubt about it, she was showing too many signs of getting above herself and she would have to be dealt with rather sooner than he had intended.

She looked up at him with the irritatingly familiar expression of knowingness on her face as he stopped beside the table in the window.

"I'd prefer one of the tables at the back, Cora. Shall we?" And without waiting for an answer, he led the way through the narrow aisle between the red-checked tables to the far corner and stood holding his own chair—the one that ensured he had his back to the room—as she went past him and settled herself.

"Well," he said and reached for the menu, "what shall we have? The cannelloni, perhaps."

"You hardly have to read that with such ostentation, Ken. You must know it by heart by now. Or is it that it's easier to look at than I am?"

There was an edge to her husky voice, and he looked up at her for a moment before letting his eyes slide away again. Oh, God damn it all to hell! She was all set for another of her probing sessions, quite obviously. The sooner the better, undoubtedly, he thought. No real reason to put it off much longer anyway.

"Are we going to eat dinner, Cora, in some semblance of peace and amity, or are you going to start the argument now? Because if that's what you're planning, I tell you right now I'm not in the mood for it. I've told you before, great involved discussion of the state of the parties gives me indigestion."

"Oh, we'll have dinner! I might as well get that much! I'll have an avocado—*with* prawns and an escalope Marsala and a green salad. And a full bottle of decent wine too. Not a half-carafe of plonk. If you can afford it, that is."

"If that's what you want."

He ordered their meal, making a point of selecting the cheapest pasta for himself, and refusing a first course. He'd lunched well, anyway, with a PRO anxious enough to get something out of him to have fed him at the Savoy. A light meal now wouldn't hurt him.

She ate very little of the food when it came, looking at him under her lashes as she left the greater part of each dish untasted on her plate. Bitch! he thought savagely. But if she thinks she can get at me this way, she's got another think coming.

But she could get at him that way and knew it, for by the time she had ordered a zabaglione, eaten barely two spoonfuls of it, and then demanded brandy with her coffee, he was in a flaming temper. And as his own anger rose, so her own edginess seemed to diminish. He paid the bill—half as much again as he usually had to shell out—and after a moment's hesitation, scooped all the change from the saucerful of silver the waiter brought.

"What, no tip?" she said softly as she pulled on her gloves. "As bad as that, is it?"

"Since we won't be coming back here—ever—there seems no reason," he said savagely and immediately felt better. A statement of intent, that was what he had made, and it had struck home. He knew that because of the sudden stillness he felt in her, and the way she got up to leave without another word when he pushed his chair back.

They walked along Charlotte Street toward the underground station in total silence. They sat side by side in the almost empty train as it bucketed its way to Belsize Park, and the climbed the hill to the flat, still without speaking a word.

She dropped her coat and bag and gloves on the elegant velvet-covered sofa and turned to look at him as he followed her into the living room. She spoke lightly. "We might almost be married, mightn't we? I used to know a man who told me you could always spot married couples anywhere—they were the ones who never talked to each other."

"But we're not." His own voice was harsh.

"No. We're not."

There was a long silence, and then she said softly, "Nor ever going to be, are we, Ken? That is it, isn't it? All this time, all this talk, it's all been pie in the sky, hasn't it?"

Almost without realizing it, he slid into the familiar pattern. "Cora, for God's sake! I've told you why, time and again—when I can—"

"Yes, I know. When you can afford to be married, then you will. A man on his way up can't afford to start on the wrong foot. Marriage too soon is asking for trouble. I've heard it all before. And me—" She laughed suddenly. "I've believed you! Isn't that funny? I really believed you. I really thought you meant you'd marry *me* when you could afford it. What I didn't understand was that what you meant was that marriage would come when you found a *woman* who could afford it, not when you had enough money yourself. Isn't that funny? You must agree it's very amusing, Ken! Here I am, a woman who uses words every day of the week as part of her stock in trade, who's been selling everything from corsets to loo paper by giving words dozens of different meanings, and I couldn't see what it was you were doing! You were telling me no more than the truth, but I heard what I wanted to hear! Oh, it's hilarious."

"Cora, you really—"

"Oh, no! Let me finish! I might as well, since there's no point any more in biting my lips, is there? Because I'm not going to get a tip either, am I? You're leaving me behind too, aren't you? Like the others?"

"What others?" He spoke carefully. "What others, Cora? I don't know what you're talking about."

"Don't you? Don't you really? Oh, come on, Ken! How much longer can you keep up the fiction? I've known for, oh, weeks. What's happening to me has happened time and again before. I tried to persuade myself it would be different this time, that I really meant something to you. But I'm like the others. Useful for a while, but not as useful as I was. It's been quite interesting, really, seeing where I fitted into your pattern."

"I don't know what you're talking about."

"Oh, come *on*! I'm an intelligent woman, you know—more than just someone to provide a sex life on the cheap and somewhere to hang up your hat! The first one or two may have been on the dim side, but I'm bright, you know that? I can see the pattern very clearly. You've always been good at trading up, haven't you? What was the first one? A shop girl? Then a typist, perhaps, or did you make the leap to a full-blown secretary? Each one a bit better-looking, a bit brighter, and certainly better off. I must have seemed quite a plum when you started with me. A professional type, with a really good job, and money to match. A comfortable flat, a good address. Oh, you must have been pleased with yourself!"

He said nothing, standing staring at her with his face carefully guarded. She stood up and began to prowl restlessly about the room, touching the ornaments on the room divider, running her fingers along the books on the shelves that flanked the fireplace.

"And what will the next address be?" she said, not looking at him. "Belgravia, this time? Or merely swinging Chelsea? Hampstead was quite a step up from Kilburn. That was where the one before lived, wasn't it? I remember, you got letters redirected from there. You've been cleverer this time, of course, never had letters sent here. So my successor won't know, will she? Will she give you a free home as well as the other half of her bed? I suppose so. You'd never make the change otherwise, would you?"

"Is that what's really getting you, Cora? Money?" He spoke softly, watching her every movement. "I never imagined you as a grasping type."

"Grasping? Me? Oh, my God!" She began to laugh then, savagely. "Grasping? Christ, but you really are—I've got to admire you, you know. It's a gift, a real gift, do you know that? You can take your own motives and swing them so far they land fair and square on me. Grasping, me? What does that make you? You may have forgotten, my dear, but I haven't yet had that birthday present you promised me. And the way you've timed this—and it is you that's timed it, not me—you're leaving me just in time to avoid having to pay for a Christmas present too. Did you work out the odds? I bet you did. I bet you assessed the sort of present I'd be likely to give you and then decided it wouldn't be big enough to compensate for having to come across with something for me. I mean, you've already had the gold cigarette case, and the links, and the watch. The most you could hope for this time was a bottle of after-shave, wasn't that it? And your new one—whoever she is—

she ought to be good for something really lush. First Christmas together and all that—brings out the best in a woman, doesn't it? Yes, I've noticed. I've had to. I've paid every bloody bill for you for over six months. And even on an MP's salary you could have managed something better than a weekly dinner at that tuppenny-ha'penny place you call 'ours.' Ours! It was ours because it was the cheapest you could find, that's all. There's nothing more sentimental about it than that."

"Are you telling me to leave, Cora? Is that it? Throwing me out?" He kept his voice as level as he could, trying to keep the elation out. It was marvelous, it really was, the way she was doing it all for him. He'd thought it would be a more complicated change, this one, but in the event . . .

"No, I'm not. I'm just accepting a fact, that's all. You're going anyway. You've been working up to it for weeks. I told you, you've traded up to a bright one this time. So I've known from the moment you first began to plan it."

He moved then, walking quietly toward the bedroom door. "There's no point in my saying anything. There isn't a word of truth in a single thing you've said this evening, but I'm not going to waste my breath in arguing with you. I'll go. Now. But remember, it's your doing not mine."

"No, Ken, don't waste your breath. Don't waste a thing. You never have, so why start now? But, tell me something before you go."

He turned and looked at her, his hand on the doorknob.

"Is she expecting you tonight? Or are you going to have to actually spend money on an hotel?"

He smiled then, a slow gentle smile. "I find hotels less than comfortable, Cora, you know that. I imagine I can stay with friends, for a while."

"Christ, but you— Oh, one of these days you'll fall over yourself, you've got to. One of these days you'll reach for the main chance and it'll be just out of your reach. And when you try to pull back and catch hold of what you were leaving behind, it won't be there. One of these days . . ."

"Perhaps," he said softly and went into the bedroom to pack his cases with his usual calm methodical order. It was almost ten now. He could stay at one of the cheaper hotels near the House for tonight. And tomorrow, before taking himself to the Sillick to see Kegan, he would phone Judith Wallace. He'd meant to hold her off for at least another month, but she was ready; and a show of eagerness on his part wouldn't be a bad thing. Not at all a bad thing.

Kegan was feeling better than he had for a long time. It was high time someone took him seriously, recognized just how much effect he had had on the thing. It had hurt, the way he had been ignored, as though he were of no greater importance than some clerk or other. Because that was how it had seemed ever since the thing had become public property.

"It's not that I wanted to be thanked or anything of that sort!" he said now. "Far from it. The help I gave Dr. Briant over this past two years, the support I gave him, I did it because I believed in the value of what he was trying to do. But what happened? In all the newspaper coverage, all those television programs, has anyone asked *me*? They put on newspaper reporters, and paid them handsomely for saying what they thought about it, put on members of Parliament—not that I don't think *you* did an excellent job, because of course you did—but here I sit, knowing more about the matter than anyone else, and who takes a moment's interest? I can't deny I'm hurt—well, not hurt as much as distressed that the public shouldn't be given the opportunity of hearing the facts I have at my disposal. Not that I didn't offer my services to J. J. Gerrard. At the time of that program I told him I would be willing to cooperate with him, and what happened? Nothing! There're people who know nothing about it appearing on programs week after week, producing their opinions on it, and I've got facts—*facts*, not opinion! To be honest with you, Mr. Gurney, I've wondered whether Briant himself had put a spoke in. He and I—well, despite all my efforts on his behalf, he's a difficult man to get on with."

Gurney let him burble on. Quite obviously he'd been storing up this spate of resentment for some time. Give him the sympathetic ear he needed, and he'd have him in his pocket. Whether or not he actually had the sort of facts Davidson was demanding was almost beside the point. He certainly knew all the ins and outs of the financing of the project from the word go, and that would be ample to start with.

". . . and I must say I'm most impressed, Mr. Gurney, most impressed. It's extremely reassuring to know that members go to so much trouble to investigate the matters they bring to the attention of the House. Most reassuring. I know, from my own position here, how vital it is to be completely *au fait* with the matter with which one deals, but I also know enough people in senior positions of the same sort who are less—shall we say less responsible? You and I, we speak the same language."

God forbid, you wet ass, Gurney thought and smiled toothily at him. "My dear Mr. Kegan, I can assure you there are plenty of members who prosecute in the House matters of which they know less than nothing! But that isn't my way, any more than it would be yours. And it is a great relief to me to know that we can discuss this on the same level, that you can give me the assistance I need. And I can promise you your valuable contribution to the structure of my bill won't go unrecognized. I will make a point of mentioning it to one or two of my good friends at Alexander Fleming House. Too often, ministries never know of the immense ability of the people they employ. People who do a good job of work, and get on with it uncomplainingly, they deserve recognition."

"Oh, please, Mr. Gurney! I want no recognition! I assure you, it's enough for me to do my job well, and know that I am doing it." Kegan's delight was so obvious that Gurney could have laughed aloud. "Now, do let me offer you some lunch. We have a most pleasant dining room for senior administrative staff, and though NHS budgets are what they are, we can provide you with a reasonable meal. And then we can settle to some solid talking."

"A delightful idea. Thank you. All I'll need to know is the precise sources of the finances for the Briant project, the way the money is tied up, and the degree of control there is over actual expenditure. I know Briant is somewhat . . . obstructive when any attempts are made to investigate him, but in your position, I'm sure that can be dealt with."

Isobel listened with apparent calmness, her face expressing only mild interest in what he was saying, her hands neatly folded, as usual, against her overall front. But her pulse was thumping heavily in her ears, and she felt a deep well of fear coldly spreading within her.

"You do understand, Miss Quinn? From today, I want you to stop hand-expressing of your milk after the feeds, in order to cut down the secretion. With the altered dosage of the red capsules, that will have the desired effect within a week. He won't be aware yet, of course, of any difference, and I want you to maintain your usual watchfulness. He is still to be fed the instant the need is expressed, as before, because he must come to the new experience totally unprepared. If there is any change now, it may partly invalidate the findings when we start the experiment properly."

He looked down at the papers on the desk in front of him. "Now, let me see those weight and physical development charts. Hmm. The weight gain spurts make a definite pattern, Barbara, you agree? No sign yet of any unevenness of growth. Interesting, though, the way the limb dimensions change? No regularity there. The right arm is clearly larger in the major muscle areas than the left, but it has appeared with a random pattern."

"He's right-handed." Isobel heard her own voice almost in surprise. Why had she told him that? She never told him anything she noticed, if she could help it, not without being directly asked. But he's not a thing, the little voice within her cried. He's a person! He's a right-handed *person.*

"Oh?" Dr. Briant looked up at her sharply. "You've noticed that? Very observant of you."

"Yes, sir," she said and lowered her eyes.

"Is there anything else of this nature you have recognized?"

"No, sir."

"Hmm. Why do you say there is a definite right-handedness?"

"Because of the way he always puts it out to me first. Sometimes it's the other one, but usually the right. And it's the one furthest away from me when I stand next his cot." She raised her eyes and looked at him. "He's very bright, and if it was as easy for him to use his left hand, he'd reach for me with it. But he doesn't. He's very bright."

"Indeed he is." He smiled thinly at her. "And so are you, to notice a piece of evidence of this sort, and correctly evaluate it. Clearly, working here with us is giving you a scientific turn of mind."

"Yes, sir," she said and looked down again, wanting to hit at his hateful cold face and narrow-lipped smile. Hateful, hateful, hateful man. Georgie's a person, not a thing you look at with turns of mind.

"So, you have it clear, what it is we want of you this week? No further expression of milk, but no changes from the infant's point of view. All his subjective experience must remain unaltered, er, he is to go on exactly as he always has."

She went to the lavatory before going into the nursery and sat perched on the lid of the pan with her hands firmly planted on each knee, staring at the pattern of cracks on the paintwork of the locked door. She had to be completely calm, completely herself, before going into the nursery and coming into the view of the monitoring cameras. She could never be really sure how much they actually watched her, but she knew the films were kept and looked at sooner or later, so she could take no chances. But here, for just a few moments, she could enjoy the relief of letting her face go, of letting her feelings come out properly.

She grimaced and clenched her teeth and shook her head violently from side to side, and then thumped each closed fist on her knees until the ache spread down toward her feet. Then, her teeth still clenched, she let a deep rumbling growl build up in her throat, quiet, yet strong enough to reverberate through her chest. And then she relaxed her whole body and let her head droop forward until her forehead was resting on her fists, still lying as they were on her knees.

She had worked out the ritual gradually over the past few days, and as usual, it soothed her, and she stood up and felt her face settle back into its normal calm lines, felt her body lose its tightness. Collectedly, she flushed the cistern and opened the door with a rattle before walking into the nursery. She washed her hands with care, feeling the camera above her head watching the process, and dried them and then rubbed in the antiseptic cream meticulously before walking over to the cot to look down at the baby.

He was sleeping, lying on his belly, his mouth lax and glistening above the damp patch on the muslin square under his head. He's been dribbling more lately. I wonder if they've noticed? I shan't tell them. I think he's going to cut a tooth soon, but I shan't tell them. He's advanced enough to start cutting teeth as early as five weeks of age. Not that it's got anything to do with them, no matter what anyone says. He's just an advanced baby, that's all. And there's nothing that odd about it, there's been lots of babies cut teeth early. I read about a baby born with two teeth already cut, didn't I, once?

She sat down in the chair beside the cot and picked up the crochet she had started at the weekend. A bonnet it was, and when she'd started it, she'd thought, What does he want a bonnet for, poor little scrap? It's not as though he ever goes out of the place, ever goes on nice little walks in a pram like other babies. What's he want a bonnet for? But she'd fancied doing one, so she'd started it. It was a complicated pattern, and she was enjoying it.

And maybe, Georgie, we'll be glad of it, what do you say? she asked him as he slept there beside her, her lips quietly folded closed and her eyes fixed on her work. Maybe we will be one of these days. There's the rompers, as well, and the little jackets. And those boots and mittens I made out of the material left over from the rompers. The thing is, can I get at them? I've tried to work out if the cameras can see the door, but it's very hard, the way they can move them around from downstairs. There must be some way of working it out, though. Some way to get the things where I might want them to be.

She let herself look at the baby while still keeping her head industriously bent over the bonnet. Don't you worry, my lovely. Don't you fret yourself. Isobel won't let them do anything to you, I promise you. Just you go on the way you are, my lovey, and we'll soon show them. We'll see if it's really going to be like they said, like he said, and if it is, your Isobel won't let them. Don't you fret you, George, my lovey . . .

They sent up cheese and biscuits with her supper that night, and she ate in her own room, safe from observation. But the cheese and the biscuits she did not eat, wrapping them neatly in a white handkerchief and then putting them tidily into her bedside table drawer. She wasn't quite sure there was any real reason for doing it, but it made her feel better, somehow, made her most secret thinking seem that much more interesting.

Mike sat waiting for Briant, his long legs sprawled in front of him, for the first time in a month feeling as relaxed as he looked. To get the chance to do a piece of his own sort would go a long way to restoring his self-esteem. It had been hell, the long and so far useless search for the girl. He had been so sure the orderly would be the key, and tedious though it had been to hang about the hospital gates like any legman, he hadn't minded too much.

But then when he had managed to spot her, walking out wrapped in a dingy brown coat, her head tied up in a scarf decorated with horses' heads, had asked her her name, and realized he'd guessed right (she looked so exactly the sort of woman who would write letters to Problem Page Aunties), only to discover she was as much use as a sick headache, then he had hit bottom.

At first he had thought she was being stubborn, putting on a performance of stupidity in an attempt to extract money from the *Echo* for the information she had, but when not even the sight of two new five-pound notes on the stained tablecloth on the café where he had been giving her eggs and chips and stewed brown tea had any effect, he had had to accept it. She had genuinely forgotten the girl's name.

"I'm ever so sorry, really, sir, I'm ever so sorry. I never was much of a one for names, like. I can tell you what she looked like. Pretty she was, with blue eyes, and—"

"You've already told me all that." Mike had tried not to show his irritation with her bovine idiocy. "But it's her name I need to know, so that I can find her address and talk to her. Look, there must be *some* place in the hospital where there's a record. She had charts and things, I imagine."

"Oh, yes, sir. Notes. Green folders for Miss Guttner, and yellow ones for Mr. Jeffcoate, and blue ones for—"

"Well, couldn't you just go and look up the notes for me? They'd have her name *and* address, come to that."

She shook her head dolefully. "But you have to have the name and number to get them. I go over to Records, see. It's over by the Path Lab, next to the Pharmacy, the blue-painted door you have to use, not the other one, that's for the girls what work in Records, and you go up to the counter, and you give them the paper with the name and number on it—Sister always gives me a paper, see, because I never was much of a one for names—and then they go and get the notes and put them in an envelope all stuck down, because notes are special, you see, and then I take them back to Sister. I'm really sorry, sir, I'd tell you if I knew, because I was that worried about her and her sweet little baby. And it's all right, now, isn't it? Sister said to everyone it was all right. I never let on it was me wrote a letter about it. Sister was that mad, she'd have gone on and on at me. But she said it was all right, the baby was in good hands, and everything, told everyone in the ward, she did. Not the patients, I mean, just us, the staff, like, and so I thought, Well, it's all right."

After that he'd tried getting at some of the nurses, was desperate enough to accost almost anyone leaving the hospital who looked as though they might be staff, and he'd drawn a blank every time. It was incredible how close the bastards were. Someone has put the fear of God into that place, he'd thought, trying to direct his anger away from himself. But it hadn't helped. To fail so abysmally at a simple piece of journalistic skill like tracking down a source of information, that had hurt, following on what he still regarded as his failure to make his mark on the Gerrard program. That he had failed was undoubted. Not a single television offer had come in from anywhere as a result, let alone from Gerrard himself.

And it hadn't been easy to tell Sefton he'd failed, either. The Old Man had behaved surprisingly well, Mike had thought suspiciously, not producing the sort of thinly veiled hostility with which he still treated Graham, and that had made it worse. Mike had been quite prepared to tell Sefton where he could put his stinking job, been prepared to take his chances on getting another reasonable berth on the Street, even been prepared to risk having to give up journalism altogether. But it hadn't been necessary.

"Look, why are you being so reasonable about this?" Mike had asked him bluntly, leaning on the spurious courage of the two double whiskies he'd swallowed before going up to see the Old Man. "You sent me to get a story, and I fell down. I expected you to raise merry hell—"

"If you expected that, your understanding of my attitude is very limited," Sir Daniel had said dryly. "I am not given to raising any sort of fracas at any time, under any provocation. I am a reasonable man. I don't deny I am extremely disappointed—extremely. But I have a high regard for your ability and I am rarely wrong in my judgments of the personnel I employ. So, if you tell me you are having difficulty in finding this girl, then I must be patient. Clearly the difficulties are very real, but you will overcome them eventually. In the meantime, you had better concentrate on Briant. I must tell you—and this is strictly for your ears and yours alone at this stage—that we have come to an advantageous arrangement with him. And part of it is that you should handle all the interviews he has consented to give us, and have all the agreed access to the child."

"I see!" Mike had relaxed then as the pieces fell into place. "Briant will play it your way, on the understanding that he deals with a man who speaks his language, is that it? He likes me better than any of the other people he's had to talk to?"

"There is no special virtue in you that makes this so," Sir Daniel had said sharply. "It reflects, rather, credit on the *Echo* that we had the wit to find a raw man who happened to have a scientific background and train him into the sort of journalist a man like Briant can work with. And having invested so much effort in training you, we are now ready to reap the benefits. Now, as I said, I still expect to get a story on the girl from you, and still expect you to try to contact her. But in the interim, we need some hard background stuff on Briant and his immediate plans for the future of his work. I have arranged that you see him tomorrow at three P.M. Don't be late. And file copy immediately after completing the interview. Good afternoon, Bridges."

But, secure in the knowledge that Sefton needed him more than he needed Sefton at the moment, Mike had pushed his advantage and prised out of the Old Man some more information about the "advantageous arrangement" with Briant. And he had gone away feeling curiously uncomfortable about it. Was it the whisky he had drunk, or the mixed sense of failure and triumph about the way his work was going, or the way that Sefton was handling Briant, that made him feel so? He didn't know, but he wasn't comfortable.

And relaxed though he now felt, waiting for Briant, enough of the discomfort lingered to make him, when Briant came into the room, greet the man with a brusquerie he hadn't intended, added as it was to a sharp surge of embarrassment at the sight of his tired face. He looks ten years older than he did at the press conference, Mike thought with sudden compassion.

"Good afternoon," George said and sat down and looked at Mike with a thin smile. A good man, none of that sickening effusiveness about him that made so many newspaper people obnoxious, he thought. And then he spoke in his usual dry manner.

"Before we go any further this afternoon, I want to be absolutely sure you've got the arrangement clear in your head. Until the child is a year old, none of these pictures you get are to be published. Without that guarantee the whole thing is off. I've got to avoid any possible damage to the project during this very sensitive first year. Nor is the baby to be . . . to be exploited commercially in any way until then."

He frowned sharply and then went on a little painfully. "I still hate the whole thing, that he will be used commercially. But I'm over a barrel."

It was suddenly important to George that this man should understand that. From the time he had first met him at the press conference he had felt a respect for him, journalist though he was, and he still had it. The man was a scientist too, albeit a non-working one, and the sympathy of fellow scientists was necessary to George. For all he was a man with a clear view of his goal and was not given to considering in much depth the ethical views outsiders might hold about his work, he was well aware that the ethical problem existed. But as long as other people in his field reconized his integrity, he could ride over the mewing doubts of people like Gerrard and his ilk.

"I know perfectly well how you must feel about it," Mike said. "In your shoes I'd be sick. You shouldn't have to depend on the money of men like Sefton to do your job. But at the same time, I think it's vital that science shouldn't operate in secret. People, even the dimmest of them, have a right to know what's going on. If I didn't believe that, I couldn't do the job I do. All I want out of you is facts, facts about what you're doing, how you're doing it, and above all *why*. I'll write them up as honestly as I can, and that will give Sefton pretty good value for his money, without splashing the infant over advertisements for baby foods."

He laughed a little bitterly. "My God, it will! He's tied me up pretty tightly too. He's got all rights in every word I write for the *Echo* on your project. He'll resell every piece I produce to Christ knows how many foreign papers and magazines. He'll recoup his investment in you one way or another, while I'll go on getting a living wage and have to settle for that."

"I'm glad you appreciate my difficulties," George said, and there was genuine relief in his voice. "Not everyone would. And that brings up another point. Sefton has agreed that his financial involvement shall be kept quiet. That's part of our deal. He's told you that?"

"He's told me," Mike said and grinned suddenly. "You needn't worry on that score. It's as much to his benefit as yours to keep it under wraps. If it gets out that he's bought the baby—sorry, I mean invested in your project—it'll throw doubt on anything the *Echo* publishes. It's important to him that it should appear the *Echo* is non-partisan, free, fearless, honest, probing, the usual crap. When the paper runs my stuff on your work, every other paper on the Street'll spit. But if they find out how I got access, they'll make mincemeat of him. No, you needn't worry about that. It'll be the best kept secret ever, I promise you."

"Good. Now that we fully understand each other, we can get on. Tell me what you want, and I'll do my best to give it to you."

"Right." Mike leaned forward in his chair and switched on his tape recorder. "We'll use this instead of written notes, if you don't mind. Saves time. What I'd like to have today is a brief rundown on your plans for the next few months."

"A tall order. In which specific area?"

"Something that will make it possible for me to reiterate that the baby is at present living in a perfect environment. I've said it before, and I'd like the chance to say it again. This child is a fortunate one in many ways."

"If you can tell your readers that, I'll be very happy," George said a little sardonically. "I'm not swayed by public opinion to any great extent, but the horror in which I would appear to be held by a section of the public does . . . irritate sometimes."

"I'll tell them," Mike said. "And where you go from here. Or will it be possible to maintain this perfection for a long time?"

"No, not for much longer. We're about to embark on phase two. Now we know that this infant has the temperament we thought he would have, that he has shown no aggression, both because he lacks aggression-making genes and because he hasn't needed to, we can demonstrate the effect of environment on creating aggression. It is aggression that I'm particularly interested in, you'll remember. I genuinely believe it will be possible to exclude dangerous aggressive behavior from human life when we recognize how it arises."

"I'll keep off that point, of course."

"Because of the ethical arguments? How will the work be applied, *should* it be applied, and the rest of that?" George bit the words back and then let his irritation burst out. "For Christ's sake, what do these bloody people want of me? When will they see that I can't fritter away my mental energies on questions of this sort? When Euclid organized geometry, did we have to stop and think that it would lead to . . . to navigation and gunnery, that they in their turn would lead to exploitation of primitive peoples and weapons that could kill at a greater distance? If he had, he'd never have got past his first theorem. Did Pasteur have to fear that his work might lead to a human ability to control killing diseases, and ultimately to the sort of death control that has brought us to the brink of overpopulating this planet with one species? When scientists have to think in that way, they emasculate themselves. Is that what these puking little moaners want?"

He stood up suddenly and began to walk about the room restlessly.

"Someone once said that Time is the destroyer, the eternal leveler, constantly trying to break everything down to its basic elements. That man is constantly fighting the ravages of Time, trying to build up what it breaks down. But the longer I live, the more I see that man is as blind and as unthinking as Time itself. Will there always be these attempts to hold back on genuine progress? Must people like me always be dragged down to the lowest common denominator of timorous spirits? Why can't they be glad they have us? Even the superstitious religious brigade should be able to do that. That was the one really useful thing that man Gerrard said, that my ability to work as I do is as God-given as anything else. If little men need such reassurances as they find in blind belief in unprovable entities that they think guide their silly little lives, then why can't they accept and believe in the value—the clearly demonstrable value—of what science does? I am not unintelligent, but I will never, never be able to comprehend these idiotic people—"

"Because they don't think in a comprehensible way," Mike said. "Not in your sense, that is. You assume that because you think with logic, that everyone else could if they wanted to, that all that is needed is the willingness to do so. Well, it isn't. Very few people have minds that operate like yours, and if you wait until the sun falls into the English Channel, you'll never understand them, and they'll never understand you. But you'll win. Scientists always have, and they always will."

"It's a small comfort at the moment," George said bleakly and sat down again. He rubbed his face wearily then and produced another of his thin smiles.

"This sort of polemic production is getting to be a bad habit. I find myself making speeches about science when I needn't. Instead of getting on with what we're here for, I let myself be carried off into . . . into pointless perorations."

"When you use words so elegantly, you make me fear for my future, Dr. Briant," Mike said, a little maliciously.

"What? Oh." George laughed shortly. "Thank you. I am not entirely of one culture, you see. I have a smattering of the other side, for all I'm a scientist. But this really won't do. What was it we were talking about before I so ridiculously interrupted myself?"

"You said you were about to embark on phase two of your project."

"Yes. Phase two. Well, we must now try to establish how aggressive responses are created in individuals who do not have a genetically determined aggression quotient. So, the next step will be to expose the child to experiences that are known to be likely to cause such responses. We'll then be able to evaluate those influences, and thus teach people how to rear their offspring so that they do not expose them to the sort of stimuli that result in undesirable behavior."

He stopped and then went on a little diffidently. "Look, it is at this point that I may be laying myself open to charges of being . . . less than kind to the infant. In order to discover which experiences frustrate him sufficiently to cause aggressive responses, he'll have to be exposed to unpleasant ones. In a way, he'll suffer more from them than the infant who meets them from birth. You see that? It will mean that we will be deliberately grafting onto his genetic inheritance some of the very responses the work is ultimately designed to remove. But I can defend this. First, I can't get my results if I don't do it, and second, well, he won't be any worse off than any other person when he reaches adult life. We all show . . . well, certain forms of undesirable behavior which we demonstrate in response to the stimuli we meet. I have a foul temper, for example. I wasn't born with it, though I suspect, from study of my own family patterns, that I have inherited a fairly strong aggressive gene from somewhere. But it overtakes me very often because of obscure stimuli, obscure because I never really know what triggers it off, not in depth. I know that idiots anger me, but I don't know *why* they anger me. It isn't enough to say it's just because they're idiots. I feel, as a sentient human being, I should be able to avoid my upsurge of aggressive anger when it comes. Well, I can't. And this infant, as an adult, won't be able to either. But as I say, he won't be any worse off than you or I or any one of a million others. It will be later generations who will benefit from the work we're doing and not him."

"And you have a conscience about it. Is that it? You'd like to be able to produce your perfect individual from this infant, instead of using him to show how other infants can be made perfect. You want to have your cake and eat it?"

"That sounds extremely unscientific," George said after a moment, and then grimaced. "Damn it. You're right, of course. If I were to be completely honest, I'd admit I care about the opinions of others, even those woolly-minded idiots I so despise. To be a prophet in one's own time and country is never a position enjoying approbation. Is it? And I know—*know*, don't merely think—that what I'm doing is of inestimable value. That isn't arrogance. The knowledge is the result of clear logical thinking. I *know* the value of my work. I *know* it derives not from some special virtue in my conscious life but from the genetic makeup I have, that my ability to think as I do and work as I do is as inevitable a part of me as the color of my eyes or the shape of my nose. But I'm still human. Still want to be . . . be recognized for what I am. Still have a conscience. And when I think about that, I wonder how much my conscience derives from . . . from a true desire to behave in a genuinely scientific manner, and how much it is rooted in the more ignoble desire for the approbation of others. I have my dilemmas, you know."

There was a short silence, and then Mike said softly, "You are a remarkable man, Dr. Briant. Yet I pity you, deeply. May I say that without offending you? Without sounding—oh, I don't know—arrogant. Condescending. Whether you're right or wrong in your thinking, I'm not really qualified to judge. But I can judge you as another man, like me, and I'm bloody sorry for you. You've got a vision and it must hurt like hell to see it as you do. And, Christ, but you must be lonely! I'm just a second-rater, hung up on my stupid little personal problems, but at least they're comprehensible to other people if I want to share them. But who can you share yours with? Oh, hell, I'm sorry. I've no right to—"

"No, don't apologize. There's no need. In fact—" George smiled then, as awkwardly as a child. "Thank you. Your degree of understanding is a considerable comfort. And as for your being a second-rater, you do yourself an injustice. You may at the moment be doing second-rate work, but the fact that you're aware of it indicates you have a first-rate mind."

They sat and looked at each other solemnly for a moment, only the soft hissing of the tape recorder on the desk between them breaking the silence. And then Mike moved sharply and said, "Well, you were about to tell me of the way you were planning to handle phase two."

"Er, yes. Yes. Well, simply, we're going to expose him to frustration. He has reached the stage of being fully breast-fed for only three feeds a day. At midday he has ten minutes of suckling, the rest of his food being given by spoon—strained meats, fruits, and vegetables, and so on—the diet planned by one of the hospital dieticians. At one of these midday feeds he will be exposed to the sight of the breast and refused access to it for a period of time. We will measure how long he can tolerate the unfulfilled promise of food, see how long it takes him to cry. We will continue to do this at succeeding feeds until he displays aggrsssion towards his nurse, with whom he has already built a marked attachment. He'll show this, we expect, by fighting at the breast, to start with, in much the same way as most infants do. Throwing his limbs about, crying and then biting as he feeds, once he is allowed to."

"We've altered the hormone dosage to the nurse to diminish her milk production, and his breast feeds will eventually satisfy him less. This will show us to what extent he is able to channel his aggression. The question is, will he merely be aggressive and continue to be so, or will he accept the loss of a familiar satisfaction, seeking gratification from other sources? Will he take more of the offered spoon foods, and reject the breast altogether, or continue to fight for it? It is our belief that because of his high intelligence he will rapidly come to terms with his changed situation, and instead of continuing to display his anger, will accept the alternative of spoon foods ad lib. We may well find it possible to wean him completely from the breast before he reaches the age of twelve weeks."

"I can see why you're a little anxious about public opinion. On the face of it, it's rather an abrupt way to handle the child. I'll try to avoid making it seem too clinical a method of treating him when I write it up. Unless I can make readers see the thinking behind it, it would be pointless to describe it, anyway. I wonder . . ."

He paused and then said carefully, "Look, I know it's part of the deal that we talk only to you and don't go prying behind your back at your staff. But if I could interview the nurse, it might help. If she can tell me the baby copes well with the experiences, then I have no doubt I can convince my readers all is well."

"I doubt you'd get much out of her, frankly. She's doing a very good job, a very good job indeed—because of her own personality faults. Well, perhaps faults is hardly the word. The point is, she's a very simple soul. Warmly responsive to the baby, but to no one else. Not a woman who thinks very much at all. That's why she was selected. I wanted a nurse who was at the lowest possible level of intelligence compatible with an ability to carry out instructions. As I've said before, intelligent thinking modifies emotional responses. This woman responds directly to the infant, as is necessary for his welfare, because she is a non-thinker. You see that? So even if you interviewed her, you'd get no opinion from her, only monosyllables."

"Oh. A pity from my point of view, but I can see what you mean. Well, I suppose the only answer then is to report as I see. You'll permit me to observe?"

"Not directly, if you don't mind. I don't want to introduce a new face at this stage of the proceedings. He's an intelligent infant, remember, and may be distracted by too many people being present when we try the experiment. But you can certainly see the film we take rerun afterwards if you wish. Will that do?"

"Admirably. When do you propose to start?"

"Next week probably. There's no urgency about it, and I can wait that long. And for the next few days I must devote myself to administration." He produced a wintry smile. "Not that I mind on this occasion. Now I have some money at my disposal, I can get some new facilities I need—some more computer availability and so on—and pay my staff properly. And I have some personal needs to deal with too. I am without a car at the moment, for example, and must waste too much time using public transport when I go from here to the universities where we use computers."

And I've got to do something about Marjorie's income too, he thought suddenly. She's getting pressing about money, and if I'm not careful, she'll make trouble of some sort if I don't satisfy her. "If you call me next week, say on Monday, I'll make a definite arrangement for you."

Mike stood up and switched off the tape recorder. "Thank you. I've enough to get on with at the moment." He paused and then said in as casual a tone as he could, "There's just one more point. I'd like to get a background story from the . . . the baby's mother. Nothing personal, I assure you, none of this emotional stuff. But I've got to do a piece on the ethical aspects, and it would add weight to your point of view if she comes out on the same side. Do you see?"

George frowned sharply. "Oh, no. I'm sorry. I could not possibly put you in touch with her. Don't ask me again, please. I must be adamant on that."

Mike nodded heavily. "I expected as much. But I had to try. You see that?"

"Of course. You too have your dilemmas."

"My turn to thank you for understanding? Well, since we seem to be in such excellent rapport, I'll—and look, don't let Sefton know this, because he'd do his pieces, but if you like, I'll let you see my copy before I file it. I'll be honest with you. I'm offering this partly to help you—knowing what will be run in the paper will forearm you—but also to protect myself. It may happen that when the subeditors get their hot little hands on my stuff, they'll muck it about to please themselves. And, well, I wouldn't want you to think I was at fault if something you dislike appears."

"I appreciate that. Very much. I feel if there is one fortunate circumstance about this wretched deal your employer has made with me it is that I am at least dealing with a scientific mind. I feel rather happier than I did."

As he drove back to the office, Mike found himself wishing that he too could feel happier. He should, God knew. He'd got this difficult man virtually eating out of his hand, would get superb material for his pieces in the *Echo* that would help him redeem himself in his own eyes, restore some of his lost self-esteem. Why, then, did he feel so depressed? Wasn't it all going for him? He'd got his job safe in his pocket because of the quality of his working relationship with this man. Why should he feel so uneasy?

Perhaps I should have settled for teaching those snotty-nosed kids after all, he thought savagely as he drove at a vicious speed through the thickening evening traffic. All these bloody ethics give me mental indigestion.

11

"My dear, it will do you all the good in the world," Barbara said bracingly. "It should be a good party, and at your age you need parties. And really, you know, you should be flattered. Andrew Vernon is quite a sophisticated young man. And he's asked *you* to go with him."

And heaven help him if he lets her know I asked him to take her, she thought. But he's an easygoing type, and he wants to keep on the right side of me. He'll be safe enough.

"Well, if *you* think I should go," Hilary said, pleased. She must care for me, or she wouldn't be bothered whether I go or not.

"Of course I do! And that dress suits you. You look charming, and it would be a pity to waste the effort that went into getting ready, wouldn't it? And anyway," she added shrewdly, "your father would be hurt if he thought you didn't appreciate having something new to wear. It was one of the things that's pleased him most about having new funds—being able to give you a few things you need."

"Yes, of course, I know that. He's been like Santa Claus, hasn't he?" Hilary smiled then. "But such a careful Santa Claus! He said he was just giving me a salary in kind and to be sure and see it that way. I told him he doesn't have to, I mean, I don't want any salary, especially knowing funds are so tight."

"Not as tight as they were, fortunately," Barbara said. "So please him and go to this party, hmm? And it will be good for you, you know? All work and no play and all that."

The door opened, and Vernon put his head around it.

"Barbara, have you seen Hilary anywhere? Oh, *there* you are! I've been looking for you. Your father's working in the histology lab, and I didn't like to bother him. Are you ready? Er, you look very nice."

"Doesn't she?" Barbara said heartily. "Now, have fun, hmm? Have you a key? Good. Come in quietly, now. I'm going to persuade your father to have an early night—he's been overworking shockingly—so don't fall over the milk when you come back in the small hours."

They went in a small flurry, Vernon winking heavily at Barbara from behind Hilary's back, and then she was alone in the office, sitting at her desk and staring at the neat pile of papers that remained of her day's activities.

Would it work? Why not? He had seemed to enjoy that evening, eaten heartily, complimented her on her cooking, had seemed really relaxed. They had sat companionably listening to Hilary's chatter, and she had been able to watch him covertly, happy to see some of the weariness fall from him. The only irritation had been Hilary's presence, that evening.

And now Hilary had gone out, and her own efforts for the whole of the preceding week had ensured there was no backlog of work waiting to be done. It shouldn't be too difficult to persuade him.

She stood up abruptly and moved to the small mirror over the washbasin in the corner. Her hair looked fine, even though she hadn't had time for a visit to the hairdresser, and the dark red of her new suit made her look—what? Attractive? She peered at herself closely. Well, she mightn't be a beauty, but she was a damned sight younger than Marjorie, for all her elegant good looks. And she was here, not sitting in sulky loneliness in an empty house. And George showed no signs of missing her, did he? None of the appearances of a man suffering from the loss of a wife he cared about. So there's no reason for me to feel in the wrong about making the most of my opportunities, is there? None at all. And he, he's so . . . Who is there who cares about him as I do?

She grimaced at herself in the mirror and, moving with a determination she wasn't really feeling, went out of the room and across the corridor to the histology laboratory, pushing the door open gently.

He was sitting hunched over the microscope, the light from the lamp on the bench throwing his nose and jaw into sharp profile, and she felt again the sudden surge of excitement that was becoming so achingly familiar. How could she have left him? she wondered again. How could she possibly not want to keep him, a man like this, so totally complete a man, with his fine mind and his tightly controlled body and . . .

He looked up and smiled fleetingly. "Oh, Barbara. Were you looking for me? I was just checking the slides on the earlier chromosome patterns. There's no doubt we were accurate, you know, none at all."

"Hilary asked me to say good night to you," Barbara said. "She's gone to that party with young Vernon, you know. She was so excited about it. I'm sure she'll enjoy herself."

He stretched and turned his swivel stool to face her. "Oh, good. I'm glad she has. Needs to get out a bit, poor child. It's been a dreary business for her, I imagine, cooped up here. It was kind of Vernon to ask her. Most kind. I hadn't thought, really, that he'd—well, you know how it is! One doesn't notice one's children growing up, but she isn't really a child any more, is she?"

"Far from it," Barbara said and moved across the room to lean against the bench beside him. "A delightful girl."

"I'm really most grateful to you, Barbara. Most grateful. The life she leads, well, she needs the interest of a woman, doesn't she? I've not much experience of girls of her age, and I do appreciate the interest you take in her welfare. So does she. She seems most attached to you, most attached."

"There's no need to be grateful. Really. I'm happy to keep an eye on her, you know? I"—she swallowed—"I keep an eye on both of you."

"Both of us?"

"Yes. You're overworking, you know. You need to get out a little too. You never relax."

"Oh, don't worry about me. I'm perfectly content. Now there's some more money, life is a lot easier. And if we hold on a little longer, surely the fuss will die down, and we'll be able to get on with the job in peace."

"All the same, you look tired." Barbara looked at his face and then dropped her eyes in confusion. It wasn't easy to keep a light tone to her voice. "Look, George, there's no urgent work to be done, and as Hilary is out, you've no one to prepare a meal for you."

"A meal? Oh, I daresay Hilary's left something up there."

"And when I heard Hilary was going out with young Vernon, I made up my mind you'd have an evening off too! Now you've sampled my cooking, you know what I can do, and I thought—Well, would you care to risk it again? I've a splendid steak just waiting to be grilled, and, er, a ripe Camembert . . ." Her voice trailed away. "And there's a rather pleasant concert on the radio this evening. I thought perhaps—"

"Oh!" He looked up at her and smiled again. "That was a most kind thought, most kind! But really, you know, I can't trespass on your hospitality again! You've already been more than generous. That was a most pleasant evening you gave us, and I can't let you—"

"But I enjoyed the evening too," Barbara said quickly. "I, er, enjoy cooking, you know? And it isn't often I get the opportunity to try my small skill on someone else. It would be, er, fun for me too if you'd come. I mean, if it would bore you—seeing me here all day, of course, you might prefer to spend the evening alone—but I just thought—"

"Oh, not at all, not at all! You're very good company. It isn't that, I assure you. I just don't want to impose on you."

"If I thought it an imposition, I wouldn't suggest it, really I wouldn't. But I'm finding so much interest in . . . in this project, and it would be such a pleasure to have an opportunity to talk about it without the constant interruptions we always get here. What with the others, and the telephone, and the monitors, I just thought it would be rather pleasant to relax and talk over a meal, you know? And you *do* need to get away from the Unit sometimes, really you do."

"Well, well, all right. Thank you very much. I'd just like to complete the checks on this series. That'll take, oh, half an hour or so."

"Fine! I'll go home then and get the grill going. You remember how to get there? And you'll be able to park the car without any trouble. There's that side road, beside the pub, do you remember? I, er, I'll expect you in about an hour, then."

"In an hour. Yes. That'll be fine. Yes. Most kind of you." He smiled at her again and turned back to the microscope.

She went to the door and then stopped as she opened it. "How do you like your steak? It's a porterhouse."

"What? Oh, as it comes, as it comes. I leave that to you. I'm sure it will be delightful, however you do it."

Outside she leaned against the door for a moment, breathing a little deeply. She really wasn't used to this sort of thing, not in the least. But it had worked very well, hadn't it? And now she had the long evening to look forward to, without Hilary, without any of the maddening interruptions that starred every day in the Unit. Just herself and George. At this moment in time Barbara was sure she was the most contented woman in London.

And now what do I do? Hilary thought bleakly. I can't just go back, not at half past nine. Daddy will know I had a miserable time, and that'll upset him. And it's not as though Barbara will be there. She must have gone by now. And even if she were, how could I let her know I was so silly? She'd think me a total washout. She was so pleased I was going . . .

Her eyes filled with sudden tears and she sniffed heavily and tucked her head down into her coat collar as she hurried along the narrow street, past the ugly little terraced houses, toward the main road winking its lights far ahead. If Barbara knew what a horrible party it had turned out to be, would she still think her a washout? Wouldn't she understand? She'd find out eventually, anyway. It was certain that awful Andrew Vernon would tell her how childish she'd been.

And it *had* been a horrible party. The crowded room, so dark she had only just been able to see the people crushed together, all talking at the tops of their voices over the thumping noise of the record player, so heavy with cigarette smoke that it made her eyes sting and water. Andrew had pushed his way in and shouted at someone, "Mandy! Mandy, I brought a girl, OK? Hilary, this is Mandy. It's her party. And this is Gary, Linda, Liz, Beaky, this is Hilary. Here, give her a drink, someone. And hey, Marilyn, I want you . . ." And he'd gone plunging away from her into the mob, leaving her standing helpless and dumb against the wall.

A girl in a clinging trouser suit, tinkling with beads, her hair trailing over eyes made up with heavy black lines around them, had put a filled tumbler into her hand and said vaguely, "Hi, glad you could come. Meet the crowd. There's some food somewhere, I think, over the other side. Help yourself." And then she too had gone away, and Hilary had sipped the drink, which tasted warm and sour and horrible, and felt utterly miserable. People were dancing, gyrating in a sort of writhing glassy-eyed, empty-faced trance that bore no relationship at all to the sort of dancing she had learned on Saturday evenings at school, when the boys from St. Philip's had come with their polished blue suits and damply eager hands to steer the seniors around under Matron's watchful eyes.

And the noise had increased, and the smoke had thickened, and then she had seen the people on the couches against the walls of the dark room, writhing and gyrating much like the dancers, but in couples and not by themselves, and hated herself for the way they made her feel. Sickened by the absorption they showed, but angry because she wasn't on one of the couches herself, revolted and fascinated, embarrassed and curious, all at the same time. A horrible feeling.

And then Andrew had come back to her and cried above the noise, "Dance? This is a great beat, hmm? Nice crowd, this lot. Don't you think so? From the University, most of them. But Mandy's Slade. They're a wild crowd, the Slade people. Great. Come on, we'll dance."

And she had shaken her head suddenly and said, "Oh, no, please, I— Would you mind if I just went? I've got a frightful headache, you know, and I can get back on my own, really. No need for you . . ." And she had shoved the drink she was clutching into his hand and plunged out of the room to grab her coat from the pile heaped on the banisters, and gone running down the stairs, trying to pretend she hadn't noticed the fleeting look of relief on Andrew Vernon's face when he'd said, "Oh, really? I'm sorry. Well, if you're sure . . ."

The air had smelled clean and good, and she had gone hurrying away down the street, wanting to cry like a baby. Sixteen, and still crying at the least thing. It was awful. At least Ian didn't know. He'd be hateful about it if he knew how she'd run out on the party. Just the sort of party he'd go to, she was sure of that. Oh, if only she could see Barbara. She'd understand. Wouldn't she?

She reached the main road and stood on the edge of the pavement, blinking a little at the brightness of the sodium lights and the shop fronts, and thought again, What do I do now? I can't go back now. Not at half past nine.

I'll walk. Just for a while. Then maybe I'll have a cup of coffee somewhere, and then it'll be late enough to go back. That's what I'll do.

She hadn't realized that she was paying any attention to the things she passed as she walked, until the name leapt out at her.

"The Briant Project," the poster shrieked in heavy blue print against a white background. And then in smaller letters: "Where Does God Stand? Come and Hear the Word of God Crying in the Wilderness of Science. Bear Your Witness for God Tonight. Eight-Thirty. Herringay Arena. Friday, November Seventeenth. Speakers. Joel B. Wayne, Pastor, The International Tabernacle of World Evangelization. Mary Esther Collins, Deaconess, The Evangelical Temple, New Jersey, USA. Silver Collection. Let God Speak to YOU Tonight."

There were more of the same posters, marching away from her in a perfect diminishing perspective, and seeing her own name repeated over and over again comforted her, made her feel real again, worth while, soothed some of the hurt of her failure to fit into the party. She walked briskly with her head held up, alongside the wall on which the posters were hung, until they curved away toward the entrance of a big building on her left.

She stopped for a moment and peered curiously at the brightly lit entrance and then, impulsively, turned toward it and went in. Why not? She had an hour to kill, at least, and it would be interesting perhaps. Something to tell her father and Barbara tomorrow.

She began to fabricate a story. A dull party, really—all those exaggerated art school people. And she had noticed the posters on her way there and decided it would be fun to slip out of the party and go and find out what these absurd religion types had to say. She could see herself telling them, sharing the deliciousness of a joke only she and they—Barbara—could really appreciate.

The place was full, incredibly full. She stood in the big entranceway, letting her eye be carried upward from tier to tier, all full of people, gray people. That was the most noticeable thing, the lack of color. When she concentrated, she could see splashes of red and blue, in people's coats, in the hats so many of the women seemed to be wearing, but the overall impression was of drab greenish gray. As though the colors of individual clothes had taken on their surroundings to become nothing.

And then she let her eyes move away, toward the center, and there was a brilliantly lit stage with a row of chairs on it, and more gray people. One of them was standing at a high pulpit-shaped desk in the center, shouting into a microphone, and she strained her ears to hear clearly, but there was just a booming echoing sound that swallowed the words the woman at the tall desk was saying.

"Welcome, sister."

She turned her head and saw a young man beside her, his face creased with a wide smile, his hand held out, and she blinked.

"I beg your pardon?"

"Welcome to you, sister," he said softly in what she now recognized as an American accent, and then as a shout suddenly went up from the audience, he raised his voice above the noise. "Come and sit down among friends. We are glad indeed to see you and have you visit with us."

He put his hand on her arm, and bemused, she let him lead her down an aisle toward a seat halfway down the serried tiers. Several people had to stand up to let her pass to the empty place, and she shrank slightly as each of them touched her gently as she went by, at the smiles they gave her, as though they knew her.

And then she was sitting, her elbows held tautly close to her sides, and she let her eyes slide sideways at the people on each side and felt oddly relieved, for they were no longer smiling at her but staring at the stage, their eyes curiously bright and yet blank. There was a middle-aged woman immediately on her left, and her mouth was hanging slightly open, the lips gleaming wetly, and repelled, Hilary looked at the stage too: anywhere rather than at the expression of eager fascination on the face beside her.

It was odd, the difficulty she found in hearing what the woman down there was saying. The boom of the microphone, the slight delay as the words tumbled over one another from amplifiers in different parts of the arena, all combined to create a curiously hypnotic effect; and the place was coldly stuffy, chilly enough for her to need the heaviness of her coat, but oppressive, the air smelling of greasily dirty human hair and carbolic disinfectant and dampness.

She tried to concentrate, to pick sense out of the words booming at her, but she couldn't, somehow. All she could concentrate on was the need to keep her body as small as possible so that she had no physical contact with her neighbors, and her knees shook slightly as she held them close together.

She began to feel a little lightheaded. I should have eaten something at that party, she thought suddenly. I had no lunch, I was so nervous about it, and I'm hungry. And cold. I wish I hadn't come in here. I wish I hadn't gone out with Andrew Vernon. I wish Barbara were here.

She sat and stared numbly at the woman on the stage and tried again to listen to what she was saying.

". . . and those of us who give our witness for God and Christ Jesus—Christ Jesus—Christ Jesus"—the words echoed, making a little song inside Hilary's head—"shall know the joys of total love —total love—total love . . ."

Pregnant pauses, Hilary thought, absurdly. That's why the echo comes. She makes pregnant pauses and they fill up with words, that's why they're called pregnant. And she wanted to giggle suddenly, feeling unexpectedly better. She still had the rather remote lightheaded feeling, but it wasn't quite so disagreeable now.

The woman on the stage threw her arms up sharply and cried in an even louder voice so that the microphone crackled as well as boomed. "Who will bear witness with me tonight? Who will fight the evil that is in men's hearts? Who will love Christ Jesus with me tonight?—tonight?—tonight?"

And again a shout went up from the audience, rolling heavily around the tight-packed tiers, and Hilary found herself shouting too, not because she wanted to, but because somehow she couldn't stop it. It came from her like a sneeze, one of those violently satisfying sneezes that made her body feel good, relaxed. And the man on the other side of her turned and smiled widely at her, and she smiled back, involuntarily, and then, realizing she had relaxed so that her knee was touching his, she tightened her body again and shrank back inside herself.

But she really was feeling much more comfortable now, not so cold, not so lonely. It was curiously comforting, being part of this huge crowd of people. After the weeks of being encapsulated in the Unit, constantly aware of herself as an individual, of the individuality of the other people there, her father, Barbara, to be one of this anonymous mass was like being wrapped in a thick soft blanket.

She became aware of the silence that had fallen and looked back at the stage expectantly, realizing without surprise that the sense of expectation was a shared one, that the rest of the audience was feeling it too.

The woman who had been standing at the tall central desk had sat down, and a tall man at the end of the row of chairs behind her stirred and then stood up, and then from somewhere far at the back of the big echoing arena, so far back that it seemed to come from the uppermost tier immediately below the green metal rafters of the arched roof, a ragged chant started, and Hilary turned her head to look upward.

The rows of people were swaying patchily, but even as she looked, the swaying became more even, until the whole vast hillside of blurred faces seemed to be moved by a wave of wind blowing over it, and the chant too became more definite, more musical.

"Joel, Joel, Jo-*el*, Jo-*el*, Jo-*el*." The sound lifted, became more rhythmic, until Hilary felt the beat of it moving her own body, and she too was swaying. Or was it just the sound that swayed her? The people on each side of her were swaying too, and she was forced to move with them; yet the chanting moved her from within, somehow, echoing inside her head, and then she realized her own lips were moving in time to the keening cry. "Jo-*el*, Jo-*el*, Jo-*el*."

The man on the stage moved forward to the dais, stood with his head held upward, his hands on each side of the desk, and then he held them up, his arms spread wide, and immediately, as though a switch had been thrown, the chanting stopped, and the audience stopped swaying, and a silence fell, so thick that Hilary heard it filling her ears with a high ringing note.

"My dearly beloved brethren, my sisters, my brothers, my beloved in God . . ."

It was a low voice, but so clear that there was no echo; every minute sound could be heard, the crisp consonants, the gentle hiss of the sibilants, and Hilary felt a shiver move through her as she stared at the figure on the stage before her. Even from her distance she could see his eyes, a clear pellucid green with the pupils so large that she could see the darkness of them, and he seemed to be looking directly at her, and she wanted to look away, embarrassed, but she couldn't. The face was so strong in its square handsomeness, the white hair above it so thick and springing in the bright lights, the eyes so compellingly wide and green and—what was it? *Knowing*. It was as though he knew why she was here, knew how horrible the party from which she had fled had been, as though he were whispering to her, "It doesn't matter. It doesn't matter."

And then he was speaking again, his gentle low voice filling the great space of the arena, filling her own body with a warmth she found deeply soothing.

"I speak to you of God, I speak to you from God, I speak to you through God. God that lies within me speaking to God within you. Open your hearts and fear no more. Let God move within you and answer me. Open yourselves to the greater good that lies above and below and about us all. Merge with me and love, the love that is God, and hear the words He has bid me speak unto you. Open thou thine ears to the voice that yearns to cry from you to me, to the small still voice that cries deep within your own hearts, ye beloved children of the great and loving and awesome Truth that is the everliving God."

As she stared at him, at the white head thrown up, the line of the jaw below the moving lips, her surroundings seemed to dwindle into nothingness, until she was aware of only the figure before her, dwarfed by distance yet filling her total viewpoint. She felt the warmth grow within her, felt as though she too were bathed in the nimbus of light that seemed to surround him.

With a part of her mind she recognized that the lighting had changed, that the illumination that had filled the arena had dimmed to darkness, that only a single glowing amber spotlight was still burning, outlining the figure of the man before her, and she realized that it was this as much as what he was saying that made her feel so removed from herself, as though she were there in the amber pool with him, just the two of them together. But even though she knew why she felt so, it made no difference. She was part of him, part of his voice, as well as part of the whole great crowd about her.

"The evil that is in some men, the free will that is the gift and the burden that God has laid upon His beloved children, that evil must be fought by us for God. We shall not take unto ourselves the giving of life. God forbids us to take life, for only God can create life. God forbids us to change life, forbids forward men from creating man in man's image, for God made man, God made us in His own image, and the evil men are the instruments of the evil one that is Satan. They seek to destroy mankind by creating men in Satan's image, and we must fight the good fight against the evil of Satan with all the strength that God has given unto us."

She stared at him, feeling herself pulled toward him, leaning forward with an eagerness that tensed every muscle, and the light about his head lightened, changed from amber to a warm rose-colored glow that gave his body a new halo that seemed to sparkle.

"O my beloved ones, beware, beware the sin of man, the depths of evil that lie in men's hearts! As we are one with God, so are we one with all mankind. The evil that lies in the scientists' laboratories lies in our own homes, at our own hearths. Think not that you can escape it by turning your backs upon it. Remember the truth that a man of God has told us: No man is an island unto himself; the bell that rings of everlasting death rings for thee, for me, for all of us. We must fight the evils of the man Briant, the Antichrist who so hates man that he takes to himself the right to destroy God's greatest creation, mankind itself. In those sinful hands lies a little child, a little child created in evil, for evil purposes. Fight the blackness of that sin, fight the wickedness of the destroyers, join me in the struggle to bring God's love back to the world that has spurned it."

The coldness had come back, had stripped away the comfort of the crowd, and she felt herself shivering, could hear her own teeth chattering, felt fear rising in her. The words were running in her head, over and over again: the evils of the man Briant, the evils of the man Briant.

It was as though the sound of her own name had been a trigger. Just as seeing it written on the posters outside had made her feel better, now hearing it spoken in those soft low tones made her feel frightened. What was he saying, this beautiful man with the green eyes and the rose-colored nimbus around him? Was it her father he was speaking of? The scientists, were they Barbara and her father?

Was it herself he was saying was evil and wicked, a destroyer?

She hardly realized she was moving until she reached the end of the row and had plunged past startled people to stand shaking in the aisle, and then the young man with the wide smile was standing there, holding out a dish toward her.

She stared at it, stupidly, heard the words coming from the amplifiers around her: "It will be a long fight, a hard fight, and we must fight it with all the weapons of the age. We must publish the word of God, in books, in leaflets, in newspapers and on television. And for this we need the money that opens the doors to these pulpits from which the word of God can be spread. Give of your hearts, my brethren, and give also of your wealth, however small, however great. Sacrifice must be made if the war against evil is to be waged."

She looked away, staring around her, and saw other young men, all holding wooden dishes, moving down the aisles and along the front, and money was tinkling into the bowls as people reached for the dishes, passed them along eagerly from hand to hand, and the young man in front of her moved closer, held his dish nearer to her invitingly, and she shook her head and shouted, "No! No, it isn't true. No!" And she pushed past him to run along the aisle to the big doorway, running until she reached the street, to stand there gulping in an effort to catch her breath.

She was still shaking, and for a moment she didn't know what to do, so bewildered was she by the tumult of confused feeling that filled her, and then she saw the row of taxis standing on the far side of the road and plunged across toward it. She'd go back, tell her father, tell Barbara, make them do something to stop that white-headed green-eyed man in there.

" 'Ere, watch it, ducks! You'll get to 'eaven a sight sooner 'n you expected, you go running through the traffic like that."

She blinked, staring at the man who was leaning out of the driver's seat of the first taxi in the row, and said stupidly, "What? What did you say?"

"I said—'ere, you look rough, ducky. You all right? Someone been gettin' at you? What's the matter?"

She shook her head. "I—nothing. Nothing. I've just got to get, got to go back, right away."

"You sure you don't want no 'elp? If someone's been trying to get at you . . ." The driver got out of the taxi and took her arm. "Want me to call the law for you?"

"No, no, it's all right. Just take me to—"

"Where, ducks? Home? Just tell me where, and we'll get you there in no time."

She blinked at him again and stopped. Barbara. It was Barbara she had to tell first. Barbara who would understand best. Daddy might—no, it had to be Barbara.

"Mildmay, Mildmay House, Concord Street. Yes, that's the address. Top flat, Mildmay House in Concord Street."

"Off the 'Olloway Road? I know, ducky. OK, then, 'op in. Soon 'ave you back with your mum."

By the time the taxi drew up at the door of the narrow block of flats, she had the money ready in her hand, three half-crowns, and she thrust it at the driver, who called after her, "Want me to wait till you get in, ducks?" But she ignored him and pushed against the main door, and then she was running up the two flights of linoleum-covered stairs, past the heavy closed doors of other flats, until she reached the top floor.

"Barbara. Barbara." She banged the knocker hard and then, unable to wait, banged it again, leaning against the wall breathlessly, and then knocked yet again, feeling tears on her face, and still shaking, reached once more for the knocker over the narrow flap of the letter box.

The door opened sharply, and when she saw Barbara's face peering around it, she pushed against the panels and said breathlessly, "Oh, thank God you're here. Thank God. I've got to tell you—please, I've got to tell you."

She hardly looked at Barbara until she was inside and leaning against the wall of the narrow foyer, and then as she took a deep shuddering breath, saw that Barbara was clutching a thin dressing gown around her, that her hair was rumpled, and her face set in a sort of furious rigidity.

"What the hell?" Barbara said, and Hilary felt her own face crumple and the tears fill her nose so that she had to swallow.

"Oh, Barbara, I'm so sorry. I had to come and tell you. It was awful, I just had to, and I never thought you'd have gone to bed. Oh, I'm sorry, Barbara."

And she put her arms out toward her, and Barbara pulled back, and then a door at the end of the foyer opened, and Hilary turned her head.

Her father was standing there, his hair as rumpled as Barbara's and his bare feet thrust into his unlaced shoes. He was wearing a skimpy green bathrobe, his naked legs emerging from it ludicrously, and Hilary stood very still, staring at him with her mouth slightly open, her face blank with surprise.

They spoke together, and she turned her head from one to the other, trying to understand.

"My dear child, what on earth?"

"Really, Hilary, we had no idea. Why aren't you with Andrew? I—we—your father, er, we were— Oh, Christ!"

"Hilary, what's happened? Why are you here? I—"

Hilary was looking now at Barbara, and the other woman's eyes slid away, and she smoothed her hand over her hair uncertainly and tried to smile, and then Hilary was backing away, shaking her head from side to side.

"No. I didn't—It really doesn't matter. I wanted—it isn't important. I'm sorry—I—"

And she tugged at the door knob, fumbling for the catch, and then it was open, and she was running down the stairs as fast as she had run up them, as above her Barbara cried out, "Hilary, Hilary, come back! I want to explain."

She almost fell over the taxi driver at the foot of the last flight, for he was standing peering upward as she came hurtling downward, and he stepped back and said protestingly, "Go easy, ducks. Don't want to send me flyin', do you? Is your mum there, all right? Thought I'd better stop and make sure you was all right."

She stared at him and then looked back over her shoulder and saw Barbara poised at the top of the flight. She turned back to the taxi driver and said breathlessly, "No, no. She's not here—not here."

"You sure you don't want me to get the law for you, ducks? You look in a right state—"

"No, no." She looked back up the stairs, but Barbara had stepped back into the shadows, pulling her flimsy dressing gown close to her. Hilary ran past the driver to the door, and he followed her worriedly.

"Please!" Hilary said and ran across the pavement to the cab. "Please, take me home to my mother. Sev—seventeen Briar Avenue, North Finchley. She'll be there. Please, take me home to my mother . . ."

12

"I wouldn't have intruded on you if I hadn't felt it absolutely necessary," Miriam said stiltedly, not looking at George. "I know how busy you are, but—" She closed her eyes for a moment. "There's really no one else. I did go to a GP, but she—well, I can't go back to her. She knows me, you see. So I—well that's why I'm here."

He's not really listening to me, she thought suddenly. I'm not being sufficiently explicit. I'll have to be more direct. Somehow.

"It's difficult to explain." She looked down at her hands tightly clasped on her lap. "But since . . . since the birth, I haven't been quite myself."

George was trying very hard to concentrate. When she had appeared this morning, just walking into the Unit, insisting she must see him at once, he had been irritated, wanting to tell her to go away, wanting to deal with this matter of Hilary and the way she had fled to Marjorie. But then he had become aware of the way she looked, and he had been shocked. She was so thin, her face so shadowed under the cheekbones and around her eyes that she looked incredibly tired. So he had swallowed his impatience and now sat trying to keep his mind on her and free of the nagging anxiety about last night's episode.

But it was difficult. How could he have been so stupid? Even if Hilary hadn't turned up in that melodramatic fashion, it would have been stupid, bound to cause repercussions. But Barbara had made it so clear that she was aware of his need, and had seemed to offer at the same time a simple solution to an irritating problem—oh, Christ, what was the use of trying to analyze it? He had needed a woman, had been relaxed by good food and wine and this heady new freedom from money worry, and she had been available. More than available, he now realized with some bitterness. Inviting. With hindsight, he saw she had planned the whole episode. And far from relieving him of his problem, it had compounded it. He had to recognize that his sexual appetite, far from being slaked, had been thoroughly aroused. When he had woken that morning from his uneasy night's sleep, his first thoughts had been not of Hilary and what she might have told Marjorie, but of Barbara, his first unguarded feeling a wish that she was there with him.

". . . and even with the sedatives, I'm no better off," Miriam was saying. "I find myself—look, this isn't easy for me, but I've got to talk to someone about it, and there's no one I can trust to . . . to understand."

"Apart from the sleep problem, are there any other symptoms?" George had dredged a little from what she had said, despite the undertow of his own thinking. "Physical symptoms?"

"I . . . I can't concentrate. Is that a physical symptom? Probably not. I've been trying to work, but I've made no progress at all. And I can't eat. And"—she swallowed—"I get odd ideas."

"In what way odd?"

She looked at him helplessly and then to the horror of both of them began to cry, her face suffusing with a patchy redness.

"Oh, my dear girl! You really are distressed." He moved around the desk swiftly and sat on the edge of it, facing her, putting a hand on her shoulder. "I've never seen you in such an emotional state! What on earth is it?"

She rubbed at her face angrily, and the crying stopped, and the color faded, leaving her with a violet-tinted pallor. "That's . . . that's just it. I've never known anything like it. I cry for no reason. I find myself thinking constantly of my feelings—me! I've never been like this in my life! It's . . . it's *infuriating.*"

He smiled at her then. "That's better!"

"What?"

"Being angry. That's more like you. And it's made you feel a little better, saying you're angry? Yes, of course it has. Anger has that effect on me too. Useful, isn't it?"

She was indeed feeling better, and she nodded, even managing a thin smile. "Yes. It does help."

"Good. Now, tell me. What are these odd ideas that so distress you?"

"I think I understand them better than I did. Something my— the GP I saw said some things that made a sort of sense."

She spoke carefully, trying to be detached, objective. "One of the reasons you selected me for the project was my . . . my sexual inexperience. You told me that."

"Yes. There were excellent biological reasons for it. And practical ones. You had no personal entanglements that would complicate your involvement in the project." He trust his hands into his pockets. "Sexual experience usually creates complications."

"Does it? I suppose so."

"Yes." He moved sharply and went back to his chair behind the desk. "But what has this to do with your present problem?"

"I, I have discovered in myself a . . . drive that I was not aware of." She tried to keep her voice colorless. "And not having previous experience of it, I don't know how to . . . to cope with it."

He became suddenly remote, leaning back in his chair, and she felt the chill in him and stopped and looked down at her hands again.

"Coping with sexual drives can be problematic, but I hardly see what relevance this has to your present situation. What precisely is it you are trying to tell me? I find myself at a loss to understand."

"Oh, for God's sake!" she shouted at him, enraged. "Do I have to spell it out? Ever since that bloody baby was born, I've been obsessed with sex! Obsessed with it, do you hear me? I sit there in my room, trying to work, and I . . . I find myself thinking about—oh, what's the use? I'm sorry I came and bothered you. I should have known better. Look, I won't come again, but since I'm here, you can give me a sedative. I've used all I had, and if I don't have something, I think I'll go completely out of my mind—such mind as I have left. You owe me that much, at least. Give me a supply of barbiturates and leave it at that."

"*I* owe you that much? What does that mean? I promised you nothing! You went into your part of the project with your eyes open. I made it clear to you that after the birth your involvement would be completed, and that, I trusted, made it abundantly clear that mine with you would be equally at an end! I don't say that I lack any . . . any reasonable concern for your welfare, but to suggest I *owe* you that concern is outrageous! I will not be subjected to these pressures, to this sort of—"

He stopped and took a deep breath, and then went on more calmly. "Look, Miriam, if you ascribe this . . . this syndrome from which you believe yourself to be suffering to the birth of the infant, I can only assure you that there is no reason why this should be so, unless—" He stopped suddenly and stared at her, frowning. Then his face cleared. "Oh, I'm sorry. I'm not thinking well at all. Of course I understand! I have been remarkably obtuse!"

She looked back at him coldly, her face set in harsh lines. "Really? How good of you to say so!"

"Yes, *that's* what it is. Post-partum depression! A common enough phenomenon in normal situations, but in yours—of course! There is ample biological evidence. Dugald's work with macaque monkeys—yes, of *course!* When an infant is removed from a mother, and lactation is suppressed, the incidence rises sharply. Now, this is easily remedied. Very easily. I'll arrange for treatment—"

"Treatment?"

"Indeed. A course of antidepressants will resolve your symptoms rapidly, I assure you. Now, if you'll just wait, I'll send over to the pharmacy."

She looked at him uncertainly. "Post-partum depression? Norma said—well, I suppose it could be. But—" Then she shook her head. "It may be as you say, and it may be some drug treatment will relieve some part of the . . . my difficulties. But this other thing—"

But he seemed to be no longer listening to her, writing quickly on a form he had taken from his desk drawer, and she bit her words back and sat in sullen silence staring at him.

Behind her the door opened, and a voice said urgently, "George, please, may I speak to you? It's important."

Miriam looked over her shoulder to see Barbara standing there and she muttered, "Good morning."

The other woman looked at her blankly for a moment and then nodded abstractedly. "Er, good morning. Excuse me, will you? George, this really is—"

George frowned at her as he folded the slip of paper on which he had been writing and said crisply, "Just a moment, please, Barbara. Will you be good enough to tell young Isaacs I want him to go to the pharmacy and bring this prescription back for Miss Lawton at once."

"Miss—oh!" Barbara looked at Miriam again and said awkwardly, "I'm so sorry! I—I should have recognized—it's just that—look, George." She turned again to him, her face twisted with anxiety. "Your—Mrs. Briant is here and says she must see you *immediately*. Unless you can see her right now, she says she . . . she'll go to see the man, er, our opposition."

She looked at George with desperate appeal. "You do know who I mean?"

"Opposition?" George said sharply. "Who do you mean? Oh, Gur— The man Kegan tried to get me to see?"

She nodded. "And you may have forgotten that, er, young man is here this morning. He's seeing some reruns of the rooting reflex film, but if she should happen to realize who he is and speak to him, she might—it really is important you see her immediately."

George stood up sharply and nodded. "Then I had better do so. Have you spoken to her yourself? Is she alone?"

"She's alone, and I didn't see her. Isaacs did. He put her in the histology lab. She . . . she gave him a most explicit message and he spoke to me about it because you—"

"Yes, quite. Well, send him to get this filled, as I said. I'll see her in here. If you will take Miss Lawton to—let me see—the small records room, and get Isaacs to show Mrs. Briant in here, and you'd better go to—oh, *blast!*" He looked uncharacteristically agitated. "This is like some bloody French farce. Go up to the nursery, will you, and stay there. I'll come up later."

Miriam felt angry again as she let Barbara anxiously hustle her out of the office and then show her with scant ceremony into the tiny cluttered records room before disappearing. Her part on the project might be over, but what right had they to treat her in so abrupt a fashion? Without her there wouldn't be any bloody project.

And then she stood holding her head between her hands, hating herself. Here she went again, tied up in knots about her personal feelings, instead of recognizing and accepting the fact that some emergency or other had arisen and that individual sensibilities had to be subservient to it. To have produced so infantile a thought as that exaggerated idea of her own importance to the project—it was appalling.

She stood still, consciously taking slow controlled breaths, and then moved with decision. There was no point in waiting for the prescription. George had been so patently abstracted that he could not possibly have reached an accurate diagnosis of her problem, and to swallow some unknown drug prescribed on the basis of so hasty a judgment would be ridiculous. She would tell one of them to tell him so and go.

The corridor outside was deserted, although she could hear voices from the office at the far end of it. A loudly shrill voice: ". . . told me exactly what she saw, and if you think . . ." And then George's deeper tones cutting in. But she couldn't hear his words clearly, even had she wished to.

She moved across the corridor to the nearest door and pushed it open. A man looked up, his face politely inquiring in the flickering half-light, for the blinds were drawn and a film was running on a screen on the far wall. He stared at her for a moment and then reached for the projector on the table in front of him and turned it off before switching on the gooseneck lamp beside it.

"Hello," he said. "Looking for me?"

"For anybody," she said sharply, not liking the considering way he looked at her. "I wish to leave a message for Dr. Briant. If you will tell him, please—"

"He's in his office, isn't he?"

"He's occupied at the moment," she said irritably. "And I have no wish to disturb him. So if you'll just tell him, please, that I won't wait for the—for the material for which Isaacs was to go."

"You aren't one of the team here." It was a flat statement.

"If you will please give him that message." She stepped back, pulling on the door knob, but he moved swiftly and held on to the door.

"I can't unless you tell me who sends it."

"He'll know. And thank you."

She turned and walked quickly along the corridor and out of the main door, but he followed her, walking along the path beside her with such long strides that she could not have outstripped him without breaking into a run. Irritably, she stopped and turned to look at him.

"Did I not make my message clear? I am not able to wait for—"

"I rather think I know who you are." He stood and looked at her, his eyebrows slightly raised. "Dark hair, blue eyes. She put it rather sloppily you know. 'Blue eyes put in with a smutty finger,' she said. Your eyelashes are dark enough to warrant the whimsy, I'd say."

"What are you talking about? If you will forgive me, I have no time to be—"

"And only people involved with the project in some way are permitted into the Unit. Now, you are not a member of the team. I've already said that and you didn't deny the fact. And you are certainly not Kegan or Dr. Saxby or Miss Guttner, and dietitians and the like usually wear a uniform of some sort—"

"Oh, for heaven's sake." She turned and started to walk away again, but again he fell into step beside her.

"And since you fit the description so admirably, you must be an individual for whom I have been searching for some time. Tell me, as the baby's natural mother—if one can use the word natural in this context—what are your views on the ethical aspects of this project?"

She stopped and looked sideways at him, and then started even more determinedly to walk toward the hospital side gates.

"You're completely demented. I imagine the gate porter will be only too willing to assist me in getting rid of you."

"And what will you tell him? That you have been recognized as the baby's mother and want the fact kept quiet? He'll be fascinated, I have no doubt. There are usually a couple of other newspapermen hanging around, and they'll be suitably grateful for his information—"

"Other newspapermen?" Again she stopped walking and turned to face him. "Ah! I see. You're one of those muckrakers, are you? If you can't get hold of any real facts, you invent them out of whole cloth?"

"Do you lie awake at night thinking up nice insulting phrases, or do they come to you naturally?" he said equably and smiled at her with great friendliness. "Oh, come on, admit it! I've hit it, haven't I? You're the baby's mother, and I recognize you and claim the five pounds—"

Suddenly, she felt as though she had been driven as far as she could go. It wasn't until she saw the red weals rising on his cheek that she realized she had actually hit him, and she stood in amazement at her own action, feeling the palm of her hand tingling.

"Oh, dear me!" The mildness of his voice didn't match the glint of temper in his eyes. "In hitting it, I get hit. I hope that made you feel rather better than I do at the moment."

He touched his face delicately. "If you're going to go about slapping people, you really shouldn't wear rings. That one has actually drawn blood."

She looked at the scratch on his red cheek and muttered, "I'm sorry. You provoked me—"

"Oh, don't apologize. I can imagine how you feel. To manage to keep a secret like yours for all this time must create strain. Enough to lead to a wholesale slaughter. I'll do the handsome thing and forgive you. If you'll come and have coffee with me and talk to me."

"No."

"Why not? You'll have to eventually."

"Indeed I will not." But she made no move to go, staring at him curiously. After George's abrupt treatment, to have a complete stranger recognize the strain she was feeling made her feel less angry than she had been. "There is no reason why I should."

"Oh, there's every reason. You see, if you refuse me, I shall simply follow you at a discreet distance. Eventually you will have to go home, and I will then know where you live. Thereafter I will stand at your door like Cesario, waiting for you if not actually calling upon your soul within the house, and every time you emerge, I shall repeat my invitation. Ergo, you will eventually accept it, since scientists are practical people, unlike us muckrakers, who are merely persistent."

He smiled again, with the same relaxed friendliness, and she looked at the redness of his cheek and thought confusedly, Why not? I've got to talk to someone, I told George that, and he wouldn't understand. Why not?

"Let me observe the social niceties. My name is Michael Bridges. I am the science writer for the *Echo* and have rather more integrity than most of my colleagues—which isn't difficult, I'll admit. I have my B.Sc., albeit from an inferior university, and you will therefore find me less irritating to talk to than people with no scientific jargon at their disposal. I enjoy Dr. Briant's cooperation—as you saw for yourself, I was seeing some of his early filmed material—which should reassure you. Do you need any other recommendations? Any further assurances that I am eminently respectable, and can be trusted not to rake too deeply?"

"Why do you want to talk to me? To write up some revolting sentimental claptrap?"

He produced a pained expression. "Oh, no, no! I wouldn't be able to write sentimental claptrap if I tried from now till the millennium arrived. Confidentially, I'm not a very good journalist. Really good ones can write anything, but me, I'm limited. Just straight science, that's all I'm good for."

"Bridges, you say? I think I might have seen some of your work. It's not bad, I suppose—"

"Do you have to be so grudging? Ah, well. At least you'll admit it wasn't too . . . mucky?"

"Oh, stop that. And anyway, most journalists are—"

"Muckrakers? How do you know? I might as well suggest all scientists are ice cold fish who don't give a damn for anything but their own work, and can't see anything beyond it. That scientists are unfeeling—"

"I am such a scientist, and it would be a much better thing for science if all of them were like me."

"Unfeeling, are you? Really? Now why are you at such pains to tell me that? I wouldn't have thought—"

"If you wouldn't have, then don't do so now. I asked you, why do you want to talk to me? If you want scientific information about this project, you'd be better occupied going back to your films."

"Ah, but you can give me better news. You're here now, and those films will wait. I suspect you won't. What do I want? That's simple. I'd like to discuss"—he looked at her closely and then said slowly—"I'd like to discuss your own work, and your plans for your scientific future. Not personal future, I promise you. But at the press conference Dr. Briant said you were returning to your own biological work. And as I said before, I'd also be most interested to hear your views of the Briant project and its possible applications. Dr. Briant's views are interesting, but those of his peers—other scientists like yourself—are equally as important."

She laughed suddenly. "You really are too transparent for words. Do you think that suggesting I'm Dr. Briant's peer will so flatter me that I'll be putty in your hands? Come, Mr. Bridges, I'm not that malleable."

"Touché." He laughed too and turned toward the gate, taking her elbow in a light grasp to urge her along with him. "Really, talking to you will be as much pleasure as it will be work. Coffee, then?"

"Just a moment, for heaven's sake. Are you always so precipitate? What about the message I asked you to deliver?"

"I'll deliver it when I go back. I won't keep you more than an hour or so! Anyway, he'll get it, won't he, when he sees you aren't there? What was it Isaacs was to get for you?"

"That's the first question I refuse to answer."

"Oh, all right. It's not a very important one, anyway. Shall we go then? Good. What's your name, by the way?"

"Lawton."

"What Lawton?"

"Mmm? Oh, my first name. Is that relevant?"

"No. What Lawton?"

"Miss."

"Try again."

"Oh, Miriam, damn you."

"Excellent. Miriam. And I'm Mike. Now, coffee."

Marjorie's head was aching abominably as she left the hospital, making her eyes feel hot and sandy, and she drove home with a recklessness that caused a narrow escape from a crash. I wish it had happened, she thought viciously as she wrenched the car clear of the oncoming lorry and just slid in under the bonnet of the furiously hooting van she was overtaking. Then he'd be sorry. And immediately she thought, Like hell. It would be just what would suit him, having me dead.

By the time she reached home and screeched to a stop in the narrow driveway, she had mentally reviewed her own violent death, attended the inquest and her funeral, observed George's remarriage to that cow of a woman, Ian's suicide because of it all, and George's own remorseful death to finish it off. Her eyes were wet with self-pity as well as aching when she flung into the house.

Ian was sprawled in the untidy sitting room when she came in, and he looked up at her lazily as she threw her bag onto the floor and then collapsed on the sofa.

"Well? Did he confess all? And did you find out where the lolly is coming from? And above all, my love, is he going to shell out?"

"He's a bastard. A complete bastard. Couldn't care less about anything, anything at all, apart from that goddamned work of his. Didn't deny a thing—not a bloody thing! Do you know what he said? It was as much my fault as his! As much my fault! They make me sick, sick, do you hear me? Men like him. All I was good for was sex, that's all, and because I wasn't available, it was *my* fault! As if—"

"*Tous les chats sont gris*—hmm? Well, there's nothing new in that, darling, is there? Come on, Rusty! You've been around long enough to know that! Surely you realized he'd shack up with someone, under the circumstances? What did you expect?"

He looked up at her with a sharply avid look on his face. "What sort of man is he, anyway, Rusty? Randy type? I've often wondered."

"Ian, don't be coarse! It's nothing to do with you."

He shrugged. "Well, you started the subject. Anyway, the important thing is, what about the folding stuff, the lettuce, the lolly? As far as I'm concerned, that's all that matters—hey, it's a bit early for that, isn't it?"

She refilled the glass she had already emptied in one swift gulp and came back to the sofa from the sideboard, holding it between both hands.

"I need it," she said. "Christ, I do. Here I am, with you and now Hilary to worry about, all on my own, and there he is, wrapped up in his bloody project with that woman falling flat on her back for him."

"Who's being coarse now? Listen, Rusty, just cool it, will you? Make yourself some coffee—it'll do you more good than gin at this hour of the morning—and let's think this thing through properly. He owes us a lot, right? He owes you the respect due to a wife"—he smirked slightly—"whether you really want it or not. He owes me a hell of a lot, since he buggered up that job for me, and any others that turn up. As long as he refuses to sign contracts, I'm hamstrung—till I'm old enough to sign my own, or you divorce him and get control of us and the right to sign contracts for me."

"I'm not divorcing him. Why the hell should I? And put that woman just where she wants to be? I'd have to be out of my mind.

I don't deny I thought of it, but why should I? Apart from anything else, it may be he's right, and this project'll make him. Maybe there'll be some real money coming in, and why should she get what I'm entitled to?"

"And that's the real point. Where's he getting the lolly *from*? Hilary said all of a sudden there's money to play with. Where's it coming from? And where's our share?"

"He wouldn't care if we starved, I tell you, he'd see us in the gutter and—"

"That gin's making you maudlin. Do leave it alone. And *listen* to me! Where's he getting it from?"

"I don't know! I tried to find out, and he just shrugged it off. Wouldn't answer."

"The thing is, is he getting it the straight way? With all the opposition to what he's doing there, you can't tell me some civil servant sat up in Whitehall and said, 'Ah! Here's a good chappie, let's ladle some of the ready into his lap.' It must be coming from somewhere a bit shady. There isn't an official body'd touch him with a bargepole, let alone give him a ha'penny to fly with. There must be some way to find out."

"Well, I tried, Ian, really I did. If you'd have come with me this morning, as I asked you—"

"Oh, no! Not on your sweet nelly. Talking to him'd be a waste of time. But, I wonder—"

He got to his feet and stretched, scratching his bare chest and yawning in a faintly theatrical way. "I wonder. There's more than one way to paddle through this mud pool."

She was lying full length on the sofa now, the glass on the floor beside her, and she turned her head and squinted painfully at him.

"What are you thinking of? Darling, do get me some aspirin, will you? I've a swine of a headache."

"What? Oh, all right. What do you expect, getting yourself half pissed at this time of the morning?"

"I do wish you wouldn't talk in that vulgar fashion, Ian." She spoke in a plaintive whine now. "You know I hate it, and I've suffered enough for one day, darling, really I have."

"Oh, all right." He looked down at her for a moment, a faint sneer on his face. "Don't go getting yourself worked up into one of your fancy sick spells, for God's sake."

"You sound like him when you talk that way. Please don't. Oh, I do feel awful."

"I'm sure you do. All right, I'll bring them when I'm dressed."

But he didn't come back to the sitting room when he had shaved and showered and carefully dressed himself in his cream corduroy jacket and black polo-necked shirt and tight trousers. Instead, he roughly shook Hilary awake and told her shortly, "Rusty's under the weather. You'd better take her some aspirin and see if you can get the place cleaned up a bit. Do you more good than lying here feeling sorry for yourself. Come *on*."

He took with him twenty pounds in cash from his secret store, which he kept hidden beneath his mattress. What Rusty didn't know about his private financial arrangements wouldn't hurt her, and he'd seen no need to tell her of his source of income from Sefton. Though I might, he thought magnanimously as he hailed a taxi at the corner of the road, I might give her a few quid after this morning, if it works out right. And it had better. That lousy bastard. He had a lot to pay for, one way and another, and Ian wasn't the man to sit about waiting for debts like that to be paid. Someone somewhere was going to shell out, and if in doing so his father copped it, so much the better.

"House of Commons," he said to the taxi driver in a lordly fashion and settled back in the cab with his booted feet on the tip-up seat in front. He thought with great satisfaction of the brilliance of the idea that had come to him, quite forgetting that it had been Marjorie who had first thought of getting at George through the MP who was gunning for him. But then, Ian had a great gift for forgetting things it was not convenient to remember.

13

"I am not prepared to discuss it," George said flatly. "Not now or ever. I want only to forget the whole episode occurred. I was stupid enough to let my private needs come between me and my work, and the results of that stupidity are my problem. Mine and no one else's."

"You can't say that!" Barbara said almost despairingly. "You can't! I'm part of it too! It was my fault Hilary was so distressed, my fault she found out and told your wife. Of course we've got to talk about it. You can't shut me out like that. Please, George, you can't."

"I can and I will. All I want now is to forget it and concentrate on work—*work*, do you hear me?"

"You don't have to tell me how important work is. I care as much about it as . . . as I care about you as a person. George, please! I love you, and—"

"For Christ's sake! Haven't I put up with enough? All my adult life I've been trying to escape it. Love! I never want to hear of it again! I want no more mewing about love, and relationships, or anything remotely connected with such emotional garbage. I've cluttered up eighteen years with it, eighteen years of fretting wastefully about a wife and two children who . . . who should not have meant anything, who should never have happened. All right. I've learned at last where my mistakes lay. Let it go at that. Leave me alone about it! You're a good worker, Barbara, a very good worker, and I'd be hard put to it to replace you, after all the time you've put into the project. But by God, if you can't control these ludicrous sentimental yearnings, you'll have to go. I can't be doing with any more. Can't you get that into your head? I've had enough!"

She was whey-faced and had to swallow hard before she could speak. "You wouldn't send me away. You couldn't."

"If I had to, indeed I could. You are not irreplaceable. I could train Isaacs to take over your work. Very easily."

"There'll be no need," she said swiftly. "None at all. I . . . I won't mention it again. But let me say one thing more, before . . . before we finish this conversation."

"If it has anything to do with your emotional needs, I don't want—"

"No, it has not. It has to do with something more basic. Sexual needs."

"I've told you—" He shouted it, and she shrank from him slightly, but then went on desperately, driven almost against her will to persist in an attempt to salvage some small fragment from the mess.

"Please, hear me out. You're a reasonable man, with a . . . a logical mind. Hear me out. And if what I have to . . . well, suggest, seems unacceptable to you, I promise you I'll *never* mention it again. I promise. But just hear me out."

He looked at her, his face dark with a blend of angry unhappiness and furious impatience. "All right." And his voice was rough and icy. "All right. I'll hear you. But after this there is to be no more mention of any personal matters whatsoever."

She nodded and then clenched her hands and thrust them

deeply into the pockets of her white coat in an effort to still their shaking. But she couldn't stop the way her neck trembled, making her head move absurdly, as though she were a mandarin doll.

"You clearly have no further need for any emotional life. I accept that. But that you have a . . . a physical need for sexual relief can't be denied. It showed last night. As a reasonable man, you must accept that."

He nodded briefly. "I have already said the blame was mine. My own stupidity."

"Not stupidity. Physiology. You can't blame yourself for being a man any more than you can blame yourself for being a scientist. And as a man, you have needs that you've got to meet somehow. Well, I have needs too, and I want them satisfied. For a long time now I've known I wanted to satisfy them with you—no, I'm not talking about love. I promised I wouldn't," she said as he opened his mouth to interrupt. "I'm being practical. Plain practical. While you were . . . you were living with your wife, I had to tolerate the way I was, and somehow live with the need. I'm practical, you know, and I couldn't see any way of . . . of getting what I wanted without causing a great deal of trouble. Well, the trouble's happened anyway, but now you say it's over. You've washed your hands of any further emotional involvement of any sort. I now want to make it clear that I am prepared to go on being . . . well, available to you, for any physical needs you have. This isn't sentiment. It's intelligent acceptance of a situation. I'll get what I need, you'll get what you need, and emotional matters won't come into it. It will be as simple a matter as telling me to collate a day's readings or organize a set of tests. That's all. Practical."

There was a short silence. Then he said in the same flat tone he had first used, "Is that all you want to say?"

"Yes."

"Very well, I've heard it. Can we now put any further discussion of the matter completely out of court and get back to what we are here for? There is work to be done."

"Yes."

"Good. Now, where are yesterday's graphs? Are they ready for the computer programming yet?"

"Not quite. I'm waiting for Isaacs to bring the charts of his timing readings on the feeding response films."

"They should be here by now."

"He was delayed this morning, you'll remember." She spoke a little nervously. "But he said he'd work through lunchtime to finish them. We could go over to histology and see—"

"Very well. And then I want to spend a little longer than usual briefing Miss Quinn. She will need clearly to understand what we are about to do. She's shown no anxiety about the change in feeding patterns?"

"No. None at all. Just been her usual bovine self. It's extraordinary, isn't it, the way she plods through everything?"

He raised one eyebrow momentarily. "I find it refreshing. Well, Isaacs, then. Shall we go?"

She followed him from the room, grateful for the way her body had stopped shaking, and feeling a good deal happier than she would have thought possible. From here on, there should be few problems, as long as she could bite her tongue whenever necessary.

But as she followed George's spare figure into the histology room, a sudden thought hit her. She'd better go and see the gyne people and get herself sorted out. Or would it be more discreet to see a GP? Perhaps it would. They were as well able to prescribe the Pill as anyone else, after all. There must be no more complications.

The sound rang through her head, cutting wide swaths of pain, channeling deep rifts which filled with the memory of the way Jenny had used to sound. She didn't want to look at him, at the redness of his face, the tendrils of hair darkened by his sweating, but she could not raise her eyes. She just sat there, feeling the heat of his body coming through her overall to her knees, and added her own cries of silent anguish deep inside herself to the loud desperation of his.

"Lift him a little closer, Miss Quinn," Dr. Briant said loudly, raising his voice above the noise. "And turn him towards you. I want to be certain that the breast fills his entire field of vision."

She moved woodenly, as though her arms were not her own, watching her square red hands slip under his small body, raise him and turn him toward her, and he stopped his squalling for a brief moment. His eyes moved and then focused again at the level of her exposed nipple, and then the gaping redness split his face again, and the sound, wailing and furious, splintered her head once more.

I can't do it. I can't do it. I can't do it. The words slid from side to side of her mind, battering at her lowered eyelids as still she watched the crumpled outraged face. But she didn't move, still sat in the same heavy posture, her shoulders held rigid, feeling the sweat on her own body under the heaviness of her breasts and around her waist under the crumpled clothes.

"All right, now, bring him closer, so that he can almost reach —not too close—now be ready to let his cheek touch your skin. Slowly, now," Briant said. And she raised her eyes for the first time and looked at him and knew the misery and hate that were filling her showed on her face, and she could do nothing about it.

But they were all watching the baby, the six of them, Barbara Hervey with her chin held high so that she could see over Dr. Briant's shoulder, Briant himself with his head poked forward, a stopwatch in one hand, the other four just as absorbed in their greedy watching of his bewildered misery. And she hated them all, and let the knowledge of her hate fill the craters in her mind that his crying was still gouging out.

"Starting *now,*" Briant said, and even through the noise of the crying she was aware of the click of the stopwatch. She let her hands obey, raising the rigid hot little body, letting his cheek touch her, and feeling her skin move under it. Immediately, the damp head turned in toward her, the red gape changing its shape, the cry changing too, becoming sharper, and then she couldn't help it and moved one hand to lift her breast toward him, offering the nipple to his seeking mouth.

"No, let him find it," Briant said quickly. "That's it. He's there. Now, hold still. Excellent, excellent."

Take it, take it, Georgie boy, take it, I want you to, please, for me, take it, not for them, for me.

But he fought and rolled his head against her, and the crying rose and fell, and still he pulled his head away, and she touched his cheek and then cradled his head in her hand, turning it toward her, and the nipple touched his lips, and she arched her back so that her breasts lifted and his mouth was filled, and then he was pulling, drawing on her and gulping, but still jerking slightly against her arm as he pumped his jaws, gradually establishing a rhythm, his eyes tight closed.

The redness of his face faded as she watched him, as she felt herself pushing peace and comfort and safety back into him, and she took a long slow breath, willing the fine tremor that was moving every muscle in her to stop.

"Well done, Miss Quinn. You controlled that beautifully. Next time, though, don't guide him as you did today. It was clearly necessary this first time, but not next time. Barbara, I want to see that rerun as soon as possible. How quickly can you get the film processed? And the blood pressure chart and the EEG and ECG, Isaacs? Can you get them graphed immediately? Vernon, I want to check your timing with mine. I think I might have been fractionally slow on the finish."

"We could rerun in an hour. Will that do?" Barbara Hervey said.

"An hour. Hmmm. How would that suit you, Isaacs? Yes? Splendid then. Everybody, please. I want to discuss all our individual observations in depth."

They moved toward the door, following Briant, and Isobel said woodenly, "Do I continue as usual, after this feed?"

"What? Oh, yes. Yes, Miss Quinn. As usual, please. Very much so. It is imperative that no further alterations in pattern be added until the next session. We want to measure the effects of today's experiment on his learning processes. Just as usual, and thank you for an excellent piece of work." He smiled at her kindly, but already he was abstracted by his own thinking, not really aware of her, and she knew it. "Not easy to get such timing right, not easy."

And then they were gone, leaving her alone with the watchful monitors and the still tense but suckling baby at her breast, and the fury and misery and hate in her seethed and moved, and then settled into a cold hardness deep in her belly.

I'm sorry, my lovely one, I'm sorry. Isobel didn't know, little one, I didn't know.

But you guessed. You guessed it would be something like this. Didn't you? You knew what they would do, just as you know how they'll be when they watch the film of it.

She felt physically sick as she thought about that, the way they could watch the suffering he had gone through and not care about it. To do so wicked a thing as they had done, to so frighten and hurt a baby who had never been frightened or hurt ever, and then to actually watch it twice over!

But all babies cry, a small voice seemed to say suddenly inside her head. All babies cry sometimes. Jenny cried. They all do.

But not Georgie, not my little Georgie. He never has, and it hurts him more to suffer. He's never suffered with me, and now they're making me make him cry, and he'll grow to hate me, not them, and it's—I can't stand it any more, and it must be meant or why else should I have been doing what I have these past days? God must have put the idea into me, just as He sent me here to look after him from the beginning. He must mean me to do something about it. Mustn't He?

"My dear young man, you really will have to be a little more direct, you know. I'm a very busy man, and I have only limited time to spare for you, I'm afraid. And although you have been talking to me here for the best part of ten minutes, I still don't entirely grasp what it is you're trying to say."

"Ten minutes? I waited for you the best part of an hour, kicking my heels here like some rubbernecker or other!"

"Indeed?" Gurney was nettled. Who the devil did this cocky little sod think he was talking to? "Well, some people's time is more expendable than that of others. And as I say, I am somewhat at a loss to understand precisely what it is you want of me."

"Oh, come on, Mr. Gurney! I made it clear enough, didn't I? Without exactly spelling it out—and I've more sense than to do that. Never know what's bugged these days, do you?"

"Bugged?" Gurney frowned. "Are you suggesting there are—that we use *listening* devices here? That's outrageous! I must ask you to—"

"Oh, all right, all right. Maybe it was a bit much to expect this place to be as with-it as all that. All right! You want it in plain easy words, I'll give it you. You're gunning for my old man, aren't you?"

"You become more and more insulting, young man. Members of this House do not go *gunning* for any one individual, as you put it."

"No?" Ian lit another cigarette and blew the smoke carelessly in Gurney's direction. "Maybe you should, but that's none of my concern. Look, are you or are you not trying to get a change in the law to stop people like my revered papa from mucking about with human life, and the rest of that rot? Because if you're not, the papers have been spreading a lot of lies about you."

"I am presenting a private member's bill that may have an effect on your father's work, yes. But I don't see that—"

"And I should think it'd be a lot easier for you if you could find out things about my old man that show him up for what he is."

"Oh?" Gurney felt his annoyance drift away. "What sort of things?"

"Like the way he's started having it off with one of the women scientists around that Unit of his, leaving my mother in a terrible state, not knowing where to turn for money." Ian looked virtuous. "You should just see the state she's in, poor soul. And there he is, loaded with cash, and—"

"Loaded? That's hardly the word, is it? I understood he was painfully short of funds to operate the project. I have spoken at some length with Mr. Kegan, the hospital secretary, and not even he, with his intimate knowledge of the project, and his access to the Unit, could show that there was any spare money."

"Ah, but he's not the Prof's son, is he? And I am. I've really got what you might call the horse's mouth, haven't I? Any news I might have to give you, you can count on."

"Why are you coming to me with tales like this?"

Again Ian produced his virtuous expression. "Well, I mean! The way he's treating my poor mother! It's enough to upset any man, isn't it? You've got a mother yourself, I daresay."

"Hmmph. Well, let me hear precisely what evidence you have and we'll see what we can do about it." Gurney reached for a sheet of paper and a pen from the desk in front of him. "Your father, you say, is—"

"Oh, come on, not so fast, Mr. Gurney! What about my side of it?"

"Your side of it?"

"Yeah! My side of it! I suppose you have to have this all legal, and so on? Got to have a sworn statement from me or something of that sort? It wouldn't be evidence without it."

"Oh. I suppose so, although you can trust me not to reveal my source of information."

"I much care if you reveal it! You can say what you like once we've come to an agreement."

"What sort of agreement?"

"The only sort that means anything, Mr. Gurney. A hard cash one. I've got my mother to think of, after all. She's got to be looked after, hasn't she? And if I don't, who will? To put it nice and plain, Mr. Gurney, what's in it for me if I tell you it all the way you want it?"

Gurney pushed the paper away from him and looked at the grinning face in front of him. Ye gods. I've met a few, but this one—

"Master Briant," he said softly. "Let me give you a little advice. You will get nowhere by going about things the way you are. To attempt to suborn a member of this House is to take a considerable risk, do you know that? And not even your youth would excuse you if I chose to make trouble because of your behavior here this afternoon. To attempt to sell information to me is an act of subornation, and I for one will have no part of it. Bought evidence may have some value somewhere, but not here. Good afternoon."

"D'you mean you're not interested?" Ian sat up straight and stared at the other man. "Oh, come on, you've got to be! You want this bill to get through, and I've been reading the papers like everyone else! You'll have to do something pretty good to get it past this lot! Fancy themselves progressives, don't they? Threw out hanging, brought in a queers' charter, abortion, the lot—they aren't going to put this through just because a few old stick-in-the-mud Conservatives don't fancy it! You've got to be interested!"

"Oh, I'm interested all right!" Gurney was beginning to enjoy himself. "But not to the extent of paying you money! You stupid little boy, don't you see what you've done? You've *told* me what I need to know! Not in detail, perhaps, but enough to start me on my own inquiries. Now I know there's more money coming into the project from somewhere, it will be a simple matter to find out precisely where somewhere is. You've *given* me what I want—free and gratis!"

Ian jumped up so sharply that his chair fell over, and he stood in front of the desk and thrust his face furiously at Gurney. "You lousy cheapskate! You dirty lousy—"

"Mr. Briant! Must I send for a sergeant-at-arms to remove you?"

"Ah, you make me sick! Too bloody mean to pay a decent rate for what you want! Well, don't think you've scuttled me, chum, because you haven't, not by a long shot! There's more than you'd be glad to pay for what I've got to tell."

"Oh? Precisely who? One of the cheaper tabloid papers, perhaps. But they won't pay you a cent until they know you've got a story in you. And once you tell them, they'll do precisely as I have and send you packing. Really, *Mr.* Briant, you'll need a lot more experience and finesse—some subtlety—before you'll make any success of this sort of thing. You're too crude even to be amusing. Do me a favor, run away and play. You're beginning to bore me—"

"Oh, am I! Well, there's others won't be so bloody bored! I'll go to—to—"

"Yes, Mr. Briant? You'll go to whom?"

"I . . . I'll go to . . ." Ian floundered and then shouted triumphantly, "I'll go to that religious lot, to what's-his-name—Joel Wayne. That's who. He's really gunning for the Prof, he is. Calls him Christ-knows-what. And they've got some money coming in, I can tell you. Lashings of it. My sister went there, do you know that? She went to one of their rallies, and it put the fear of God into her and no mistake—for all she fancies herself so scientific—and they were raking in the cash hand over fist there. Oh, *they'll* pay for what I've got to give 'em. The more evidence they've got of the old man's sinfulness, the better they'll like it!"

He laughed suddenly, his original good humor apparently quite restored.

"My God, Gurney, I ought to be grateful to you. Your cheapskate ways'll lead me slap bang into some real lolly! You'll be kicking yourself for turning me down, that's what you'll be doing. And don't you bother to come after me when you've changed your mind either, because *that's* all you'll get from me!" And he thrust two fingers up at him, accompanying it with a jerk of his chin, and then slammed out of the room, leaving Gurney to recover his equanimity.

At first he found himself infuriated by the boy's behavior, feeling more ruffled than he would have cared to admit by the total lack of awe he had shown. God damn it, MPs were not people to be treated like that! How dare he be so incredibly insolent? But then he felt some genuine amusement at the juvenile way the whole thing had been handled. Even though Ian was only seventeen, he need not have behaved in so absurdly childish a fashion, assuming an ability to wheel and deal that he wouldn't have as long as he had an arse to sit on. Gurney was somewhat given to thinking in juvenile obscenities himself when he was disturbed. When I was his age, he thought with malicious pleasure, I'd have been able to run rings around half the Establishment with a story like the one he's obviously got at his fingers' ends.

Undoubtedly it was a salable story. The question was, would that stupid yobbo be able to sell it? The religious thing—of course, he was right there. It might indeed be just the sort of fuel they needed to keep their flames burning. And from many accounts, they were extremely lucrative flames.

He moved to the window of the small office he had borrowed for the afternoon and stood staring out at the Gothic buttresses and their attendant pigeons, thinking hard.

This needed careful working out. He had embarked on the bill not because he really gave a damn one way or the other about Briant and his work. For his part, Briant could keep a thousand babies in test tubes or cages or whatever, and welcome. But the project had seemed a heaven-sent opportunity to make his mark, to make himself felt. For his three years in the House he had no more to show than a measly consultancy to a second-rate public relations firm, and a badly paid monthly column in a local newspaper in the constituency. The whole point of letting Daphne put him up for the Selection Committee and steer him through the by-election to a seat (and his lips curved slightly as he remembered Daphne) had been the fringe benefits. But what fringe benefits were there for a virtually apolitical backbencher? The first real chance that had come his way had been his drawing of a place in the private member's bill ballot, and then the Briant furor.

And it should have been the walkover it had looked like being; Davidson's obstructive behavior had been a most unpleasant surprise. He hadn't expected to have to face so many bloody complications. But they were there all right, and unless he found a way to overcome them, the success of the bill was far from being a foregone conclusion. And if it failed, where was the opportunity to get at the real honey he knew lay waiting to be scooped up by an MP with an intelligent eye to the main chance? Indeed, this latest development needed careful thinking out.

So, let's think straight. These evangelists are pulling in huge audiences for their rallies, ever since that American arrived to take over the movement that had started with a few spontanous meetings in places like Trafalgar Square and Birmingham's Bull Ring. They were making a lot of money, manipulating a hell of a lot of people. And if there is one thing the great British public is likely to rise to, it's any suggestion that foreign pseudo-religious movements are making hay out of them. Remember all the flap there was about the Scientologists?

Now, if I can convince enough people here in the House that there are parallels, and that the Wayne lot are manipulating the public directly through fears engendered in simple minds by the Briant project, surely that should swing a lot of sympathy my way? And if I can show that the Wayne people are prepared to use any weapon they can get their hands on, even to the extent of allowing young Briant to sell them dirt about his father, that really would be ammunition.

I'll have to move fast, he decided. Young Briant was already on his way to Wayne, wherever Wayne might be. It might take him some time to track him down, but on the other hand, it might not. I've got to get to him too, as fast as possible.

Where do Americans stay in London? he asked himself and then grinned. The Regent Palace if they're tourists, but Claridge's or somewhere like it if they've got money to play with. I'll start at the top end and work down. And he hurried out of the room for the members' lobby and the telephone directories.

14

He bought some chrysanthemums, great shaggy-headed copper-colored ones, and felt slightly foolish when he was back in the car looking at them on the seat beside him. It had been the action of an impulse, and now he wondered whether it had been a bad one. She seemed so—what was the word?—crisp a personality, uninterested in the sort of approach that would appeal to most women. Her clothes neat and well fitting but with no suggestion that any real care about their effect had gone into their choosing, her face quite free of cosmetics, all had pointed to the sort of person who would scorn gifts of flowers. Yet, underneath he had had a dragging awareness of a different something about her, and it was perhaps that that had made him stop at the brightly colored stall in the dwindling light of a Camden Town afternoon to buy the exaggeratedly beautiful flowers.

He grimaced a little as the heavy smell of them hit him. A bit like formaldehyde, he thought as he waited for the traffic lights to change. Quite suddenly he was back in the chemistry laboratory at the college, with Carrie standing beside him, impatiently directing him toward the results she had herself already achieved so effortlessly. Carrie. There were things about this girl that were very like her. Carrie too had been good-looking and seemed to scorn it. She too had been quick in reaction, had a much swifter mind than his own.

This is a hell of a time to remember Carrie, for Christ's sake, he thought irritably, letting in the clutch. But he could not banish the memory. She had initiated him into so much, what with the way she had helped him plan his degree work and organized his living accommodations for him. And she had taught him how to make love too, directing his virginal fumblings with much the same ill-concealed impatience with which she had directed everything else. It had hurt him to realize how calmly and practically she had used him, while he in his stupid innocent fashion had let himself care for her a great deal. When she had been offered a plum job and accepted it without a moment's hesitation or a backward glance at the year they had lived together, he had suffered agonies of outraged misery.

And though there had been other women since, none of them had ever quite matched that first experience. Some had had the urgent sexuality Carrie had offered without the accompanying intelligence that sharpened his pleasure in satisfying it. Some had had the quickness and wit he valued but lacked the sexual initiative she had conditioned him to expect in a woman. It was always the passive ones he abandoned most quickly.

But why now was he thinking about Carrie and her successors when he was on his way to get a story from this girl? The coffee they had shared had completed the breaking down of the barrier she had seemed to have against talking about the project, and she had agreed readily enough to this further meeting this evening. But it was a story he was after and not a girl as such.

Or was he in fact attracted to her? He parked the car at the end of Albert Street and sat staring ahead at the elegant patterns made by the façades of the old terraced houses with their cockleshell fanlights. Was he attracted to her as a woman? There was no other woman around at this time apart from the green-eyed girl who lived in the flat above his own. She had made it clear she was interested if he was, and he had played with the idea of starting something there. But he dismissed her now. Anyway, there was never any sense in getting involved with people on one's own doorstep; it created too many complications. And perhaps this handsome but somehow drab girl he was about to see was exerting some sort of a pull on him.

Maybe that's why I thought of Carrie, he thought somberly. Science had been her thing too, albeit chemistry and not biology, and there were those other similarities. But why compare her with *Carrie,* who had caused him so much pain, and not with one of the others, who had been strictly for laughs? Was it because this one made him feel he could become emotionally involved with her? But that didn't bear thinking of. He had managed very nicely without getting hung up on any one girl these past dozen years and more, and he was certainly unlikely to change so established a living pattern now, not at his age.

He left the flowers on the seat, filling the small car with their reek, and walked purposefully up the street, looking for the house. The hell with it. He'd play the bloody thing by ear. The main thing was he'd got her, and she was going to give him good copy.

She had been standing waiting at the window for some time when she saw him walking up the street with his long loping strides. He's a bit flatfooted, she thought suddenly and then looked at the shape of him. Shouldn't I feel something about the way he looks? It's supposed to be important, that, remembering the way Norma had used to waffle on about the appearance of the various boys who had occupied her thinking during their shared college days. But it doesn't seem to mean a thing.

She felt curiously remote, and it comforted her. It was almost as she had been used to be, this detached considering attitude, and she let her mind stretch itself tentatively, exploring the feelings that had so bedeviled her these past weeks, much as one explored an aching tooth with one's tongue, risking the exquisite stab of pain it might cause.

But there was no response, none of that sickening surge of feeling that had so distressed her so often, and she relaxed. Decision had been the treatment she needed, and to hell with George and his facile diagnosis and offer of tranquilizers! Her painful thinking ever since Norma's hectoring had crystallized at last, and now she knew precisely what she had to do. The solution to her problem was within her reach.

She looked down at him as he came up the worn steps past the rusted lacework of the iron railings and thought suddenly, Suppose he won't? I've made the decision, but he is part of it, after all. Suppose he refuses? But Norma had made it clear in her exposition that such a response was unlikely.

She drew the curtains and looked briefly around the dim room as the bell pealed, and then turned on the table lamp in front of the hissing gas fire, adding its yellow glow to the redness, and collectedly walked to the door and pressed the intercom button.

"Yes? Who is it?" She was pleased with the calmness in her voice.

"Bridges," came the thin voice through the microphone far below on the front door jamb. "Mike Bridges."

"Come in. Top floor. The front flat." And she pressed the button to release the door-opening mechanism.

She was sitting on the sofa beside the fire in the pool of light thrown by the lamp when he came through the door she had left open for him and stood for a moment looking at her after he had closed it behind him.

"Good evening," she said. "You keep good time. I prepared sandwiches and coffee. Will that be adequate for you?"

"You needn't have bothered," he said and shrugged out of his coat. "I had planned to take you out to eat."

"There's a hook behind the door. No thank you. I prefer we should stay here. Do you mind?"

"Not in the least. I live on sandwiches and coffee anyway. Is it good coffee, or instant muck?" He smiled at her as he came and sat on the sofa beside her. "I'm a shocking coffee snob."

"It's percolated Blue Mountain, a medium grind. I too like my coffee well made. Black or white?"

"Black, please. Thank you. Dear me. Pumpernickel! You have exotic tastes in bread."

"It was all the shop had," she said absently, giving him his mug of coffee. "There would appear to be a demand in this district for foreign foods."

"And for sweet-roasted ham too. Excellent. This is an odd room."

"Odd? In what way?" she leaned back, cradling her own coffee mug in both hands.

"It's so . . . impersonal. No sign of the impact a personality usually makes on a room. Or perhaps you haven't lived here long?"

"Five years. Ever since I came down from University."

"Oh? Then you aren't the sort of woman people call a homemaker, is that it?"

She shrugged. "Perhaps not. I've never thought about it. I've been too busy working."

He looked at her with real curiosity. "You've always been in research? You must have good grants."

"No grants. I have a small income left by my father. It's adequate to my needs." She smiled thinly. "Were you hoping to paint a pathetic picture of devoted science in a garret? I'm sorry to disappoint you."

"No, not at all. But I'm always curious about people's money. I've only got what I earn, and I know how bloody little of it there is. I'm very impressed. I rarely meet people who live on private means. Quite the aristocratic touch."

"Seven hundred a year isn't very aristocratic."

"But it means a reasonable capital, doesn't it?"

"I don't really know. It's a trust fund, handled by my bank. Why are you so concerned about it?"

"I'm not. I'm just . . . making conversation, I suppose. May I have some more coffee?"

"There's no need to make conversation, is there? You have questions to ask. About my views on the ethical aspects of the Briant project? Help yourself to sugar."

"Yes. But I find myself rather more interested in you, as a person. Or does saying that alarm you? You accused me this morning of planning to write sentimental claptrap."

"You've changed."

"What?"

"This morning you were . . . gay. Flippant. Now you seem to be more—oh, I don't know. Solemn."

"That was technique this morning. I needed to get over your suspicions, and the flip approach works best. But if you prefer, I can turn it on again. I keep it on tap."

"No. I think not. The, er, approach you are using now fits better with my own ideas."

"Oh?"

Deliberately, she put down her mug and leaned back in her corner, looking in her characteristic way at her hands clasped in her lap.

"You're interested in my personal response to my part in the project, as well as my views on the ethics of it."

He too abandoned his coffee mug and leaned back, folding his arms and looking at her bent head. She's the one who is different, he thought, puzzlement creeping into him. Quite different. Relaxed? No, not that. Far from it. But she even looks different. As though her edges were more clear-cut. This morning there was a sort of fuzziness to her outline.

"Of course I'm interested," he said. "I said so."

She looked up and returned his gaze very levelly and then smiled briefly, and it lifted her expression, softening it so that the thin cheeks rounded, blurring the sharp planes of her face.

"You told me you're a scientist too. And as a scientist, you should be able to accept what I'm going to say to you without too much surprise."

"I'm already surprised. You're so different. This morning—"

"This morning I had a problem. Now I am on the way to solving it, with your cooperation."

"Oh? And here was I thinking you were solving my problem."

"And what is that?"

"A boss who wants a story about you."

She shrugged that away. "You must put it in abeyance. I'm not really concerned about it right now."

"Then why did you agree to see me this evening? Isn't that the whole purpose of this discussion? Why else am I here?"

"As far as I am concerned, you're here to help me solve a problem that has become . . . irritating. It's interfering with my work, even my health, which has always been excellent. And meeting you this morning was a most fortuitous circumstance, I now realize."

"Do you always use such pompous language when you're about to ask favors?"

"Pompous?" She frowned. "And who said anything about favors? As I understand these things, what I want of you will be as much to your benefit as mine."

"You're beginning to irritate me. I can carry on circular conversations with the best of them, but usually such talk is only necessary when neither side has anything much to say. If you have got something to say, why not just get on with it? And for God's sake, try to stop wrapping it up in *New Statesman* journalese."

"I'm sorry," she said stiffly. "Very well. You know that I entered into the Briant project on a short-term basis. That is, my function was to—well, incubate the infant. After the birth I was free to return to my own interests."

"Yes."

"Do you find anything . . . odd in my willingness to do this?"

There was a long pause, and then he said slowly, "In some ways, of course. Who wouldn't? For a young woman to . . . to surrender herself to so intense a personal experience while apparently expecting no personal involvement, it is odd in normal terms."

She nodded. "A fair point of view. At first I was thoroughly annoyed by it, when it was made in newspapers and on television. It had seemed to me a perfectly reasonable thing to do, in scientific terms. I couldn't see what people were getting at, accusing me of . . . of unnaturalness. To me, science is as natural as breathing. I simply couldn't comprehend what place personal feelings had in the matter."

Again she looked up at him and smiled thinly. "Well, I was wrong. Because of my lack of experience in . . . in matters of . . . of feeling, I was basing my attitude on inadequate knowledge. Most unscientific of me—"

"That's better," he said softly.

"What is?"

"You're embarrassed. I still don't know what it is you're getting at, but it's embarrassing you, and I find that refreshing."

"It isn't easy for me to talk of feelings. I . . . I have never cared much for indulgence in emotionalism. It has always seemed to me to be so wasteful and messy, and—" She shrugged. "Well, I have been forced to see that it is impossible to eradicate all emotionalism, however much I might wish to do so."

"Are you unhappy about the baby?" There was a gentleness in his voice, and she looked at him in puzzlement.

"The baby? No. Why should I be?"

"Why should—for heaven's sake, girl, women who have babies, no matter under what circumstances, usually feel *something* for them."

"The baby is in good hands. Why should I be worried?"

"You don't feel anything for him at all?"

"Oh, an interest in the information the infant is providing, certainly! If I hadn't been interested in the project as a project, I would hardly have become involved, would I? There's no reason why I should feel any emotional rapport with the child, though. I never saw it, and—"

"So Briant was right about that much. Mother love doesn't arise spontaneously. Certainly not in you. Well, all right. If it isn't the baby that's worrying you, what is?"

"My. . . my own responses."

"Oh? In what way?"

She spoke in a low voice now, still looking at her hands. "Since the birth I have discovered in myself a need I didn't know existed. According to a—someone to whom I talked about my changed—the way I have been feeling—it is biologically, er, triggered off."

She looked up at his face and then slid her eyes away again. "It seems that for women reproduction and sexual activity are inextricably linked. That experience of one without the other creates problems—"

He laughed suddenly. "Well, of course! It isn't possible to have one without the other!"

"Isn't it?" She sounded suddenly angry. "Don't be so stupid! Of course it is! Even with the . . . with the sexually sheltered life I've led, I've heard about contraception! It is certainly possible to divorce sexual experience from reproduction, and from some of the reading I've been doing lately, it seems to me that some of the social malaise of which we hear so much derives from it. And"—she spoke with a sharp bitterness in her voice—"and look at me! I've done something really different. I've divorced reproduction from sex! Haven't I? The whole bloody world knows it, including you! George was hardly secretive about the fact that I was an unsullied virgin, was he?"

She stood up suddenly and moved to stand in front of the fire, leaning her arms on the mantel shelf above it and looking down at the hissing red-blue jets. He looked at her back, so vulnerable in its rigid control, and wanted to touch her, to make her relax. She ought to cry, he thought. Which was an odd idea for him, for he disliked seeing a woman weep.

"And Norma told me that was the root of my problem. She said—"

"Norma?"

"Oh, Norma Gould, a GP I know. I . . . I went to see her about the way I was feeling, and she said—oh, not in so many words, but she made it clear, and it makes sense."

She turned now and looked at him very directly. "My trouble is that I need to complete a physiological cycle. Normally, a woman has sexual experience and thereafter produces an infant. This total activity releases her, relieves her of a biological need. Until I entered the project, I was quite unaware of the existence of this need in me, as an individual. But having the child seems to . . . to have triggered off the mechanism. And I now know that until I . . . until I close the circuit, as it were, I will feel as I do now."

He was sitting up very straight now and staring at her. "I am not certain that I understand just what it is—look, I don't want to jump to a conclusion, but are you trying to tell me, are you asking me to—" He stopped and shook his head in frank bewilderment. "I must have misunderstood you."

"I'm asking you to provide the sexual experience I have never had," she said in a level voice, still looking at him very directly. "To complete the pattern for me."

"But why me?" he said stupidly.

She moved then to cross the room and stand beside the desk in front of the curtained window, her back to him.

"There isn't anyone else I could ask."

"But—"

"Oh, think it out for yourself!" She turned and looked at him again, and there was irritation in her voice. "If I were the sort of person who . . . who had people on tap to provide this experience, I would hardly have reached the age of twenty-six without having had it, would I? The very thing that made me suitable for the project—well, one of them—was my bloody virginity! I think I realized—oh, it was three weeks ago—what it was I needed, but what could I do? March out into the street and pick up the first man who walked along and say, 'Please, sir . . .' Do be logical!"

"So as soon as you met me this morning, you decided in cold blood to—"

"No, I didn't. It wasn't until I talked to you in the café that it occurred to me."

"Do you like me?" he asked abruptly.

"Like you? I haven't thought about it."

"Look, if you said to me you fancied me, that you took a look this morning and thought you'd like to go to bed with me, it'd make sense, in my language. It wouldn't be the first time it's happened. Times have changed, and plenty of girls these days"—he shrugged slightly—"put it on a plate, to be crude. But this, to suggest I should oblige you like some—oh, I don't know. You make me feel like a stud bull, for Christ's sake! What sort of man do you take me for?"

"But men don't have to be involved with the women they have sex with." She sounded genuinely puzzled.

"Who told you that?"

"Norma. She said men operate in a different way. And she should know. She's always been very interested in—"

"It may be true of some men. And if I were honest, I'd admit there have been plenty of times I've been involved—sexually involved—with girls I didn't particularly care about. But I've got to *fancy* them, for Christ's sake! There's got to be something, some sort of spark."

Her face was expressionless. "And you don't find me—you don't feel you want to help me. I provide no spark."

"Oh, there's nothing wrong with you! You're a good-looking girl, and—oh, my God! You make me feel so—I don't know." He stood up too and began to move restlessly about the room, rubbing the back of his head so that his hair ruffled absurdly. She watched him silently.

"I don't know," he said again. It was quite extraordinary, the confusion he felt. He should have been repelled by her cool invitation, or angry because of her apparent lack of interest in him as a person, yet there was no sense of repulsion, no anger in him. There was, rather, a thickening nervous excitement, a feeling of being painfully young and helpless mixed up with a sense of inevitability, of *déjà vu*.

He suddenly saw himself sitting at the shabby table in his room at Mrs. Constatine's, struggling with the mathematics of an experiment in chemical analysis and looking up to see Carrie sitting on his bed, her arms around her knees, gazing at him with a half-smile on her face. "Come here, Mike," she had said softly, and he had got clumsily to his feet and crossed the room to her, frightened suddenly. And she had put up her face and said commandingly, "Kiss me, Mike." And he had stood and stared helplessly at her, until she had put up an impatient hand and pulled him down beside her.

He shook his head irritably, pushing the memory away. The twenty-year-old innocent he had been was dead and long since gone, had no relevance to the here and now, to this crazy girl beside the desk, looking at him through those dark lashes with still intentness.

"I don't *know*," he said again and looked at her, and she looked back silently.

"You're quite mad," he said uncertainly.

"But you will, won't you?" she said, and it was a statement of fact.

There was surprise in her when he spoke, for she had been lying bemused and relaxed for what seemed a long time, safe in her own sense of remoteness.

"I'm sorry," he said heavily, and she turned to look at him.

"Sorry? For what? If apologies are due at all, it's from me. I did rather—well, it was my decision."

He was sitting hunched up with the counterpane pulled over his knees and with his arms around them, staring at the wardrobe on the far wall. "I . . . I didn't show you the sort of . . . concern I feel I should." He turned and looked at her then. "You are very inexperienced and it would have been kinder in me to have been gentler, less impatient. But you—"

He frowned and looked away from her. "You surprised me."

"In what way?" It was curious how peaceful she felt, and there was a sudden stab of pleasure in realizing that she had an academic interest in what he was saying. Indeed, she had been right; she had solved her problem and could think well again.

"I said I needed to feel something for a girl. That I wasn't the sort of man to behave like a bull in a field. I said it because I . . . I don't think I knew certainly. Now I do."

"Knew what?" She yawned suddenly and pulled the counterpane closer around her shoulders.

"I find you—you are a very attractive woman."

"I imagine most women are in this situation."

"No. I don't mean just sexually. I mean attractive to *me*. You made me respond more than I would have expected myself to respond to someone I hardly know." He looked at her again and said with sudden awkwardness, "You are very like the only woman I've ever really cared about. A long time ago, when I was at University."

"Perhaps that's my good fortune, since it made you able to solve my problem for me."

"Is it solved so easily? That's an absurd idea."

"What's absurd about it? You've done just that. I feel better than I have since the birth. Better than I have for a long time."

"That's post-orgasmic euphoria."

"My dear man, who's being *New Statesman* now? Nonsense. I had a need, you provided a means to satisfy it, and I can now forget it."

He stared at her and then shook his head in disbelief. "Ye gods, how naïve can you be! Do you honestly think you can shut the book on one episode like this and say that's that?"

"Why not? I've managed perfectly well for many years without any sexual involvements. I don't imagine I've changed that much. Having the baby had an unfortunate effect, maybe, but it was temporary. It was simply a matter of finding how to . . . well, complete the pattern. So now it's complete."

She smiled then with real amusement. "It may have been a reversal of the usual procedure, but I don't think I need worry about that."

She moved sharply and got out of bed and picked up her clothes. "I'll dress in the bathroom, and you can dress here. Then I must pay my debts, mustn't I? You want your story, and you're entitled to it, on the understanding of course that you don't publish my name."

She moved across the room and into the small bathroom and after a while went on talking through the open door. "I'm sure you'll appreciate why I must insist on anonymity. It really would be impossible to do any work if your colleagues came pestering me, wouldn't it? And I suppose I must keep my promise to George and protect my identity."

Her voice hardened. "Although I'm annoyed with him, I must confess. He refused this morning to—well, no harm done."

She came back into the room to find him silently tying his shoe laces. "In fact, it's perhaps as well. I doubt if I could have found so . . . swift a solution in discussion with George! I indeed owe you a debt of—"

"Is that all you can say?" He seemed to explode into anger, and she looked at him in surprise. "You'll pay your *debts?* Christ, what am I to you? A male prostitute? Someone you can use and then pay off like some bloody—"

"Why are you so angry? I told you what I wanted, and you provided it. The least I can do is cooperate with you in my turn. What is there in that to anger you?"

"How would you feel in my shoes? If I had walked in here, told you I needed a woman and that you'd do as well as anyone, and how about it? And if I then offered to give you something in exchange for being so accommodating? How would you feel if I had done that to you?"

"If I had consented to cooperate, how should I feel? It sounds perfectly reasonable to me."

"Reasonable! My God, you're—I don't understand how any woman could possibly behave like this! It's the most unnatural thing I—"

Her jaw tightened, and she walked into the living room, and he followed her furiously.

"—unnatural thing I've ever come across. I've known plenty of women in my time, but never one who could coolly offer to *pay* me in some way for—"

"Why not!" She turned on him, angry in her turn. "If men can buy women for sex, why shouldn't I do the same thing? Not that I made any such offer! I simply made it clear I was willing to cooperate with you in appreciation of—"

"Services rendered?"

"No! In appreciation of your assistance with a problem that was a nuisance. That's all."

"That's all! You treat me like some . . . some—"

"I really don't understand you." She tried to sound reasonable. "What is it that makes you so furious?"

"What is it that—look, I—" and then he stopped and sat down heavily on the sofa and put his head between his hands.

"I don't know," he said after a long pause. "I simply don't know.

At first, I—oh, I don't really know why I'm here. Why I agreed to do as you wanted. Why I'm so angry. You've got me into a state of complete confusion."

"I'm very sorry indeed if you're upset. But you must see there's no reason for it."

"I told you in there that I find you very attractive. I'm not given to—look, it's been a long time since any woman has had on me the effect you have. Does that mean anything to you?"

She looked at him and then shook her head. "No. I'm sorry if that distresses you further, but no. I'm not the sort, you see." She moved away from him, across the room. "I don't make relationships. I never have. I don't care what people think about me, what effect I have on them. Since I never have, I doubt if I ever shall."

"Don't you? Yet you wanted a sexual relationship enough to—"

"This evening has had nothing to do with relationships," she said swiftly. "It was a simple solution to a problem. That's all. I'm sorry if I've . . . if I've had a personal effect on you. If you want a relationship, you'll have to look elsewhere. I'm just not interested in you in the way you seem to have become interested in me. I'm sorry about it, but there it is."

He looked up, anger rising in him again as he recognized the note of kind dismissal in her voice. But she seemed unaware of his reaction and went on in the same patiently explanatory manner. "Look, can't we look at this reasonably? I'm a logical woman, who worked out logically the structure of a problem and sought the logical solution to it. As a reasonably intelligent man, surely you can recognize the intelligence in me, and—"

"Intelligence! Ah, balls!" He was so furious he could hardly control the pitch of his voice. "You make me puke! You hide behind a great overblown notion of your own brilliance, kidding yourself you're some unique creature that—for Christ's sake, you're no better than the rest of them! I've been pulled into bed by women just as bright as you think you are, I can tell you. And if they had to kid themselves, they did it more honestly, telling me they loved me, or I loved them, or some such thing! But this phony garbage about intelligent logical thinking—who the hell do you think you're talking to? Some mindless idiot you can blind with your lousy science? Who the hell do you think you are? I'll tell you what you are."

He took a deep breath and then said deliberately, "You're no better than a whore. You had hot pants and didn't know what to do about it. You wanted a man—any man—and you covered up the honesty of that with a load of crap about rational thought. If you'd walked out into the street and said to the first man who came along, 'Please, sir,' there'd have been some decency in you. But you chose to sell yourself like any prostitute, using the science you pretend to care so bloody much about for currency. Much you care about science, to use it to buy yourself the going-over you wanted! Much you care, you lousy stinking *whore*."

The sense of peace, the resumption of cool academic thinking that had been with her since she had got out of bed, began to shake and splinter, and she felt the weight of confusion that she had been fighting all these weeks pushing back through the rifts, and fear rose in her.

"No. I've had enough! I don't want to hear another word about it! Get out of here, do you hear me? Get out! I *should* have just got some man from the street. I should—get out! Leave me alone! Just go away and leave me alone."

She ran to the door and tugged his coat from it and threw it at him and then pulled the door wide.

"Get out, and leave me alone! I don't care what you feel, what you think, anything about you! I don't want to know about why you agreed to do as I asked, or why I—get *out*!"

She knew she was shrieking like a fishwife, and she didn't care. She had to get rid of him, free herself of the weight of his feelings, desperate for the safety of being alone inside herself again. She had to be free of this man and his probings, free of him to be free of herself.

But he stood and stared at her, his expression oddly triumphant, and she had to find some way to rid herself of him immediately, urgently. And with a sudden inspiration she shouted, "I won't give you your bloody interview, not now or ever. But I'll pay you in hard cash. If you won't take what I offered—and you've earned something this afternoon—I'll give you a check. That should clear the slate."

And she moved across the room toward the desk, but he moved more quickly and pulled on her shoulder and swung her around, and with his open palm and then the back of his hand he hit both sides of her face hard.

"And you've earned that! You're not the only one who can pay debts!"

And then he was gone, leaving her standing very still in front of the desk, her hands hanging limply at her sides.

15

"But of course I turned him away, Mr. Gurney. Sad as I was for the poor boy, I had to turn him away." Wayne shook his head in gentle regret and smiled, his face illuminated with kindness. "I would have been happier to try to bring him to a knowledge of the good that I know lies beneath his unprepossessing exterior, but he is not at present accessible to the voice of God. But one day, one day, I trust, he will find the road to Him."

Gurney was trying not to let the man see he was conscious of the fascination being projected at him, but it was extraordinarily difficult. The soft voice, the beguiling lilt of the accent, American, yet, unusually, in no way irritating to him, the cleanly handsome lines of the face, all conspired to make him feel wrapped in the warmth of the man's personality. It took a considerable effort of will not to let him see how determinedly he had to fight against it.

"I doubt if he wanted the sort of help you have to offer, Mr. Wayne. He was looking for something far more concrete."

"Oh, I was aware of that, Mr. Gurney. I could hardly be otherwise. He was quite absurdly blunt in his demands. I guess, from your visit with me this evening, that he made you the same offer? Yes, of course he did. Poor young man."

"May I too be blunt, in my own way? Why did you send him away? I would have thought that the information he had to offer would be of value to you."

Wayne smiled again. "Would you, Mr. Gurney? How little you understand of the ways of God! You know, I could ask you, Mr. Gurney, why you sent him away. In your position, didn't he have something to offer *you?*"

Gurney smiled thinly. "It might seem so. I'll be honest with you, if you will be equally honest in return."

"You don't have to barter for my honesty, Mr. Gurney," Wayne said gently. "It is a free gift offered freely by every God-loving man, and I will give it you as to every other man, as to God Himself."

"You need not preach at me, Mr. Wayne."

"My talk of God embarrasses you? I'm sorry for that. Very well, I will try not to embarrass you further at this time. Since God is part of everything I do and say, whether I mention His name or not makes no matter. You were about to say?"

"It was not embarrassment I was feeling. However, I was about to point out that I sent the boy away for two reasons. Primarily one very basic one. I could not, even if I were willing to do so, give him money. I have none available to me. Members of Parliament in this country are not exactly affluent. Unlike"—he looked at the other's benevolent expression with smiling malice—"unlike, apparently, men of God in your country."

The benevolence did not falter. "And the other reason?"

"To personally discredit Dr. Briant in so . . . so puerile a Sunday tabloid fashion would not necessarily give my bill the support in the House that it needs."

"And yet, realizing that, you are surprised that I too rejected the boy's offer? Wayne said softly. "You do me an injustice, Mr.

Gurney. If your publicizing of such unpleasantness would have the effect of damaging your cause, is it not obvious to you that it would be as damaging to mine?"

"No, it isn't. Members of the House do not care particularly about the moral fiber of individuals. As long as private reprehensible behavior remains a private matter, then we do not concern ourselves. We don't take notice of it unless we are forced to do so. But you are different."

"In what way am I different, Mr. Gurney?"

"Oh, for Ch— for heaven's sake, you aren't dealing with sophisticated politicians! Your arena is the public market place! You have to influence the thinking of simple people, who care a great deal about private behavior. There's nothing the Great British Public finds more enthralling than the peccadilloes of well-known people. They'll lap up every word they can get, and when there are no more juicy titbits, set about raising a great howl of protest that such things should be publicized! Now, I am going to be very direct with you, Mr. Wayne, and I'd appreciate an equally direct answer. I want to know whether you—your movement is in fact trying to put a stop to Briant. If you are, then we're playing the same game in the same court. It is necessary to me to know where I stand."

"Mr. Gurney, my Tabernacle is dedicated to one thing and one thing only. The spread of the word of God. We wish no more than to see all men within His loving arms again. Of course, since God hates evil—and the work of Briant is very evil—we too must hate evil. That is as crystal clear as it can be, would you not agree?"

"I'm not a religious man, so such explanations mean little to me. If you won't give me a direct answer in terms comprehensible to me, let me tell you how I see your . . . activities."

He leaned back in his chair and narrowed his eyes slightly. "Well, Mr. Wayne. I see you as a very clever man. Extremely clever. I believe, after talking to you here, that you are quite as sophisticated as the members of the House. Despite the innocence of the words you actually speak, I feel there is in you as broad a streak of intelligent cynicism as there is in me. Your actual words belie you, you know, when I look at you, when I observe the way you use your voice and your undoubtedly powerful personality, and above all when I look around me."

He waved his hand at the room in which they were sitting, at the heavily draped windows, the thickly carpeted floor and weightily expensive furniture. "If it isn't costing you the best part of two or three hundred pounds a week to keep you and your entourage in this hotel, I'd be very surprised. And it is obvious that money of that order is hardly coming out of your personal pocket. It's the money that is contributed by the followers of your movement that supplies this luxury, isn't it? And you get them to provide it by using your personal gifts of persuasion. I am a politician, Mr. Wayne, not one of your Trafalgar Square simpletons to be dazzled by charm and sweet words. We're cut out of the same piece of cloth, are we not?"

He leaned back in his chair and looked at the other man with his eyebrows slightly raised. Bluntness verging on rudeness was a technique that had worked many times before, and it would work with this man, he was quite certain. Man of God, my fanny! he thought and added a faintly insolent smile to his expression.

There was a long pause, and Wayne sat quite still, showing no hint of the way he was feeling. Then he too smiled. "Do you expect me to deny that money is available to me through my work with the International Tabernacle? Why should I? In my country, sir, we do not equate money with sinfulness. Our great society was founded by God-loving, God-fearing people who because of their piety and love of goodness were given by God the gift of wealth. It is only since we turned away from the good ways of the past that we have been visited by the plague of terrible poverty, and the hatred and internal strife it breeds. I understand the people of my country, Mr. Gurney, and because I do, I make sure that the Tabernacle I founded and now guide and control—under God's guidance and control—is financially viable, and is seen to be so. I would never deny, even were my conscience to permit me to do so, that God has given me the ability to live as I do. He has given it me in order to bring His children back to Him. When simple-hearted people see the success of the Tabernacle, in terms they understand, why, they see that love of God is the same as success! And they turn to me, and listen to me. And when they listen, why, they listen to Him through me. As I said to you before, Mr. Gurney, how little you understand the ways of God!"

Gurney caught his lower lip between his teeth and gently shook his head from side to side in a careful sketch of wide-eyed admiration.

"Oh, that is beautiful! Quite beautiful! I've heard some elegant explanations in my time—but that one! My dear man, I flatter myself if I say we are cut out of the same piece of cloth! My own gifts of persuasion seem very puny beside yours. What a politician you would make!"

Wayne smiled his gentle smile again and shook his head. "No, Mr. Gurney, I would not. My powers of persuasion are not mine but God's and could not be used for such unimportant ends as political activity, if by politics you mean the small concerns of small men. If I am persuasive, it is because God is persuasive. If you cannot understand that, then indeed you are in the outer darkness."

"It's not so dark that I can't see," Gurney said tartly. "I don't care how often you trot out your high-sounding God-palaverings. You are precisely what I suspected you were, Mr. Wayne—an extremely astute businessman with his eye to the main chance, like everyone else. You've hit on one of the richest veins there is, and you're exploiting it for all you're worth, and getting worth more and more in the process. Well—"

He stood up, and picked up his briefcase from the sofa beside him. "As well as you know your countrymen, Mr. Wayne, so do I know mine. And while I don't deny that you have a powerful following and that it is as potentially lucrative to you as the one you have at home, you won't have it for long. In this country, we don't so much equate money with sinfulness as equate poverty with virtue. There is a difference, you know! And when I make people see what I have seen in talking to you—that you came here to exploit the people of this country by hunting down one of this country's scientists, and that all you are after is the money in their pockets—well, you will see what the results will be. Now perhaps if one of your *delightful* young assistants will give me my coat, I will relieve you of my company.

Wayne made no move, looking up at Gurney with the same kind expression on his face, the same relaxed yet tidy look about his posture.

"Tell me, Mr. Gurney, why are you so anxious to discredit the work I am here to do? You said yourself that it might be that we were—how did you express it? Most elegantly, I recall—ah yes, that we were playing the same game in the same court. Now, if this is so, why should you decide that attacking the work of my Tabernacle would be of value to you? There is a certain ambivalence in your motivations, I feel. It isn't clear to me whether you are projecting a positive point of view and want to guide your country away from the dangers implicit in the work of men like Briant, or whether you want what you suspected me of wanting—to put a stop to Briant personally. That is what his son seems to want, but I would have thought you were above that sort of childish spitefulness. Or is it just that, Mr. Gurney? Is there, together with that cynicism to which you make such proud claim, a streak of spite? Do you hate Briant for succeeding in doing what he wants to do? Do you hate me for succeeding in my work? Ah, Mr. Gurney, you are much in need of the love of God, whether or not you are prepared to admit it!"

"So I hit home!"

"Why do you say that, Mr. Gurney?"

"Because you allow yourself the luxury of a personal dig at me. Spiteful, you suggest? No. There's no percentage in being spiteful. And there's nothing in the least ambivalent about my—what was the word—*motivations*. I want only to control the work of scientists of Briant's ilk because I have a healthy fear of its possible outcome. I hold no personal dislike for the man. If I did, wouldn't I have used young Briant? My situation is a simple one. I have a difficult bill to get through the House, against the opposition of a bunch of woolly-minded so-called progressives who will fight it just because a man of my political color has put it up. I'm known to be well to the right, and that complicates the issue. I need to use every possible weapon I can in my personal fight to do what I think should be done. If exposing you would make no difference to my campaign, I wouldn't bother to waste my time on it. But it may help. So I'm afraid . . ." He shook his head in mock regret. "There it is."

He turned to go, but before he reached the door of the big room, Wayne's soft voice was speaking.

"I too have an understanding of the mood of the people of this country, Mr. Gurney, even after so short an acquaintance with it. You are absolutely right in what you say."

Gurney turned and smiled widely across the expanse of deep yellow carpet. "Oh, I'm sure I am! I know a manipulator when I meet one! But you aren't being very skillful to admit it so easily."

"I am admitting the accuracy of only one of your statements. The ordinary people of this country are very susceptible to chauvinism, as you so clearly know. If you try to canvass support for your bill by suggesting I am personally making money out of British anxiety about a Britisher and his project, then you will undoubtedly damage the work I hold most dear. It is not as undoubted that you will help your bill, of course. Is it?"

And he in his turn smiled widely. "You know that as well as I do, Mr. Gurney. Now, let me suggest something for you to think about. If you will permit me? You will find it to your interest."

"Well?"

"Come and sit down again, my friend." Wayne patted the sofa invitingly. "No need to be so formal, standing there. We can talk this over like gentlemen, can't we? Of course."

Gurney sat down again willingly enough. I've hit him where it hurts, he thought exultantly. Otherwise he'd have let me go.

"You want to stop me from saying anthing about you and your movement—forgive me if I find words like Tabernacle somewhat absurd—that might damage the takings? Is that what you want me to think about?"

Wayne sighed softly. "You still see me as a charlatan, don't you, Mr. Gurney? That saddens me, you know. It saddens me very deeply. Well, God and I know I am no charlatan. But sometimes, for God's work, I have to use a language deriving from godless attitudes I cannot share. I will now use yours. Please listen very carefully, Mr. Gurney."

Gurney settled back in his seat, prepared to enjoy himself.

"Well, now," Wayne said comfortably. "It might seem in some ways that we indeed desire the same ends—control of the evil work of Briant and men like him. But you have seen a way in which you can further those ends by going against me, rather than with me. You could gain support for your bill by smearing me. But I, Mr. Gurney, am not concerned only with putting human controls on the evils of science. I am more positive than that. My avowed aim is to bring mankind back to God. To me, Briant and the baby he has in his hands are God's instruments, His way of leading mankind back to—"

"Spare me that, please."

"It is necessary for you to understand. If you damage me in order to get your bill through, you may halt Briantism for a while, but not for long. But if I succeed in *my* work, why, men like Briant will never again come to cause trouble! God will have won. And since Briant is an instrument of God and must be used in this way, I know I must convince you that you should abandon your attempts to stop Briant in *your* way. Only my way—God's way—must succeed. Your bill's passage would offer false reassurance to lost souls. It is necessary at present for Briant to continue to operate as he does. God will find a way to stop him when His time is ripe, when the peoples of the world have been brought back from the dangers of evil."

"You're certainly consistent, Mr. Wayne. No matter how often I make it clear I've seen through your smoke screen, you still puff great bursts of it at me. It really is most tedious."

"One day I trust that God will help you to see that I speak only the truth. Is it so difficult for you to believe in my sincerity? Can you not see beyond the apparent richness of my daily life—the mere unimportant details of that daily life—to the truth I have given you? God works His will in many ways, my dear Mr. Gurney, no less through ways that may seem bad as those that are obviously good. If a show of riches brings folk to God, and thereby brings more riches, which again brings more unhappy souls into the fold, cannot you see the good? And if finding a way to persuade you to stop lobbying your bill—or whatever it is you do in your House of

Parliament when you sponsor such things—keeps open the doorway to God, why then, no matter how bad a way it may seem on the surface, then it is a good one. In God's work, end indeed justifies means. When all the sheep are safe in the shepherd's hands, then we can gladly abandon our hunting in the ways of the wolf—"

"Just a minute. Let me get this clear. You want me to *stop* my bill? Are you quite—"

"No, I am not mad, Mr. Gurney," Wayne said equably. "I am speaking your language, you will recall. So, I offer you not what you at present reject, although it is the greatest gift I have to give you—the love of God—but what you care about. Mr. Gurney, this organization could make valuable use of the assistance of a man of your caliber. If you will abandon a career which I believe has not been a markedly distinguished one hitherto, I can recompense you most handsomely. As you said yourself, men of God in my country are much better provided for than members of Parliament in yours."

"I—you're offering me a job?" Gurney's voice soared to an almost ludicrous squeak. "To *buy* me off? Good God Almighty—"

"Precisely, Mr. Gurney. Shall we discuss?"

At first Ian had felt thoroughly ill at ease, sitting waiting in the richly furnished yet heavily drab room at the front of the house; but then he realized that this was precisely why he had been put there and immediately felt better. The lousy bastard, he thought. The lousy bastard. He could just as easily have seen me there in the office, couldn't he? But no. Makes me come here to his house, and then tells that great ugly wog butler to keep me waiting, just to make me feel bad. Well, it won't work. Not on this baby.

He pulled another of the heavy chairs from its place at the big central table, put his feet up on it, and lit a cigarette, throwing the match deliberately onto the floor. So far it hadn't exactly been a successful day. Gurney first, that cheap lousy—ah, what did he matter anyway? The most that he could have given him would be a measly few quid; it was as well he'd refused. But that Wayne man—that hadn't been so good.

To start with, he'd been so smooth and made him feel so relaxed that he'd almost lost sight of what it was he was trying to do. For

Ian it had been a most unnerving experience, to be so overwhelmed by a man. He understood dimly now how he had contributed to the state Hilary had been in when she had arrived home distraught and incoherent. That was some guy, that Wayne. For a few moments it had occurred to Ian that it might be worth trying to get in there, when he had seen the obvious way money was part of it all. Wayne seemed to use a number of young men, and they had all looked sleekly well-off; why not Ian himself as one of them?

But then as Wayne went on talking to him, probing at him, he had realized that he would never be able to keep up the right front. The man obviously meant every word he said when he went on and on about his bloody Tabernacle and God and the rest of it. If, as Ian had assumed, the man had been a phony, it would have been different, worth opting in on a good racket. But he very rapidly came to the conclusion that Wayne was straight, that he really cared about his dreary religious guff, and that was something Ian could never go for.

Anyway, in the end it had boiled down to a flat nothing doing. Wayne just wasn't interested in what Ian had to sell, which left just one possibility. The thing he now had to try and work out was how the man would have to be handled. Did he offer to talk, or not to talk? That is the question.

He let his mind drift away into one of its favorite places, watching himself on a stage, his handsome head thrown back, the melody of his voice rolling through a packed auditorium, the adoring faces staring up at him—

"You will come wid' me to Sir Daniel."

He jumped slightly and reddened with anger at his own response. Bloody cocky sod, he thought, as he followed the big dark man in his short white jacket across the black and white squares of the hall, still trying to make me lose my cool. Well, it won't work. I'm not scared of him or his lousy boss.

"You wanted to see me urgently, Briant. You will have to be extremely quick. I have a dinner engagement and I can give you just a few minutes."

Sir Daniel was sitting behind a red-leather-topped desk in the big somber study, a glass of sherry in his hand, the moving light from the coal fire across the room gleaming redly on his shirt front. In spite of himself, Ian had to admire the quiet elegance of his clothes, the pearl studs under the white tie, the way the black jacket sat snugly on the erect shoulders. The man looked so marvelously *rich*. To be as rich as that, and to look like that—great great, great. One of these days . . .

"You'll want to hear what I've got to say," he said and sat down, hitching his trousers neatly as he crossed his legs with assumed nonchalance. "It's good stuff."

"Well?"

"I'm running out of money."

"Indeed? In what way is that statement to be regarded as good stuff? You've had a good deal from me, and I will need excellent reasons to provide more than I have agreed to already."

"I've been thinking about why, you know," Ian said. "Why you want me to keep quiet about . . . things. What good does it do you to stop me from letting people know my old man isn't much cop as an old man?"

"That is no concern of yours."

"Oh, I don't know! I wouldn't say that. I mean, I've got to think of my future, haven't I? I'm going into the theater, aren't I? And it takes a while for talent to be recognized. I might have to sit around for a bit waiting, so I've got to make the most of my opportunities, haven't I? Make sure I've got a few bob to live on. So if I find out I've got something useful, well, I've every right to use it, haven't I? So it is my concern. I mean, I know it's useful to you not to let people know it was the great Dr. Briant's little boy that got nicked with a handful of pot, but I don't know why. So, if I've got something else—useful—in the same way, well, I mightn't realize it, might I, if I don't know why? Do I make myself clear?"

"No. You are making yourself very tedious." Sefton pulled a sliver of gold watch from his waistcoat pocket and looked at it pointedly. "Very tedious. Be so good as to come to the point."

"Oh, sorry, I'm *sure*. Wouldn't want to waste your time, would I? That'd never do—"

"Look, Briant. I really cannot waste time on your heavy-handed juvenilia. If you have something specific to say, then say it. Or go away. I have no intention of playing games with you. What is it you want to tell me?"

"Sell you, you mean," Ian said softly. "It's something about my old man that'll make a bomb for me, anywhere I fancy offering it. The thing is, will you offer enough for me to say nothing about it, or will someone else pay more for the chance to spread it about a bit?"

"What do you know?"

"Oh, no, *Sir* Daniel. I don't get caught that way twice. Offer first, story second."

"Oh? And who has already sent you packing?"

Ian reddened. "Who says someone sent me packing?"

"You did. Come along now, Briant. Get down to it or get out. And be very careful. It may be that I no longer have any use for your silence. It may be that you could talk yourself right out of what you already have, rather than into more. I repeat, therefore, stop this infantile way of talking and get down to it. I am not prepared to play a role you assign to me in one of your adolescent cinematic fantasies, merely to please you."

"The Prof has got a woman," Ian said sulkily. "And he's got his hands on cash, a lot of cash, from somewhere, and it's pretty obviously a shady deal. So what are you going to do about it? Use it and pay for the information, or cover it up and pay for that?"

"Cash? What do you mean, cash?"

"The woman's one of the—"

"I am not concerned with the woman. He can have a whole seraglio for all I am interested. What cash are you talking about?"

"He's got cash. I told you. Bought a car, paying full salaries to his bunch of scientists—including his bird—got my sister a lot of new clothes, the whole bit."

"Do you know where it's coming from?"

"Ah!" Feeling he had a grip on the situation at alst, Ian relaxed. "That'd be telling, wouldn't it? I've got to keep something in the bag. You cough up, and then, maybe—"

"You don't know."

"Oh, yes I do."

"Oh, of course you don't. If you did, you wouldn't be sitting here. But that is by the way." Sefton sat in silence for a moment, twisting the slender sherry glass on the blotter before him. Then he said abruptly, "If I choose not to pay you, what will you do?"

"Go to . . . go to the *Clarion.*" Ian lifted his chin. "You're not the only pebble on the beach, you know."

Sefton looked at him, his face closed and thoughtful. Then he produced a narrow-lipped smile.

"I despise you, Briant. You are a thoroughly slimy, nasty, pusillanimous object, and I find your presence in my house as intolerable as I would find the presence of any other parasite."

Ian, scarlet, opened his mouth, but Sir Daniel rode over him imperturbably.

"And I am not prepared to put up with your presence anywhere near me for any longer. I am rich enough to indulge myself, and I will do so now. I will pay you sufficient to get you not only out of my house and out of my sight, but completely out of this country. Not because I in any way fear you, or think you can be of any use to me, but because you make my gorge rise. You have a passport of your own, or are you, as a minor, still on your father's?"

"I've got my own," Ian muttered.

"We must be grateful for that. It will shorten the time in which we must tolerate your revolting presence amongst us. Tomorrow you will go to the *Echo* offices, to the cashier's department, with your passport. You will give it to Mr. Gorton, who will obtain a visa for you, and a permit to work in the United States. You will then be given a one-way air ticket to San Francisco, and sufficient funds to maintain you for a month. Now get out, and never on any account let me or anyone else in this country be forced to suffer your revolting company again."

He leaned forward and picked up a pen and pulled a sheet of paper from the rack in front of him and began to write. Then he stopped and looked up.

"Your parents, for whom I feel a deep pity, will eventually be grateful to me for what I have done. However, I wish them not to know at this stage that they have cause for gratitude. You will not, therefore, tell them, or the whole arrangement is ended. Is that clear?"

San Francisco, Ian was thinking. 'Frisco, where it's all happening. Where the whole scene is, where the action is. San Francisco. Oh boy, oh boy, oh boy—

"Is that clear, Briant?" Sir Daniel's voice was icy cold, but Ian felt no chill at all. He stood up and stretched and grinned and said cheerfully, "Great by me! I'll write Rusty—the old lady—from the other end. You'll let me do that? She'll raise no end of a stink if I just disappear."

Sir Daniel shrugged and returned to his writing, and Ian went, slamming the door behind him. And after a moment Sefton pulled the telephone toward him, and dialed the *Echo* office number.

16

I don't believe it. I don't believe it. It isn't true, it can't be. He can't mean what he said.

"Is that quite clear, Miss Quinn?" Briant said again, and his voice was sharper. "I know it is a little difficult for you, but I have explained fully why it is necessary. Do you understand just what it is you must do today?"

"No, sir. Not properly," she said dully and looked up at him, away from Georgie, lying in her lap and looking at her with the alert considering stare she knew so well. "Not really." He drew a sharp breath that hissed slightly through his teeth and turned away irritably, grimacing at Barbara Hervey standing beside him, and she stepped forward and leaned over Isobel and spoke in a soft but very clear voice.

"We have to see what will happen if he is treated just like any other baby, Miss Quinn. It's no different to what happens to hundreds, to thousands, of babies every day. Every mother has to punish her baby sometimes, you know that."

"But he hasn't done anything, has he?" she said, her voice still dull and heavy. "It's not like it's being naughty, wanting his feed."

"We know that, Miss Quinn. Of course we do. But mothers often smack their babies for crying. They think it's naughtiness, you see, even if we know it isn't really. And we don't want you to hurt him—at least, not really, you know? It's just a little tap on his bottom when he cries, that's all. I'm sure you can manage that for us, can't you? Of course you can. And we know it's difficult, when we've trained you always to handle him so gently. But it won't damage him in any way and it is necessary to the investigations we're doing here. As Dr. Briant explained, it's no different to what happens to lots of babies—to what happened to you, and me, and everyone else when we were babies. This won't bother him any more than it did us, you know? So let's start shall we? Just unbutton your blouse now, there's a good girl." Barbara moved then, turning her head to look at George and the other four, standing watchful and with barely concealed impatience in front of Isobel's feeding chair.

"Er, I'll stand behind her, shall I, George? Just to help if necessary."

"What? But I want *her* to—oh, all *right*. But keep well out of his line of vision, you understand? I don't want him to doubt the source of the stimulus in any way. It must come from the same source of his satisfaction if we're to get any ambivalence effect. So keep well back, right?"

Isobel felt the warmth of her behind her back, and then felt Barbara's body come closer, lean over her, reaching for the buttons of her blouse, and she raised her shoulder sharply.

"Let's start, shall we? That's right."

Slowly, Isobel began to fumble at the buttons, feeling her fingers cold and clumsy, as though they were inanimate, like the buttons themselves, never taking her eyes from the baby's face.

His gaze shifted, moved downward, and then it started. His mouth opened and closed, and his eyes got smaller as his face crumpled up with eagerness, and he was trying to lift his head toward her as her breasts were exposed.

And the crying came again, as sharp as a needle, cutting into her ears with hot pain, and he was squirming, trying to get closer to her, and Dr. Briant's voice rose above the noise, exhorting her, loudly and insistently. "That's right. No, *don't* lift him, don't lift him. Let him cry. That's right, hold it till he's had a full minute of it—a full minute. Vernon, you signal it. Hold it, Miss Quinn. Well done, Barbara . . ."

She had tried to slide her hand under his body, tried to help him so that he could reach the nipple he was screaming for so piteously, but Barbara's hand was strong and heavy on her elbow, holding her back, and she could only sit in anguish staring at him as he lay on her lap rigid with fury and misery and the need of her.

"Fifty seconds, fifty-five, sixty . . ." Vernon said.

And George called sharply, "Right! Now, Miss Quinn, *now*, do you hear? Just a tap, that's all."

Barbara's hand on her elbow tightened, and Isobel felt her arm rise, the hand feeling dead and lumpy at the end of it, and then they were all calling at her above the noise of his screaming: "Now, now! Just a tap!" And she had to, because she couldn't fight them any more, and with her left hand she held up his feet so that his bare bottom was clear of her lap, and she let Barbara swing her arm back for her, and then felt the contact between her palm and his skin, as sharp and ugly as the wailing, squalling noise that was filling her whole body with pain and misery.

And then he screamed louder, and his face, already so red, seemed to darken, becoming bluish white around the gaping blackness that was his mouth, and then there was a thick sickening silence as he fought to catch his breath again before screaming even more furiously.

It seemed to Isobel that she was sitting in a deep tunnel, with a tiny gap of light far above her, inside which she could see it all happening. It was as though she were an outside observer sitting helplessly watching the misery of the woman and baby far above her in that tiny square that was the top of the pit in which she was buried, useless and helpless and hating and hopeless. And it happened again, twice more, the baby's attempts to reach the breast, the other Isobel, the one she was watching, holding her shoulders rigid and letting herself be forced into smacking at the narrow little buttocks. And then it ceased, and they let her lift him, just as she had that first time, let him see the breast, and then she was arching her back, the Isobel in the gap at the top of the tunnel, and it was as though she were moving now, coming up toward the top of the darkness. And the square she was watching grew, expanding slowly until she was there again, reunited with herself, and the baby was at her breast suckling and pulling at her in enraged hunger, and the sound of his crying was only an echo in her head, rolling around and around and hitting at her ears and eyes with pain.

"Good girl, good girl. You did that splendidly. Didn't she, George? Splendidly, and I know it was difficult for you. Well done, Miss Quinn."

"Yes, indeed, Miss Quinn, well done. That really was a most dramatic series of responses—most valuable. And you can see, can't you, how quickly he's adapted? No breast refusal this time, once it became available. Excellent."

She let them talk on, hearing their voices rising and falling about her, keeping a curious rhythm with the rise and fall inside herself as she thought about it, thought painfully, for the words wouldn't come into her mind as they usually did, only pictures.

She saw the drawer in her bedside table with its neat parcels of leftover food, the little heap of clothes she had made for him, all tidily arranged alongside her vests and stockings. She saw herself holding Georgie in her arms, moving slowly along a dark tunnel, just like the awful tunnel she had been sitting in this afternoon, but this tunnel was a good one, not a frightening one, for it wasn't deep down, but ran straight forward . . .

". . . allowing an hour to process this film, and time to set up reruns of the first session, will that be possible? All of you, then, in an hour. All right Barbara? And, er, Miss Quinn." Briant turned and looked down at her as she sat in her usual heavy posture, the baby held closely in the crook of her left arm, her other hand cradling his head. "Now you've seen the method, I'm sure next time you'll be able to manage it without Miss Hervey's help, don't you think so?"

"Yes, sir, thank you," she said, but she didn't look up, keeping her head bent over Georgie's intent face. But now words were forming in her head, making a soothing rhythm that seemed to fit the sounds of their footsteps as they went away and the door closed behind them.

No more, my lovely one. No more. God's on your side, our side, Georgie, my little lovely, and I'm all ready. In an hour, when you're fed, and they're watching it again. Just an hour, my pretty one, my lovely one . . .

There was exhilaration in him, a refreshing sense of deep satisfaction, as he leaned back in his chair and looked across the desk at them, apparently quite unaware of the weariness, the longing to get away, that filled all four of them.

"A most constructive afternoon's work, most valuable indeed. It has helped me decide on the date of a preliminary paper. I hadn't planned to report on the conception and its selection, or on the birth, until I had some certainty that our first extrapolations were being supported by demonstrable results. Now, what would you say? Would you regard publication of a preliminary report as at all premature?"

"It might get the popular press going again," Isaacs said. "I imagine they're watching *Nature* like hawks. It might stir them up all over again, and we all know how you would feel about that."

Vernon looked irritably at him and then sideways at George. "Dr. Briant can handle them, though, can't you, sir? And whenever it's published, there'll be a response of that sort. So you might as well—"

"George." Barbara's voice had a sharp edge to it and George turned his head and looked at her, sitting very erect in the chair beside his own.

She was staring across the room at the monitor screen that showed the nursery, her forehead creased with puzzlement.

"How long since anyone looked at the nursery monitor?" And the other four people facing her over the desk turned and looked over their shoulders, moving in a ragged chorus line, and George said, "I haven't been noticing for—what's the matter?"

Barbara moved swiftly, leaning across the desk to reach the row of buttons that changed the image showing on the monitor from one to the other of the four cameras in the nursery, and they all watched as the picture rolled and then changed. The cot was empty, as they had seen when she had first made them all look at the small screen. The chair beside the bathing table was empty, and so was the feeding area, and so was the entire room view that camera four showed from its vantage point high on the ceiling.

"Christ!" Isaacs said and pushed his chair back so that it fell over, and then they were all moving, plunging past one another, crowding the doorway, and pounding up the stairs, swept by a corporate sense of incredulity.

Isaacs stood back at the top, pushing Vernon to one side as he came up to his level, and the others stopped too, so that it was George who moved forward and pushed open the nursery door and went in first.

They stood clustered in the center of the silent room, staring at the blank furniture, the blind black eyes of the cameras, the empty cot with its gently pulsing mattress and the blue coverlet crumpled at its foot, and there was a silence wrapped about them, a stillness highlighted by the lazy twistings of the mobile over the cot.

George moved then, back out of the door to the corridor, with the five of them trailing after him, their faces blank with disbelief, and again they crowded around him at the door of Isobel's room, seeming to find it necessary to be close together.

The room was neat and empty, the bed smoothly blank, the small dressing table with its crocheted beige mats tidily centered on the polished wood, the cheap alarm clock ticking loudly on the bedside table.

It was Barbara who saw it, and she pushed past George to cross the room and pick it up from its place under the clock. A piece of yellow paper, with one edge torn, and she looked at it and then gave it to George, who took it mutely and turned it to read the big round letters that marched across the crumpled surface.

> I am taking Georgie away with me owing to the way I think it is bad for him to be here. He does not like it. He will come to no harm with me. I have always looked after him and he knows me best. Please to hold my pay for this month as my notice. I am taking the clothes I have made for him but also some of the disposables because he must have them. I remain. I. Quinn (Miss). PS. I am not sorry about this because this afternoon was very bad for him.

"I don't—it isn't *possible,*" Barbara said stupidly. "It isn't *possible.* She can't have—how did she get out? How—"

Isaacs, who had taken the piece of yellow paper from George's lax grasp to read it, passed it to Vernon beside him and said defensively, "We were talking, going over the data—"

"We couldn't have watched," Vernon said swiftly. "Could we? We had our backs to the screen the whole time. Only you and Dr. Briant could have seen—"

"It just never seemed—we always watch the reruns, select what we want. Who thought to watch in case of something like this? I don't *believe* it," Barbara said piteously. "George, for God's sake, what are we to *do?* It's so *incredible.*"

George was standing very still, staring across the room at the bedside table, his face expressionless, and Vernon said tentatively, "A search? Where do we look? How long since she went? She could be anywhere."

"We were sitting talking for two hours." Peter Amato spoke for the first time and looked at the girl behind him, standing next to Ralph Davis and Vernon. "Do you remember, Elsa? I showed you my watch, because we were supposed to be going to a . . ."

His voice trailed away as he looked at George's unresponsive back, and he flushed and moved closer to the girl standing silently behind him.

"The film ran for twenty-three and a half minutes," Davis cut in eagerly. "I noticed that because I wanted to match it with tomorrow's—the timing, I mean, I thought I'd—well, it was twenty-three and a half minutes, so she could have gone any time this past two and a half hours . . ."

And his voice too trailed away as he looked at George, still standing silently in the doorway of the small room.

"George!" Barbara's voice was rough with anxiety. "What do you want us to *do*? We've got to do something."

"She warned me." George's voice was almost unrecognizable in its flatness. "She warned me, Marjorie warned me, and I ignored it. If I'd listened—two years or more it's taken, and, oh, my God!" And he took a deep breath and closed his eyes, and Barbara put out her hand and touched his shoulder, her face so twisted by distress that she looked like a caricature of herself.

"Oh, my dear, please," she said, and he snapped his eyes open and turned and pushed past them toward the stairs, and they followed him like a flock of overgrown nervous hens.

"We'll have to get the police after her right away," Vernon said breathlessly as they reached the ground floor. "Sir? Shall I—"

"No! Let me think. Barbara, come into the office. You four—for Christ's sake, keep out of the way, will you! I'll tell you in a minute what—Barbara, come here." And George flung himself at the door of his office, Barbara scuttling behind him.

"If we call the police, we'll have the whole story all over the place—and what will that do?" He paced the room, uncoordinated movements making him seem stiff and clumsy. "Christ, how could I have been so *stupid*! How could I have let such a thing happen? It's mad, mad not to have realized she might—I was so sure the woman was incapable of— Barbara, what the hell shall I *do*?"

He looked at her, his face anguished, and she put out her hands toward him and then dropped them to her sides, a sense of inadequacy swamping her. She shook her head helplessly. "I don't know, George, I don't *know*. We've got to get him back. But even if we do, after this, how can we go on? She's . . . she's broken the schedule, completely broken it. Even when we get him back, how can we find out what effects—could we? I mean, supposing we can get him back within twenty-four hours? Wouldn't that be all right? We could do a complete rundown on everything, and with all the data we've got we could run a complete comparison, isolate the possible effects of this, allow for them—George? It's not perhaps as bad as we thought—if we get him back quickly?"

Her gradually developing hopefulness seemed to communicate itself to him, and he stood still and took a deep breath and looked at her for a long moment, his eyes considering. Then he nodded with some of his normal briskness.

"Yes, yes, you're absolutely right. It isn't irremediable. I was so shocked for a moment I couldn't think clearly. But—look, how do we start? Assuming the longest time she's had—what was it Davis said? Two and a half hours"—he looked at his watch—"and it's now almost eight. We discovered his loss at—what was it? Just after seven-thirty? She must have gone some time after five, at the start of the rush hour."

"Which would delay her, surely?"

". . . and there can't be that many women with babies in arms using rush hour travel. She may have been noticed. It should be possible to find a lead."

"But not on our own," Barbara said heavily. "It will have to be the police. Can you get them to keep quiet?"

"I'll have to try. But—" He shook his head. "We've no choice. If it gets out, it gets out, and that's all about it. Just keep those bloody reporters away from me, somehow, if it starts. Thank God at least Bridges couldn't come today. I'll have to put him off seeing tomorrow's rerun somehow, unless—oh, to hell with that, we've got to get this moving, right now."

The two women sitting beside her had stopped talking to each other, and she felt their eyes on her and eased her arm gently against the weight of him, pulling the blanket higher to shade his face even more, and thought confusedly, I'll have to think of somewhere soon. He'll be getting hungry again.

"What a good little baby." The voice was edged with curiosity. "Not a peep out of it in all this time. Shockin' isn't it, the way you 'ave to wait in these places? Is it a boy or girl, then? An' not too ill, I 'ope?"

She raised her head and looked at the face beside her, a thin sharp face, the eyes probing, and involuntarily turned her shoulders to hide him and shrank back, staring stupidly at them both, at the fatter face peering over the bony shoulder of her immediate neighbor. Her tongue felt thick and dry, and panic welled up in her. I mustn't talk to anyone. I mustn't talk—they'll know who he is and take him away.

The two women exchanged a glance, and the fat one said softly, "It's one of those immigrants, doesn't talk no English, that's what it is." And the other one widened her mouth in comprehension and turned back and smiled and nodded exaggeratedly and said loudly and slowly, "Nice baby, nice baby?" And she put her hand out toward the burden in Isobel's crooked arm.

But she reared back, knowing her fear was in her face, and the thin woman made a face and shrugged and turned away to her neighbor.

"Bloody foreigners, come 'ere, usin' our 'ospitals for free. Makes you sick, don't it? 'Oo'd be a poor bleedin' taxpayer? Bad enough they can't talk properly, can't even be civil. You'd think I wanted to pinch her bloody kid, wouldn't yer? Bleedin' likely that is! Got enough little buggers o' me own." And the two of them laughed raucously and then put their heads closer together and went on gossiping, leaving Isobel trembling with reaction.

She looked up at the clock on the cracked white tiles of the waiting-room wall. A quarter past nine. He'd be wanting a feed soon, and she'd have to go somewhere. The waiting room was emptying now, only half a dozen people still sitting in lumpish patience, and even as she looked around, sliding her eyes sideways in an effort to be unobtrusive, the two women beside her got up in response to a beckoning nurse who had appeared at the swing doors and went importantly into the casualty room. The nurse looked back over her shoulder, and her eyes moved over the waiting-room benches. Counting people, Isobel thought. I'll have to go soon, or they'll talk to me, and then—I'll have to go.

She saw the police car opposite the main gates as she moved out into the lamplit street, and she wanted to run. But she was stiff with the fatigue of the fear that had filled her for the past hours, still feeling the residue of the attack of shaking that had forced her to stop in the mercifully crowded casualty waiting room so short a time after she had walked out of the Unit, with no plan in her mind, only a stubborn need to go.

She could only move stolidly onward, unable either to hurry forward or turn back, and the policeman sitting in the front of the car let his eyes move over her and away without showing any concern. And she thought suddenly, It's because I'm fat. Georgie's so small in his blanket and I'm so big he didn't even see I was carrying him, only saw my bag on my arm. And she felt better, even a little elated, as she reached the end of the street and merged with the hurrying crowds of the big main road, letting herself be swallowed up, just another part of the mass that was London.

"We've got every railway station, every bus station, every main outlet there is under surveillance, sir," the Inspector said patiently. "And I've put as many men as I can spare on checking rooming houses and hotels. But without a description of what she's wearing—"

"I've told you already half a dozen times that we can't—"

"Yes, sir. You don't know. But you see the size of the problem. There's over thirteen million people in the Greater London area alone, and by now"—he squinted up at the clock ticking ponderously on his office wall—"almost one A.M.—she could have covered a lot of ground. Got a lift, perhaps. Who knows? We've alerted all regions, but more than that . . . unless you let us try radio, as I suggested, and of course television when it starts tomorrow—later today, that is—"

"Christ, we've got to get him back before then, man! We've got to, or—"

"I can't do more, sir. We could broadcast a message, as I said, in the first bulletins, and that often works the oracle. It's up to you—at present, that is. Mind you, if we don't find her soon, we'll have to take it into our own hands. Abduction, you see. The way you feel about publicity is understandable, but abduction—it's a criminal offense, and once we're called in, we've got to treat it as such."

"You'll have to let them, George," Barbara said softly. "It's obviously true what the Inspector said. If they didn't find her in the first couple of hours, every further hour that goes by makes it more and more difficult. It'll have to get out or we'll never get him back. George?"

He got up and shrugged on his coat. "Oh, all right, all right. Broadcast your message. If it's the only thing you can do. But for Christ's sake, let me have some protection from the press, will you? A few men at the hospital—"

"I haven't got men to search *and* to do that, sir," the Inspector said stolidly. "But I'll do my best for you. I'll see you at the hospital later this morning then, sir. The first message'll go out with the six A.M. bulletin."

"It's been very good of you," Isobel said again. "But I must be going now. And thank you for the supper last night and all. I'd pay you if—"

"Forget it, ducky." The woman pulled her dressing gown closer and yawned widely. "Forget it." She peered through the open door at the thin morning darkness of the street and shivered.

"Sooner you nor me, ducks, at this hour. Sure you won't 'ang about a bit longer? Well, it's up to you. And you take my advice, ducky, and shop the bastard. Throwin' you out like that, an' a poor little baby an' all! You got your rights in common law, you know. I've 'ad some with the sods, and I know. You've got your rights. You tell the fuzz, ducks. Give the bastards somethin' to do instead of goin' after workin' girls and driving 'em round the twist."

She laughed and it spluttered into a cough, and Isobel murmured quickly, "Yes, yes, I will. And thanks again, I'm ever so grateful." And she went out of the door to move as quickly as she could along the dirty pavement.

The woman in the dressing gown went back to her frowsty kitchen and turned on the gas under the kettle and lit her first cigarette before switching on the radio.

"It's not a lot that's really much use, sir." The Inspector, who looked as fresh and clean-shaven as though he'd spent the whole of the night in bed, making George very aware of his own crumpled red-eyed weariness, sounded gloomy. "There's usually a few cranks claim to have something, but this time there's been a real barrage. Calls from Edinburgh and Glasgow, seventeen from Bristol—even a bloke in a tuppenny-ha'penny village near Truro. Almost three hundred altogether. There was one I was pretty hopeful of. A brass, er, a prostitute living on this patch claims she gave a bed for the night to a woman with a baby, supposed to have been thrown out by her man. But then she wanted to know who was paying for the lead—so there you are. There's plenty of those. Think there's a reward, you see. But we'll check 'em all. Every one of 'em. We'll get the child, sooner or later."

And I hope it's alive when we do, he thought, as he nodded at George and went out of the Unit and back to his car. The longer she's gone, the worse the chances are. Spinsters and babies—God, but I hate these cases.

"I had to finish surgery first, Miriam. I came as quickly as I could, but I had to clear the surgery. Now what is it? My God, you look grim. Come on, now, tell me about it. You were almost incoherent when you phoned."

Miriam looked up at her stupidly and opened her mouth and then closed it again and shook her head and let the tears come again, spilling down her face, excoriating her aching eyes.

"I can't. I—Norma, please—I'm ill. Please—"

"I can see you are! I can see. Now just relax, love, just relax and tell me what it is."

Grunting slightly, she lowered her heavy body to her knees and put her hands on Miriam's, tightly intertwined but shaking uncontrollably, and peered up at the ravaged face. "Tell me about it." And her voice was professionally soothing.

"It—all for nothing, all for nothing. It made me into a whore—that's what he said, said I was a whore, and it's true, and now it's all for nothing, all for nothing at all. I'm ill, help me, Norma. I'm ill—"

"Who said you were a—look, put your head forward, like this. That's right, on your knees. And breathe deeply—deeply—good girl. You'll feel calmer in a moment. Deep, now, and again. Good girl. Now, come on—to bed. Come and lie down in bed, and you'll be better soon."

Awkwardly, she led the shaking body across the room into the bedroom and heaved her up into the crumpled sheets and blankets, and Miriam lay there, her eyes closed, and some of the color came back to her face as Norma brushed the hair back from her sweating forehead and murmured gently to her.

Then she opened her eyes again and said, "Norma?" her voice sharp with fear.

"I'm here. I'm here. Now tell me. What is it? What happened to do this to you? You'll feel better if you tell me."

"My face feels stiff. I can't feel my face properly." Miriam was touching her lips with one shaking hand. "I was so sick, and it hurt so, and I can't feel my face properly."

"I know. Just tell me. I'm listening."

"He said it, you see, and I—it should have been all right. *You* said it would be all right, so I did—"

"I said what would be all right?"

"I had to finish it properly. A woman has to have a man if she has a baby. You said, didn't you? So I did, and he said I was a whore, I ought to have got someone from the street, anyone, and I thought it would be all right after him and it wasn't. And—oh, my God, it was all for nothing, all for nothing. It was on the radio this morning. You heard that? It was all for nothing." And the tears came again, and she rolled her head from side to side on the pillow. "It was all for nothing, all for nothing, and I did it and—"

"Stop it, right now. Stop it!" Norma said sharply. "You're not making sense. Now calm down, do you hear me? And tell me what it is, properly. What did I hear this morning? What was all for nothing?"

"The baby—it's gone, and the whole thing's ruined, it must be, now it's gone. And he said—"

"What baby? Who said?"

"Mike. I did what you said, and I got a man. Because of the baby. I should have told you about it, but how could I? But you said a man, so I did. And he told me to get someone off the street, and I did—horrible, horrible, horrible."

And again she rolled her head on the pillow, and this time Norma sat and looked at her and said nothing. Then she sighed softly and went back to the living room for her bag.

"I'm going to give you something to relax you, Miriam." She

found the syringe and began to draw up the dose. "Just a small prick now—keep *still*—good girl. You'll feel better soon, and you'll sleep. Good girl."

She sat beside her for a long time, watching, and gradually the restlessness stopped, and the whimpering died away, and then she was sleeping. Softly Norma stood up and went into the living room to pick up the telephone and dial a number.

"Psychiatric Unit, please," she said quietly and looked back over her shoulder into the bedroom. Miriam was lying still, her heavy breathing clearly audible, and Norma spoke a little more loudly.

"Dr. Galleyman, please. John? Hello. Norma Gould. Fine, thanks. Yes, he's fine too. Look, John, I've got a patient for you. An emergency. Can you find me a bed? Mmm. To be quite honest, I don't really know. She's in a very hysterical state—some sort of explosion or other. I'm not sure whether it's exogenous or not—she's quite incoherent. But there seems to be a paranoid element in it. She's claiming to get messages from the radio. Quite. No, I don't think she's hallucinated, but it's difficult to assess in the state she's in. The thing is, she's an old friend, a very bright girl, and this is most uncharacteristic behavior. Completely bizarre for the personality I know her to be. What? Oh, no. I'd much rather get her into your unit than send her to Friern. Yes, exactly. What? Oh, yes. I've given her Largactil. She'll be easily handled, I think. I'll stay with her anyway, until you send an ambulance. Right. Name—Miriam Lawton. Yes, L-A-W-T . . . yes. Age, er, twenty-six. Albert Street . . ."

17

"Right, Gorton, with that settled, there's something else. The young man I sent to you last week—remember? Going to San Francisco. Yes. When? Hmm. I see. Can't recoup that, then. What about the money—how did you arrange that? Ah! Excellent, excellent. Now I want you to make some new arrangements. Cable them. Yes, this morning, and cancel. That's right. Cancel. They are not to give him a penny, you understand? Did he have any actual cash from you? Well, he'll have to settle for that, though it won't get him far. My dear Gorton, that's his problem! At least we won't waste any more money on him. Right. Thank you—oh, and by the way, it's still not to be known, by anyone. Yes, yes. Of course. I was not suggesting you would. Just repeating the fact that the instruction still stands in spite of the cancellation of the funds. Yes."

He flashed the intercom, after he'd hung up the phone, and said crisply, "Send Bridges in now, will you? No, no coffee. This won't take long. And then call Graham and say—exactly, now—Sir Daniel's compliments, and would he be kind enough to come and see him in his private office in fifteen minutes to join him for lunch. Right? And book a table for us at the Garden—no, er, make it the Savoy. Yes."

Mike took the initiative as soon as he was sitting down, facing him over the desk.

"I'm sorry about it. Very sorry. But I couldn't find the girl, and it's obvious to me that I'm not going to be able to. So I can't get you the story."

"I am not concerned about that." Sefton leaned back in his chair and looked at Mike consideringly. "The time for that has passed. You must surely realize that?"

"Passed? How do you mean?"

"The child's gone, for heaven's sake, man. Use your head!"

"Missing at the moment, yes. But they'll get him back."

"Are you sure? I wish I were so sanguine. The woman's obviously mad. You realize what the outcome can be? She's been on the loose for three full days. And you know as well as I do that the longer the time is, the more likely it is she's panicked. Every policeman in the country searching, the whole damned population watching for her—do you know how many calls a day *we're* getting? They're jamming the switchboard. No, Bridges, the time has passed for what I had originally planned. It is my misfortune that Briant had so little control over his project. He's destroyed my investment with his wretched stupidity. Destroyed it utterly. My task now is to cut my losses, cut them as finely as I can."

"I see. You're relinquishing your support of Briant?"

"Indeed I am. Only a fool remains on a losing side, and I am not a fool, even if my judgment has been awry on this occasion."

"So, where do we go from here?"

"I know where *I'm* going, Bridges. The question is, where are *you* going?" And he smiled thinly.

Mike frowned sharply and lifted his chin to stare at the smooth square face. Then he said very softly, "Suppose you tell me."

"I am not enjoying this, Bridges. Not in the least. It is always distressing to me when individuals suffer because of other people's ineptitude. But this is virtually out of my hands. My duty is to the *Echo* and its readers. I must find a way to help my readers understand why it is necessary for us to change our—tack, shall we say?—without losing too many of them. If only Briant had been the capable man I had believed him to be." He shook his head sadly. "But something went wrong with him. Perhaps his private problems came between him and his work and affected *his* judgment. Who can say? Whatever it was that caused the situation, it inevitably has repercussions and unfortunately, it happens that individuals are caught by them, and suffer through no fault of their own. I am suffering personally. No man enjoys knowing he has lacked shrewdness, failed to accurately foresee an outcome. The infant, one is forced to fear, is suffering or has suffered some—well, we must wait and see about that. And you—"

"Yes? What about me? Do tell me. I'm positively panting to hear of the role you've assigned to me in your—"

"Come, now, Bridges, there's no point in taking that tone. There is nothing personal in any of this, and you must see that. Let us be gentlemen about the matter—"

"OK. So I'm a gentleman. And I want to know what the bloody hell it is that you're planning and that affects me. A little less of the best butter and a bit more solid information would—"

"James McClarrie is coming to me from the *Clarion*. Not as good a science background as yours, I know, but he has written some excellent anti-Briant pieces, and with the right handling of the publicity about his decision to join the *Echo*'s team, I think our readers will—"

"Accept me as a scapegoat. Is that it? You'll make it look as though the *Echo*'s point of view was based on *my* attitudes, that all your drum-beating for Briant was *my* idea, and that now the thing's gone sour, I've been chucked? Is that it? Christ, but you're a bastard, Sefton! I wrote the stuff I did entirely at *your* instigation. At the start of the whole thing, I was prepared to give you straight-down-the-middle stuff, no judgments, just straight factual reporting. But you turn me into a commentator, and now because you—my God, but you're a bastard."

"An undignified exchange of personalities is of small value,

Bridges. I will forget your remarks, since you are naturally distressed at the thought of leaving the *Echo*. I—"

"Bloody big of you! You'll forget! Big deal!" Mike was on his feet, his face white with fury. "Well, I'll tell you something. I'm not so conveniently good at forgetting. And I remember something you'd very much like forgotten! The fact that you financed Briant. Oh, boy, that'll interest a few people."

Sefton raised his eyebrows and said gently, "I agree. It would. If it were true."

"If it were true! You know you—"

"I know what constitutes truth, Bridges. Mere statements do not. To have the real ring of, er, verisimilitude, one needs evidence. Documentary evidence. And there is none."

"You entered into a contract. The legal—"

Sefton smiled again. "You must think me remarkably stupid, Bridges. Without making any admissions, let me ask you to consider a hypothetical situation. *Suppose* a man such as myself drew up a contract without external legal aid, having sufficient knowledge of legal methodology to do so. *Suppose* the other party to such a private contract lacked similar knowledge and therefore accepted it. And *suppose* in exchange for an assurance that the first party would not demand any restitution of monies paid under it, for which that first party had not received fair recompense, the second party agreed to return the contract copy he held? Where would be any documentary proof that the arrangement had ever been made?"

He leaned forward and spoke in a very quiet voice, his eyes fixed on Mike's face.

"Mr. Bridges. Let me warn you against making any such wild statements as you seem to envisage. In the absence of any real proof, you would be hard put to it indeed to make any defense should a case be brought against you for libel, or slander, or both. I make myself abundantly clear? I trust so. And now . . ."

He leaned back again and once again produced his affable smile. "And now we will put this unfortunate few minutes of conversation quite out of mind. I am a fair man, Bridges, and you will find that Gorton has for you a check that takes into account the sterling work you have done in the past, and the sad ending of what has been a comparatively harmonious relationship between us. I have gone to some pains to ensure that you have no case to take to the NUJ. The Father of your Chapel is a most, ah, intelligent man. And having seen the amount of your copy we have decided to spike this past few days, and knowing of the failure to get the girl's story —well, I really wouldn't try to make this a union matter, my dear boy. Hardly worth the trouble."

"My failure to get—oh, my God!" Mike began to laugh, throwing his head back, and Sefton frowned and reached for his intercom. "Mr. Bridges is ready to go, if you please."

When the door opened behind him and the tall secretary came in to stand heavily beside him, Mike was no longer laughing but staring somberly at the man at the desk.

"Goodbye, Mr. Bridges. I trust you will soon decide on your future. I wish you all success in it, wherever it may lead you."

Sefton bent his head to his desk, and the secretary stood back with exaggerated courtesy to leave a clear way to the door. Mike looked back when he reached it and stared for a moment at the man behind the desk and then shrugged.

"Well, Sefton, you old bastard, there's one thing I've got out of this that you didn't get your filthy hands on, and I'm grateful for that. I failed to get the girl's story! Oh, boy, oh, boy! That's really beautiful."

The door opened, and Mike turned to see Graham standing hesitantly in its opening.

"Your secretary isn't in the anteroom, Sir Daniel—oh! I'm sorry if I—"

"My dear Graham! Do come in. I'm quite free now." Sir Daniel stood up and came around the desk, his hand outstretched. "Now, my dear fellow, a little sherry before we go?"

"Er, thank you." Graham looked slightly puzzled, and Mike laughed again and said viciously, "You'd better take it, chum. With the sort of licking you'll be expected to do for the next little while, you're going to have a right crappy taste in your mouth without something to take the edge off!"

And he slammed through the door, taking immense pleasure in

elbowing the secretary to one side so violently that he nearly fell.

I'm so tired, Georgie, so tired, all the way through to my middle. So tired. I'll tell my mum about it, and she'll give me some . . .

She shivered and shook her head, trying to clear it. It was so silly, the way she got all mixed up, sometimes feeling as though she were Georgie and seeing her mum's face as clear as if she were there, and then knowing she had been dead these years and years, but hearing her talking.

She rummaged in the big bag on the seat beside her, looking for—what? She had already forgotten, even as she stared into its cluttered mess of diapers and bits of food in screws of paper. It was getting harder and harder to think properly, to remember what it was all about. It had been for so long, all her life, it seemed, that it had been going on, walking from place to place, with Georgie getting heavier on her arm, and her feet hurting so that she felt the ache deep in her belly, across her back, merging with the ache in her head. If she could only find a proper bed to sleep in instead of park benches and all-night launderettes—though they were at least warm—that would make all the difference. Just to lie down instead of sitting and walking and then sitting again. Somewhere warm and safe and soft where she could lie down and sleep.

There was a rhythmic beat coming from somewhere, and she listened to it, and the sound of it merged with the thought of a soft safe warm bed, with the thought of lying in the cot with the pulsing mattress. No, *Georgie*, lying in the pulsing cot, not herself. Georgie . . .

The beat softened, merged with the high sweetness of violins, and she blinked and quite suddenly her head was clear again and she stared around at the big high-vaulted concourse, at the hurrying people sweeping past the smokily dim lights of the platform barriers, the knotted groups clustered around heaps of luggage, the long slow-moving trucks driven by grubby-looking men in shapeless uniforms, the bright cases of neon signs and bookstalls and coffee trolleys, and for a moment panic came back. How long had she been sitting here? Had someone noticed her, noticed Georgie bundled in his thin blanket on the seat beside her, started wondering, connecting her with the placards by the bookstalls, and their shrieking "Briant Baby! Latest Developments!"?

". . . the seven-fifteen from Cardiff, due at platform seven, now running forty-nine minutes late. British Rail regrets . . . signal failure . . ." The voice boomed its muffled echoes, and then the music rose again, thin and sweet, blending with a smell of coffee from the stall at the end of the row of benches on which she was sitting. I'm hungry, she thought suddenly. I'll have to eat something or my milk will go off and Georgie—I'll have to eat something. And she turned again to the bag beside her, remembering what it was she had started to look for.

It was darker suddenly, and she had to peer closer into the bag. There were still some biscuits, weren't there? There should be, somewhere. And then maybe with some coffee from the stall she'd feel better, and it would be time to find somewhere to feed Georgie. He was still sleeping, but soon, he'd be hungry, and they said he must never cry for a feed, didn't they? But the darkness in the bag moved and she knew with sudden sick certainty that it was a shadow and looked up, staring at the man looking down at her, and felt her face stiffen with fear. He was wearing a dark overcoat and holding a soft hat in one hand, the other plunged deep in his coat pocket, and she thought, He's a policeman. He smells like a policeman and he's noticed . . .

"Excuse me, madam, just making a routine check."

"It's running forty-nine minutes late, they said, didn't they?"

"I beg your pardon?"

"The Cardiff train—running forty-nine minutes late? It's shocking the way they keep you hanging around in these places—and my baby'll be getting hungry soon."

She leaned sideways and picked up the bundled Georgie and looked over him at the watchful face staring at her and suddenly held the bundle out invitingly.

"I'll have to phone home and tell them—running forty-nine minutes late, and they'll be worrying. But my baby—Jenny—will you hold her for me while I go to the phone? I won't be a minute."

He looked at her carefully for a moment and then relaxed his watchfulness and shook his head and smiled thinly. "Sorry, madam, can't help, I'm afraid. One of these ladies, maybe." He turned his head briefly to look along the lines of self-absorbed people on the benches and then back to her. "Or try the Ladies'—someone there'll oblige, I'm sure. Waiting for someone on the train, are you?"

"My mother. The Ladies', yes, that's what I'll do. Thanks." Awkwardly, she stood up, hefting Georgie to her other arm, and picked up the bag and moved away, feeling his eyes on her back, consideringly, but he didn't follow her, and when she reached the far side and the door marked "Ladies' Waiting Room," she looked back and saw him bending over and talking to a woman with a pushchair beside her. And she giggled inside her head and thought, Silly, silly, silly. That baby, it's at least a year old. Doesn't he know that? That's not Georgie, and he let me go because he didn't know that. Silly, silly, silly.

God is on our side, Georgie, she said silently as she plodded heavily down the steps toward the lavatories. Every time, He does it, puts the words there, makes them come out right, every time. I wish I wasn't so hungry.

She stood for a moment in the cold whiteness of the lavatory area until the fat overalled woman with a towel over her arm took a penny from the girl who had gone clattering down the stairs in front of her. When the attendant had clicked open one of the heavy doors and gone in to wipe around the seat, she moved quickly across to the far side and fumbled a penny from her bag and was inside before the woman could notice. As long as they didn't see you go in, they couldn't tell how long you'd been there. She couldn't stand it again, having them bang and bang on the door, and then open it from outside and stare at her perched there with Georgie at her breast. That time, the woman had been all right, she'd had six herself she'd said, and you couldn't just feed them any old where, could you? And she kept her lavs as sweet and clean as any, so no harm done. But she couldn't face that again.

She heard the busy repetition of creaking and slamming doors from outside and relaxed. Busy places were the best every time. She'd be able to stay here a long while, long enough to get him fed.

And after that, maybe, she'd be able to think of somewhere to go where she could sleep. Maybe.

"What makes you think I can help you?"

"You're the only Norma Gould in the book. The only doctor, that is. She mentioned your name once. You do know her, don't you? And if you're her doctor, you should know what's going on. So why not tell me?" He frowned irritably as she stared at him, doubt on her face.

"Look, what's the mystery? The woman in the flat below here told me she'd gone in an ambulance." His voice sharpened. "What happened? Did she—what did she do to herself?"

"What makes you think she did something to herself? I'm sorry to seem uncooperative, but you must see I can't just—wait a moment. *What* did you say your name was?"

"Bridges. I—"

"No. Your first name."

"Michael. What—"

"Ah! Mike. We've got nothing out of her since she was admitted, but she did say—yes. Mike. How long have you known her?"

"For God's sake, what is this? I go to see a girl, no one seems to know where she is, just that she was taken ill, and I come to you because you're the only lead I have, and now you—look, what is it? *Did* she do something to herself?"

"No. But I'm interested to know why you should think she might have done. I'm not just being unnecessarily curious. We need to know, you see. It would help in her treatment. The thing is, she's had a breakdown, for want of a better word. I admitted her to a psychiatric unit. It would be a considerable help to get some background information about this illness. And you might be able to provide some of it. So, before I can decide whether or not you should be allowed to visit her, I'll need to talk to you. Later, the psychiatrist looking after the case will want to interview you too, if you're willing to help. But I'm an old friend of hers, you see, so I'd like to talk to you first. So, could you tell me please, how long you've known her? And then how she has behaved in recent weeks? It really would be a great help."

"It's completely beyond me. The woman can't have disappeared into the ether! With all the fuss there's been, the television appeals, the newspaper publicity—pictures of both of them have been plastered everywhere for the best part of five days. How inept can your people be not to have found them yet?"

"The pictures aren't all they might be, Dr. Briant. You admitted that yourself. Taking stills from a video tape recording, you don't get the definition, you see. And a baby—well, you know how one baby looks very like another! I remember, when my second was in hospital, and we went to see her. Three months old she was, and do you think I could easily pick her out of a wardful?" The Inspector shook his head. "No, Dr. Briant, you can't say my men aren't doing their damnedest, because they are. If there's one thing really gets my boys going it's a baby case. And this woman—Quinn—she's so damned *ordinary*! You walk into any supermarket any time today and you'll see a dozen who could be her. I keep telling you, we're doing our best. We can't do more."

George stood up and walked across the room fretfully to stand staring out of the window at the courtyard. "It's not as though the woman were all that bright, for God's sake! I may have misjudged her bloody emotional state, but I know I didn't misjudge her mental capacities. She hasn't the wit to evade a really determined search, she'd walk straight into trouble the first—"

"Ah, that's where you're wrong, Dr. Briant, quite wrong. The dimmer they are, the more likely they are to get away with it. Give me your clever villain and I'll nail him. But your daft ones, the ones who plan nothing, walk off the street into the first likely looking crib, bash the back door in and help themselves—they get away with it. The harder they try to plan things, the more they use their heads, the more likely it is they leave a trail as wide as . . . as the M-One. But the dim ones—it's because they don't see trouble coming that they avoid it so easily—walk right through it, really. We'll catch ten smart embezzlers for every stupid shoplifter we manage to nobble. It's like I said, Doctor. We're doing our best. We can't do more. But now we've got your people involved, it may speed up. So far your Miss Hervey's covered the North London area hospitals and nurseries and the like; we'll take her across the water this afternoon. And with your other people—well, we should have made a direct check on every abandoned baby in the country within the next week—"

"The next week! I tell you frankly, Inspector, unless we get him back sooner than that, the whole thing will have been a waste of time. I'm already very doubtful about the possibilities of salvaging much out of the—oh, God damn it all to hell! Two years, two years to end like this! It's more than—"

The Inspector paused at the door and stared back at him, a faint frown on his face. "You do want to find him, no matter what, of course?"

"What? Oh, I suppose you'll have to go on. But unless you get him back here very soon, my own feeling is"—he shrugged—"there won't be much point in it."

"I thought you were worried about him. The baby, I mean. If he were mine, I'd be—well, I don't know much about the science of it all, but he's a baby, after all, isn't he? I'm a father myself, and I know how I'd feel in your shoes."

"Yes. Yes, of course," George said. "But *soon.* That's the whole point of the operation. *Soon.*"

The Inspector looked at him for a moment and then said, "Yes, sir," and his voice was flat with dislike.

George woke suddenly as the light hit his eyes, and he blinked stupidly into the glare, aware of the stiffness of his neck, the pins and needles in the arm that had lain crumpled beneath the weight of his body in the chair.

"Who—what is it? Have you got him?" he said thickly and tried to focus his eyes on the shape of the figure by the door.

"It's me."

"What? Hilary! What are you—I'm sorry, I fell alseep. I haven't had much sleep these past days. What is it?"

She stood sullenly beside the door, her hands in her coat pockets, her head down so that she need not meet his eyes. "I didn't want to come but she made me."

"What? Oh, I'm sorry. I can't think straight. I'm still disorientated. Give me a moment or two." He stood up and crossed the room to the basin in the corner and began to wash his face in cold water.

"What time is it?" He dried his face roughly and turned to look at her.

"Half past nine." And this time she looked up at him and her face changed. "Oh, Dad, you look awful! As though—"

"I've been— well, you know what's happened, I suppose."

"Yes. I know."

"Is that why you came?" He smiled thinly at her, suddenly glad to see her standing there. "You must be as distressed as we are here."

"I didn't want to come. She made me."

He frowned. "Your mother? She sent you?"

"She's been trying to phone you, for days, ever since Ian went. They wouldn't put her through."

"We've refused all calls except official police ones. Ian—what's that about Ian?"

"The cable came this morning. He . . . got a job of some sort—in San Francisco. That's where he cabled from, anyway."

"San—what? How the hell did he get there?"

"I don't know." Hilary sounded sullen again. "I don't much care. I don't care about anything. I just want to be left in peace." She looked away from him, her mouth held in an ugly line as she tried not to let the crying start again. "I don't care about anything any more."

"Look, my dear, I know how distressed you were the . . . the evening you left the Unit. I've wanted to talk to you about it, but you weren't here, were you? Your mother told me—well, I know you've been made very unhappy about things, but—"

"I don't want to talk about it!" she said violently. "Not now or ever. I wouldn't have come, only she made me."

"My dear child. I'd be as content to say no more about an unnecessary and unfortunate incident as you. I would never force you to do anything against your will, and I—well, I assumed you wanted to stay with your mother. But if you would prefer to return here to me, well, then we'll forget all about it."

"I came because she made me," Hilary said again, mulishly.

He frowned. "She wants you to come back to the Unit?"

"She wants you. She doesn't care about me." She looked at him and then at the floor. "No more than you do."

"That's most unjust! You know I do."

"It doesn't matter. Nothing about me matters. You've got . . . *her*. And she—" She swallowed. "I won't talk about it. I've told you what I was sent to tell you, and"—again she swallowed—"so I've told you. She says you've got to come right away."

"Your mother?"

"Yes! I *told* you. She wants you. She's ill."

He looked at her for a moment and then walked back to his desk and sat down heavily.

"Ill: I see. That was her exact message?"

"Yes. She's ill, and you've got to come."

"I see. Now, you tell me. Is she ill?"

"I said so!"

"No, your *mother* said so. I—one doesn't want to be harsh, my dear, but you know as well as I do your mother has been . . . well, using her health as a weapon for a long time. I would be the first to admit that once she was ill, but her kidney disease has been under control for a long time now, and there have been so many times when I—when she has caused me to be anxious about her health when there was no just cause. So I'm asking you, is she ill, or does she merely say she is?"

"I don't know. How can I know? She says she feels ill, and she seems—oh, don't ask me. I was sent to tell you, so I've told you."

"Please, Hilary, try to be adult about this. You aren't a child any more. You know the situation between us. I wish it hadn't happened, but it has, and there it is. I must tell you I have made up my mind that I won't suffer any more at your mother's hands. I'm sorry for her, deeply sorry. I know she's unhappy, but there is nothing I can do about it. I can't change the situation an iota, not in any way that would satisfy her. And for that reason I am not prepared to be—I won't let her confuse my life any further. And I suspect that she's . . . using a threat of illness to confuse me now. Can you understand that?"

"When people tell me I've got to be an adult about something, it usually means I've got to say what they want me to, and not what I really think. I suppose you want me to say she isn't ill. Well, she said I had to be an adult too, and she wanted me to tell you she *is*. I just want to be left in *peace*. I don't know what I'm supposed to say—I wish you'd both leave me alone."

She was crying now, painfully, her face red and creased, and he put his hand out toward her, but she shook her head furiously and sniffed heavily, turning her head to wipe her cheek roughly against her coat collar.

"Oh, Hilary, I'm sorry. You shouldn't have to—I'm sorry." He stood up and came around the desk toward her and put an arm across her shoulders, and for a moment she resisted. But then she relaxed and turned her head and rested it against him and abandoned herself to her tears, weeping noisily and luxuriously.

He let her cry for a while and then gave her a handkerchief from his pocket and led her to a chair before going back to his own and leaning across the desk to smile carefully at her. "Better now? Good girl. Now, listen, my dear. Just let me sort things out, and then we'll say no more. You'll stay here, just as you used to. And when"—he frowned then for a moment—"when we get the baby back, and it can't be long now before they find him, we'll go on as before, hmm? But just tell me—*is* she really ill? Or is this just another of her . . . usual episodes?"

She looked at him and then wiped her eyes again before sitting staring at the desk, her forehead slightly creased. She thought of Marjorie, of the awfulness of the way she had lain for hours on the sofa alternately crying and moaning, and then sleeping heavily. She thought of the bleakness of the uncared-for house, the loneliness of it, of the misery of the past few days compared with the way things had been when she had lived here in the Unit.

"Well?" George said, and she looked up at him and smiled a little waveringly and closed her mind to the memory of Marjorie's puffy red face, the way she had so often vomited with horrifying noisiness in the lavatory, the way she seemed to have aged ten years in a few days.

"I think she's been drinking rather a lot," she said, and George nodded heavily.

"I can quite see she would turn to that. But that's all? I mean, if she's drinking a lot, it would account for—oh, damn it, how could *you* know? If she has genuine symptoms, you wouldn't be able to tell. Well, either way, she's not fit to be responsible for a child of—"

Hilary made an odd sound, half giggle, half sob. "Now I'm a child again, so it doesn't matter what I say, does it?"

"What? Oh, well, that was fair, I suppose. I am trying to have it both ways."

"Well, I *am* a child. I *am*. I'm no good at all this business. I can't tell people what they ought to do, or what's true or what isn't. I'm no good at working things out. I want to do what I want, not what other people keep saying I ought to."

She began to cry again, and he felt a momentary twinge of irritation, and then an immediate surge of guilt. She was quite right, of course; how could she cope with so complex a situation? It was cruelly unjust of Marjorie to use her as a go-between in this way. Drinking, and letting the child see it—it was outrageous. Ill or not, it was outrageous. And of course she wasn't. It was just another of her wretched play-acting ploys, and he couldn't, he wouldn't, suffer it any longer.

He rubbed his face, suddenly aware again of his deep fatigue, and said heavily, "It's all right, Hilary. Forget it. It's not your problem. You go on up and make yourself a hot drink and go to bed. I'll deal with this."

He sat for a long time after she had gone and then picked up the telephone. He began to dial a number and then, with sudden petulance, slammed down the phone. To hell with her. If she was genuinely ill, she could call a doctor for herself. He had enough to worry about right now. From here on, Marjorie was her own problem.

18

It was cold, so cold. A heavy cold that weighed on the back of her neck and pushed her body down against the hardness of the slatted seat, that pressed up against her feet cruelly, so cruelly that she whimpered a little with the pain of it.

He stirred in her arms at the sound, and she looked down to peer at his face and felt a sudden leap of fear. He wasn't there. All she could see was the buttons of her coat strained across her chest, and then she whimpered again, but now with relief. She had forgotten, so silly to have forgotten. She had managed to tuck his small body inside her coat, to button him against her and keep him warm, to stop people seeing him.

Not that there was anyone around who could see him, not here. A good place, this, a private place, although it was such a cold one. A *good* place.

She lifted her head and listened, but it was still the same. The faint rattle of the twigs on the bushes as the wind moved through them, the hissing sound above as the wind went upward to reach the leafless trees, the hoarse whispering rumble of traffic coming from somewhere very far away. And it all looked the same, the darkness stretching away into patches of heavier darkness that were empty flower beds and clumps of shrubs, the faintly glowing deep gray sky reflected away on her right in the shifting dull gleam that was the water.

When you're a big boy, Georgie, we'll come to this park in the daytime, and we'll sail a little boat on the water, that's what we'll do, won't we? When you're a big boy, and they've stopped looking for us. When you're big . . .

He stirred again in her arms and gave a thin muffled cry, and she pulled at her coat and peered into the darkness inside it. She couldn't see his face, but she could feel a faint warmth from him, and she lifted him closer to rest her cold face against him. But he wasn't as warm as she had thought, for his cheek was as cold as her own, and she murmured, "There, there, my lovey, soon make it better, soon . . ."

With fingers doubled in size with the cold she fumbled at her clothes, unbuttoning her cardigan and then her blouse, pulling at her breast so that he could reach her, and she tried to make him open his mouth, to take the nipple and start feeding, but he rolled his head, and she held him close and said again, "There, there, my lovey, soon be better, soon . . ."

This time he managed it and began to suckle, but after the initial awareness of the pull on her, the cold came down again, and she could feel nothing but the ache in her legs and the hardness of the seat. But it didn't matter. As long as she knew he was feeding, it didn't matter.

She leaned her body forward as a sudden sharper gust of wind curled into her clothes, touching her bare skin, and moving awkwardly, bent her knees closer by tucking her feet more under the bench, so that he was enveloped by her body. It was a comfortable position, she suddenly realized with startled pleasure. She hadn't tried sitting like this before. To curve her back forward seemed to relieve the ache across her shoulders, to bring more warmth to her belly, even to make her feet hurt less, and she let her head droop further forward in gratitude for the comfort.

But it didn't last long. The cold came back, the aching, and this time she moved sideways, lifting her feet awkwardly up onto the bench, resting her back against the curled iron armrest, still keeping her knees bent to keep Georgie safely pressed against her body.

And now it was really easier. Much easier. By moving her buttocks slightly sideways she could rest her head against the back of the bench, could hide herself from the coldness of the wind. This way it didn't matter that she could hardly feel the positions of her own arms and legs, because the back of the seat held her safe, held her crooked arm firmly so that Georgie's face was held close against the safety of her body. He seemed to be happier too, for he didn't move, just lay in her arms quietly. She looked down once more, feeling sleep creeping toward her from the darkness beyond her safe bench, trying to see his jaws pumping, to gain the familiar pleasure of watching him feed, but she couldn't see him properly in the dimness. But it didn't matter, not being able to see. He was here, safe with her, and no one would come to take him away from her, not from this safe, quiet place. A good place. Not so cold any more. Not now she was getting used to it.

The sleep came nearer, stepping gently toward her out of the darkness, bringing the soft blackness with it, moving up the bench, around it, and then lightly over her, and she closed her eyes and let it cradle her and Georgie, let it make them both warm again.

"Mr. Bridges, I've told you as clearly as I can that it would not be to Miss Lawton's interest to be visited by you now. Later, perhaps, when she has had sufficient treatment to be able to cope with the situation, but not now. Surely you can understand that?"

"I understand what you say, but I take leave to disagree with you. I may not know as much about clinical psychiatry as I might, but surely the support of friends is an essential part of treatment? And she has so few . . ."

The heavy man in the white coat leaned back in his chair and looked consideringly at him, and Mike looked back defiantly. He couldn't have explained why it was that he was being so dogged about this, why he had spent so much time convincing Norma Gould that his concern for Miriam was genuine, why he had felt it so necessary to persist in his demands to talk to the psychiatrist in charge of the case. But it was necessary. And he wasn't going to give in now and go meekly away without seeing the girl, without talking to her.

"Tell me something, Mr. Bridges," Dr. Galleyman said. "Have you wondered why you should be so anxious to see this girl? On your own admission, you hardly know her. I am aware of course of, er, the extent of your involvement with her. We have managed to obtain quite a comprehensive history. But even so, your involvement, though intimate, was of a very short duration, wasn't it? Now, you say you know little about clinical psychiatry, yet surely you must realize that your own needs are being expressed in this anxiety? That you are not being . . . well, merely friendly. I feel it is possible that in some way you are seeking an answer to a problem of your own as much as trying to offer help to my patient."

"Oh, for Christ's sake! Haven't you enough patients? Do you have to fill in your spare time analyzing their visitors?"

Dr. Galleyman smiled. "Belligerence is an interesting response, Mr. Bridges. Quite diagnostic in some cases. May I suggest to you that you analyze yourself? I certainly don't wish to. As you say, I have quite enough work to do without adding to it unnecessarily. I suggest the possibility that you have a personal need in this situation in order to save my time, in fact. Until you have some insight into your own motives for this stubborn refusal to accept the reasons for waiting until Miss Lawton is able to cope with a visit from you, clearly you are going to make a considerable nuisance of yourself. And since you are far from being a fool, and seem, as far as I can tell on so short an acquaintance, a reasonably well adjusted individual, I will offer you a few ideas to think about. Now—"

He began to count on his fingers.

"One, I suggest to you that you feel guilt because you think that your acceptance of her sexual advances precipitated her present state of frank illness. Two, I suggest you feel guilt in a more general way since you were, as part of your job, a supporter of the man whose scientific activities led to Miss Lawton's belief—based though it was on erroneous thinking—that she had a need to make those sexual advances to you. Three, I suggest you are driven to expiate your sense of guilt by throwing it back at Miss Lawton, either in the form of an apology, or in the form of a denial of what you subconsciously feel is your share of the blame.

"Well, if I am right, I can tell you this. First, your contribution to her present condition was nothing like as important as you think. She would have reached this stage of florid breakdown even if you had not had intercourse with her. Second, to take to yourself a . . . a corporate guilt about the use of her in Dr. Briant's project is pointless. If there is any need for such guilt, it is indeed a corporate one, that is, should be shared by every individual in our society. And third, she has quite enough of her own problems with which to cope without being burdened by your need to either apologize or deny blame."

He smiled gently at the silent man on the other side of his desk. "You are right in your recognition of her need for the support of friends. She will need it, but not until she begins to get better. If you can spend the next few weeks coming to terms with your own problems, then by the time she is ready for you, I will be more than happy—indeed, eager—to allow you access to her. In the meantime, I am sufficiently interested in her future welfare to offer you the chance to come and talk to me here from time to time. I believe it will be possible to help this very interesting girl to recover from the emotional illness toward which I believe she has been moving for some time, and which was hastened in its onset by her recent experiences. And part of her recovery will undoubtedly consist of—shall we say?—the hope of meaningful relationships in the future. If you relate to her as much as I suspect you do—and I am not sure you are yet aware yourself of how emotionally involved you are—then Miss Lawton has an excellent prognosis. An excellent one."

He stood up and moved toward the door to open it and stand back invitingly.

"It is up to you, Mr. Bridges. I hope you now see the situation as clearly as I would wish you to. There is a very good outlook for both my patient and for you. If you will *be* patient. And now if you will forgive me, I must send you away. I have some work to do."

She woke to a thin grayness that filled every part of herself as well as the landscape around her, and sat staring stupidly around, her mind clouded with bewilderment. And then she knew the heavy ache in her legs that had woken her, felt it change, become actual pain, and remembered.

Awkwardly, she moved, heaving her legs clumsily off the bench, until they were resting on the ground and shrieking their hurt at her, and then she flexed her shoulders slightly and looked down to see if Georgie was still asleep.

He didn't move against her arm as she eased it away from its cramped position against her body, until with a clumsy twist of her shoulders that dropped her arm lower, his head fell away from her breast and lolled heavily against the crook of her elbow.

"Hello, my little lovey, did I wake you?" she murmured aloud. Then she slid her other hand under his head to turn him so that he was lying on her lap and she could look into his face.

He was patchily red, the skin creased around his mouth and nose into deeply indented white lines, and his eyes were half open, the narrow edge of bluish whiteness matching the color of the creases.

Poor Georgie . . . doesn't want to wake up. But it's time to wake up, time to find another safe place to be, or they'll be coming here as well, Georgie.

She moved her knees against the ache in her legs and his head rolled again, lax and curiously weighty, and she lifted him and tried to hold him against her breast, but the heaviness of him seemed to defeat her, seemed to defeat him too, for again his head rolled and she peered at him in the thin gray light and whispered, "Georgie? Try to wake up properly, Georgie. Don't play games with me, Georgie, don't frighten your Isobel."

But he didn't respond, lying against her arm with a chill weight that matched the feeling in her body, and she stood up with agonizing slowness, hearing the muscles shout their agony at her, and held him close and whispered again, "Don't play games, Georgie."

Again she looked at him, and now his head was twisted awkwardly against the buttons of her coat, and she eased him away from her then, and with one stiff icy hand tried to arrange his head comfortably against her, pulling at her clothes so that his cheek with its red and blue-white patches was against the fabric of her cardigan.

But she knew now. She knew, yet she did not know, for she spoke again, louder, hearing her own voice, hoarse with cold, filling her ears against the silent voice inside her that was crying aloud words she would not listen to.

"Sleep a little more, my lovey, sleep a little more if you want to. Your Isobel won't wake you."

She began to move, dragging one leaden foot in front of the other, pushing away the deeper gray of the concrete path so that the monotoned landscape around her moved, the trees and bushes that bordered the path going past her in jerky slowness. And as they went, they muttered with their own whispering voices at Georgie, telling him to wake up and not to play games, to wake up and not to play games, to wake up . . .

The edge of the path was shimmering now, and the voices whispering at Georgie stopped being whispers, became a liquid murmuring that took up the same refrain, as the water of the lake glimmered and moved and pulsed its way past her, and she turned her head to look at it, at the moving silveriness of it, and saw its pulsing, lifting and falling in gentle grayness.

Pulsing and shifting, moving gently and grayly, murmuring and pulsing . . .

You want to sleep more, Georgie, you want to sleep more, my little lovey? Do you want to sleep in your soft beating bed again? Poor Georgie, wanting to sleep.

The water beside the path moved even more slowly, turned itself so that it wasn't edging the path any more, but lay across it, filling her vision in front and below as well as on each side, moving up her legs, weighting them ever more heavily, pulling downward with a murmuring insistence she could not deny. An insistence she did not want to deny, for she could feel Georgie in the crook of her arm pulling himself down toward it, and she said aloud, just as the weight of him met the pull of the water and lifted the pain from her, "Georgie."

"But suppose they don't get the child back. What then? You've lost your—what was it you called him? The instrument that will lead man back to God. And I—"

"And you are afraid you will lose what I offered you? Isn't that it? Isn't that why you are here this evening?"

Joel Wayne's voice was as urbane as ever, and he smiled at Gurney with great sweetness. "As I said to you before, my dear Kenneth, how little you comprehend the ways of God if you think I will abandon you should matters arrange themselves so that I have no further obvious use for you. For a man of much basic talent, you are sadly lacking in true understanding."

"I haven't said yet that I'm prepared to accept your offer," Gurney said a little sulkily. "But obviously I want to know where I stand in the event of—well, the Briant project failing. That's reasonable enough."

"Oh, eminently reasonable, in your terms, Kenneth. But your terms"—he shook his head sadly—"they always let you down, do they not?"

"I don't know what you're talking about."

"Don't you?" The other man stood up and moved across the room to the coffee trolley beside the couch to pour cups for both of them. "Well, then, my dear friend, let me explain."

He came back with the drinks and sat down beside Gurney, his every movement filled with friendliness.

"As I see you, Kenneth, all your life you have been rather like Aesop's dog. You remember that unfortunate animal? He was crossing a river, a bone clutched in his jaws, and he looked down and saw reflected in the water another dog, carrying an even juicier and more toothsome bone—or so he thought. And desire for the better bone overcame him, and he opened his jaws to seize it. And lo, the bone he was carrying was lost, swept away in the flood, and with it went the shadowy bone he had yearned for. Is it not what has happened to you many times, dear Kenneth? You seize what appears to be a great prize—or at least the promise of one.

And then, even before you have time to explore the reality of the prize you hold, you drop it in favor of one that looks more promising, more immediately productive of the treasures you long to possess."

"A very facile analysis on the basis of a very slender acquaintanceship, Wayne! If it weren't so amusing, I'd be justified in being very angry at so—"

"If you are not angry, then there is indeed great hope for you, Kenneth. In fact, of course, you are angry, are you not? Yes, of course you are. But there is still hope for you. The hope of the love of God. It is there, waiting for you to accept it—"

"Oh, for crying out loud! Do you have to start on that again? I told you, as far as I'm concerned, that cat won't jump. I don't believe one word of your pious mouthings, couldn't care less about God or—"

"If that were true, you would not be here, trying to make sure that the shadowy bone you saw in my offer is real enough to warrant dropping the bone that is your bill. Oh, I have no doubt that you have assured yourself you are interested only in the money you can get from joining me. That you *think* you couldn't care less about God. But you care. You cannot help but care, dear man, since God cares for you. As long as He does, even those that seem to reject Him are destined to accept Him. And that includes you."

"Look, can we leave this? It's a waste of time, and if you want to waste yours, mine is too valuable to me. I came only to . . . to find out what you will do if the Briant project comes to an end. That's all."

"Then I will tell you that if it does, it is God's will, and that in His own good time—very precious time, too—He will tell me what to do. And when I know, I will tell you. I will be here when you return to accept my offer of God's love. And you will return, you know. You will return."

And again he smiled his smile of ineffable sweetness and finished his coffee.

19

George was already sitting at the big board-room table when they came in in twos and threes, barely concealing his impatience as they settled themselves around the expanse of gleaming mahogany. None of them looked directly at him, although several of them muttered, "Good afternoon," as they passed his chair, before sitting and murmuring at one another while they waited for Sir Peter Apthorp to start the proceedings.

He came in last of all and, without apologizing for his lateness, cleared his throat and spoke crisply from his seat in the big carved chair at the head of the table.

"Well, gentlemen, ladies, we have just half an hour to deal with this matter. As you probably know, Briant has asked for an extraordinary meeting of the hospital medical committee, since he wishes to put a motion to us. George, will you explain what it is you want us to discuss, if you please."

George leaned forward in his chair and set his elbows firmly on the table, clasping his hands on the blotter in front of him. He spoke to his hands, not raising his eyes to the faces that stared silently at him.

"You will all know, of course, what has happened to the work upon which I have been engaged this past two years. We have lost the child who provided all essential research data, under exceedingly unfortunate circumstances. What I want to talk to you about is the future of the work to which I have devoted myself. It is my firm wish to continue my research. The loss of the present experiment is a grievous loss, but not an irremediable one. I could return to the stage at which I was some thirteen months ago and initiate a new conception, another infant, and recommence my investigations. What I want of you—as my medical colleagues—is your support in achieving this."

"How do you mean, support?" Catchpole, the cardiologist, stirred in his seat beside George and spoke gruffly. "What possible support can we give you? Your speciality is a pretty esoteric one, as far as I'm concerned, anyway. I doubt there's much help I could give you—or for that matter anyone else could."

He looked around the table, his shaggy eyebrows raised. "Miss Guttner, maybe, as an obstetrician, Saxby there, of course—their fields impinge on yours. But what can Cale do, for example? Otolaryngologists, like cardiologists, can hardly—"

"I'm coming to that," George said. "I must make it clear that I want professional support from you, not direct clinical assistance, of which I have ample and for which I have been and still am most grateful." He sketched a bow in the general direction of Miss Guttner and Dr. Saxby. "Professional support in the face of lay administrative opposition."

A faint rustle moved around the table, and he felt for the first time some diminution of the faint hostility with which they had been filled.

"You have all suffered at some time, I am quite sure, from the idiotic attitudes held by our masters in the Civil Service. They control the purse strings, and any attempts we make to further the work of our own specialities is doomed, time and again, by the ridiculous sanctions they inflict on us. They are trying to impose an intolerable sanction on me now, and I'm asking you, as my professional colleagues, to stand up and be counted. To refuse to accept the embargo they are attempting to put on me and my work."

"Who are *they*, George?" Neufeld, the psychiatrist, lifted his head and spoke softly. "Sounds a bit paranoiac, doesn't it, to talk vaguely of 'they' and their interference?"

George's lips thinned. He had never been on any sort of terms with Neufeld; how could he be when he had made no effort ever to hide his scorn of his specialty?

"I mean specifically Kegan," he said shortly. "And the management committee he holds in his pocket—"

"Now, just a minute, George," Sir Peter said acidly. "Watch your tongue. I am myself a member of the management committee."

"I'm well aware of that, Sir Peter. Well aware. But I am equally well aware that you are the only medical member of that committee. That for the most part the membership is made up of . . . of jumped-up grocers and plumbers and men of that ilk, with as much understanding of the realities of medicine and medical research as I have of . . . of fly fishing. You cannot deny, can you, that Kegan has the ear of the bulk of that committee, and that any motion he wants to put through it gets through, and no argument?"

Sir Peter said nothing, staring owlishly at George's tight angry face.

"And that being so, I can tell you—those of you who are not on the management committee, that is—that he delivered to me this morning an ultimatum. My research unit is to be closed forthwith and all hospital funds withdrawn. In other words, I am to give up my research totally, as far as the Sillick Memorial is concerned. And you know as well as I do that my chances of finding another hospital that will permit me to establish a new unit are slender, very slender indeed. Other hospitals, just like this one, are bedeviled by civil servants, and they—if you will forgive a moment's paranoia, Neufeld—will respond to me just as Kegan and his crew have done."

"So what do you want us to do, George?" Jennifer Victor, the ophthalmologist, leaned forward from her place at the foot of the table. "Because I agree with you—we *are* overcontrolled by lay people here. But what do you want of us?"

"A firm avowal, from the medical committee as a whole, that you won't tolerate this sort of interference. That you believe the work I am doing to be of importance, and that you are prepared to back me in my demand for the chance to continue it. That's all."

"And how precisely do you propose we set about giving that support? Do we threaten some sort of . . . well, industrial type action? A strike?" David Little, the newest general surgical member of the committee, raised his sleek eyebrows at George. "The mind boggles somewhat at the thought of eminent physicians and surgeons marching up and down in front of the Admin Block with placards reading, 'Unfair to Old George.' "

"Oh, for heaven's sake, Little! This is not a matter in which flippancy has any part. You know as well as I do that if the medical committee, as a body, were to make it clear they were not prepared to tolerate this lay interference with medical affairs, even Kegan and his crew of lickspittles would have to capitulate. Important as they are in the running of this place, the medical staff is still of some weight! Or do you admit defeat and accept that these bureaucrats have indeed full power over our activities?"

He slid his gaze around the table and felt again the swing of mood. He had touched on one of their most sore points. He knew how much resentment they had of the lay side of the hospital's staff. And he pressed his advantage home.

"Look at this matter in a spirit of enlightened self-interest, for God's sake! Let them get away with demolishing me, and who knows where they'll stop? Next time it'll be a clinical unit they'll try to run their way. And that's medical anarchy of the most dangerous sort, you must agree!"

"He's absolutely right!" Jennifer Victor said excitedly, her round cheeks reddening. "Isn't he? Look what happened in my department six months ago! The management committee, without so much as a by-your-leave, let alone any consulting with me, axed three of my clinics, just because they said they couldn't afford the clinical assistance I needed! My waiting lists have doubled since then—doubled! That was the thin edge of the wedge, if you like.

And if they're now trying to get George out, what happens next? To your unit, for a start, Dr. Catchpole—you haven't got your hypothermia equipment yet for your open heart surgery, have you? What chance of getting it if we let them get away with this now?"

"And of course there's the dialysis unit, isn't there? Or will you be able to get that through, since you're on the management committee yourself, Sir Peter?" Cale asked a little waspishly. "I know how long I've been waiting for my new audiology equipment."

George leaned back, well satisfied, and let them go on. He had touched them on the raw, as he had hoped he would. Fill them with fear for their own pet projects, and he had them. There could be little doubt, he thought now, as he looked from one animated face to another as they loudly talked over one another's voices of the hindrances they had themselves suffered, that they would give him the support he needed. Just a matter of time now.

And it would be better to let them use that time without his presence. He was disliked on a personal level by enough of them—and was well aware of that dislike—to ensure that his presence was likely to act as an irritant. Let them talk exhaustingly of the principle involved, and then act upon it, and he would be able to start work again soon. He thought briefly of the available data sitting in the Unit; it should be possible, with really hard work on the part of the whole staff of the Unit, to establish a pregnancy within the next three months. And with the research results of the Lawton pregnancy still fresh in their minds, they should be able to make an even better job of the whole thing . . .

He stood up, and the talk around the table faltered and died away.

"You'll find it easier to reach your decision if I go away, I imagine," he said and produced one of his thin smiles. "I am confident I can rely upon you, as professional colleagues, to give me the help I need. Thank you, Sir Peter, ladies and gentlemen."

There was a moment's silence after he had gone, and then Neufeld said softly, "Of course, there is one thing you all appear to have forgetten in the discussion we've had so far."

He smiled around the table. "George, of course, sees the situation in black and white—and I must say again, in my opinion a black and white somewhat defined by a tendency to paranoiac ideas. He suggests, does he not, that it is perhaps spite that activates the management committee, or that some power battle is being engaged upon. But we surely are more practical than that? We do appreciate, do we not, that the real villain of this piece is not the faceless bureaucrats of which George spoke so . . . movingly, but good old-fashioned money. There just isn't enough cash to do all we know should be done here. Not enough for your hypothermia units *and* your dialysis unit *and* your eye clinics *and* George's research project. Now, as I see it, we know beyond any shadow of a doubt what value there would be in these facilities for which we have all been pressing for so long. And I have done my share of pleading too, for as you know, I have long wanted to establish a day hospital psychiatric unit here. We know that they would have immediate clinical applications. But what immediate clinical applications can there be in George's very expensive work? It is undoubtedly a project of, er, great scope. Great *possible* value—or so George has been at some pains to tell us over the past couple of years. But it will be many many years—if ever, of course—before George's researches can bear any edible fruit, if you will forgive a clumsy metaphor.

"If it were simply a case of saying to Kegan, on George's behalf, that there must be no lay interference with his work, it would be simple, and our duty would be clear. We would, of course, have to say it. But it would be a case of saying, would it not, that we are prepared to put our units in abeyance in order that this work of George's can go on. Don't you think it is *this* we should be discussing rather than George's, er, resentment of the power that is exercised by the holders of our purse strings?"

There was another silence when he stopped speaking, and then several of them leaned forward and started to talk again, with even more animation than they had shown when George had been there to observe it.

It took every atom of control he had not to bunch his hands into fists and hit out at them, at their avid faces and flashing cameras and waving notebooks, but he knew it would not help matters if he did. There were too many of them, and there was no way of avoiding them. They had been holding the place besieged for so long, and he couldn't stay in the Unit any longer.

Kegan had made that abundantly clear yesterday, clearly taking a malicious delight in pointing out with suave mock regret that he would be forced to obtain police aid unless he left the Sillick's premises on time, and that he had not only the support of the hospital management committee, but also that of the medical committee.

"You will be committing a trespass if you are here after ten A.M. tomorrow, Dr. Briant," he had said with oleaginous sweetness. "Out of my hands now, you see. A committee matter . . ."

And the bastard had probably tipped off the press about that too, for there seemed to be far more of them here now than had been besieging the place this past few days. And the only way to get through them, to clear a way for Hilary, shaking and crying behind him in the lobby as she stood by their meager luggage, was to tolerate their nagging greedy questions.

And since he still had to face the discomfort of telling Hilary that she had to be left out of his plans, the less she suffered now the easier that would be. At least he had only Hilary left to talk to, with the embarrassing mawkishness of Barbara's response to his announcement behind him. There was this gauntlet of vultures to run, Hilary to deal with, and then . . .

"How do you feel about the tragedy, Dr. Briant?" A man with a microphone managed to thrust through the mob, and George reared back and looked at him with cold dislike in every line of his face.

"Precisely as you would expect me to feel. Let me through, please."

"Sir, why did Miss Quinn do it? What happened to make her abduct the baby? According to one of your staff, it was because of a piece of experimental work she was directly involved in. Do you agree with that?"

"I cannot comment on any remarks made by ex-members of my staff. I have no more knowledge of why the woman did it than you have."

"What was the experiment? Is it true the child was—"

"I have no comment to make on the work that was done here. No comment."

"But there must have been a reason for—"

"Oh, for Christ's sake man! She was unbalanced in some way! I can't—"

"Unbalanced? Then why did you appoint her?"

A man with a camera flashed at him as another reporter with a microphone pushed aside the first questioner. "Couldn't you have avoided this if you had investigated her more in advance?"

"I *did* investigate her! It was not possible to foresee such an attack of . . . of unbalanced behavior."

"Would you deny, Dr. Briant, that throughout this project you have consistently discounted the human aspects of the work you were doing?" This came from a woman who had managed to wriggle her way through the other people surrounding Briant, and the shrillness of her voice cut over the shouted questions that were coming from all directions, and made them hush for a moment.

"Isn't that so, Dr. Briant?" she went on insistently. "The accusations of inhumanity made about you are proven by this tragedy? If being in a position to actually *see* what was done to this baby was enough to unhinge a woman who at the start was perfectly normal, fit enough to be employed by you in so important a post, wasn't the public outcry against you justified?"

"That is complete nonsense!" he said furiously. "Malicious nonsense! I did not at any time do anything to the baby that could have been construed as inhuman! He was observed, that was all, *observed*. He suffered no more distress than that suffered by any baby unfortunate enough to be born to the average stupid woman. In so-called normal families, babies are exposed to the experiences and the frustration that breed aggression from the moment of birth—the moment of birth, madam! This child was exposed to such stimuli only two or three times in his life, and that mildly—"

"It couldn't have been that mild, or the poor woman wouldn't have been driven to act as she did by it. Isn't it likely that she loved the baby so much that—"

"Loved it? *Loved* it? Sentimental idiocy prompted that remark, madam! If she had *loved* the child so much, would she have murdered it? Would she—"

"Just a moment, Dr. Briant!" a man shouted from the back of the crowd. "To call her a murderer is outrageous! The Coroner's report said that the infant was dead before he went into the water! He died of a combination of cold and suffocation! The post-mortem showed that. The Coroner said he was probably overlain while the woman slept on the bench where they found her bag."

"I know that, sir! I know it perfectly well!" George was white with fury. "But to remove a carefully protected and nurtured infant of so young an age from a perfect environment and then to expose him to days and nights spent in the open air, in winter, was tantamount to murder! And the fact that she committed suicide is an indication of—"

"There's no proof her suicide was a deliberate act," the woman reporter cut in again. "If she woke and found the baby dead in her arms, she must have been in a desperate state. It could have been she—"

"I will not comment any further on this. I will *not*. All this is pure surmise, and I refuse to waste—"

"Sir, will you then comment on Joel Wayne's statements to the press? He says the child was an instrument of God, that his death was a direct act of God, and he is getting enormous support for his point of view. How do you feel about being the cause of so considerable a religious—"

"I cannot comment on that, either. My knowledge of religious matters is as scanty as yours is of science. You may be prepared—you and the people you are supposed to represent—to make judgments on the basis of your ignorance. I am not. I am a scientist, and the way superstition chooses to manipulate my work is no concern of mine!"

"Calling religion superstition sounds like a comment, Dr. Briant," the man with the microphone said with smooth swiftness. "And such a comment from you is likely to alienate public sympathy from you even more, if that were possible."

"I can't help that," George said icily. "Public opinion matters less than nothing to me in the work I do."

"Maybe not, sir, but may I point out that the baby's death has had the effect of rejuvenating interest in Mr. Gurney's bill to control projects such as yours? And now that Mr. Gurney has publicly announced his own intention to work in the future with Mr. Wayne, the current religious fervor will ensure the bill is very likely to get an unopposed second reading. And if that happens, what are your chances of working in this country in the future?"

"Won't you have to give up research of this type, in the future?" Another man managed to make himself heard above the noise. "Will you admit you were misguided to embark on it in the first place? And can you tell us what your future plans are?"

"Whether the bill gets through or not is a matter of supreme unconcern to me. And my plans for the future, since they do not involve working in this country, are of supreme unconcern to you," George snapped.

"Why?"

"Where are you going?"

"What's happening, then, to . . ."

They were all shouting at once and pressing closer, and enraged, George raised his hands and pushed hard against the nearest body and shouted, "Be quiet! Get out of my way and let me get—be quiet!"

"We're entitled to an answer!" one of them roared back. "You mayn't be guilty in law, but a hell of a lot of people hold you responsible for what happened to that baby and that woman! You've got to answer."

"I haven't *got* to do anything!" George shouted. "And any such accusations will—who said that? Unless it is withdrawn immediately I—"

"All right, all right!" George strained to see who it was, but the press of bodies was too great. "I'll withdraw, but answer us! What are your future plans? We've a right to know. The people of this country have a right to know what is done by a British scientist."

"You've no *right* to anything, do you understand that? None at all! It was your stupid misinformed comment that stirred up most of the trouble I've had with this project. And—"

He took a deep breath and stopped and then said loudly, "All right. All *right*. If you'll be quiet, I'll tell you what I'm going to do in the future. And then you'll see what effect your badgering of me has had. You'll see just what effect the lack of intelligent understanding of my work has had. You'll see why this country loses its best brains to more enlightened parts of the world."

Immediately, there was a hushed expectancy, and he stood for a moment in silence before speaking with great deliberation. "All right. I do not deny that I misjudged the temperament of the Quinn woman. That I should have foreseen that she might develop so close an emotional attachment to the child that she would behave in so . . . so destructive a fashion. I do not deny that the monitors covering her and the baby were not observed as closely as they should have been at the time she abducted the child. I cannot deny these facts. But I can tell you why they happened."

There was a heavy silence, highlighted only by the distant roar of traffic, and he stood there, the cold wind ruffling his hair, staring at them with disdain in every line of his body.

"Throughout this work, which was pure research, pure science designed for worthwhile ends, engaged in because I wanted to demonstrate a way to improve the quality of human life, I have been hampered—cruelly hampered—by lack of intelligent support. I have had to waste far too much of my energies in scrabbling for money. I have had to settle for inadequate staff both in terms of quantity and quality. I have had to settle for inadequate equipment and an inadequately secured environment. I have had to tolerate the meddling greed of small-minded people seeking their own puerile satisfactions in battening on the mind and work of a better man, and because I was so hampered, I was also deflected. Had I been able to give my total concern to my work, and not part of it to worrying about such things as money and public opinion" —he let the sneer show on his face as well as in his voice—"then I would have foreseen what might happen with Miss Quinn and avoided it. I would have been able to report properly on my work, and thus keep the public, about which you say you care so much, accurately informed of what was happening. And this public of yours would have been able to take a pride in the fact that one of its own scientists was doing work that, carried through, could bring considerable renown to the country that supported it.

"But because of the mindless opposition with which I have been bombarded, this has all gone by the board. So"—he gave a thin and almost triumphant smile—"so, I am no longer prepared to waste my efforts in such a country. I am withdrawing from any sense of national pride, which I once had, I assure you, which I once had. I am working in the future in a country which has offered me a well equipped unit, ample staff and funds, and total protection from the badgering of uninformed people like yourselves. In future I will work in the solitude true science needs."

"*Where?*" someone called from the mass of people around him. "America? But they're as outraged as we are! And even with the sort of money available in the States, they can't guarantee your solitude, not after the fiasco in this country."

"Not America. Yugoslavia."

"Yugo—? But that's part of the bloc of—"

"I don't care what its political color is. It's a country where funds are available for constructive science of the sort I want to do. Where hard-working men are allowed to work, and helped to work, and not held back by the stupid little fears of the uninformed, where—"

"Where politics and science work together," someone said softly in the momentary hush that had fallen.

"Where ideas are given room to grow, and science is valued as it should be," George snapped. "Where facts and the proof of them can be demonstrated properly, and not buried in a mass of emotionalism masquerading as public concern. I've said before, I don't give a damn about political ideas. Only about *science*. That's what I'm here for, that's what I exist for, and all that matters to me from here on is that I be allowed to get on with my work in peace. And I have no doubt whatsoever that the day will come when you will bitterly regret, you people who condemn what you don't understand because you are afraid of truths too big for you, you will bitterly regret the loss of what I and men like me could have given to you."

"But even there—even there, won't the fact that you have failed with the project you started here mean something? Won't they see the failure was caused because you didn't take enough account of the human aspects of the thing, and—"

"Failure?" He raised his head and stared at them, letting his eyes move across their faces, recognizing but not touched by the expressions of revulsion, of anger, of fear and dislike, or pity and frank loathing that invested them.

"Failure? How can it be regarded as a failure? I have learned a vital fact. I know what must not happen next time."